BEFORE I SLEEP

BEFORE I SLEEP

D. A. Russell

To dreams, and illusions.
And the wisdom to know the difference.

iUniverse, Inc.
Bloomington

Before I Sleep

iUniverse books may be ordered through booksellers or by contacting:

iUniverse
1663 Liberty Drive
Bloomington, IN 47403
www.iuniverse.com
1-800-Authors (1-800-288-4677)

ISBN: 978-1-4759-4472-3 (sc)
ISBN: 978-1-4759-4474-7 (hc)
ISBN: 978-1-4759-4473-0 (ebk)

Printed in the United States of America

iUniverse rev. date: 08/16/2012

Contents

This book is dedicated to Rob and Stephanie, who have given me life and joy every day since they were born. And special thanks to Pete who never stopped believing, and to Lisa and Dean who provided a much needed kick in the butt to get this published.

Prologue

Those soft evening winds that only seem to be found in the cool hills of New Hampshire gently signaled the coming end of the day for New Ipswich. Even to those who had spent their lives here, and had perhaps hundreds of times felt the soft touch of evening's quiet, it could never become a time to take for granted. Sounds and smells and feelings and colors all blended on such a night to produce a special beauty and tranquility that would rest gently in mind long after evening's end. Those who lived there never spoke of it, yet all knew that the touch of such an evening would be something saved and cherished, no matter how far you went from this place.

New Ipswich, of all the towns that lie nestled in the shadows of Mount Monadnock to the northwest, has always managed to escape the future. So many of the once-beautiful towns nearby had grown and prospered, and then paid the price that inevitably follows such success. Yet, New Ipswich remained locked in the 1950s. The center was called a "four corners" and was not much more than that. If you happened to prefer another gasoline to Mobil, you would have to travel a bit. Matt's station was the only one in town, and no one was concerned by the monopoly. There was a post office, a small general store, and of course a church or two. But, in the valley that held New Ipswich, mostly there was a special kind of quiet that a Frost or a Copland always heard so much better than the rest of us.

Close to the four corners was a home that was in many ways a reflection of the history in that valley. It was a home that twisted and turned in many directions, as one addition after another had been added over the past century or so. For many of the more recent years, it had been the home and office of Doctor Richard Freeman. There were few in New Ipswich who had not seen their lives cross his, and hundreds of the young and old of New Ipswich had rested under his roof. The home was now owned by someone new, an old man who lived there alone, the latest to share in its warmth. Inevitably, he too would move on and another would come. Yet, the echoes and shadows of all those who had lived there were something that continued within the walls, something that was forever. The house would always remain, and all the echoes and shadows would always have shelter there.

In the rear of the house was a homemade shed carefully built to the dimensions of a sixteen foot sailboat. The shed was crafted with a typical New Hampshire economy of form and materials. It was designed to protect the boat, and be a place where the boat could be readied for the next season. The wooden sailboat was a perfect match for the place. It was at least twenty-five years old. If you looked very carefully, the hull would reflect many years of wear, but you would also see the care that had gone into the boat over the years. It had been repaired, painted, and polished by the old man who grimaced as he turned from his cramped position at the sound from outside.

The sound had not been loud, but the old man both sensed it and realized that it did not fit the sounds of this night. He placed his brush on the ground, wiped his hands on the towel that hung on the boat cradle, and slowly stood up. Instinctively, as he had done so many times long ago in places with names nearly forgotten, like Borneo or Corregidor, he let his mind replay the moment. He tried to judge the nature and direction, and most of all the meaning of the sound. Once again, for reasons he had never been able to understand, he knew immediately and with certainty that this sound could only mean death. Somehow, sounds that should have been buried fifty years in his past had returned.

The old man worked his way past the boat and out of the shed. Stopping at the entrance, he waited for the slight noise of the hinges to end as the door swung open. For just a moment he was back in the heat of the Solomon Islands, was twenty-three again, and could feel the weight of binoculars around his neck to sweep the fields before him. He carefully listened for any repeat of the noise. The old man's eyes, now in bifocals, creased as he scanned the area where he knew the first sound had come. The only response was silence. Even the night wind had stopped.

The old man paused to consider his choices. Without taking his eyes from the woods, he realized that both the house and the nearby car offered alternatives to entering the woods. With certainty he knew that what lay there would extract a price from someone. The nature of the price, and the payer, made little difference to his choice. As the decision formed, for just a moment the words of a friend who had once served with him in the jungle flashed into his mind. "Bill," he heard the voice from so long ago say, "Sometimes I wonder just how much of a damn fool you really are. Could you stop, no matter what, if your antiquated sense of honor told you to go?"

"Johnny," the old man murmured, "I'm seventy-four years old and on my way back into the jungle. What would you think of me if you could see me now?"

Carefully, he began to move towards the stone wall that separated the rear of his property from the hills and forest to the west. Without conscious thought, he picked his way through the asparagus beds at the base of the wall that had taken him so many years to develop. Thirty yards beyond the wall, lying in a slight depression filled with fallen leaves framed by Mount Monadnock looming in the distance, he found the man.

There was no movement of the body at first. The man was spread-eagle without shoes or shirt in the dead leaves. The bare back was lined with welts and gouges. Caked and damp blood mixed as it seeped from the many wounds. In the small of the back, just above the right side of the waist, was the obvious sign of a bullet hole. With a great sadness the old man realized that death, if not here already, could not be far away. His eyes closed briefly as he remembered those times before when all he could do was stay with a friend, comfort, and wait, when both knew that bandages or help were too late.

It had been that way with Johnny. Help had never come. His platoon was dead around him. The old man would get a silver star for what happened that day, yet he could never wear it. It lay, dust covered in the back of a closet, representing only failure and pain to him. Nothing could erase the memory of holding the body of his friend in his arms until he died. He had tried with all his strength to will life back into Johnny, to hug him so closely that the angel of death itself could not claim his friend. The medics found him there, still beside the body two days later. No one else from the platoon was left.

The old man stooped, laid two fingers on the man's neck, and felt a weak pulse. He pulled off his old gray flannel shirt and covered the man before gently turning him over. The man on the ground was so young, the old man thought, as he carefully checked the pockets for identification. All of the pockets were empty. When he finished and looked up he found the man's head slightly lifted, with eyes open, looking intently at him as though both judge and jury of some form.

"Please," the old man said as he reached to support the head. "Lie back." The old man carefully scooped up dirt and leaves to form a crude pillow. "Help is coming," he lied easily. "Just rest. Who are you?"

The eyes just looked back at him. Again the old man knew that he was being judged. The eyes looked away to dart from tree to shadow to tree in the nearby area. Finally, they returned to look at the old man, and reflected a small measure of trust.

"Whoever they are, I'm not one of them," said the old man. "I'm here alone. Please let me help you."

The words from the dying man just barely escaped. "Before . . . I . . . Sleep."

The old man misunderstood. "No son, you're wrong. Listen to me. This is not yet your time to sleep."

The dying man's eyes closed tightly, as if concentrating, and then opened with an intensity that shook the old man. From too many times past the old man knew that death was here, and that the man on the ground knew it, too. Both knew that there was no time left for all the words that cried inside to be shared. A legion of names, a hundred remembrances, and so many apologies would have to wait. The old man felt his eyes involuntarily water as he remembered being there to hear such words before. As always, he was shaken by the power of hearing words that were to the dying person the only words that could be chosen to leave behind. They were the words that a person would trade for his life.

"Before I Sleep," the dying man forced. "Before . . . I . . . Sleep . . . You must remember. Before I Sleep!"

The old man reached to comfort the dying man. "I understand," he said, just as he had always said before to those whose words, in dying, made no sense to him. "I'll never forget. 'Before I Sleep.' I've got it."

The dying man's eyes closed once more, and then opened slowly and evenly. The old man saw a change in the eyes, and realized that the dying man understood exactly what was happening.

"No. You can't understand . . . It's too late." The dying man's voice came out remarkably strong. "Too many will die." The eyes shifted to look over the old man's right shoulder, and then blanked forever.

"He's right, you know." The voice from behind the old man was flat, and as matter of fact as a traffic report. "It's far too late."

The old man knew that the voice had to belong to the boy's hunter, but he did not turn immediately. First, with gentleness, he closed the dead man's eyes and swept the hair from the dead man's forehead. He positioned the head on the makeshift pillow and slowly pulled the shirt over the man's face. Only then did he slowly rise, and turn to the voice.

"I guess I'm getting old, after all." He said quietly, almost to himself. "Johnny was right, a damn fool, to boot. There's a time I'd have realized there must be someone else."

Within seconds the old man knew that he, too, would die today. He saw that the eyes of the newcomer leaning against the maple tree were cold and hard. They looked more like the calculating eyes of a bird of prey than of the thin, stark man who looked back at him. For just a moment, in the second or two before all the years and sights and times allowed him to regain his control, the old man understood what the rabbit must feel just before the talons of the falcon strike.

While the pose appeared almost casual, the old man saw in the newcomer that cat-like alertness that had always marked certain men as predators no matter what the surroundings. Even had he just met the newcomer at a tea party, or on the streets of Boston, the old man would have known he faced a killer. There are patterns, he realized, that don't change, whether here in his gentle woods or back in the violent jungles of Borneo.

"You're good. Very good," said the old man as he faced the newcomer. "I didn't hear a sound from you." He looked down at the body on the ground. "I take it that the boy wasn't just babbling? He was trying to tell me something. Something that cost him his life."

The newcomer did not answer right away, and never took his eyes away from the old man. Over the past fifteen years the newcomer had killed many times, in many places, and had learned even as a teenager that you never take any adversary for granted. Instinctively, despite the overwhelming advantage, he recognized the old man before him as something different, something special. He stared at the old man and saw none of the fear that always cowered in the eyes of his victims. Instead the old man was looking past him, through him, with an expression that showed little. With a start that years of training kept hidden far below the surface, the newcomer realized that the only emotion he could sense in the old man's eyes was strength, perhaps touched by wry, sad humor. There was none of the fear in the old man's eyes that he had expected to find. They were eyes that he had seen before.

Once before the newcomer had faced such a man. In all the years of killing in what seemed like twice a full lifetime by the time he had reached thirty-three, the newcomer still remembered standing before someone who commanded such respect as did this old man. The newcomer had been a child then, caught in the adult game of Mideast war. The remembrance of the cool eyes that looked at him, saw the grenade in his hand and yet chose to let a boy live when a man would have died, were something that never left his memory. Amidst all of the anger in him, the seething that consumed his life, nothing could ever touch him like the memory of that face long ago. Since the age of fourteen he had wished for nothing more than to be able to have the peace and strength that is found behind such eyes.

Finally, the newcomer spoke. "Old man, you've seen death before today." The words were as close to tribute, as near to a salute, as he could give.

The old man turned his head to look around his forest. He saw the maple grove that had been such a good provider of syrup over the years. He looked towards the shed. He could just see the nose of the boat that had helped to fill so much of the years since Susan. He thought of friends and places. When he looked back at the newcomer, he thought again of the patterns he had seen in hard men anywhere.

"Death doesn't change, son. It merely learns new ways from us to go along with those it already knows. I think you know that." The old man's eyes locked with the newcomer's. "And yet, there never is a shortage of those who would try to teach it more."

"I'm sorry, old man." The newcomer reached his left hand inside his lightweight jacket and drew out a silencer-equipped gun. "You just were in the wrong place today, though the place makes no difference when your time has come. When Allah chooses you, he will find you. Today he chose you."

The old man felt the wind pick up again. The sounds of the evening enveloped him once more. He turned and looked at all the beauty that had been his to share for so many years, and had to smile. He thought of people, and faces, and most of all he remembered laughter. He remembered the laughter of friends and the laughter of soldiers. He remembered the precious laughter of children. He remembered the sound of the woman he would always think of as young, despite all the years growing old together sharing both laughter and the touch of lovers.

A wry smile came to his face as he realized that it was his turn for selecting those words to trade for life. He thought of all that had shaped him, and all that was important. He thought of the woman most of all. As the newcomer raised his weapon, the old man finally realized what he must say.

"Son, do what you must do. It's my time to visit old friends. There's nothing more to be done, before I sleep."

Chapter One

Rob Stephens stood well away from the soccer field and watched with satisfaction as the boys continued with their scrimmage. To those watching, he did not appear to move, as though he was carved there. He could have been part of the scenery or a piece of the hillside. He stood halfway up the slope, where the field had been cut out of the hillside when Wendlandt Academy first opened back in the early 1950s. The field never seemed to belong there. It looked as though the slope should have continued down to the school buildings a quarter mile below. The effect was much like a child's sand castle where, with an easy stroke of a shovel, a mesa could be formed at will.

Wendlandt Academy was a small private school nestled in the foothills north of Mount Monadnock in the summer village of Dublin, New Hampshire. Dublin's population would swell in the summer, only to shrink back in the winter. The population's yearly tide was caused not by lunar forces, but by the summer influx of the "Flatlanders" from places like Boston and Long Island. Few flatlanders ever even heard that term used, let alone knew that it applied to them. But, they all wore it as clearly as though they wore name tags. To the locals, the flatlanders were accepted in much the same way that one finally learns to accept a slushy winter day. Some of the more senior Dubliners could even admit that they were used to the annual mass birth that began each Memorial Day. But all of the locals also knew that special feeling that happened each Labor Day when the flatlanders began their migration back south. It was like when you finally stop holding your breath.

There was, of course, one day each year when the flatlanders were truly appreciated. That usually occurred in late November, or early December, when the year's property tax rate was established and tax bills mailed out to all those Boston and New York addresses.

Rob Stephens, even when he first appeared in Dublin six years ago, was never mistaken for a flatlander. The locals could easily recognize directness and a measure of reserve that made that label senseless. To those who did get to know him, to the degree that anyone did, there was no simple label that applied. Stephens was a difficult person to categorize. Myrna Glover, who had lived in Dublin for eighty-one years and had been on the staff at Yankee Magazine for more than forty of those years, got the closest to defining the enigma. Myrna was someone whose opinions meant quite a bit around Dublin. She was one of the very few who were accepted by both the year-round and summer groups. Some called her a historical landmark, though never to her face. Her purposeful stride and ever-present scarf, usually a royal metallic blue color, were local fixtures. A joke first heard nearly thirty years before had claimed that "When Myrna goes walking in her blue scarf, even the summer mosquitoes step respectfully aside."

Myrna was not the first to wonder about Stephens. But few would question that she was the first to realize that he didn't easily fit any of the more usual molds. He first came to her attention when she started hearing others talking about him down at the Post Office, or at Ben's Store. Often the locals would speak of meeting him on the Pumpelly Trail up Mount Monadnock, or sitting on the big rock at the east end of Dark Pond, or climbing the small rock face near the cemetery. Many had seen him in what appeared to be his favorite place, sitting by Emerson's Seat on the old Lost Farm Trail south of Bald Rock. "Rob," she said, "is a puzzle. I can tell you so many things he is not, but I'll be damned if I can tell you exactly what he is. However, there is one thing that I can smell from talking to him. You can trust him. That covers a whole lot of ground as far as I'm concerned."

The boys at Wendlandt didn't even realize that there was a puzzle to be solved. In the manner of children, who often seem to see things that far more experienced adults no longer can, they awarded him the nickname of "Q." It was a shortened version of "Q1," which had been shortened, in turn, from "The quiet One." The name had been earned his second year at Wendlandt, during the winter when two of the boys had been caught with their local girlfriends inside the boarded up Dublin Lake Club. Breaking into the flatlander summer club might have been overlooked, as some degree of interplay between the academy boys and local girls always had been tolerated. However, when the party goods were found to include marijuana, the always simmering feud between town and school erupted. Even when it seemed clear that the girls might have provided the marijuana, a town meeting was called by the angry residents. For more than two hours, the town and school had battled. The local residents insisted that the boys be ". . . arrested and locked up for years." The school insisted that ". . . more local police effort be spent checking out the girls." Yet, despite all of their public posturing, even the most hopeful of those at the school knew that the boys, John Hardy and Bill Parsons, would at the least be expelled.

It was nearly 11:00 that night when Rob Stephens rose from his seat. Unlike all those shouting around him, Stephens said nothing. He simply stood, waiting patiently for the chance to speak. For nearly five minutes, no one paid any attention to him. He stood with his left arm crossed in front of him to support the elbow of the half raised right arm. As calmly as a diner signaling for a waiter he stood quietly, holding up a single finger to request a moment to speak. That was when Myrna Glover, without knowing it, gave Stephens the label that boys would later apply.

John Hardy, sitting in what he would later describe as ". . . the executioner's box awaiting my sentence" while the words flew around him, was near her front row seat.

"Glover had to be the worst of them," he told his friends many hours later back at the dormitory that night. "I think if she had her way, that witch would have gutted me on the spot to make sure I couldn't get near any more of her townies. But suddenly when I looked up at her and she was just staring at Stephens, not saying a word. Pretty soon she started to point him out to the others around her. Before I knew it, the place had gone silent, and everyone was looking at him. No one else could have noticed, but she nodded her head to Stephens. Her head barely moved. Then, I'll be damned if he didn't nod back to her. His head couldn't have moved more than half an inch. It was some kind of signal. Whatever it meant, those two understood each other. I swear they both had been waiting for the right time, and somehow now was 'it.' Then she said, 'Let the quiet one talk. I think maybe this one has words I want to hear.'"

"Stephens didn't say much," Hardy had continued four years ago when telling his friends about that night. "His voice was soft, but I know for a fact that everyone there heard every word. He looked down the row of aldermen, looking right into eyes of each one. 'Many people are going to be hurt because of this night,' he said. 'These two boys, the girls, the school, the town, maybe all of us. I know that if we search hard enough we'll find someone to hang. But, so far in all the talking there are no answers. Perhaps real answers are impossible.'"

"Then Stephens paused for about ten seconds," Hardy had continued. "He turned around and looked right at Bill and me. I swear he could look right through to our underwear. I think he was adding up everything he knew about us, and that the total would be the most important judgment in my life. I couldn't breathe. I wanted to say something, but I had no idea what to say. Before I could even begin to think, he turned away and finished up what he had to say. 'We've said everything we can. We did that in the first few minutes here tonight. You can only say the same things so many times before the only thing left is to make a decision.'"

"You clowns could never understand it," Hardy had continued in the dorm later that night. "Here was someone who just had to stand up and others listened. Others knew. 'The Quiet One' she called him. Yet, she was like all of the others. That 'quiet one' was plenty loud enough to get every bit of her attention. When Stephens turned and looked right at Glover, I knew right then that the evening was over. You see, he knew somehow that she was the key. It was weird. It was almost as though those two were the only ones in the crowded hall. 'Ma'am,' he said, 'I'll deal with these two boys. I'll take responsibility for them for the rest of the year. If I cannot solve the problem, I'll return them here, to this hall.' Stephens then just waited. At the time, I swear no one said anything for about two days. It could only be seconds. Nothing seemed to happen. Every one of those townies was just looking back and forth between Stephens and Glover. Everyone else just watched the two of them, until finally she nodded again. The same as before. If you weren't watching closely, you would miss it. She nodded just once. Then she got up and stood there for a couple seconds, and said 'I'm satisfied. Let's get on with it.' And she walked out of the hall. The hall filled with the sounds of nodding and mumbling, and then others got up and started to leave. Pretty soon, there was nobody left but us."

"When the rest had left, Stephens came over to us. He didn't even raise an eyebrow. No yelling. No threats. He just looked at us and said 'Let's go, you gentlemen know what you have to do.' That was it. I remember walking back up the hill to the dorm. I couldn't get out of my mind the sight of Stephens just standing there, the 'quiet one.' Well Bill and I are going to be choir boys for the rest of the year. We have to be. Not because of force, you see, but because he gave his word for us. I'm going to tell you guys something," he was to continue, "I learned something tonight. I don't even know exactly what yet, but I did. And it's important. You just let people know, anyone messes with Stephens, they're gonna have to come through me."

For the rest of that year Hardy and Parsons had, indeed, been choir boys. And in the years since, Stephens had become "Q" to new classes of students. When he first learned the name, from another faculty member, the legend was sealed at Wendlandt. Stephens had let loose with a burst of laughter that soon infected all around him in the faculty lounge. The four others there, resting in the sanctuary of paneling and bookshelves, were swept up in the genuine humor of the laughter. "'Q-1' is it? I like it!" he had laughed at a joke that no others could possibly understand. "What incredible irony. The 'quiet one.' I think that of all the names I've carried over the years, this is the first I'll enjoy wearing."

All of that night was far from Stephens mind as he watched the soccer practice. He was proud of the boys and they always knew he was, even though it was very rare that he would offer a "very good" or, the ultimate, an "excellent, gentlemen." Despite its small size—the senior class had just fourteen students this year—Wendlandt had always been a competitive team. For the past three years, a string of coaches at places like Exeter and Mount Herman had walked off the field shaking their head at a loss when they had expected a walkover.

On the field, the boys were working hard at a four-on-three box drill when Stephens saw the sedan pull up to the administration building down the hill. Even while calling out to the boys to ". . . mark up better, you're not covering the floater," he carefully watched the two men get out of the car. He saw both of them scan the area in a way that Stephens immediately recognized. Well before they had completed their scan and started into the building, Stephens knew the men were seeking him.

Stephens closed his eyes briefly, and then started down the hill towards the field. He saw the men leave the building, and return to the car. "All right, gentlemen. Let's get together."

As the boys walked over, Stephens began to pick up the loose soccer balls and place them into the red and blue ball bag. He could see the look of puzzlement on the faces of the boys who expected another hour of practice.

"Mr. Stephens," asked Chris Miller, "did we screw up that much?"

"No guys. It's time for me to bag it today. I've got visitors coming." He looked at Ned Mendoza, his center half who seemed more an assistant coach than a player at times. "Ned, run these turkeys through a three-on-two against goalie for half an hour. Then laps, boys."

The car pulled up at the edge of the field. Mendoza walked over to Stephens as the rest of the team moved back onto the field. He knew that something had changed. Looking at Stephens, he felt a growing uneasiness.

"Q, you all right?" Over Ned's four years at Wendlandt, he and Stephens had developed a closeness that always surprised Ned. No one ever seemed to get close to Stephens, yet by mid way through Ned's second year the two of them would often be together. When asked, Ned would usually give a stock answer. "I don't know. I guess that we both just happen to have some of the same interests. It's no big thing." But he could never understand why or how it evolved. And yet, if pressed, he would have discovered that the relationship was one of the most important parts of his life. There were many times, usually after an evening in the loft over the study hall when the two spoke quietly or read silently, when Ned would leave knowing just how hard it would be to explain why these nights were so special.

Stephens had no trouble understanding it. It had started with sports. He saw intensity in Ned, a drive and determination that mirrored parts of himself that none at Wendlandt would guess existed. Yet, even when Ned was quiet and reserved, his normal manner, somehow anyone around him could still sense the strength inside. A person like Myrna Glove would have no problem understanding Ned. If she ever met him, she would soon realize he was another "Quiet One."

"Of course, Ned. There's no problem." He nodded towards the two men who were now leaning on the outside of the parked car. "It's just that my visitors are here early. I really didn't expect them until later."

Even at a distance he knew that one was Harvey Green. Green always had a way of looking as though he fit in no matter what the situation. Even here, as odd as the two of them should have looked parked by the field, Green looked more like a faculty member watching his school's team practice than someone who had in the past ten years probably been in more hot areas than all but a handful of the Company's men.

Stephens had always liked Green. Even had they both not shared the same enjoyment of soccer, they still would have been drawn together. Green had never fully lost his English accent. On those few times when his excitement showed, usually only when watching a taped soccer match of Manchester United versus Arsenal on PBS, he would slip back to sounding like an extra in the street scene of My Fair Lady. The outside forward position would become a "win-ger," complete with two syllables and a hard "g." Taking a shot on goal was "having a bang at it" and resting was "taking a blow."

Green was a throwback, a simple person. He was a person who never seemed to say much, but when he did it was invariably worthwhile to listen to his words. He was a few years older than Stephens, and like Stephens Green looked older than he actually was. Time always paid particular attention to the faces of people like Green. It left its mark there, its footprint, a visa stamp of its own to mark all the places he had been. Green could blend in as easily in a crowded train station as at a board of directors meeting. Somehow, he just seemed like everyone's old friend.

The other person by the car could never blend in. The image of the perfect banker was obvious even from 100 yards away. The whole picture, from the sharp gray fedora and hand-carved briar pipe right down to the $250 wingtips that Stephens knew must be there, marked him as Carl Sanders. Even across a field, and after six years, Stephens found the old feelings welling back up again. He remembered that last day, in Sanders' office, when he told Sanders of Foster's death. He remembered the eyes of Sanders, eyes that did not even find the information to be important. They were eyes that just accepted the news as though Stephens were reporting nothing more than the prime interest rate. He remembered the all too easy answer, "Stephens, people get hurt in our business every day." And most of all, he remembered Foster. He remembered holding him, cradling his head like a child, trying to will away the death that both knew had come for Foster. And he remembered Green's words the damp, cold day they buried Foster. "Rob, even if we really do believe in all we do, does it matter? Does anything ever change? Do we just replace one hard man with another?"

The wind had picked up, blowing out of the southeast over the lake, when Stephens focused back on the present. It would be a cold night.

Perhaps the first real frost of the year would come. Already, trees at the highest elevation were starting to turn, and the incredible colors of a New Hampshire fall were not far away. The boys had begun their three-on-two drill and he could hear the voices calling to one another. "Your ball . . . help back here if you need it . . . pass square." As always, the sounds of the kids playing seemed to put everything into perspective. Stephens had always known that there was no place he could be more content than when surrounded by the open, innocent sounds of children.

"Ned, it looks as though I'd better get moving. I don't think they'll just go away."

Ned looked at the waiting men, and then back at Stephens. Ned saw a person standing there who seemed to be someone new, somehow different. Ned still saw the "Quiet One," but there was something in the way Stephens was looking at the two men that Ned had never seen before. Had Ned been there that night four years before, he might have recognized the same intense look of judge and jury that Stephens had given to John Hardy and Bill Parsons.

"Who are they, Mr. Stephens?" Ned was beginning to worry. "Do you want me to tell them you're busy?"

Stephens handed the ball bag to Mendoza. Slowly he rolled his sleeves back down and carefully rebuttoned his cuffs. Finally, he turned back to Ned. Ned saw that Stephens had reached his decision. His eyes were smiling again. He reached out, and very briefly rested his hand on Ned's shoulder. "Thanks, Ned. But I can handle it," he said. "You take care of the guys. I'll catch you later." He lowered his arm, and began to walk across the field.

In the instinctive way of the young, Ned realized that his friend had just said goodbye.

Chapter Two

The walk across that field seemed to be one of the longest Stephens could remember. Here at Wendlandt he had finally achieved a measure of peace. He enjoyed hiking the local hills and cross-country ski trails. Often he would climb up to his favorite resting place near the summit of Mount Monadnock, where he could sit and feel the gentle wind blowing past the aged granite that formed Emerson's chair. He would be able to see Boston, ninty miles away to the southeast, with the giant reflecting towers called Hancock and Prudential impudently mimicking the sun. Below would be the gentle valleys that seemed to roll and call with a tranquility that Stephens could find nowhere else in his past. On such days all of the years before would blend and fade away. All of the voices that called, the faces that beckoned, the sounds and images and smells and feelings that followed him would be swept aside for a while. He felt that there was no other way to cleanse the snakes from his mind than to let the soft quiet of Monadnock wash over him.

When he had come to Wendlandt six years ago, the school was a chance to start over. He had been thirty-two years old then, and could never seem to remember what it was like to be a child. The satisfaction from teaching a small mathematics class, and the enthusiasm that flowed from the boys whenever they were playing soccer, were a tonic long needed.

The two men leaning against the car did not change their positions as Stephens approached. While both were motionless, it was for very different reasons. Green and Stephens had little need for handshakes to mark the bond between them. The nature of their friendship did not recognize the years between visits. When you have been enough places together, and have shared enough fears, there are few words that have not been aired. The important things had already been said before, and such facts are never changed by time.

Sanders remained motionless as a signal to both Green and Stephens. Very little Sanders did was not carefully planned to send a message to anyone watching. Stephens smiled inwardly as he saw he had been right about the wingtips. He was not at all surprised to see Sanders' shoes had once again defied the laws of nature. No one in the Company had ever seen a spot on Sanders' shoes. They invariably looked as though he had just spit-shined them. As ever, he completely fit the nickname awarded to him a dozen years earlier by Stephens. There were very few people at the Company who didn't refer to Sanders as 'Nieman Marcus.' It was one of those nicknames you can never escape, and would always enrage Sanders if he overheard it. The more senior people at the Company knew that it was not the name itself that caused the anger. Indeed, Sanders liked the comparison. But the fact that it was given to him by Stephens made it intolerable.

"Hello Harvey," Stephens said as he drew near and stopped at the front of the car. Green leaned against the front fender a couple feet in front of him. Beyond Green, leaning against the rear passenger door, was Sanders. "I've seen you look better. You been sick or something?"

"Your right halfback drifts too much, Rob," Green answered. "But then, you never really did understand the game. Too bad there isn't some British blood in you."

"Well, from the looks of it, you're close to retirement. When you do, you can come teach me." Stephens smiled with Green. It seemed so easy for them both to step back six years together.

"Cute. How folksy," interrupted Sanders, pointing with his pipe as though he were Spielberg and Stephens a bit-part actor in a scene. "Get in the car, Stephens. We have a little ride to take. You two can exchange your pleasantries on the way back to Boston."

Sanders reached for the car door as though the stage direction was finished and now all the players should move to their stations. He stopped, his hand carefully frozen in mid flight, as he realized that neither Stephens nor Green had moved. "Let's move it, Stephens. I don't have all day to waste here in the boondocks."

Stephens looked directly at Sanders and said nothing for a few moments. His face was nearly expressionless except for the smallest trace of anger around his eyes. Finally, the eyes softened and laughed at the scene around him. "Well. I'm fine, thank you. How nice of you to ask.

And yes, it's such a lovely day." Green made no effort to hold back his smile at Stephens' reply.

Sanders stepped back away from the car, dropping his hand from the handle. He spun to his right, and called forth what he knew was a suitably piercing stare. "Listen Stephens. It wasn't my idea to come here today, and I'll be damned if I'm going to start letting you give me shit again." He stabbed the air with his pipe in the general direction of Green. "But there are some people back in Virginia who are convinced you aren't washed up. Instead of doing any of a few hundred things one hell of a lot more important, I get to play chauffeur. So, mister, get your ass into this car and let's get it over with."

Stephens saw the green and brown wave as a soft breeze off Dublin Lake worked its way over the hillside. It was a gentle motion that swept over the trees that patiently waited for winter. It passed, and then died. The hills were still again.

"Sanders, I know little details were never your bag, but I'm gone. I'm on the outside. Terminated, but without prejudice. Can you follow any of that?" There was the smallest trace of pleading in his voice. "I made my choice, and I don't plan to go back. Carl, you're going to have to go to this dance without me."

Sanders eyes tightened. Nothing in Stephens' words, or voice had made any difference. The voice hardened further. "Mr. Stephens, I *own* your dance card. It never expires. You know the system. If it isn't me, it will be someone else."

Stephens looked away from Sanders. His eyes swept the hillside, searching for a return of the breeze and the friendly wave in the leaves. He looked down the hillside at the school buildings, two with welcoming hands of smoke escaping from the chimneys. It was beginning to get dark. Dusk was here. Soon, the night would come, and his sleep would bring an extra measure of the old faces and sounds.

Stephens considered what had to be the reason for their arrival. He turned back to Sanders. His voice softened. "I'm sorry, Carl. I knew you would come. I guess I knew it two weeks ago. The coincidence was a little too much for you to overlook. But I've already thought it over. I'm out. I plan to stay out. There have to be a dozen others you can put on the Robbins affair."

Sanders stopped, frozen. For a moment he forgot about the mask he had chosen to wear. "How the hell did you know about Bill Robbins? Who talked to you?" he spat.

Green was not at all surprised. Both respect and a smile of satisfaction mixed on his face. "You always could figure things out, old buddy."

"Listen Sanders, one of my soccer kids could have figured out that it was a pro job. Not many people get shot around here. Even fewer buy it the way Robbins did. Our local constabulary might not match your lab teams, but the chief down in Jaffrey still was good enough to recognize the rifling marks of a slug that passed through a silencer."

"You're guessing. Maybe a good guess, but still a guess."

"We don't need these games, Sanders. There are two more factors that seal it. First of all, I knew Robbins. He used to own the Peterborough Theater." He turned to face Green. "You know, you would have liked Bill Robbins. I talked with him at the theater half a dozen times. He was a lot like the two of us."

"One thing I do know, the first factor, is that there was no motive. No one has found a hint of a motive. The guy lived alone and couldn't have been a threat to anyone. Robbins had to be killed because he saw something. Nothing else makes sense. Someone like him isn't going to be killed with a silencer by an angry relative." Stephens gave a small laugh, just a self-deprecating shot of breath through his nose. "Even if I had missed all of that, even if there was any doubt at all about it in my mind, there is the second factor. Joe Techman."

Sanders no longer was making any pretense at cool. "How did you know Techman was in on this?"

"Obviously you don't read the Peterborough Transcript, Sanders. If you did, you would have seen the photo on the front page the day after the funeral. Even I could recognize Techman there. Now why would old 'Slow Joe' be at a funeral in New Ipswich?"

Green looked at him in appreciation of the analysis. "Well, here I thought you had done something clever in working this out. You didn't tell me we left a roadmap for you." Sanders said nothing.

"So I knew two weeks ago that someone might give me a call," Stephens continued. "I wasn't exactly hiding here. It was only a matter of time before someone would remember I was here. The coincidence would be too much. I'm just sorry you wasted your time."

Stephens turned to Green. "I'm glad you came, Harvey. Maybe the trip was a waste, but old farts like you and I tend to drift too far away from one another. Maybe it's just the way we look at priorities." He thought back to an old joke between the two and had to laugh again, as he always did, no matter how many times it was said. It recalled many times and places for the two of them, but would never be understood by anyone else. "At least my queen doesn't wear a dress."

Stephens turned and started back towards the soccer balls that were piled in their bags, like cairns marking a mountain trail, on the far side of the field.

"Stephens, get your ass back here!" called Sanders as he started to follow. "I'm not going back to face Bradford empty handed. If I have to, I'll personally drag you all the way myself."

Green reached out quickly, and with a strength that would not be expected by anyone judging his appearance, locked Sanders' arm. All the gentleness and good humor that were such a natural part of him were gone. He swung Sanders around to face him with such force that the perfect gray fedora spun off and tumbled over the grass to end up under the car.

"You've forgotten a lot in six years, Sanders. Don't you *ever* forget who that is out there. That 'ass' you want to grab has paid his dues more times than any of us."

Sanders pulled his arm out and down in a violent motion described in the training manuals as the optimum way to get out of a 'one-handed arm attack.' The movement had no apparent effect. The grip held and he remained firmly locked in Green's grasp.

"You were the one who insisted on this guy," Sanders charged, turning his attack to Green. "Remember? 'He's the only one who can handle this, Mr. Bradford, sir.' Well, look at your hero run. He can't get away fast enough, can he? If it's all right with you, *Mister* Green, I'd just as soon take my chances with someone I can trust to stick it out."

Green loosened his grip. Sanders started to reach to massage his arm when he saw the look on Green's face. The reaching hand stopped half way to its target.

"Sanders, I stood next to that guy in 78 when you dropped the two of us into Athens without cover, and half of Nidal's best knowing we were coming. He knew it too, but he still went into that airline luggage area. He did it alone, Sanders. I was down with my leg half shot off. Your goddamn 'help' didn't exist, and we were out of time. Stephens knew he couldn't wait. By the time your promised cavalry came over the hill there would be no targets left and those hostages would be dead. He knew you had blown it, but he went in anyway."

Green looked over at Stephens who was now halfway across the soccer field. He shook his head as he thought back to the scene in the airport. "Nine men died that day Sanders, and not one was a hostage. Had it been anyone lees than Stephens they all would have died. Christ, I'll never shake the picture of him walking into that room alone. There are damn few things in this life that scare me, but I never want to know what happened there that night."

Green moved closer to Sanders. Their faces were less than six inches apart. "He never reported your little screw-up there, did he Sanders? And you sure never bothered to clear up the story. You ended up as the hero, instead. You and I both know your nuts should have been left on the Director's doorstep. If it had been my choice they would have been, but Stephens overruled me. So, don't you *ever* question that man. Not again. Not once. There are too many people like me around that owe him. Too many that would come to his side anytime, anyplace he called."

The two stood there for half a minute. Neither moved. Their eyes were locked together. Finally, Green stepped back and moved towards the car to retrieve the hat that was now behind the front wheel. Sanders slowly let his breath escape, and turned to glance at Stephens in the distance. He rubbed his arm to work out the soreness.

This time, it was Sanders' voice that had a trace of pleading mixed in with the directive. "It was your idea to come here, Green. Why don't you talk to him?"

Green dusted off the fedora, carefully wiped a small patch of dirt off the bottom of the rim, and handed the hat to Sanders. He walked over to the driver's door, opened it, and with some reluctance reached in and grabbed a large manila envelope.

"You can stay by the car," he said as he straightened up. He looked across the field at Stephens. "I'll be the Judas, here, today."

Stephens saw Green approaching. In the distance Sanders was back in the car sitting alone in the front seat. The boys were making little pretense anymore at practicing soccer. Their 3-on-2 drill had died a natural death some time before. The boys stood in a small circle near the 18 yard 'D,' occasionally passing a single ball between them. At any given time at least half of them, though pretending to look down at the ball, stared first at the car, and then at Stephens and Green.

"Harvey, how the hell did you end up babysitting Marcus?" Stephens asked as Green reached him. "You're kind of hard to picture riding herd on desk jockeys. Or are you the new shoe shine king?"

Green knew there was no seriousness in the barb. "I screwed up good, Rob. The bastards promoted me. I have your old job now. I work for Sanders."

"I'm sorry for you, Harvey." He looked over towards the car. "Some things never change."

Both stood waiting for the other to continue. Both, for many of the same reasons, wished that there were a way to avoid what would come. Stephens nodded towards the kids out on the field. "They know something's happening, you know. It's so easy to underestimate kids. They're tougher than we were. A lot more streetwise. And I think that for many things, things involving people and feelings, they are better and faster than us. A few more years older, and they'll lose it. But for now, they still can instinctively judge people and events with a clarity I envy."

Stephens called out to the boys at the far end of the field. His voice was again that of coach. "All right, gentlemen. You're not going to get much accomplished that way. Let's end it for today. Hit the showers." The boys delayed, and then started to walk slowly in the direction of the buildings. Ned Mendoza broke away from them and headed towards Stephens.

"Ned, I'll get the balls. You hit the showers before you tighten up."

"Q, you sure you don't need some help?" Ned asked, hoping somehow to be allowed to impact what was going on.

"No thanks Ned, you head back. I'll be by later."

Ned paused while he furiously tried to think of any possible way he could stay.

"*Later*, Ned," Stephens called out.

Ned shook his head. "Later, coach. Later," he said to himself too softly to be heard. Then he turned and walked off the field towards the dorms that lay at the bottom of the hill.

Stephens said nothing, until Ned disappeared from sight. Finally, he turned back to Green. He knew that no more delay was possible. "Harvey,

I really can't help you here. Please don't ask. I made my choice six years ago and I haven't regretted my decision since. Don't force me to rabbit on you two. Harvey, look at this." He swept his arm around at the field, the lake, and Monadnock. "I waited thirty years to find this."

"Rob, I'm not here just because I work for that clown," Green said sadly, realizing the impact of what he was about to say. "I'm here because we need you. And I think that you might need to do this, too."

"Harvey, I'm not having withdrawal pains. I don't 'miss the action and excitement.' Oh I don't doubt this one is more than just a routine project, but I assure you I feel no need at all to be a part of it. But, if it will help, I'll share an observation or two with you. I got to know Robbins pretty well over the past couple years. We used to sit and talk up in the small office just off the balcony in the old Peterborough Movie Theater. The balcony was always closed. His office was a step out of the past. It was plastered with hundreds of the bright yellow flyers he distributed to advertise the movies. I think, at heart, there were few things he enjoyed more than his version of being the 'country innkeeper.' But in his case, his inn was a movie theater."

"We'll, he was a long way from being just an innkeeper. He was different. He never brought it up and I never pushed, but I'd be willing to make book that he was something a lot like Company once. Even at his age there's no way some hopped-up kid walked up to him and took him out. I tell you Harvey, I know this doesn't make any sense for a guy his age, but I feel certain that it took a least a sanction-4 to get him."

Green's voice went flat. Even before the words began his expression said, 'I'm sorry.' "We think it was a six."

Rob went cold. His stomach seemed to tighten. Suddenly he realized why Green's manner had bothered him so. He knew that there was only one way that Green's presence could make sense. "I know I've been away for some time, but back then there were no more than two dozen sixes in the world, and they generally didn't spend much time taking out old men in the woods."

"Rob, Techman wasn't the only person at the funeral. We had someone running optics cover. He brought back a lot of photos. All but one was useless. It was among the last he took. He picked out a car parked about a quarter mile away from the cemetery. It was a stock Buick, but it had tinted side windows. He fired off a full roll of the new 1420 hi-res film on that car."

Green held out the manila folder. "We got a silhouette, Rob."

Long before his hand touched the envelope, before he reached inside, Rob knew who would be in that picture. There would be a lean, hard face. It would be a face that seemed to be drawn tight with no fat, no wrinkles. The eyes would be deep-set and hawk-like, and the mouth would show no expression. There would never be a sign of expression from the one who chose to be called Falconer.

"I'm sorry. You know that only something like this would bring me up here. We all thought he was dead. Christ, Rob, we all thought you had evened the score for Foster. Everybody was certain was Falconer was in that building—and that you had finally taken him out. We all were so sure. There's been *nothing* for the last six years. Not even a hint of him. Now he's back. We don't think even Arafat knows he's back. Moussad insists he's dead, and that you got him. And now he appears almost in your backyard. Hell, half the guys who are in on this think you're the target."

Green rubbed his eyes. He looked very tired and very old just then. "Rob, my gut tells me he's on his own this time. I think he's playing his own game. It's either personal or he's renegade. That's why I think you're the target. I think it's payback time."

Stephens stared beyond the picture in his hand. As always, part of his mind calmly looked at the big picture around him even as the rest of his brain was furiously calculating the possibilities and details. He already knew that there was only one path left open for him. The past six years had been just an interlude, just a break between the acts of a play. Most of all, he knew that he had made promises that he had to keep before the peace of Dublin would ever again be possible.

"Rob, out of all of us you're still the only one who was able to match up against him. No one else even got close. You always understood Falconer. You could get inside his head. None of us could. You were so close to nailing him three or four times. I think you might be the only person on this earth he fears."

"And as if we needed it, there's more. We're pretty sure that a kid named Jim Peterson bought it in the same area around the same time. His last contact was the day Robbins died. We haven't found a trace of him since then. He had been helping treasury on a routine check of a presidential threat. Some young girl who works at an ice cream place down in Jaffrey called Silver Ranch phoned in for him. She said Peterson drove into the parking lot like a mad man, passed her a message, and then jumped back into his car and sped off. She said he was scared stiff, and he took out heading down route 124. That's the road to New Ipswich. It happened the same day Robbins was killed."

"The message had just the Virginia panic number, and one line. It said, 'Falconer is at A-12.' Well, 'A-12' is a mail drop Peterson uses. We found nothing but a coded letter hidden there. No one can figure out what the hell it means. It seems to be a progressive book-reference code, and we don't have the book."

"Rob, something very big is going down here. I'm worried. It's more just the coincidence that you're here. I was the one who asked to look you up. Sanders wanted no part of it. I went past him to Bradford. You can imagine what Sanders thought of that."

Green waited for a few moments before finishing. He started to reach out his arm, as though contact would somehow help. "Rob, we need you again," he said with great sadness. "My God I'm sorry. I really am." Green let his arm drop back to his side.

Stephens looked over at the empty soccer nets, and then at Monadnock in the distance. The sky was clear. A part of Stephens' mind thought about the glorious night sky that he had looked forward to enjoying—one with Orion standing powerfully standing astride the heavens and Cygnus gracefully flying its timeless path. It would be the kind of night when Stephens liked to walk the cross country ski trail that wandered toward Harrisville before looping down across the road and back to the school. It would be the kind of night when he and Ned might sit together in the loft. It would have been a good night to read Frost.

"Harvey, it's hard to just walk away from a place like this. It stays with you," Stephens said. He pointed to Dublin Lake in the distance. "Do you know that on some mornings the loons still dance there in the early mist? I've seen them twice now. There may be nothing of more haunting beauty than that sight."

Green said nothing. He had known all along what the outcome of the visit would be. No matter how important it was, no matter how much he could convince himself that it must be done, he hated the choice he had forced upon his friend.

"There's an old Indian legend, Harvey. It claims that you can never die on a day when you wake to the dancing of the loons."

It was late dusk now. In another half hour, darkness would take over. The car with Sanders seemed to be miles away on the far side of a huge plain. As they walked towards it, Green asked himself if even the return of the Falconer could justify what he had done.

Stephens wondered if the loons would ever dance again for him.

Chapter Three

Leaving Wendlandt went much easier than Stephens had expected when he started down the hill flanked by Green and Sanders. The soccer boys were still showering in the locker room in the basement of the dining building, and would be tied up for another half hour. The showers were very much a part of the flavor that would always be Wendlandt. Every year, the older boys would regale the new class with the story of the long-departed professor's wife who would pass through the area two or three times each month when the boys were in the showers. She would carry her glasses in hand, firmly aim her head at the ground, and sweep through the steam from the open showers like an ocean liner through the sea fog. Invariably she would call out "It's okay boys. I can't see a thing without my glasses." But those sitting on the rough wooden benches could look up and see her eyes constantly sweeping around the room.

John Hardy, who would be the central figure three years later in the town meeting, concocted the simple plan to write "Hello Emilie" in lipstick on his chest and await her arrival. It took six days of waiting, giggling, and crude jokes among the boys before she swept through the room again. Near the door as she was leaving she called back in surprised voice, "Come on John, you know that's spelled with a 'Y.'" Then, she stopped cold as she realized what had happened. Three weeks later, after the boys' call of "With a Y!" had followed her everywhere she went, her husband left to take "a great offer" for a public school opening in Manchester.

Stephens had few things to collect in his rooms on the first floor of the Old North Dormitory. All of the fulltime staff carried the additional responsibility of being dorm masters. Since he was single, he had been assigned to the smallest of the faculty suites. Yet the bathroom, small bedroom, and sitting room were all that he needed. He had a place to sleep and to read. The small kitchenette in one corner was rarely used. On most days he would eat in the main dining room with the boys. Sunday mornings were different. On that one day he would make his own meal of scrambled eggs, sausage, and English Muffins. The morning would be spent attacking the Boston Globe and New York Times crossword puzzles.

There were no photos or mementos of the past in his rooms. Despite that, there was a friendliness and warmth to the sitting room that made it a special place. The soft-hued paneling and shelves full of books softly cradled the old easy chair and lamp that were at one end of the room. Lying open, face down on the small table next to the chair was the second book of the Tolkien Trilogy *Lord of the Rings*. It was the third time he had read the fantasy of honor and adventure that has captivated so many over the years.

It took less than five minutes for Stephens to fill a small athletic bag with the few things he would need. He knew that Tolkien, or any of the other books that he had looked forward to reading over the long New Hampshire winter, would do him little good where he was going. His last stop before leaving the room was to go over to the bookcase and remove an old, dog-eared copy of a mathematics book. This was the one book in the room that he knew he would need. The spine read Finite Mathematics by Kemeny and Kurtz. He wondered, as he opened it and removed the handgun and two clips of ammunition, whether John Kemeny had ever studied the mathematics of ballistics.

A quick phone call had set up a brief meeting with Headmaster Gillespie. The discussion was awkward and short. There was no way Stephens could offer a reasonable explanation for the emergency leave of absence he requested. Gillespie walked to the window and looked down at the car parked below, motor running. "Rob, whatever it is, when you're ready to come back we'll be here." He turned back and looked directly at Stephens. "The position will stay open, Rob. For as long as it takes."

As the car pulled away, he saw Ned emerging from the locker room. Ned started over the commons at a trot for the quick run up to the Old North Dormitory. After perhaps a dozen strides, he stopped when he saw Stephens in the departing car. When the car had pulled out of sight, Ned stood there alone for several moments. Then he began the long, slow walk to the empty dorm.

The next morning the three men approached Folkes Farm in the northern tip of Virginia. They were driving a muddy, green, five-year-old Ford station wagon bearing the Folkes Farm emblem. They had driven to Nashua where a helicopter awaited to fly them to Logan Airport in Boston. The last Delta Airlines flight took them to National Airport in Washington. They spent the night in the suite that was always on hold for Agency use at the Washington Plaza Hotel. The hotel had become a favorite of Company people ever since it had recruited a top quality general manager from one of Boston's best hotels a year earlier. Green and Sanders left Stephens alone that night. Both knew that there would be plenty of time the next day to provide any of the details that were not covered during the car ride to Nashua.

The one hour drive that morning had brought them to the CIA's antiterrorism headquarters, known as ATQ by the few who knew of its existence. Folkes Farm was more than 150 years old. It was just a few miles north of Centreville and lay in the heart of all those Civil War names known to school children everywhere. To the west stood the Bull Run Mountains with the Bull Run River flowing east to join the Potomac. Harpers Ferry was to the north, Manassas to the south, and a host of other battlefields lay in the distance.

As the station wagon pulled up to the outskirts of the farm, Stephens looked in the distance to see a building more reminiscent of an episode of *Dallas,* or a remake of *Gone with the Wind,* than of anything he would expect from the CIA. So much of the agency approach was reflected in the scene. The typical shell within a shell, fake within a fake, con within a con. The farm was very little of what it appeared to be.

Stephens turned to the back seat where Sanders had sat alone for the drive. Sanders had said next to nothing for the entire trip. "We having lunch with Clark Gable?" Stephens asked.

"Things haven't ground to a halt without you, Stephens. We've made quite a few changes. Time does move on, you know." Sanders waved a hand to encompass the entire farm. "This is the new ATQ."

Stephens turned back to Green.

"Rob, ATQ is now a lot larger than you remember," said Green as they approached the main gate into the farm. "They moved it out of Langley four years ago, and hid it here. The locals have no clue. To them, this is just the home of Mr. and Mrs. Clayton Welbrough Pierce the third. I tell you, I hope that when I'm ready to retire I can have this job. It would sure beat the hell out of teaching you soccer. How would you like to be paid to look rich, act rich, be rich, keep totally clean, go to every social event in the state, and live on a ranch raising thoroughbreds?"

The car pulled to a stop next to a small hut that held a sleepy looking ranch hand. The hut stood at the gateway to the ranch. A ten foot chain link fence stretched out of sight in both directions. Two antique smoked glass carriage lamps stood on wrought iron posts just inside the gate. Stephens looked first at the estate in the distance, and then back to Green. "You've got to be shitting me. This is just bizarre."

Green rolled down the window and held out his pass to the ranch hand in the hut. Sanders, in the back seat did the same. "Morning Harvey, Mr. Sanders," said the ranch hand as he carefully studied the passes of the two men. "Who's your friend?"

"He's with us, Sam," answered Green. Green lightly rubbed the left side of his forehead as he waited for Sam to inspect the passes. The small motion was necessary, since there was a third, unidentified party in the car. Until he saw that exact movement, Sam was required to assume that the third party was dangerous and was forcing the other two to enter the area.

Green reached out to accept the returned passes. "He wants to be adopted by the Pierces."

"Sorry, Harvey," said the ranch hand as he opened the gate, "I've got seniority on that opening when it comes up."

The car pulled through the gate and started down the road towards the main house. Though the estate was just about one half mile straight in front of the gate, the road curved far to the left as you entered. A large pond blocked any direct route to the house.

"This place used to be a safe house until '84," said Green. "The Pierces have lived here since '86. Now it's ATQ. There's about five times as much below ground as you see up here, buddy."

Stephens looked back over his shoulder towards the gate. "You have one old guy guarding the main entrance to ATQ?"

Sanders spoke up from the back seat. "You never used to take anything at face value, Stephens. I thought that was your big secret to success. Don't ever trust anything."

"Don't take Sam lightly, Rob. He's a Sanction-4," explained Green. "Under that counter, never leaving his right hand is an Uzi specially fitted with armor-piercing shells. The whole hut is steel lined, except for a small panel in front of the Uzi that's just eighth inch veneer. His foot is always on at least one of the two deadman switches by his feet. And all of us were on 'Candid Camera' all the way."

"The lanterns," asked Stephens?

"Yup. And with the firepower in the upper floor of that house, we could floor this sucker and still wouldn't even get close to the house before this old Ford would be scrap metal."

The car wound its way past the far end of the pond and began to curve back towards the estate. They passed a pasture filled with cows. Beyond it, to the rear of the house, was a paddock where two beautiful horses grazed. Between the cows and the horses stood a magnificent barn. Behind it was the dairy processing plant.

The dairy cows and the horses were vital to the security of the place. Folkes Farm actually was a working dairy farm. Its milk traded throughout the area and was featured at smaller markets like the IGAs that still spotted the area despite the large food store chains. Every day a dozen milk tanker trucks pulled up at one of the three rear entrances to the farm. Local neighbors were proud of the farm. It had achieved commercial success without drifting away from its historical legacy and beauty. None of the nearby house and farm owners would have guessed that some of the trucks that visited were fakes and had never held milk. They would bring supplies and people into the area. During construction of the underground labyrinth below the plant, the hollow tankers had been used to transport building materials in, and excavation dirt out.

The thoroughbreds, along with the Pierces' famed art collection, explained the tight security around the farm. People for miles believed the view of the farm that was carefully maintained by the CIA. It was well known that the Pierces ". . . absolutely hate all the security, and probably would have had none of it if they hadn't lost that beautiful Renoir several years back." The two famed thoroughbreds, Notre Dame and Strasbourg, would be reason enough for the extra security.

Mr. and Mrs. Clayton Welbrough Pierce III were, in their own way, a microcosm of the Washington, Georgetown, and Virginia scene. Their fortune had come ". . . from old money, oil they say, back before the damn Arabs ruined everything." They were well known and respected by Virginia

Society. Mrs. Pierce was head of the Bull Run Ladies Volunteers, whose generosity in support of children was the backbone of at least three private schools. Mr. Pierce ". . . has the ear of the President, himself" and had been at many White House affairs. Often Pierce had been asked to run for elective office. Always his answer had been that ". . . I'm a simple man. Let others screw up the country." A social event anywhere in a hundred miles could well be judged by whether or not the Clayton Welbrough Pierces had been invited, and whether or not they attended.

In reality, Mr. and Mrs. Pierce actually were married. In all the years they had grown into the role, they had nearly forgotten their real names of Pete and Joan Buxton. She had been head of Ciphers Department for nine years before they had been transformed into the Pierces. He had been an undistinguished mid-level member of the records section. The job Green called the "best in the company" had fallen to them because of a twist of luck. Of all the possible candidates who were vetted, the Buxton/Pierces were the only couple who had no children and no remaining family in the country.

Green did not stop at the house itself. "Farmhands don't pull up to the front door, Rob." Just before he came to the house, he turned left and headed between the house and barn towards the milk processing plant in the rear. The building looked like a huge local hockey arena. It was built of metal sheeting and had been painted a bright, clean white. Above the huge pair of swinging doors at the South end of the building was the familiar dark green double-F emblem of Folkes Farm.

Green pulled the car up to a small parking area that held less than twenty cars. A small white sign indicated "Employees Only" with a "Visitors" sign pointing to the end of the building. Once they had pulled around to the side of the plant, he could see another building in the distance that had two milk trucks in the process of being filled.

"Rob," continued Green, "This plant actually does produce milk, though a hell of a lot less than you'd guess from the number of cartons you could find in stores. We also own a second plant down in Lynchburg that also processes milk from dozens of smaller dairies. By the time they finish each day, our shipments have magically tripled." Green pointed to the fields where hundreds of cows grazed. "More than half of what we have on this farm aren't milkers at all. A little shot of something once a month or so and they stay clean and dry. That keeps the need for people down. They just graze, and require about a third of the people any of the locals would guess."

The three walked to a side entrance labeled "Office."

"What's that building out back?"

"That's supposed to be the loading station and where our full-time ranch hands sleep. A few of our people do sleep there on a rotating basis. If all the bessies on this farm were milkers, we'd need to keep that place full. As it is, most of the people who arrive here never have anything to do with the cows. They just head straight down to the complex. But the number of people and cars looks about right to the locals."

"We split the herd into three parts and keep them in different parts of the ranch. There's more than 1200 acres here, you know. We have two more buildings just like this one in other corners of the farm." Green pointed to the nearby herd. "This is the real herd. We hire locals to help work it. The locals never have anything to do with the other two herds and have no idea both are dry. Now who would suspect anything here when we hire locals all the time to wander around. The cars that pull up each day make perfect sense when you look at all the processing from this and the other three plants. Remember, there are three other entrances, too. Every building has a tunnel that connects to the main complex."

The three men walked through the door into a small general office area. A receptionist near the front door smiled warmly. "Good morning Mr. Sanders. Mr. Green. Are you here this morning to see Ms. Chambers?"

Green had only met Ms. Chambers a handful of times since he had been pulled to ATQ from his field position. He doubted that he would add to that number today. Ms. Chambers ran the actual milking and herd operations. The reception area led to the farm offices that were available to the non-ATQ farmhands, employees, vendors and job applicants who came to the farm. Only one of the offices led further into the complex as entry to ATQ.

The same precaution shown at the front gate was used here to ensure the entry was not being forced. The receptionist would always operate on the assumption that one or more of the people in that office were outsiders. Until the third party that the receptionist did not recognize was identified, a standard litany would be followed.

"Yes we are, Millie," said Green massaging his neck in the 'safe' signal. "Can we go ahead?"

"Of course, sir. You know the way," she said once Green and Sanders had vouched for the third party and have given the day's safe signal.

Sanders led the way out of the office area and down the hall past several single offices that were all occupied. These people, though Company, ran the day to day operations of the farm activities. At the end of the hallway was an office door leading to a small executive reception area. The brass engraved plaque beside the door identified the office as that of "D.L. Chambers, Executive Director."

Inside the door they were greeted by another smile, but Stephens immediately recognized it as the calm, assured smile of someone experienced in a good deal more than just office operations. She was drawing her hand back from the phone as they entered. Their arrival had been advised by Millie. Green saw the small light flash on the leftmost button of the phone next to the hold button. However, it did not indicate a call on hold. It was the result of the metal detector in the doorway that had easily picked up the presence of the weapons Stephens and Green carried. In one corner a small TV camera covered all activity in the room.

Both Green and Sanders displayed their Company passes. This time there was no signal of any sort from Green. As soon as he heard the click of the door locking behind him that would prevent any accidental surprise, he said "We'll be going below, Pat. This is Mr. Stephens. He will be going down with us."

"Your friend appears to be carrying a weapon," she said, rising from her seat and turning to Stephens. "Sir, would you please give it to Mr. Green until you're at your destination?" She opened one drawer and removed a small metal detector from it.

Stephens withdrew the weapon and handed it to Green. He looked back at the door and realized just how solid it was. The meaning of the faint click had not been lost on him. "Simple, but effective," he offered. He held his arms straight out to his side as the woman walked over to him. "Ma'am, I'd say it's a pretty safe bet that you're not here just to fetch coffee and run the copier."

She did not answer until she had completed her search. Only when she had carefully checked out any indication of metal, and any area of his clothing that she might question, did she turn her cool eyes towards Stephens. Her voice was completely level. Stephens thought he could detect a tiny spark of humor in her eyes, but there was not even a trace of anything in her voice other than the professional assurance that marked the most senior of company people. "That would be a very safe bet, Mr. Stephens."

She returned to her desk and motioned to the left of two doors at the far end of the office. "Please go ahead gentlemen." She waited until the door had closed behind and the elevator began to take them to the lower levels of the complex. Only then did she release the lock on the hall door to the office.

It took less than half an hour for Stephens to complete the formalities of being readmitted to the Company. Sanders, two days earlier, had been confident enough in the outcome of the meeting at Wendlandt to begin the process. He dropped Green and Stephens at Records Department and headed for the Director's office to report. In many ways, the forms and paperwork that were required were not much different from those of a new employee beginning at General Motors or IBM.

When Stephens finished, he and Green walked through the hallway that lead to the briefing room at the far end of the underground complex. It was a wide hall, with both single offices and wide open landscaped office areas on either side. Many eyes followed them. Occasionally Stephens saw a face he remembered. He did not know most of the current staff personnel. Many had been hired during the rapid growth of ATQ in the six years after he left. Even when Stephens was with the Company, very little of his time had been spent in the headquarters. He knew that he was "field," and that he would always be field. Staff was an area to avoid for him, an area whose politics and procedures he never really understood.

When a nod or small wave had been exchanged with one of the few who recognized Stephens, the person would wait until Stephens had passed, and then move quickly to the nearest desks to point him out to the rest of the staff. Soon there was a small murmur of voices as the news spread. ". . . did you hear . . . that's Stephens . . . you mean, *the* Stephens, Rob Stephens? . . . I thought he was dead . . . were you there in 73? . . . did you hear about Athens in 78? . . . Stephens, the one with Foster? . . . you mean there really is a Rob Stephens? . . . my god, wasn't he the one who . . ." By the time Stephens reached the large conference room at the far northwest corner of the underground complex, most of the normally self-controlled staff was either gawking down the hall or on the phone to pass the word to distant parts of the complex.

There were five people waiting in the conference room when Stephens and Green arrived. At the head of the table was John Bradford, the head of ATQ and one of the eight Deputy Directors of the CIA. His was the smallest of all the CIA divisions, but also the most rapidly growing. Bradford liked to tell new ATQ recruits, in their initial orientation week, that ". . . ours, regrettably, is a classic growth industry."

Until 1975, the antiterrorist group had been just a small section in the fourth branch of the CIA. Bradford, Patterson, Sanders, and Stephens were the first four members. Green transferred into the group a year later. By 1977 the operation reached a size where it was split into a separate directorate with Bradford at its head. In 1981 it had left McLean, Virginia to move to the newly completed ATQ at Folkes Farm.

Folkes Farm had taken nearly two years to construct, because most of it would be underground. The key to the construction was the placement of the three buildings overhead. First, a terrible "accident" had to be carefully planned to burn down the original barn. Then, when the barn was rebuilt, the new farmhand barracks and the plant were built at the same time. The surrounding local residents could only sympathize with the Pierces when a porous limestone bed was 'discovered' under the proposed site. The limestone would not meet new building codes to support a building, so an excavation would be necessary to remove the limestone and refill the area to make a firm foundation. Once the three building were up, a large part of the underground area was already in place. The additional underground work over the following years used the false, hollow milk tankers to remove the telltale dirt and bring materials to the site.

Four of Bradford's six section chiefs comprised the remainder of the people in the conference room. Bill Sanders was the head of Mideast Operations, or MIDOPS. MIDOPS had become the most important of the three operational sections. Sanders was responsible for liaison with other CIA directorates, a field staff of thirty-one agents, and internal staff of eleven. Harvey Green was his head of field operations, Stephens' old position.

Joyce Patterson was a remarkable woman. She ran the catchall group responsible for all other parts of the world. TERROPS handled anything not Mideast or domestic. Russia came under this group. South America was the current main concern. Patterson herself was in her late forties, and was stunningly attractive. She was a Smith Rhodes Scholar who studied psychology in her year at Oxford. More than anyone else in the directorate, Patterson created an air of stability. Her calm logic was legendary. Her first class three assignment in 1967 had led to the discovery of what was then the highest level mole ever found in the West German government. For seven years she had been in East German operations, and had worked her way up to station chief. She was one of the hand-picked original four that formed ATQ. All who worked with her knew that it was only a matter of time before she would soon be "one of the eight."

Pete Jacobi was head of domestic anti-terror activities. USOPS was a new section. It had been formed in 1984 after the Beirut embassy bombing and had the distinction of being the only CIA activity authorized within the United States. Only the senate panel that oversaw CIA activities was aware that it existed, and even that panel had very mixed feelings about making an exception to the absolute ban on domestic CIA activities. All but two of the senate panel had first insisted that the FBI could adequately handle any such duties. "If they need help," the senators would argue, "there is no reason the CIA could not provide 'advice and assistance' if requested."

It had taken a rare visit by the President to Capitol Hill to change their feelings. The President, Jacobi, and Patterson had met for nearly three hours in secret with the panel. Jacobi and Patterson had presented compelling arguments about the need for a single responsibility for antiterror activities. They pointed out the FBI's obvious inability to directly carry the investigation outside the United States where the terrorist activities originated. They presented charts and facts and figures about the growing incidence of terrorist activities and the potential for domestic terrorism. Despite this, the panel would not budge. Only when it was clear the discussions were at a dead end did the President order Jacobi to reveal the specifics of the "McJeannet affair" that had occurred earlier that same week.

McJeannet had been a high-profile target on the ATQ watch list ever since the Munich Olympics massacre. When the FBI forwarded a set of photographs to ATQ as part of the routine preparation for the President's visit, Green recognized McJeannet's face in one of the photographs of the visitor's gallery. Acting on Green's warning, the FBI caught McJeannet just as he was leaving the gallery. McJeannet had left his briefcase in the gallery. FBI bomb squad experts had quietly entered and removed the case just moments before the timer had reached its setpoint. Two members on the senate panel had turned white when they suddenly realized the real meaning of the well publicized "gas tank explosion" just outside the capitol building only two days before.

Pete Jacobi, though young for such a position by Agency standards, was very good at his job. In the first eighteen months of formal operations, Jacobi's small USOPS group had been credited with uncovering and stopping eleven planned domestic terrorist operations.

Jim Lowe headed ciphers. He had replaced Joan Buxton when she became Mrs. Clayton Welbrough Pierce, III. Missing from the meeting were the remaining two section chiefs. Dorothy Chambers was responsible for ATQ security, the Pierces, and the daily operations of the farm. Ed Harrington headed up administration and records.

Stephens smiled as he looked at the familiar faces in the room. Patterson and Bradford were among the very best. Green was one of the few people in his life he could trust "at my back when it's dirty." Even Sanders, despite all of the friction, was valuable because of his strong analytical skills, and the uncanny ability to spot patterns in information that everybody else would miss. They were pros. He turned to Bradford. "When I left here, John, there were only a dozen of us in the whole bloody group."

"Rob, when you left, there were at lot less terrorists." John rose from his chair and shook hands with Stephens warmly. "We're a long way past the time when you, Bill, Joyce and I could take on the world and win most of them." Bradford pointed to a chair between Patterson and Jacobi. "You know most of us here. You might remember Pete Jacobi. We doubled with him back when he was in 4th. He joined us a few months after you left. Jim Lowe came about two years later when we finally added our own ciphers section."

Stephens greeted each of the two in turn. Then he walked around the far side of the table to the open chair next to Patterson. Stephens had always had great respect for Patterson. He reached down and rested a hand on her shoulder as he passed. She reached up and touched his hand. "Welcome back, Rob. Enjoy your vacation?"

"Yes, Joyce. I did. You should try it sometime."

Stephens took his seat between Patterson and Jacobi. Bradford walked over and closed the door before starting the meeting. "Okay. We have a lot of ground to cover. Bill tells me that Rob has been briefed on the basics.

In a nutshell, we're sucking wind here. We've got a threat on the President none of us understand, a page of code no one can crack, two dead people, and one resurrected corpse."

Bradford sat back down in his chair and opened a folder. "About all we know is that somehow this is all tied together. Next week the President is in Boston. I've done everything I can do except slap him upside the head to get him to postpone it. Christ, it's just a lousy endorsement speech for god's sake, not a State of the Union Address. But he won't budge. He's going."

"Let's start with you, Jacobi. Bring everyone up to speed on what you're doing about all this."

Jacobi was the youngest at the table. He was in his mid-thirties and never ceased to be the target for humor labeling him as 'the kid,' or 'rook.' On this day he looked a good deal older than any at the table had seen him look before. Jacobi was tired, and the missing Jim Peterson was his man. He had not yet reached the point where he could just step away from such a loss. For the past three days he had not left the complex. When possible, between analyses of reports coming in, he napped in the infirmary.

Jacobi got out of his seat and walked to the projector at the end of the room. He dimmed the lights and displayed a slide onto a screen that had dropped from a recess in the ceiling with a quiet whirr.

"This is the first threat. Secret Service got it October 13th. You can see that they might consider it fairly routine. They get a couple like this every day."

Stephens straightened in his chair when he got to the end of the note. The final phrase in the message stood out as though the only words on the page.

"It was postmarked out of Keene, New Hampshire. They ran a standard check on it, found nothing, and put it into the "Die-a-natural-death" file. In fairness to Treasury, it would be easy to blow this one off."

Jacobi stepped through the next three slides. "There are three more of these. One is from Fitchburg, Massachusetts and the other two are from New Hampshire. Nashua and Manchester. All are about the same with the same demands about our bases in Greece, activities anywhere near the Gulf of Sidra, and the West Bank. The last one says the President will die on his trip to Boston if there is no agreement first."

Jacobi turned off the projector and turned the lights back up. He walked back to his seat. "The second one arrived on the 22nd of October.

The next two were in November, one on the 2nd, one on the 11th. After the third one, Treasury asked us for help. My deputy section chief, Miller, put Jim Peterson on it."

Stephens continued to stare at the wall where the slides had been displayed. The final phrase in all four messages had been the same—"And remember, no matter how long he must search and soar, the hawk inevitably strikes." That phrase had always been the mark of the Falconer. It was his own proud proclamation when he wanted his victim to know that nothing could change the future.

"How could that be missed?" Stephens asked of no one in particular. "How could such a sign be missed. Have we all forgotten the Falconer?"

Jacobi sat down and shook his head bitterly. "Those four letters were here more than two weeks before Jim Peterson disappeared. Rob, we had them in here for two weeks, and no one noticed anything unusual. The 'hawk' thing didn't mean anything to me. Falconer was just a name, a six year old name of a dead man. I never was on any of the Falconer cases. As far as I can see at least fourteen people saw those messages, and not one of us thought they were anything special. I didn't even bother to bring them to the staff reviews." His voice trailed off. "If I had, John, Bill, Joyce or Harvey all would have caught it. I just didn't know . . ."

John Bradford interrupted. "Pete, any one of us might indeed have caught it, but there is no way in hell something like that should have been brought to our attention based upon what was known. Hell, after Pearl Harbor there were probably a hundred books written on what 'should have been done' to avoid it, but not one I've seen showed how a lone person with isolated facts could have logically come to a conclusion that would have changed a damn thing."

Bradford reached into his pile of notes and pulled out his copies of the four threats. "The fact is, no matter how callous this sounds, Treasury gets dozens of these a week. Other than a phrase that would only mean something to a few dozen people in the world, there is no reason these would stand out. Deputy Directors simply don't get bothered with routine Presidential threats. Nor do you run to other section heads on trivial matters. So we can waste as much time as we desire on second guessing, but it won't change a thing."

Bradford laid the notes back on the table. His expression softened as he looked at Jacobi. "Pete, despite all the computers and the codes and all the failsafes we try to build, it all comes down to people. Humans have to make judgments based upon the facts they see, and how they see them at the time. Sometimes we make mistakes. *And sometimes, all the facts aren't there when we need them.*"

No one spoke for a few moments. It was not for lack of sympathy or for lack of understanding. They pauses because no matter how much experience sat at that table, none of them had ever discovered a way to push away the doubts and feelings when they failed. The feelings could sometimes be controlled, but could never be eliminated. Even when all the logic in the world proved conclusively that events had to be as they were, no one had ever found how to escape the endless doubts that crept into the dark edges of their thoughts.

Jim Lowe broke the silence. "I assume it's the location of those four postmarks that sent Peterson to New Ipswich?" Lowe was rarely in key staff meetings, unless his ciphers section played a direct role in the investigation. He was never comfortable being there. Lowe was a very quiet person who was much more at home with the mathematics and precision of his code duties than when he had to come face to face with the real-world impact of his responsibilities. "Manchester, Nashua, Fitchburg, and Keene all form a quadrilateral with New Ipswich at its focus."

Patterson could not help a slight inward smile at Lowe's clinical choice of terms. "From the briefing papers I saw that doesn't narrow things down much. Within that *square* are Jaffrey, Peterborough, Marlborough, and even your Dublin, Rob," she said turning to Stephens.

"If we include towns the size of New Ipswich on our list, that box has another dozen or two candidates for us," Stephens answered. "It gives us nothing by itself. The key questions are why New Ipswich, why Robbins, and what happened to Peterson?"

Patterson turned to Bradford to continue Stephens' thought. "Any of the briefing papers you've had your people send up to me indicate nothing special about New Ipswich. It's just a small, sleepy town. Most people who live there work somewhere else. The only decent sized firm, a matchbook company, closed down ten years ago."

"Peterson has got to be the key, Pete," stated Bradford. "Let's turn to him for a bit. Please bring everyone up to date on what he was doing before we pulled him and reassigned him to the Treasury request."

Jacobi turned to Stephens. "This is something you might know about, Rob. It's from your own back yard. Peterson was on a simple vetting mission to look at the actions of a harmless antinuclear group called the '11:55

Clan.' The top banana is someone named Charley Pillsford. He lives on Brattle Street in Cambridge, but also has a summer house in Dublin."

"I've heard the name of the group, but that's about it. I don't remember ever meeting Pillsford while in Dublin."

Lowe provided another of his rare comments. "I know that group. They're the ones behind that referendum against any nuclear R&D in Cambridge. They got our recruiters thrown out of Harvard."

"Those are the ones," Jacobi continued. "The name comes from the 'doomsday clock' idea. There's a group, I think they're in Minnesota, or somewhere? They keep track of how close we are to a nuclear war. When the clock hits 12:00, boom."

"Last time I heard anything about it, they announced that things had improved and they were moving the hands back a minute or so," said Lowe. "Is that the same group Peterson was studying?"

"No. One of the few things we *do* know is that the two groups are totally different. Peterson's group just stole the idea for the name, as far as we can tell," said Jacobi. "The 11:55 Clan in Boston seems to be pretty mild stuff. They're into protest and demonstration, but no terrorism. One of Peterson's first reports indicated he thought they were pretty sincere. I can't see any way they could tie into Falconer."

"What you're saying, Pete," interjected Bradford, "is that they're exactly the right type of vetting assignment for the first solo by a class two."

"Right. That's why we chose them," said Jacobi, turning to Stephens. "Rob, it's been standard practice since '81 to age a class two field agent on an easy one like this. Up until that point they're never out of sight of a three, or higher. We send them out to check out something harmless like Greenpeace or Save the Whales. They don't have to know that we usually don't even look at the reports they file other than for critical training review. Jim Peterson was a natural for 11:55. He was brought up in a little bedroom town near Worcester called West Boylston. He knew the area."

"Doesn't make any sense that Falconer would have anything to do with kids," said Stephens. "Any chance he's got another Emily in the group?"

"I guess it's possible," answered Patterson, "but I think it's pretty unlikely. What would be the benefit? Where are the . . ."

Jacobi interrupted. "What's an 'Emily?'"

"Just a long shot," answered Bradford. "Emily Bertasi was an agent of ours he turned. While it's never bought us anything, the only chink in Falconer's armor we've ever found is an uncanny ability to seduce women.

He's involved women in his affairs, even when it had to be a huge risk, two or three times in the past. Every time they were so smitten that they never had a clue what he was up to."

There were a few seconds of silence before Sanders spoke. "I don't see it. They're mostly college kids." He shook his head. "I don't see it."

"What are the stats on Peterson, himself," asked Patterson.

Jacobi sorted through the pile of papers in front of him. He pulled out a sheet with a light green tint that marked it as from the personnel records section.

"He's been with us four years. Held a lot of promise. Houghton was the class four on his baptism runs." Baptism was a term for the time a new field agent spent in the field with a senior agent. "He gave the kid high marks. Let's see. Specifically cited for self-control and judgment. He was red-tagged in his third year as a possible candidate for rapid field advancement." Jacobi turned to the back side of the sheet. "He came to us fresh out of school. Boston College. Education major. He had one special characteristic. He had a baby face. At age twenty-five he would have no problem passing for a college student. He could have even passed for being high school student on a good day. He had a knack for being able to blend in with almost any young crowd."

"According to this, he answered one of our ads in the Boston Herald." Jacobi looked around the table. "I wonder if many people would ever believe how many people come to us that way."

"What did you think of him?" asked Bradford. "Was he reliable? Can we take his reports at face value?"

"I think he was solid," answered Jacobi. "He was much better than the typical rookie class two. We underestimated his reports because he was new. If we had taken him seriously, this would be a very different type of meeting."

Jacobi sifted through the papers to find a specific field report. "His last report in was from Jaffrey a couple days after we pulled him from the 11:55 stuff and put him on the Treasure assignment. He was staying at the 'Quiet Pines Motel.' He claimed he was getting close to something." Jacobi searched the text for a specific reference. "He said 'very little to report yet, but was close to something that might be critical.'"

Jacobi carefully put the sheet back on the table and squared the pile of papers. "Miller took the report. He told me that same day, half joking, that 'this kid Peterson has a major league case of NKS."

Stephens leaned over and looked quizzically at Patterson. "NKS?" he asked quietly.

Patterson smiled and raised one eyebrow. "'New Kid Syndrome.' We've added a few acronyms since you left, you know."

Stephens rolled his eyes and then turned back to hear the rest of Jacobi's report.

"Miller filled me in later," continued Jacobi. "Peterson had claimed that he was close to something that was 'too important to discuss on an open line.' Miller and I both wrote it off as the usual attempt to look important on the first solo."

Jacobi looked around the table for support and agreement. "We all just missed it. You all have been there. All of us have seen that kind of new-kid exaggeration a few dozen times each."

Green was the one who answered. "Pete, it's easy to look back now and see all kinds of answers. At the time I doubt either Miller or you even knew there was a question being asked."

"There's one other piece of information we added just yesterday," Jacobi continued. "Cadbury was pretty close to him. They were hired at the same time. Cadbury had desk watch all that week. He took both of Peterson's calls. Before Miller got on, he and Cadbury spoke for a couple minutes. Cadbury says that when he routinely asked Peterson how things were going Peterson said '. . . if I'm right, what I'm on will make everyone back there forget all about Rob Stephens.'"

All heads around the table involuntarily turned to look at Stephens. Stephens looked up and turned towards Green. "Kids," he said sadly, shaking his head.

"What's his official status at this point," asked Patterson. "Is he dead, or missing? Could he possibly be deep cover? Could he be a drifter? A rabbit? How do we classify him?"

"There's no body, so at least one theory would have to be either deep cover or drifter," answered Jacobi. "I can't support the drifter idea though. There's nothing in his past to indicate that he was anything but solid. If this kid was burned out, or was going through the 'in-or-out crisis,' I read him as the kind who would just out and say it. I don't see him running home to momma."

"Does he have family?" asked Patterson.

"Records say he lost both his parents while he was in high school. His older sister pretty much raised him. They sent someone to visit her, but she could give us nothing."

"Then that leaves deep cover as at least a viable alternative," stated Patterson.

Jacobi answered, "Maybe. That's the best of the two alternatives. But, frankly, I'm not sure it washes. That photo of the Falconer changes everything."

Stephens rose from his chair and walked over to a low credenza against the wall. He picked up a glass and a pitcher of ice water. The condensation from the pitcher flowed down and dripped noisily on the tray as he filled the glass. He knew that he had to pass a death judgment on the young Peterson kid. He knew that despite all the realism in that room, despite all the years of experience, none of the others had yet gotten to the point where they could state the obvious.

"If that is the Falconer, then Jim Peterson didn't have a chance." He turned back and looked at the others around the table. "We sent a little boy to stop a great white."

When Stephens returned to the table with his glass of water, Bradford asked Lowe to present his information. Lowe walked over to the projector. "Let me show you the sheet of code we got from Peterson's drop. I believe Harvey picked it up."

"When we got the call from that young girl at the ice cream stand she gave us the message from Peterson that 'The Falconer is at A-12,'" explained Green. "Because of the name Falconer, Pete called me in on it. The A-12 reference was to a Jaffrey Post Office Box we had opened. The only thing I found there was an envelope with this page of code. The lab found nothing special about it. All they could tell us is that they're pretty sure Peterson didn't write it."

Lowe inserted a slide and started the projector. "This is the message. You can see it's handwritten."

The screen showed a paragraph of numbers with an occasional word intermixed. The whole page was filled.

"This is what we call a 'literary sequence code.' It is unbelievably simple and totally uncrackable unless you know the exact book, page and word that define the start of the code. Let me give you a little example."

Lowe called up the next slide in the sequence. "Here's a simple example to give you an idea about what we're up against."

22 21 17 9 house 17 2 3 11 fence.

"Looks simple, doesn't it. But it makes no sense to anyone. That's because each number refers to a specific word in a book or magazine. You pick a book, and a starting point in that book. The first word is number one, the next is two, and so on."

"Let me show you what this message means. We took a simple example." Lowe switched to a new slide:

1	2	3	4	5	6	7	8	9	10	11
Mary	had	a	little	lamb	whose	fleece	was	white	as	snow.

12	13	14	15	16	17	18	19	20	21	22
Every	where	that	Mary	went	the	lamb	was	sure	to	go.

"Now, if you know this poem is the key, the code is simple." He put a new slide on the screen. This slide had the decoded message on the bottom of the slide.

Go to the white house that had a snow fence.

"See, the 22 stands for 'go' and the 21 for 'to,' etc. Since the words house and fence aren't in the poem, they're written in. Of course we could have easily chosen a longer section of a book that offered a better vocabulary so that 'house' and 'fence' would be in code, too."

Lowe flipped back to the original coded message from Peterson. "We don't know what this says, what it means, or where it came from. We need the book and reference. That's the beauty of this kind of thing. You can just about publish your basic top secret message in the local newspaper. If you're really cocky, you can even reveal the name of the reference. Then, when you want to allow someone to decode the message, you phone and tell them the key. For example, the code in our newspaper might tell the world that the reference was 'Last of the Mohicans.' The phone call would reveal that the key word is 'Chapter 11, paragraph 14, word three.' That defines what word is '1,' in the code and the rest is easy."

"Do we have any idea at all about the key?" asked Patterson.

"None, unless there's something new in the last hour," answered Lowe, looking to Bradford for confirmation. Bradford nodded in agreement. "We're running a check of anything associated with the Falconer before, but even if he uses the same reference book, the chances of finding the key phrase are ridiculously small. We could even find the key, and miss it. A year ago I saw a clever twist on this kind of code for the first time. Every other word was intentionally pure gobbledygook. The idea was fiendish. Even if you had the key, after you tested it by decoding the first few lines. You'd see nothing but nonsense and would quit and try something new without realizing you had it!"

"I appreciate your effort, Lowe, but it's a waste of time," said Stephens with certainty. "The Falconer won't reuse an old code."

"Then we're back at the beginning again," said Bradford. "The key is the Falconer. We have to assume Peterson is dead, and that Falconer caught him, probably after he stole this sheet. There might be a chance Peterson's a prisoner, but that's pretty remote. Falconer has never taken prisoners unless there was a very good reason, and none comes to mind here no matter how I try to think of one. An educated guess says Falconer might be somewhere near New Ipswich. He is probably going to try and kill the President in Boston next week."

"Look, just to eliminate a possibility, is it possible that this has nothing to do with the Falconer?" asked Patterson. "Is there any chance that photo is of someone else? Every time I go over this I come back to how much it hinges on whether or not the Falconer is really alive."

"Joyce, we've drawn a total blank there," said Sanders. "That silhouette, and that phrase about the hawk, are the only pieces of evidence that he's alive. That's pretty soft stuff. All the hard evidence, everything else we have, says Stephens took him out in '78."

"John," said Patterson, turning to Bradford, "one of my people has an interesting theory that deserves a bit of consideration. It's the idea of Walt Jarva." One of the reasons for all the respect and trust people had with Patterson was that she always made certain that credit for good ideas was properly given. "He came up with a concept based upon the premise that this is not the Falconer, and that the Falconer is, indeed, dead. If you accept that idea for the moment, then we should concentrate on identifying someone who was close to the Falconer cases, who would know that hawk trademark, and who might even be able to do something with some kind of a phony silhouette to throw us off."

Patterson looked around the table. "Keep in mind that the photograph only shows an outline. We're basing a lot on the shape of a profile. We don't have enough contrast or detail in the picture to see anything more than a shadow."

Patterson turned back to Bradford. "I'm letting Jarva run with this one, John. He's got three of my people down in records today looking for any tie-in, no matter how strained. We're trying to cross check every past name with their current locations. Walt is even checking the turn file to see if it could be ex-agency."

"Good idea, Joyce," said Bradford. "It's at least worth a shot. We have nothing better to go on yet."

"Look," said Green, "out of anyone at this table I probably have the best reason to be sure Falconer is dead. I was there in London with Rob closest to the explosion. That *was* the Falconer. He was in that building and there is no way he got out."

Green looked around the room, and down at the desk. Finally, he studied Stephens' face. "Maybe Jarva is right, but my gut is talking to me again. And I'm pretty sure Robs is, too. Right now I have nothing but uneasy feelings. I've got ghosts walking on my bones, Joyce. The facts all say this can't be the Falconer. But, I know it's him. I can't tell you how, but I *know* the Falconer is up there somewhere."

Stephens looked up and nodded. "It's him, Harvey. I can feel it, too."

"You two were both there, I've only heard about London," said Bradford. "The files don't offer much. What happened there?"

Stephens thought a while before answering. "It was a lot less than the stories. I was there, yet I don't recognize half the hype I've heard since. Joyce and Bill somehow put a couple pieces of information together and figured out that the Falconer was there. Harvey and I went in with a kid, Pete Fitzmorris. We killed a few of Falconer's people, and thought we killed Falconer. Fitzmorris didn't make it. Nothing more than that. Except now it looks as though we were wrong about killing the Falconer."

"It was a little more involved than that, Rob," said Patterson. She turned to Bradford. "In early '78 Moussad ended up with one live terrorist out of the six that attacked that West Bank settlement where all those children were killed. I was invited into the interrogation. Moussad had their usual level of concern about the Geneva Convention," she said wryly. "They claim that might have something to do with why they always learn more from their captives than we do."

"One piece of information was about a planned strike by another group in London. It clicked with a few other bits and pieces. Bill was the first one to see it pointed to the Falconer. Between us, we tracked down a location in a London apartment building. That's when Harvey and Rob were called in. Fitzmorris was only Sanction-four, but he was the only S-4 or above we could get there in time to help. The three of them decided to go in before Falconer had a chance to move."

"Between the three of them, they took out seventeen people. The Falconer was trapped. After all the years of trying, they had him. All that needed to be done was to wait him out. Stephens backed off and sent Green out to seal the rear of the building. Fitzmorris was supposed to cover Rob while Rob worked his way down the hall towards the Falconer. But Fitzmorris decided to be a hero and tried to rush in alone. He was killed before he made it even halfway down the hall."

"It was so unnecessary," said Stephens, thinking back to that day. "It was over. The kid didn't have to die. All we had to do was wait for help. We had plenty of time. To tell the truth, even after Fitzmorris went down I still thought we had a lock on it no matter how long we had to wait it out. Falconer was pinned. Joyce and Bill were already in the air with all the help we would need to sterilize the building."

"Then, Falconer just blew himself up," continued Stephens. "Whether it was an accident, or an attempt to get us, I don't know. He called down the hall and said, 'I am the Hawk, Stephens. No matter how long I must wait, I will inevitably land.' I thought he was absolutely mad. Then thirty seconds later that whole end of the building went up. I was forty or fifty feet away and the blast knocked me out for three days."

"When I finally came to I should have first thought of Fitzmorris, or maybe about the fact that I was alive. But I didn't. Instead, my first thought was that Falconer was finally dead." Stephens exhaled sharply, a characteristic burst of air through his nose that was half laugh and half self-derision. His voice was very soft when he continued. "It justified everything for me. Everything I had done over the years. We had finally ended an evil I could barely comprehend. A legend was down. People were safer now. It meant I could be done with it all . . ." His words trailed off.

Green provided the end of the story. "I saw Falconer just before the blast. He fired a full clip at me while I was in back of the building. In a way, that might have saved me. I burrowed as low as I could behind one of those big trash dumpsters. It ended up protecting me from most of the blast. Debris and furniture was raining down all around me. But let there be no doubt about it, the whole end of the building was gone."

Stephens looked down at the pile of papers in the briefing folder in front of him. He carefully and deliberately lined them up and squared them off. "You know, in all the years since, I never questioned that day. There was no nice clean body to identify, but in a blast like that and parts of a dozen people spread around, no one expected one. I never even doubted it before now."

"None of us did, Rob," said Sanders. "We've found nothing. Even knowing where to look, and what to look for, there isn't a single scrap over the past six years that can be tied to him. I gave two of my people the crazy assignment to blue-sky anything over the past six years that they could stretch to include him. That didn't work. Moussad has nothing. They think I'm out of my mind. Rob, we even took the risk of contacting Trueblood and Kingmaker. They both had nothing. Kingmaker was absolutely certain that the Falconer was dead. He actually had the stones to pose the question to Arafat, himself!"

Trueblood and Kingmaker were the highest placed of the very few CIA moles in the Mideast. Contacting them was a major risk, and was never even considered unless the circumstances were critical. Both moles were controlled by Sanders. Trueblood was only a mid level administrator in Khadafy's government. Kingmaker was the ATQ's most important single asset. Kingmaker had reached the inner circle of Arafat's council.

"Then we're back to square one, again," summarized Bradford. "What we do have is six days before the President arrives in Boston. That gives us six days to retrace Peterson's steps and find a few answers."

Bradford looked around the table. "Does anyone have anything more to add?" No one answered. "Then let's get to it. Sanders, please wait for me in my office." The people at the table rose and started to collect their papers to leave. "Rob, wait here for a moment, will you?"

When the rest had gone, Bradford and Stephens were alone in the room.

"I'm sorry Rob. I really am. But you can see why we need you. If this is the Falconer, and we have to assume it is, then having you back gives us a chance. It evens the odds again, Rob."

"John, why is he back? There has got to be more to it than what we see. In all the years he never telegraphed his blows like this." Stephens reached for the pile of notes and picked it up. "Four messages? One was enough. Sent from towns near where we got the photo? Showing up so we *got* a photo?" Stephens dropped the folder with a gentle plop. "He must have *wanted* to make sure this got tied to him. Is he daring us? Is it a con? We wait in Boston while he blows up the Golden Gate Bridge? It just doesn't make sense. It didn't from the first time Green told me about it. I can smell it. Damn it, I can feel it."

"Don't blame Harvey, Rob. I had already decided to call you in when he came to me."

"I don't. Harvey would not have come had he felt there was any other choice."

"Could you be the target, Rob? Is all this revenge, a giant red herring just to smoke you out?"

"No, I don't think so. Green threw that out to me. I thought about it quite a bit. But the Falconer is a pro, John. We've never faced anyone else even close to being in his league. He slips out of traps, walks right into the tightest areas we have, and has the scary ability to put together successful plans no one else could. No, getting me would be too personal for him. He's not going to allow emotions to cloud his actions."

"You did, Rob. Aren't you here because it's personal? Aren't you back because of him? Why should he be any different?"

Stephens stood up slowly and walked over to the water pitcher again. He stopped in front of the credenza, and never did reach for the pitcher. He looked down, blankly at the water glasses, and then finally looked up at Bradford.

"No, John, it's different. It's more than that. It's just that Falconer's death was a turning point for me. It was the catalyst for changes long overdue. John, when he died it meant that I had met all of my obligations. It meant I could finally leave. Now that he's back, all that changes. It's not really personal. It's just that my freedom is somehow tied to the loss of his."

Bradford stood up, picked up his papers, and walked to the door. He stopped with his hand on the handle. "Rob, I'm sorry, but I'm still glad to see you back. Joyce and I have missed you. We've needed you many times. You're the best we've ever had. You know, you probably would have had my job by now. When this is all over, maybe you'll stay this time."

Stephens didn't answer for a moment. When he did, his voice was very soft. "John, it would never work for me. I deal in blacks and whites. Everything must fit neatly into one or another of those two pigeonholes. But there are too many grays out there for me to handle in your job. Falconer is a black, and I'm a white. Or maybe I'm the black, and he is the white. I don't know. But either way, that makes it clear-cut."

Stephens looked down at the floor. His eyes focused on times and places well in the past. "I know I'm the only match for him. Do you think that makes me proud? To know that of all the killers, of all those who would claim that title, I'm really no different? Only better than most? When you look at it without the fine 'noble causes' and from below our pedestals, what really makes me any different from them?"

"Rob, you're different because it hurts you. You're different because you can never take it lightly. You're different because you continually do what you think is right, no matter how much you want to do something else. Rob, it's always been the cruelest irony—for someone with all your skills, your nature is exactly wrong for what you do the best."

Again Stephens did not answer right away. "Did you ever read T.H. White, John?" He did not wait for an answer. "I used to love reading his *Once and Future King* about King Arthur. The passage where Arthur and Merlin spoke of 'might and right' was always something special. God how I understood. Arthur's self-purgatory, his questioning how far he could use force to accomplish something 'good' seemed to be written just for me."

Bradford said nothing, just listened.

"Then, one day, I saw the flaw. White had missed the whole point. You see, he never realized that the black knight might be asking himself the very same questions. And maybe I am the black knight in Falconer's eyes."

Chapter Four

Stephens sat quietly in the passenger seat of the light blue sedan as they passed just south of Rindge, New Hampshire on the way north to Jaffrey. Even the events of the two days down in Virginia could not overshadow the glorious splashes of color in the hills around him. This was one of the most spectacular fall foliage seasons since that rare combination of early frosts and sun-filled days lit up the forests of southern New Hampshire in 1972. The hills rippled with color this year. The rare burst of the bright yellow-orange of the maples jumped out like countless beacons everywhere they drove. And when their trip passed one of the old graveyards that dot the New Hampshire back roads, Green and Stephens would be treated to the most special of all fall colors.

Old-timers in New Hampshire might never care to understand the chemical reasons for it, but the fall colors in the hardwoods shading a graveside always were brighter and warmer than the leaves anywhere nearby. Every so often a "... smart-ass college boy from MIT or something" would try to explain the enriched soils and potassium concentrations, and the lack of farming or other activities, that kept the soil rich in graveyards. But if you had been lucky enough to have enjoyed fifty or sixty New Hampshire falls, you learned that it was more than that. It had to be. Perhaps, if you stripped away the science, Robert Frost had been right. Frost had never finished the poem about it he had started on a scrap of paper once given to a friend:

> It is a sign, these leaves
> that brightly mock the fears
> of shades that haunt us so
> of what might lie below

The path to retrace Peterson's steps would start in Jaffrey. The only solid information they had was centered there. New Ipswich, where Bill Robbins had been killed, would be the second step of the trail. Past that, neither Stephens nor Green had more than instincts to go on. Virginia had provided few answers. Even the questions that were raised in the series of war councils seemed more to contradict one-another than to frame the problem. There was an underlying sense of helplessness that was almost nonexistent under normal conditions. The denizens of Folkes Farm lived under the conviction that they could at least shape, if not control, events around them. But this was a very different time. The newly risen ghost of the Falconer changed all the normal rules.

For more than twelve years the Falconer had been untouchable. He had been the one factor that could never be controlled. Eleven known kills and four major assassinations had been credited to him. There were a half dozen more kills that were suspected to be his work. He had first appeared in Munich at the 1968 Olympics, though his role wouldn't be known until years later. No one who saw the worldwide press coverage caught the significance of one brief scene among all those broadcast on television screens in more than seventy countries. Eight years later, the newly retired head of Israeli Moussad was home with his grandchildren watching an ABC Wide World of Sports rebroadcast. He suddenly sat forward in his chair with such intensity that one of the children ran to her mother shouting ". . . Mommy, Mommy, come quick. Grandpa is sick." What he had seen was a face, unknown back in 1968, that now would set in motion Moussad's highest alert level. The Falconer was one of four names on a very select list of people who, when spotted, would force immediate reassignment of all available personnel to capture or kill the target. The Moussad agent saw one face in the crowd, standing not more than ten feet from reporter Jim McKay, that was different from any others. The face was totally expressionless. The eyes swept the crowd, McKay, and the events 200 yards away in the athlete's quarters. The person wore the athletic garb of one of the nations assigned to living quarters near the Israeli team.

Throughout the first half of the 1970s the Falconer loomed in the shadows of every major success scored by Palestinian terrorists against the West. Time and again he outwitted, and then eluded, the best of the world's agencies. He was always one step faster and one move quicker. One night late in 1974, in the closest the CIA had ever gotten to capturing him, he was trapped on the upper floors of an eighteen-story building in the heart of Beirut. After a full search of the roof area in the darkness, two guards had been left there while the remainder of the team went down to help the search on the floors below. The next day both guards were found dead. Both had been strangled. Each had traces of dried blood in the faint outline of fingers around their necks.

In the light of morning searchers found a small edge of brick just below the lip of the roof, just big enough for someone to hang on by the ends of his fingers. The edge was caked with smeared blood from Falconers ripped and torn hands where he had locked onto that brick to hang there just out of sight while the Company searched the roof a few feet away. It was the same dried blood found on the necks of the strangled guards. Few in the Company could even imagine the pain in his arms and hands the Falconer must have endured, silently, as he hung in the dark over the street eighteen stories below. He had watched while the search swirled around him, waiting for the chance to pull himself back up over that edge.

In June of 1976 the Falconer was a key, unknown member of the events at the airport in Somalia. As with Munich, his plan had been so carefully crafted that his role was not discovered until months after the daring rescue mission of the hijacked plane by the Israeli commando team. Despite all of the publicity, and the in-depth screening and debriefing of those rescued, no one at the time identified the Falconer as one of the passengers on that flight. He was actually thought of as a hero by many of the passengers, and was treated for cuts given to him in a brutal beating by one of the Palestinians. He had been ". . . badly beaten trying to protect an old woman . . . a very brave man." Many of the passengers were struck by his humble nature as he avoided any publicity for his actions.

Four months later, during a November Moussad review of the July rescue, the "hero" was identified as the Falconer. It was only then that the lingering key mystery surrounding the death of three of the hijackers in the final hours of that raid was unraveled. The three had been shot and killed when, according to passengers, ". . . they were about to give in . . . they were actually looking for something to use as a white flag." Not discovered, until two days later, was that the bullets that killed the terrorists were from a silenced handgun that didn't match anything used by either the terrorists or the Israeli commandos. Two weeks later, the disassembled pieces of a weapon that did match the slugs were found in the waste tank under the rear lavatories of the Air France plane. The leaders behind the hijack had publicly vowed that there would be no surrenders during that hijacking, and that "... this is to the death ... we will be martyrs, if needed." Even the leader of the Palestinian terrorists on the plane had no idea that the Falconer was also on board, and that he was there to ensure that the boast of "no surrenders" would be fact.

The Munich and Somalia affairs were just two of the major events guided and shaped by Falconer. Both the CIA and Moussad grudgingly recognized him as the best there was. In the years leading up to the 1979 raid by Stephens and Green in London, there was a growing feeling that Falconer was invincible. A mystique developed over the years. There were persistent rumors that the name "Falconer" was a reference to a royal birth. Countless reports of sighting him—never with hard evidence and never verified by teams dispatched to the area—fostered the belief that he was all but invisible when he wished to be. On three separate occasions top intelligence community agents confirmed his death, only to find him very much alive on a later date. No significant act of terrorism or unexplained murder could pass without his name surfacing as the person behind the act.

Even without the celebrated seduction of Emily Bertasi, the assistant section head in Berlin, his reputation with women would have been legendary. Bertasi's affair had allowed the Falconer to gain entry to a Berlin safe house to plant a highly sensitive listening device in the bathroom toilet float just before a critical off-the-record session of the Vietnam Peace Talks. During her interrogation after her role was discovered, she summed up the attraction. "I knew *what* he was, long before I knew *who* he was. He was so hard, and strong. He was in such control. Yet, underneath there was a little boy who needed love, someone who could be changed. You couldn't turn away from the incredible pull of that little boy inside. It was impossible. Only later, too late, did I discover that the little boy doesn't even exist. It's only a face he wears when he needs it."

Thus, when the Falconer was thought to have been killed in London, the impact on all at the company was dramatic. It was like that feeling near the end of a horror movie when the monster finally has been killed and the beautiful young woman is safe. You can feel your breathing slowly settle back to normal. Your muscles ease and the tenseness slips from your shoulders as you settle back in your chair. But like the classic end-of-movie twist like a *Halloween II* thriller, the reappearance of the Falconer meant the respite was false. The members of the Company felt much like the movie viewers do when, just as they are calming down and relaxing after the death of "Freddie," he comes back to life and crashes through the window for one last effort to claim his victim.

There were few in Folkes farm who did not yet know that the Falconer was back, no matter what level of security surrounded the case. The word spread quickly. Until Stephens and Green resolved the matter, one way or the other, it would be difficult for anyone to concentrate on the other duties at hand. Even the uplift given by return of Stephens could not fully lighten the mood. There were always the nagging doubts that could not be pushed away when you tried to gauge which of the two would walk away this time. There were few in ATQ who would question that Falconer and Stephens were equals. They stood far above any others on either side. They were, perhaps, two sides of the very same coin. But there was one major difference that could not be escaped. Stephens had self-imposed limits and constraints, while the Falconer had none. If the "famous final scene" would be in a setting where ruthlessness made a difference, the Falconer would have the edge.

Things had irrevocably changed at ATQ. Everything else seemed unimportant for the moment, until the screen flashed "The End" and the lights came back up in the theater.

After the flight to Boston, Stephens and Green had been assigned a car from the FBI carpool in Boston's North end. The carpool was nestled in the midst of the private parking areas and rental car lots that filled the area to serve Logan Airport travellers. The sign outside the yard identified it as Shamrock Industrial Rentals. If you happened to notice the lot while eating at Rosie's just down the block you might make a note of it for your next trip, because it always seemed to have cars available. But should you decide to inquire about it, or look them up to give them a call, you would get a stock answer. "I'm sorry. All our cars are booked well in advance by our regular customers."

The trip from Boston up to Jaffrey took a little more than two hours. Stephens had Green take the side roads, even though it would add an extra half hour or so to the journey. Rather than the more common route on the main highways that led through Nashua and Peterborough, they took the smaller back roads that approached Jaffrey from the south. They traveled out Route 2 until, just past Fitchburg, Route 12 led north towards New

Hampshire. When they met up with Route 202 in Winchendon, Jaffrey would be just a few miles north.

The whole reason for the choice of routes was a brief, two-minute portion of the trip that would never be seen on the shorter way. Just a few miles south of Jaffrey, in a wide-open area of Route 202 after the driver rounds a curve, Mount Monadnock looms full and open to the northwest. Pack Monadnock Mountain flanks the road to the northeast. For those two minutes, a driver is stunned by the panorama of hundred square miles of grandeur. In the fall, when the reds and oranges and yellows of the turning foliage sweep aside all greens except the rugged pines, it is a truly magnificent sight. Stephens had first discovered the stretch of road three years earlier while coming back from a soccer game with the boys. The small diversion today seemed to Stephens to be a good way, if there could be such a thing, to start what was certain to be bad business.

When Stephens and Green reached Jaffrey, they turned east on 124. The first stop in their effort to retrace Peterson's steps would be at the roadside ice cream stand where Peterson had handed his "Falconer is at A-12" message to a startled girl who worked there. After Silver Ranch, they would continue on to the Bill Robbins home in New Ipswich.

About three miles west of Jaffrey, they found the Silver Ranch dairy sprawled on the right side of the road. A few hundred yards farther down the road, just past the entrance to the Jaffrey airport, was the Quiet Pines Motel where Peterson had stayed. Stephens and Green had rooms reserved in the same motel.

"I was expecting a little ice cream stand," said Green as they pulled in. Silver Ranch was hardly that. Rows of windows, a large picnic area, and an enclosed area full of tables and benches allowed it to handle many times the volume of the Tasty Freeze that Green had envisioned. Silver ranch was known for many miles around. It had been the site of countless first dates for the kids from Dublin, Jaffrey, Peterborough, and a dozen smaller towns. The chances were very good that any first solo trip with a brand new driver's license was to Silver Ranch.

It took only a few moments to find Sue Matson. A phone call from Boston that morning had asked her to meet with "two members of the law firm of Bannik, Warren and Graves." She smiled at the two men as she stepped out of the side employee's entrance to the kitchen, wiped her hands on the now messy apron around her waist, and walked over to where they waited.

"Hi," she said cheerfully. "I guess one of you must be like Mr. Jones."

"That's me," answered Stephens, warmly, resisting the strong urge to say he was not only *like* Mr. Jones, but he was *the* Mr. Jones. He reached into his jacket and pulled out a calling card that identified him as Walter Jones, a senior member of the law firm. "Thank you for meeting with us, especially on such short notice. But frankly, we wouldn't be here if we weren't very concerned about our friend Jim."

"I suppose it's really like none of my business, but this man was a bit, like weird, you know," she replied. "I can't figure out what was happening. I mean, like maybe this is what you call 'privileged,' but I'd really like to know what's up?"

"Well, Ma'am, I guess it really wouldn't hurt anything to tell you. After all, Jim did come to you," answered Stephens. "Jim Peterson is one of the best there is in researching corporate merger and acquisitions. He's been working on a merger involving one of the biggest companies in the state."

"Hey," she interrupted, "is that the thing with, like, New Hampshire Ball Bearing and the Japanese? I heard about that! Wow. That's big stuff around here. No one can believe the Japanese are gonna really, like take over you know."

"Ma'am, I can't comment on that," said Stephens. "I really can't tell you the name of the company. That's pretty confidential and we could blow the whole deal if we said much."

Stephens looked over to Green. Green continued the idea they had carefully gone over on the ride up. "The Japanese get really finicky about leaks. Jim Peterson was supposed to set up a key meeting with the head man of the Japanese conglomerate who insists we call him Falconer so there is no chance his name and company could leak out. That message told us the meet was on for the 12th of the month. The problem is, we haven't heard a word from Jim since then."

"Our Boston office has been on the phone to every police station for miles trying to see if he was in an accident," added Stephens. "We're trying to track him down, and frankly a lot of us are concerned. Jim is a good fellow, and well liked. I can't stand the thought that he might be off the road somewhere."

"I can't tell you guys any more than I've already told your people. I mean, like this guy just pulls up and like plays a James Bond bit on me with the note! That's about it. All of us were like having a riot saying he was a secret Russian spy! Now that you guys have been here, I'm going to have to tell my friends it was just some, like big business thing. What a bummer."

"How like Jim!" said Green. "For a junior lawyer, he always did kid around a bit! But I still don't understand why he didn't make the call himself."

"I don't think he planned to give me any note when he first pulled up. I mean, like he was paying for his dog when he suddenly turns to me and asks for a phone. He was, like really bothered all of a sudden. He kept looking over at the parking lot."

"What was he watching?"

"Nothing. I mean, like there were cars and stuff, but nothing else. So he writes the message on a napkin and hands it to me." Sue Matson rubbed her right hand with her left as she thought back. "He squeezed my hand so hard that it hurt. Then he grabs a twenty from his wallet, gives it to me, says it will like cover the phone call, and like runs for his car. Even with the call, it's the biggest tip I'll ever see around here."

"That sure sounds weird, Ma'am, even for Jim," said Green. "I've seen him in negotiations with IBM that were as hairy as they come, and Jim never lost his cool. Did you ever figure out what he was looking at? Did someone follow him out of the lot or anything?"

"I sure don't know," she answered with that look only a teenager can give when telling a 'grown up' something that should be obvious. "I mean, like we get hundreds of cars in here. I mean, like maybe two or three pulled out when he did. That's no big deal!"

Stephens handed her his business card. "Well, we do appreciate the time. Thank you. If you think of anything, please give me a call here. If I'm not there, they'll get a message to me."

The young girl slipped the business card into a pocket on the apron. "Okay, mister. But this is like getting pretty silly. I mean, like between the cops, and all your people bugging me, like what else can I say?"

Stephens didn't say anything. He just looked over at Green.

"Gee, I remember hearing that one of our people talked to you a week or so ago, but I didn't know he phoned you back a second time. I'll have to get on our people about that. We're sorry for bothering you so much."

"It wasn't the same guy. In fact, it wasn't a guy at all and it wasn't a phone call! Your company must be really screwed up. It was that woman who works with you two."

"Ken," said Stephens to Green, "do you suppose that they sent old Mrs. Crowley over from the Nashua office and didn't bother to tell us?" Stephens turned to the girl. "I guess everyone is so worried they're all looking for Jim. Was it Mrs. Crowley? She's about fifty or sixty, really short, with short gray hair."

"Not even close!" she answered. "I mean, she wasn't nearly that old. Maybe she was about your age, that's all. I think her name was Marilyn. She was, like really pretty. And her hair was long and brown."

"Oh, of course! I think that must be Mary Ann, not Marilyn! Mary Ann Weller. She's in Nashua too," said Stephens. "She's a close friend of Jim. I'm not surprised she was here. She probably took some time off to help on her own."

"Well that explains the picture bit," said the girl. "At first I figured she was here instead of you guys. But when I asked her she like didn't even like know you two were on the way up here. She must have shown that picture of him to most of my friends before she got to me. When I asked her why she didn't come right to me she said she had lost my name, and was really like embarrassed. I mean, like I guess she didn't want anyone to know she was helping, too. Was she his girlfriend?"

"I don't think so, Sue," answered Stephens. "I think you're right though. She was probably helping and was just embarrassed we were coming up the same day." He glanced briefly at Green before continuing. "Did she seem to have any idea where Jim was?"

"No. She just asked all the same things you did. She didn't tell me about the like Japanese bit, though. She pretended someone had left him a lot of money. I didn't buy it, though. I guess she didn't want to leak the big Jap deal, right?"

"Mary Ann would never let something like that leak out in the middle of delicate negotiations," answered Green.

"Well, I mean if it helps, like I think she was staying over there," said the girl pointing to the Quiet Pines Motel. "Maybe she's still there and you can catch her." She reached in the pocket to get the business card Stephens had given her, glanced at it, and then put it back in the pocket. "Mr. Jones, I like gotta get back to work here."

"Thank you again," said Green. "We do appreciate the time."

As she walked back to the kitchen area, Green and Stephens headed back to the car. Once inside, they sat quietly for a few moments before either spoke.

"Do you think it's worth going back to push for a description?" asked Green. "I sure as hell couldn't think of anything more we could have tried without getting her suspicious."

"Me neither, Harvey," said Stephens. "You know the current Northeast staff, I don't. Is there anyone active even close to what she said?"

"No one in ATQ. But all we have here is that we have a woman, long brown hair, pretty, in her mid to late thirties who's asking about Peterson. There are one or two that might fit out of Boston FBI, but we should know if they were on this."

"Anything in the briefing papers you saw?"

"Nothing there either."

Stephens put the key in the ignition and started the engine. "Let's turn this over to Virginia and see if they have anything. If not, we lucky stiffs get to endure Ms. Matson's painful version of the English language one more time."

"If I have to hear one more '. . . I mean, like I sure do, like you know' from her," said Green, "then I might just, I mean, like puke."

"I'm like with you, like fur shurr," deadpanned Stephens as he pulled out of the lot. Green made a retching sound into his jacket pocket.

Chapter Five

A minute later, they stopped the car in front of the Quiet Pines Motel and walked into the office to register. The motel was small, just ten rooms, five flanked on each side of the central office. Three years ago the owner had added an ice machine that sat just outside the main entrance on a narrow porch. It was rarely used. The motel was like so many in the North Country that reflected the dream, always just out of reach, of the small innkeeper. You could just about always find rooms available at Quiet Pines, and today the lot was once again empty when Stephens and Green pulled in. Despite all of the beauty in the hills around the area, there was no real draw that would help fill the motel. There was no big ski area in winter, or resort area in the summer. Unless there was a big wedding that filled up a home, a visitor usually stayed with family or friends when visiting Jaffrey. Salespeople tended to stay over in Keene or up in Peterborough or Nashua where there was more business.

The owner of the Quiet Pines would never give up, no matter what his accountant might advise him. The motel grounds were always neat and groomed. Every morning, and at least once later in the day, he would head outside with a canvas bag in one hand and a stick with a nail on the end in the other hand to pick up the napkins and paper that would blow over from Silver Ranch. Every week, he would dust and polish the log slices with carved mottoes that decorated his office walls. For $29.00 a night you would get a clean room, a working color television, and a quiet, restful place to sleep. On a real good night, three or four of the rooms would be occupied. Anytime the owner logged a week of less than ten rooms sold, the regular Sunday morning bookkeeping routine would have to include the small tan ledger he kept on the top shelf of his closet. The ledger recorded his remaining savings since he bought the business fourteen years before. On the previous Sunday the account had dipped below $5,000 for the first time. He had started with $73,000.

"Morning, gents," said the man, smiling warmly as he looked up from the paper he was reading behind the desk. "Pretty day isn't it." He didn't wait for an answer. "How can I help you guys?"

"We have reservations for two rooms, Jones and Kelleher."

"Oh yes. Sure thing. You must be the Boston lawyers I've been expecting." The man scanned through a card file on his desk. "Here it is. When your secretary called, she said you'd want a quiet room. Don't get many big city lawyers out here. What are you guys up for? Buying land?"

"No. We specialize in business law. There's a company near Nashua we're helping in a big stock deal. Normally we'd stay near there, but a friend of ours recommended you. Jim Peterson?"

The man laughed. "Now I tell you, I really owe this Jim Peterson a dinner. Why, he's sold more rooms the past few days than I have. Just last night his girlfriend came here to meet him. Had to have the same room he stayed in before. And then, if that isn't enough, she waits all night for him and he never shows!"

"Well I'll be," said Green. "I didn't know Jim was seeing anyone special. Real pretty, huh?"

"You better believe it. If she was waiting for me, I'd sure as hell be on time! This morning, she must have asked me three, four times if he had called. When I had to tell her 'no,' she asked me if I had any idea where he might be and where he liked to go when he stayed here. The only thing I could think of was that he sometimes ate over at the Ranch." He handed them the registration card to fill in. "I suggested she check with some of the girls that work over there. One of them might know more." He shook his head. "I don't know if she had any luck, though. She said she had a picture of him with her. That would help."

"Is she's still here, I'd love to meet her."

"Nope. Checked out this morning. Too bad. Nice lady, that one."

"Well, I'll have to give Jim a ration of crap on this one!" said Green, slapping the counter as he laughed. "Why, he's hidden her from all of us." Green turned to Stephens. "Walter, this could be great! We've got to get her name and send some phony roses or something! I'm never going to let Jim live this down!"

Stephens immediately got caught up in Green's idea for a joke. "Ooo, even better idea! When we go fishing up at the lodge with Jim next week, let's set him up!" When Stephens turned back to the man, he had the ear-to-ear smile of a prankster. "This will be too much. You have to give us her name. It's too good to pass up."

"Well, I really shouldn't. But seeing as you two are friends from the same company . . ."

The man searched through a small pile of cards for the right one. "I still should have it here. I keep these around for a few days in case a check doesn't clear." He stopped and pulled one from the pack. "Here it is. And after all, he *is* the one who sent you here," he said as he handed Stephens the card.

"Ken, get this. It's someone named Marilyn Folkes," he said as he memorized the information on the card before handing it back. He was very careful to avoid touching the area around the signature or near either of the upper corners. "Let's set up something tonight to burn dear old Jim!"

As the man turned to pull the keys for the rooms, Stephens reached over and palmed the card.

"Just head out and all the way down to the left. I put you both together at the end away from the road. That's as quiet as it gets."

"We do appreciate it," said Green as they started out the door.

The two walked toward the rooms with their bags. "It'll be dark in another couple hours," said Stephens. "We should get a move on if we want to check out the Robbins place." Stephens stopped outside the door to his room. He carefully removed the stolen registration card from his pocket and handed it, by the edges, to Green. "Why don't you call Virginia for a courier for this card? I doubt it, but there's always the chance the lab might find something."

"Cute choice of last names, don't you think," said Green as he reached out and just as carefully took the card. "What the hell is she trying to tell us with the 'Marilyn Folkes' bit? I've got to tell you, that makes no sense at all to me."

"Harvey, old friend, for the past five minutes I've twisted and turned that name every way I can think of. But I can't figure out that one for the life of me. You just don't wave a red flag like that, unless you intend for it to be seen. So it obviously was intentional, but why?"

Stephens unlocked his door. From old habit he stood to the side as he pushed the door open. Without conscious thought Green had also taken a step to the side, away from the opening. Before he moved, Stephens listened carefully for sounds in the room. Then he moved slowly to the side so that additional slices of the room came into view. When he had scanned the whole room, he reached out and pushed the door the rest of the way until it was flush with the wall behind it.

"You've got to be really good, or really stupid, to leave a signal like that," said Stephens when the door had opened fully and the empty room awaited. "It she telling whoever came that she was expecting us? Is it a clue, or just some macho game?"

"The Falconer?"

"I don't see it. That might be the only thing I'm certain of. There's nothing to gain from it. Falconer would be a lot more clever if he was trying to lead us somewhere, and wouldn't waste time with empty gestures. When he throws down the glove, there's usually a grenade in it."

"Then what's left, Rob. Another ghost?"

"She's got to be a third party, or a free agent. I'd put my money on someone in the Bureau who's still bent out of shape that we're working domestic." Stephens reached for his bag. He looked up as an idea hit him. "Christ. Maybe it's Moussad again. I don't care what the hell Bradford and Sanders think. I don't like the idea of them working the States no matter how much help they give us. And anyway, we just end up spinning our wheels covering the same ground."

"Sometimes I wonder how much time we spend chasing our tail on things like this," said Green. "You're the math whiz, Rob. Do you think you and I have traveled down our millionth dead end yet?" Green walked the few feet to his door. Sanders waited as Green pushed open his door.

"Maybe this is it," called Green when he looked back. "Step right up folks, introducing dead end number one million and one."

"You might be right, Harvey," said Stephens. "But it seems to be just about the only end we've got at the moment."

The two entered their rooms to drop off their bags. It took about ten minutes before they met back at the car and headed over to New Ipswich.

Even though they both knew exactly where the Robbins home was, Stephens made a point of stopping to ask for instructions at Matt's Mobil station in New Ipswich. There was no doubt that in so small a town their presence at the Robbins home would be known within minutes. Often the easiest way to accomplish something you don't want seen is to do it right out in front of everyone. By the time they pulled into the driveway of the Robbins home just a couple hundred yards beyond the gas station, half a dozen residents already knew about the ". . . two lawyers, with their clipboards and briefcases, up from Boston to inventory poor old Bill's estate." The previous day the "Head of Estate Litigation" from Bannik, Warren, and Graves had contacted the local police chief to give him a heads-up about the visit.

Getting inside the home took only a few seconds. The sturdy bolts and locks a practical New Hampshire native used were little problem to someone like Harvey Green. Under normal conditions, he would save only a few seconds if he had the actual key. Just as the lock clicked to signal another easy success, Stephens waved with his clipboard at a passing car. The driver gave a brief nod in return, and then stopped staring at them and sped up to a more normal speed for the highway.

"Looks like they wanted to be sure, Harvey," he said as they stepped inside the door.

"Too bad more neighbors aren't like that. I wish mine would watch my house once in a while."

The inside of the house was dark and quiet. Bill Robbins had no local relatives and no one had been inside since the place had been sealed after the initial police investigation. Neither Stephens nor Green had any delusions about what they would find. It was, indeed, at best a long shot. But, over the many years together they both had succeeded more often than others, because they were willing to do the dog work that others would not do. While it was a soft lead, the coincidences were too many to overlook. Even without the silhouette of the Falconer at the funeral, the fact that the Robbins and Peterson events happened at the same time and in the same general area would have demanded Stephen's attention. The unusual nature of the Robbins murder, combined with the Falconer's silhouette, made him certain that Peterson and Robbins were somehow tied together.

There were two reasons that led to Stephen's low expectations for the search. The first was Robbins, himself. Everything that Stephens knew about Robbins, or that the research team at the Agency could discover, indicated a man who could not possibly be part of anything involving the Falconer. He instinctively knew that people such as Robbins are consistent throughout their lifetimes. The second reason was the Falconer. If he had been involved, he would leave no signs of his passing.

Inside the front door there was a dining room to the left, a den to the right, and a hallway and stairs straight ahead. It was a traditional old New England colonial that went back to the 1800s. The dining room was large with rough beams spanning the ceiling. The stairs were narrow, wooden, and took a sharp turn at the top from a time when stairs did not have to be designed to pass a king-size mattress or prebuilt bookcases. Green started up the stairs to check out the second floor. The sounds of his footsteps were firm and solid, without the creaks and snaps of modern flooring.

As Stephens entered the den he was immediately struck by the warmth and beauty and gentleness of the room, and by how much it reflected the nature of Bill Robbins. It reminded him of the small office off the balcony of the Peterborough movie theater where a few times he and Robbins had spent an evening talking about Bogart, or music, or Nixon, or any of the host of other topics they shared. The den was in the northwest corner of the home and had two small windows, both heavily curtained so that even in the late afternoon sun little light entered the room. The soft light that did peek through seemed to cause the walls to glow as it bathed small patches of the oaken boards. The walls were not veneered paneling. They were formed of oak planks, fitted tongue-and-groove, worn and lightly finished to give a depth and texture that was special. The knots and knurls were not just shiny patterns. You didn't have to touch them to see their contour stand away from the wood.

The room did not have a ceiling light. Next to both the old brown leather couch and the cracked, red leather easy chair, were brass floor lamps. On the end tables, by the seats, were piled issues of Yankee Magazine and National Geographic. Open face down on the seat of the easy chair was the National Geographic issue that was filled with photos of the sunken Titanic. It was easy for Stephens to like the room. He could picture spending a quiet evening there, perhaps reading silently, with the sounds of Mozart playing softly in the background.

To someone who did not know Robbins, many of the items in the room would appear to contradict one another. It was almost as though the room reflected two, or perhaps three different people. There were bits and pieces going back forty-five years, with no clear pattern tying them together. On one wall was the skin of a small black bear. Just beneath it was a photograph of a young Bill Robbins, his foot on the bumper of an early 1960s gray Willy's station wagon, with the carcass of a dead bear on the hood. Across the room, opposite the conquest of the hunter and the photo of the victor, were his collection of framed original letters by Emerson, Thoreau, and Lincoln. On a small wood bookcase was a black and white picture of eight soldiers on the deck of a troop transport. All stood arm in arm. Each had signed the photo. In one corner, in the biggest handwriting of all, was the sweeping boast "To Bill the dreamer: We're almost home!—Johnny M." Just inches from the picture, pinned to the wall, was a yellowed, two-by-three inch clipping from a newspaper. It was headed *Words for the Day*. The saying was that of John Updike; "If men do not keep on speaking terms with children, they cease to be men, and become merely machines for eating and for earning money."

To Stephens there was no inconsistency at all to the items in that room.

It took only a few minutes to search the drop-leaf desk in one corner. Everything in it was neat, and ordered. Letters and photographs were all organized and bundled by rubber bands. More envelopes held receipts and kept track of budgets. A dog-eared copy of a 1952 book on savings rates and schedules was strapped to a large manila folder containing bank deposit receipts. Current bills were neatly stacked in the main open section. None of the items provided any insight into Stephens' search.

Before Stephens left the room to go into the living room beyond, he stopped by the door and smiled. He was glad that he had come to this room. It reflected the quiet confidence and easy contentment of an old man who could look back on his life and be happy with the patterns he saw. For a moment, he felt a twinge of jealousy for Robbins to have achieved such contentment. Then, just as quickly, it went. Instead, replacing it was the feeling that comes only when you know you are at ease with a friend you trust.

Just past the den, through a second door, was a huge living room that would have been called a "great room" back when the house was first built. The house was roughly in the shape of a 'C.' The front door was in the middle of the 'C' with the den and dining room in one foot and two downstairs bedrooms in the other. The great room and kitchen filled the middle. Wooden beams laced the ceiling. Windows filled both long side walls. The west side of the room looked out over the boat shed and towards Mount Monadnock in the distance. The east side was filled with plants and indoor trees. In the early morning, the dawn sun would flood the room and the plants.

Short of beginning a destructive search, none of the rooms on the lower floor yielded anything of interest to Stephens. For the first time he could remember, he felt as if he was trespassing by searching a place. Every time he opened a drawer, or studied a picture, or glanced at a letter, Stephens wanted to apologize to the man he had known. It took close to an hour before he was sure that the search of the first floor was a dead end.

At the rear of the house were two small rooms and a back stairway to the second floor. "Harvey," he called as he heard the sounds of paper being moved not far from the top of the stairs. "I've got nothing here. You have anything?"

"He's got a desk up here with two file cabinets. I'll be a while, but there's nothing yet. Everything so far says he's just your basic, garden-variety, good citizen. Maybe just a bit better than most."

"Short of pulling off the wallboards, this place is clean. When you're done there, check the basement. The entrance is in the kitchen. I'm going to look outside. There's a garage and a shed with a boat. I'll meet you back in the basement."

Stephens left the house by the side door that used to be the entry to the doctor's offices in the two downstairs bedrooms before Robbins moved in. The shed doors were slightly open fifty feet away across the driveway. As he crossed towards the shed, Stephens noted that it was starting to get dark. "I should have started outside, first," he thought. Then he changed direction and turned to walk around the house before he lost the light.

Stephens walked back to the front of the house and down the far side. He really had no idea what he was looking for. All of the police reports had indicated that a thorough search had come up empty. He could see nothing that stood out as he walked the well-kept lot. It was only when he finished, and turned back towards the boat shed, that the small part of his mind that rarely failed him signaled that something he had seen was not right.

For as long as he could remember, Stephens had been able sense patterns in things, and somehow know when something did not fit. When a problem needed to be solved all his feelings, facts, and ideas would sift and churn in some back corner of his mind, until the answer would surface. Often he would not be aware of the effort. He knew that when a problem could not be solved, the only approach was to let it sit. A solution, if there was one, would inevitably come. He never thought of it as a gift. It was just a quirk, a twist, a gimmick to him. It was just the way his mind worked best. And now, as he stopped cold in his tracks a few feet from the shed, he knew with total certainty that something he had passed during his walk did not belong there.

Stephens turned back and began to retrace his steps, looking with even more intensity to identify whatever it was that had triggered his feeling. At the left rear corner of the lot he found it. Here was a small thing, an unimportant looking thing, but one that the full police investigation and the first Agency covert sweep team had missed. He, too, had looked right at it and missed it. In the midst of an asparagus patch were two ordinary footprints.

The prints should not have been there. It seemed very unlikely that Robbins would make them. An asparagus patch takes years of care to develop and mature. It seemed totally inconsistent to Stephens that someone with the care and precision shown in the den and house would walk through such a patch, unless there were very unusual circumstances. Stephens doubted that the investigating police left them. They led towards the wall, but not back. If they had been made by the police search, there would be steps returning. Stephens squatted down and studied the prints. While he never had mastered the ability to accurately date such prints, it was clear that they must have occurred in the right general timeframe. At the newest, they might be three or four days old. He doubted that they could be more than two or three weeks old. Robbins had been killed ten days earlier.

Carefully avoiding the prints, Stephens began to move slowly into the forest. In a precise pattern of squares he intently scanned the ground looking for any slight trace, any break in the natural patterns. It was almost twenty minutes later, when darkness was getting close, that he found what he was looking for. It was a single impression of a heel near the base of a large maple tree. The heel had sunk into the soft earth and was on a sharp angle. It had been made by someone standing there, leaning against the tree, facing towards the house in the distance.

Stephens stepped behind the tree and looked in the direction indicated by the position of the heel mark. The outline of the house and shed could be seen, but were largely screened by the tall bushes on the yard side of the stone wall. Three big pines blocked out most of the house itself. He realized that the position must have been chosen to view something closer at hand that was not blocked.

Very slowly, on his hands and knees, he used the last minutes before darkness made further search impossible to work his way around the tree. About ten feet away from the base of the maple tree he found a small depression filled with leaves, and with an unnatural mound of dirt at the end closest to the house. He delicately picked away leaves, until he found matted leaves and earth near the bottom. He realized that most of the top layer of leaves had been added later. Whoever had covered the depression had done it very carefully. Stephens had walked right past it moments before he had discovered the heel print.

In the leaves at the bottom of the depression he found the dried blood. Reaching into his pocket he got one of the small, plastic Ziploc storage bags he always carried. He had been told countless times by the Agency lab boys that they were "not clean enough or sterile," but they had the advantage of always being available when needed. You didn't have to requisition them, and then wait for someone to make a supply run. Any grocery store carried them. He carefully picked up samples of the leaves and blood, and slipped them into the bag.

As darkness moved in, Stephens knew there was little more he could do in the woods without equipment and help. He would have to call for a repeat lab sweep. The team could be on the site by the next morning. He stopped and looked back at the maple tree and heel mark. He could picture the cold eyes of the person who had first orchestrated, and then watched, as death unfolded on the forest floor. It was then that Stephens finally knew with certainty that the silhouette in the photograph could only be the Falconer. The last small trace of skepticism slipped away.

For a moment, Stephens could not counter the sadness that overcame him. Part of it was the finality of the decision that was now, irrevocably, made for him. The faint hope that he could walk away from this was gone. And he felt another measure of sadness when he realized that the last thing his friend Robbins had seen was one Stephens knew all too well—the eyes of the hawk as it dives to claim its prey.

Chapter Six

Stephens stooped down and picked up the plastic bag. His knees were dirty and covered with pieces of the dry, brown leaves. The creases in the knees of the expensive suit were a lost cause. As he brushed the dirt and leaves away, he realized that he would have a very hard time, should anyone drop by the home just now, explaining why the "good Boston lawyer" looked more like a gardener than a staid barrister. He carefully worked his way back to the wall and crossed into the yard a few feet to the right of the asparagus bed.

As he moved back towards the boat shed, he saw the soft glow of light from the upstairs bedroom windows where Harvey was searching. Green had not yet made it down to the basement. Stephens considered going in to tell Green about his findings, but knew it could wait for the moment. Green was a professional, one of the very best. The effort and quality of his search would not change given the new information. Stephens could finish with the shed and garage before returning to help Green with the basement. There would be plenty of time after he was done to bring Green up to date, and then to call for the Agency sweep team.

The door to the shed was part way open as he approached, and it swung easily to his touch. Stephens could not help but notice how well the shed fit the patterns of the house. It was solid, and weather-tight. Each door was held on by four large hinges firmly anchored into the door jamb. The hinges were well oiled, and held the door perfectly level. The door made almost no sound as it glided open.

Stephens stepped through the doorway, and then stopped while he waited for his eyes to adjust to the darkness inside. The shed was about thirty feet long and fifteen feet wide, and in the initial darkness he could not see to the far end. To his right, on the side wall, he could see the faint outline of a wall switch. He walked over towards it. Just as his hand reached the light switch and clicked it on, he detected the faint smell of perfume in the darkened room.

"Please don't move," said the woman's voice from behind him in the corner to the left of the door. "Just stand there, exactly as you are."

Stephens obeyed the words, exactly. He did not move. He stood there, with his right hand frozen to the light switch and his left hand at his side. He wasted only a few seconds telling himself that he should have known better, that it was a stupid rookie move, and that years before he would never have been trapped so easily. It did not matter to him that it had been six years since he had last used what the Agency, in level-two rookie training, called the 'drop dead skills.' He long ago had learned that excuses, no matter how good, could never change facts.

The voice was cool and direct. The woman had no need to use volume to make up for any lack of authority or force. The voice had a quiet confidence to it. It was the voice of one who was used to being heard. It was the voice of someone who didn't need to embellish words or tone to give a command. It was a voice that Myrna Glover, back in Dublin, would have respected.

The part of Stephens that could always stand apart from the action and watch the events unfolding around him could not help putting a totally incongruous twist to his analysis of the voice. Despite standing there in the shed with an unknown danger behind him, a danger that might well be tied to the Falconer, that small part of him *liked* the voice. The voice called up the image of a soft fireside with two people lying nearby as the flames reflected and danced on a pair of wine glasses. Borodin called gently in the background.

"May I lower my hands? No moves, just lower them."

"No. Just leave them where they are."

"Can I turn around, at least?"

"No. I like it better this way," said the voice behind him. "Who are you?"

"My name is Walter, Walter Jones. I'm with Bannik, Warren and Graves down in Boston. I'm handling the Robbins estate." Stephens stepped smoothly into the role. "Now Ma'am, this is kind of scary for me. I mean, who are you? I know the Robbins' estate pretty well, and the only woman in those files is a sister, well over seventy, out in Chicago. You don't sound like you match that description."

In back of him he heard a small laugh of genuine amusement. It was not the kind of a laugh that is shared among friends. It was the laugh a parent might have when the child, covered with paint, says 'No Mom, I didn't play with the paint.' But there was warmth to the sound, and a slight throatiness. And, once again, the laugh triggered a brief replay of the fireside fantasy. It was as though that small part of Stephens was not watching the shed anymore, but instead was watching some foolish, poorly cut movie that flits from one scene to another without any thought to the plot at hand. For perhaps a full second Stephens concentrated on the smell of the perfume, before he focused back on the situation. One thing was very clear to him once he did. The woman was not buying anything he was saying.

"Mr. *Jones*," she said, emphasizing the name Jones with just a small dose of sarcasm, "I've once or twice had occasion to deal with lawyers. I've never once found a lawyer on hands and knees searching a forest."

"I don't get up here very often," answered Stephens. "A walk like that is nice. And I thought I might find some samples for my son's rock collection."

The soft laugh was repeated behind him. "Damn," he thought as the laugh triggered the fireside scene for yet a third time. "You're more than rusty, Stephens, you're getting downright senile."

"Mr. Jones, you're not a lawyer." Her voice was back to the tone of absolute certainty he had heard when he first entered. There was no trace of amusement in it any more. "You have nothing to do with the Robbins estate. A poor, innocent Boston lawyer would have spun in indignation to face me when I told him not to move."

Now the voice turned cold and hard. "There is only one kind of person who would know better than to move, and who would stand there frozen all this time. You can only be one of two things. One is bad, the other worse. The question for me is, which are you? Who are you, Mr. Jones? Why are you really here? This time, you might just tell me the truth."

Stephens knew that the time for the role of lawyer had ended. Events would now have to unfold a different way. The truth, or at least one of the always available shades of truth, was necessary. Without conscious thought, from all of the facts over the past few days, and from his own intuition, he chose the path to take.

"That's a question that could go both ways. I could ask you the same things, *Marilyn*."

He was rewarded, one more time, with a small bit of the laugh. This time it was subdued, just a slight punctuation to go along with a nod of her head. "Well, you seem to have done your homework. Not a bad guess. But since I'm the one with the gun, why don't you go first, Mr. Jones."

Like a chess player double checking his calculations before a planned series of moves, Stephens took one last brief look at the path he had chosen to take. Throughout his life, he had always been very good at accurately sensing the nature of people. On more than one occasion that skill had saved his life, or the lives of those around him. There were fine patterns, and distinctions that were invisible to most others, but were very clear to Stephens. They would let him quickly label a person, and place them into either his 'black' or his 'white' pigeonhole. There were only two colors in his spectrum. There was no room for grays. A middle choice, if permitted, would imply doubts, or questions, or indecision. The range of actions he would usually have to consider required a clear-cut and sound judgment. And all too often in his business, there were only seconds to choose between the two labels.

It was the single biggest difference between himself and the Falconer. He would always make the judgment *before* choosing a course of action.

Instinctively, he knew that the woman behind him should not be taken lightly. She had a measure of self-control and strength that set her apart. He knew that there was fear there, but it was contained and pushed back where it should be. Her fears would temper her actions, but would not dominate them. He had little doubt that she could use her gun if it was needed. But just as certainly, he was sure that she would be filed under the pigeonhole that carried the label 'white.'

"I'm looking for a friend of mine. He's a young kid who has been missing for some time. There was a report that he had been seen up in this area. It is important for me to help find my friend."

The voice of the woman, in response, confirmed his assessment of her. The voice was quieter, and more intense than before. "And just who was your friend?" she asked.

"His name is Jim, Jim Peterson. You and I are looking for the same person. We talked to the same young girl at Silver Ranch that you did. The one who said he went in this direction when he rushed off. My guess is that you saw the same possible connection with the Robbins murder here that we did."

There was quiet behind him. Stephens could not even hear her breathing. For nearly two minutes, neither spoke. The silence dragged out. The only sound from the woman, and that only twice, was the faint rustle of fabric as she moved ever so slightly. Stephens stood with his arms up and to the sides waiting for the woman to finish her analysis, and to hear the results of her judgment.

"May I turn around, Marilyn?"

There was no reply. He waited, and then slowly dropped his arms. It was a careful movement that made sure his arms stayed out, away from his pockets or jacket. He kept the hands stretched out and moved them first forward, and then down, like an orchestra leader motioning for the violin section to play just a bit softer. When they reached his side, he waited another few moments before he moved one foot slightly. He stopped and waited once again. When there was no reaction, he turned around to face the woman.

When he turned, he saw the woman standing in the corner ten feet away. He watched as her eyes that had been staring down at the ground, looked back up at him. As she moved, the light passed over her face, revealing the soft green of her eyes. Her long brown hair hung loosely and fell midway down her back. Her face, on the surface, reflected only control and calm as she looked directly at Stephens. But in her eyes, just under the surface, he could see sadness and doubts that were fighting to escape. Although her right hand still held a small 38 caliber pistol that looked like a prop out of an old Dragnet film, Stephens was truly surprised to find that it seemed unimportant. For the moment, the gun and the death it could represent didn't exist. For the moment, all he could think of was how very beautiful she was.

The woman raised the gun in her hand by a few inches, until it pointed to the middle of his chest. Any doubts or questions that might have been in her eyes were pushed aside. The strength and control that had been there when Stephens first entered returned. She stood facing Stephens across the packed dirt floor of the shed. Her voice was cold and hard.

"You still haven't answered my question. Who are you, really? And why do you search for Jim Peterson?"

"My name is Stephens, Rob Stephens," he said.

The gun in her hand dropped just a fraction of an inch, or two, as for the first time in the conversation the woman was startled. Then, as quickly as it had occurred, the hesitation was over. The gun came back up to point directly at his heart.

"Jim Peterson didn't know you," she stated with certainty. "You two never even met."

Once again, the signals all confirmed Stephen's feelings. This was not, in any way, a person to be taken lightly. "Marilyn, sometimes you don't have to know someone to be a friend. I do know *of* him, and I am truly looking for him, to help him. I'm not his enemy, and I don't think I'm yours."

The woman stood and looked closely at Stephens. She stared intently at his face. She reviewed all of the words, and their tone and manner, from the past ten minutes there in the shed. She thought about all of the things she had heard, and all that she knew. Finally, she too came to a conclusion. She slowly and gently nodded 'yes.' Then, without hesitation or second guessing she lowered the gun and returned it to the right-hand pocket of the blue quilted vest she was wearing.

"Yes," she acknowledged. "You *are* Rob Stephens. It all fits."

Now it was his turn to be surprised. "I would remember if we had met before?"

"Oh, we haven't met, but I do know you. Maybe in the same way that you say you know my Jim," she said with sadness, now looking past Stephens to a scene that only she could see. There was a thin edge of tears in her eyes. "He's told me about you, you know. We would talk and talk about what he wanted to do. He'd talk about you the way most kids would talk about some stupid baseball player. He wanted to be like you more than anything else in this world."

Stephens knew that there was nothing he could say that would help. He now knew who she was. The Agency reports had indicated that Peterson's only remaining family was an older sister who had raised him after the death of their parents. They had been very close, according to the reports. She had been interviewed shortly after Peterson had turned up missing. The sister's name was Cynthia Lebart.

"I am sorry," he said gently. "Then you must be his sister. Cynthia Lebart?"

"Yes," she answered quietly.

Stephens knew that there was no way he could explain what happens to people like Jim Peterson. There was no way to explain why they made the choice to be what they were. He could not make her understand the ghosts, or the visions of glory, or even the cruel, false mirages of a distant grail that might drive them. No matter how he could try there was no easy, quick way to make it appear any better, or any different, than it was. He could only stand and wait, and let her continue at her own pace.

"Is my brother dead?"

"I don't know, Cynthia," he answered gently. "That's why we're here. Right now a lot of Jim's friends are out looking for him."

Anger flashed and sparkled behind the last small bit of tears. "His friends? This is nothing but little boys playing spymaster games, isn't it? Stupid little games, but the bullets are real, aren't they?" She stretched out her arm and pointed at Stephens. "And he wants to be like *you*? What did it get him, Rob Stephens? Did you two save the world this time? Did we bravely stop a war? Did your damn little boy spymaster games save some important life, Rob Stephens? Was it a life more important than Jim's?"

The tears were completely gone now, swept aside by the intensity of the anger. She stopped pointing at him, and folded her arms tightly in front of herself with her shoulders hunched forward. It was that characteristic gesture of self-comfort that women find so easy to use, that helps so much when the reasons for events and deep sadness cannot be understood. It's a gesture that somehow bypassed men over the ages.

"Jim was a kid, for God's sake. He wasn't even thirty yet. And you guys sent him out to play Cowboys and Indians when he had a plastic gun and there were real Indians out there. Can you sleep with that, Rob Stephens?"

Stephens knew that there was no way he could comfort her, no matter how much he might want to try. Yet, he needed to try, because he knew she was right. Those same questions had never been far from his thoughts in all the years he had been with the Agency. He raised his arms toward her and took a step in her direction.

"No!" She threw the word at him as she took a step back. She dropped her arms and clenched her fists at her side. "You're no different than any of them."

Stephens stopped after one more step. "Cynthia, we're trying our best to find him. I don't know that he's dead. If he is dead, I can't say that *any* reasons can ever be worth another life. But I know this would be close to justifying it." He moved his hands in an aimless up and down motion as he searched for the any words that might help explain what was happening. "You see, I had left those 'little boy spymaster games.' I would still be out if Jim had discovered anything even a hair less important. I had to come back to help."

Stephens reached up with both hands, and in a gesture a little like praying he used his index and middle fingers to rub the corners of his eyes. He felt very tired just then.

"That's why I'm here," he said with resignation in his voice. "I don't think anything less could have called me back."

The stiffness in her pose slowly dissolved. The tightly balled fists loosened and her shoulders eased back to normal as the anger slowly dissipated. She put both hands inside her quilted vest and turned to face him squarely. It was difficult now for her to direct all the anger she felt about her brother towards the person standing before her. She felt as though she knew Rob Stephens after the years of hearing Jim speak about him. In a way that was not unlike Stephens' view that had mixed the events in the shed with an imaginary fireplace scene, she too was suddenly involved in two very different scenes.

Despite the reality of the events in shed, she realized that she had always wanted to understand more about the Rob Stephens that she had heard about in conversations with her brother. Jim had been fascinated with Stephens from his first days with the agency, and had seemed driven to try to understand the strange mix of images in the stories he had heard about Stephens. She was the one person Jim felt he could talk to safely. It surprised her as she suddenly realized how much she needed to complete the picture of what Jim had tried to explain.

There had always been a contradiction in the way that Jim told the stories about Stephens. On one hand, he had told of the one person the Agency had to match up against the worst enemies, and the darkest situations, and the hardest of times. And yet, on the other hand he told of someone who could walk away from it all at a time when others would need to bask in the glory of the position they had earned. He had spoken of a person who could not accept his role at the very same time he knew his role was vital. He had told of the person who, to avenge his friends, had walked into places and faced things that she could not even begin to imagine.

As he stood in front of her, she looked at him in a very different way than she had just a few minutes earlier. The shed, and the place, didn't matter. For a few moments, she knew it was all right to put her cares for her brother a little bit to the side. She looked at Stephens, and reviewed all of the words and feelings that still echoed in the shed. She found that she liked Rob Stephens. She understood why, until then hidden under the surface, she had always wanted to meet him.

"You know, you and Jim were a lot alike. I wish you had met. You two would have been friends." She looked directly at Stephens. "Do you know what he once told me about you? The one thing that stood out most?" She did not wait for an answer. "He told me that he was one of the only people who understood you. That he could understand how one who cared so much, and so hated what he had to become in order to succeed, could find it possible to kill. It was because you always believed in those around you more than you did in yourself."

For one of the rare times in his life, Stephens felt helpless standing there. No part of him could come up with the words that he needed.

"If Jim is dead, would you tell me, really, if you knew?"

Stephens thought about the question before he answered. He decided that the truth was more important than secrecy, or roles, or any of the games he might normally play. And he felt that she deserved the truth. She had come this far, and then had the courage to stand alone in the darkness, while she waited for the killer of her brother. That counted for something.

"Yes Cynthia, I would," he answered. "I might not be able to tell you exactly how something happened, but I will tell you if it happens. It will be small comfort, perhaps, but it's all I can offer."

She looked carefully at him. She turned, and reached over to sweep her hand over the bow of the boat. It left a clear shiny patch amid the light dusting of sawdust from the work Robbins had been doing to get the boat ready winter storage. The faded gold letters of the name "SUSAN" now showed clearly against the varnished wood beneath. When she turned back her face had softened.

"Thank you," she said. There was the beginning trace of a smile. It was the sad half-smile you share with a friend who is there when you need him.

"I always knew that Jim told me more than he should about what was going on at the Agency," she said later, as the three of them sat in the great room of the Robbins home. "Please don't think badly of Jim for it.

It never hurt anything. He just needed to talk sometimes, and I was the only one he had."

The three had joined in the great room. The search of the basement and the garage could be put off for the night. There now was more than enough justification for a full sweep, and the lab boys could add both areas to their list for tomorrow. The team would do a much better job of it than he and Green could ever do. By the time Green returned downstairs after making the call to set up the sweep, events were already in motion back in Virginia. The team would fly into Boston that same night. By first light in the morning, three light blue vans of what would appear to be an EPA field team would pull into New Ipswich to take acid rain samples. One of the sites in town being tested would be the Robbins home.

Stephens and Cynthia Lebart sat at opposite ends of a long couch that was positioned nearly in the center of the wide room facing the windows in the east wall. There was a maple drop-leaf table behind the couch. The surface of the table was barely visible under a profusion of green from all the plants that were in two long copper pans on top of it. Most of the plants were beginning to show the effects of a week of neglect. There was a wide space between the table and a low bookcase that sat beneath the western row of windows. In front of the couch was a round slate table on wrought iron legs. Two easy chairs flanked the table. Green sat in the left-hand chair, with the door to the den a few feet behind him.

"He didn't tell any secrets," she continued. "It just wasn't easy for him sometimes." Cynthia had removed her blue vest, and sat in the corner with her knees tucked up under her, seemingly unbothered by the scrutiny and questions of the two men nearby.

"How long have you been up here," asked Green?

"Just since yesterday. I knew where Jim was staying, so I had a place to start." She swept her hand around the room. "This place was more of a guess than anything else. I spent a few hours yesterday reading back issues of the local papers. One thing that helps a lot is that in a town this size is that the weekly police reports, each Thursday, are a big event. The only thing at all unusual I could find was the Robbins murder."

"Why would you tie Jim to that?" Green asked.

"I didn't at first. Not until the next morning. I had this place in back of my mind only because it happened the day after I last talked to Jim. When I went through the newspapers, I was looking for anything unusual that happened around the same time. Maybe an accident, or a hospital case, or something like that. But when that girl at the ice cream stand said he headed towards New Ipswich when he left, and that was the same afternoon of the Robbins murder, I decided I had to check it out."

Stephens settled back further in the couch. Instinctively he took a position, facing to the side, where he could alternate glances between Cynthia Lebart and the rows of windows on each of the side walls. The woman was a remarkable combination of things, and he found that he very much enjoyed the chance to just sit, and watch, and listen to her. He was surprised at how easily she slipped by the natural checks and barriers he set between himself and others.

It had always been difficult for him to get close to others. For as far back as he could remember, he had always chosen the role of loner. It had been much easier for him that way. Those few he called friends, like Green, were rare. Like all things important to him there was no middle ground to his relationships. To Stephens, a friendship meant a commitment once the basis for trust and respect had been found. It required time to evolve, and once it did, it would deserve time to grow. In his job he had little chance for the first, and could never guarantee the second.

It was even more difficult, somehow, with a woman. He never seemed able to find the mix of things, the combination of traits that was so important to him. It wasn't that he didn't enjoy the appearance of someone as attractive as Cynthia Lebart. He did very much. It was just that it was just a part of what was important to him. Long before appearance could attract him further, the woman would have to become a friend. That, alone, would be a difficult first step. The step from friend to lover had only happened once before.

As he sat and listened to her, Stephens realized that what attracted him already included a combination of things beyond appearance. It was her confidence, the cool reason behind her words, and the way her deep green eyes locked on his when she spoke. In many ways, she was a lot like Joyce Patterson back at the agency. "Two sides of the same coin," he thought. Cynthia wore a beige turtleneck sweater over her jeans. A snapshot could have given the impression of an older college student. But in person there was both a confidence and an underlying authority that was more like that of a senior corporate executive.

"That's when the two of you pulled up. I had only been here for a half hour or so." She looked over at Green and her eyes sparkled with humor. "From what I saw of you, Mr. Green, based upon how soon after you got to the door it opened, you did an awful lot better than I did getting inside." She glanced over at Stephens to include him in the small joke on herself. "Don't believe what you hear about the incredible power of a woman's bobby pin. It doesn't work that way. At least it didn't work for me on the back door."

"Don't let it get to you," answered Green. "Just for the record, I've never been able to get a bobby pin to work either."

"So you were watching us all the time we were here," said Stephens.

"I had no idea who you were when you pulled up. At first, I thought you might be police, or family. But when I saw you through the window going through everything, I begin to think that I was lucky to have been out of sight in the shed when you pulled up."

"I didn't have a choice," said Stephens to Green, pointing at the windows. "No curtains here like there are in the den."

"How did you get in here without being seen?" asked Green. "I didn't see a car parked nearby."

"That was the easy part. I just walked right in. My car's about a quarter mile up the road parked in a turnout." She turned back to Stephens, and he could see the humor in her eyes again. She laughed easily when she looked at him. "Remember your line about the walk in the woods to get rocks for your son's collection? That was beautiful! The great part is that's how I actually did get here. Or at least almost that way. If you check the shed you'll find a grocery bag full of thistles, ferns, and leaves in there. Its mine."

Green and Stephens looked at one another. Stephens raised one eyebrow in appreciation for what he expected to come next. He didn't mind at all that she was laughing at him.

"You see, I *was* walking in the woods picking up things. I parked up there, and casually worked my way down the road. It happens all the time. No one in New Hampshire gives a second look to '. . . just another nature lover.' When I got here, I waited for a quiet time and just walked in."

Stephens shook his head as he commented to Green. "I wondered why that line about the rocks was such a disaster. It was lame, but it wasn't *that* bad."

Chapter Seven

Neither Green nor Stephens was able to accept Cynthia Lebart's presence at face value. Both had no doubt that there had to be more to her visit to the Robbins home than appeared on the surface. When they had been alone upstairs, briefly leaving her alone in the great room before the call back to Virginia, Stephens had been certain that she knew a great deal about her brother's investigation.

"Harvey, it makes no sense that she was here, unless she already knew the Robbins home was connected to Peterson," Stephens said to Green while Cynthia waited downstairs. "You don't piece that together from some newspaper article the way she said."

"I know," Green answered. "That's a lot of dots to be connected without a map."

"And it's been a long time since I walked into something as well handled as what she did in that shed," Stephens added. "She couldn't have known we were coming, yet she took every step once we did show up as though we were very dangerous. She was expecting definite, major-league trouble. Harvey, she already *knew* about the Falconer. I'd stake my left one on it. Now it's up to us to find out why, and how. If I remember right, she's something in computers. I'm not going to underestimate her, but there is no way a computer jockey can drop a class six, even a very rusty one like me, unless she was expecting a six."

"I'll call Virginia," said Green. "Let's see what they know about her."

When Green came down from placing the call, he had the advantage over Stephens of a fast review of what little the agency had on file about her. The person Stephens had called a 'computer jockey' headed up the third largest data processing facility in Massachusetts with a staff of more than 200. She worked for a major defense contractor in the high-technology belt around Boston. She was a Vietnam widow who had never remarried after the death of her husband during the 1968 TET offensive just outside of DaNang. He was a member of 37th Signal Battalion that abutted the huge DaNang air base. In a two-day period of rocket attacks from the hills just west of the field, 122 people were killed around DaNang. Alan Lebart had died in the first minutes of the first attack. There was nothing special in his death. No heroism or glory. Just another death, preceded by many, followed by more.

Green was the first to decide that things had eased up enough to ask the more difficult questions that were hanging. All he had heard, so far, still didn't all fit together. He now understood exactly why Stephens had shown so much respect for her actions, but why she was there was not so clear. There were two key questions that had to be pushed. The first was to determine how much she really knew. After having the chance to listen to her, he was more convinced than ever that she knew a great deal about Jim Peterson's search. The second was to determine her motive. Of that, at least, he had a working theory. Green had concluded as he listened that she had been ready, and quite willing, to shoot Stephens out in that shed. That meant the motive might be simple revenge. It also was a further indication that she knew enough to know revenge was needed.

"How much did you know about what Jim was doing," Green asked. "From what I remember reading, when our people talked to you a week ago, you couldn't tell them much. Now, all of a sudden, you're up here yourself. What changed your mind?"

It was very subtle, but both Green and Stephens saw the instant change that occurred when she heard the question. It was as if a filter had been dropped. She was guarded, and more careful. From then on, she would think about her answers for just a second or two longer than she had before.

"He was my brother, and he was missing. That's all there is," she said as she glanced from one to the other. "Would either of you have done any differently?"

"Of course not," said Stephens. "It's just that we hope you remember something that can help us. Maybe something about what he was doing, what he had found, who was involved? You must have some idea why he's missing, or you wouldn't be here, would you?"

"Maybe you two are just overlooking the obvious," said Cynthia. "I already told you I knew Jim was Company. I knew that he was into something big. I knew what he did, or at least a little about it. Then two people who even I can spot as very, very senior Agency come visit me. They ask tons of questions. And it's pretty clear Jim is in trouble and they didn't know where he was."

"What did he tell you he was doing?" asked Green. "Why would you call it big?"

"Because that's what he told me," she answered. She thought for a few seconds before choosing what to say next. "He called collect from the motel the night before he disappeared. 'Sis,' he said, 'I'm going to be able to write my own ticket around here. I've done it. I found the biggest name in the agency files.' When I asked him more, he just boasted that 'I'll be up there with Rob Stephens. I'll be the one to close the Stephens file.'"

"Did he tell you the name?" asked Stephens, softly.

"No," she said. "He said he wouldn't share that with anyone, not even with me. It would be too dangerous."

Stephens noted the slight hesitation, again, before she answered.

"He was so excited," she continued. "It scared me. There was something awful about it."

"Did he mention any names?" asked Green. "A code name, perhaps, or an odd phrase? Like, 'skyhawk,' or 'the major,' or 'Falconer,' or maybe 'yellow one?'"

"No," she said with, again, the slightest hesitation. "The 'yellow one' rings a bell, but I don't think it has anything to do with my brother."

Again, Stephens was certain that she was lying. Those little signals and patterns were all there for him to see. But he couldn't figure out a reason for her actions. "Did he give you any idea of the places he had been," he asked.

"I went over that with your people. The answer is still no."

Green reached into his jacket, and took out the copy of an old photograph taken eight years before in what was now the bombed out lobby of the Beirut Hilton. He glanced at Stephens before he moved, and then he reached over the slate table to hand it to her.

"While you've been up here, have you ever seen this man?"

This time it was clear that the face meant something special. Her eyes tightened, and she stared at it as though trying to burn it into her mind. Stephens was certain that he had seen a flash of triumph when she first saw the picture. "You've seen that face before, haven't you?" he asked.

Cynthia quickly looked up and shook her head smoothly. "No. He's an odd-looking one, though. But I've never seen him. Should I know him?"

She didn't wait for an answer. She looked back down at the picture as though wanting to insure that every feature, every part of the face, was memorized. Stephens watched as she finally handed the picture back to Green.

Stephens knew that they had reached the critical point where either cooperation would follow, or where they would reach a dead end. "Cynthia," he began, "you've got to level with us. Eventually you're going to have to trust someone with this. You say Jim used to talk to you about me? Well then, you know I've done this for far too long to miss when someone doesn't want to tell me everything."

"I've told you everything that I know," she insisted. "I'm just here to look for my brother. He's my brother! I intend to find him."

"This is more than just a missing person. I think you know very well that Jim had fallen into something way over his head. For God's sake Cynthia, it might be way over mine," he pleaded. "Let us handle it. Walk away from this."

"Let you handle it?" she asked with no effort to mask the sarcasm in her voice. "Let you find my brother for me?"

Stephens and Green looked at one another. Neither could understand the reason for the disdain in her voice, or the start of the anger in those eyes again.

"Yes," answered Green. "We have a whole team of people standing right behind us. I know how much you care. But you can only hurt things here. Let us handle it. Please."

She ignored Green and leaned forward towards Stephens. The anger that had flashed briefly was gone. But her voice remained intense, and very certain of what she chose to say. "Look. I know you two are different. I feel much better, now, than I did. It feels good to know I have help now. But I still have to look for Jim myself. To do the best I can. He and I both need it." She glanced at Harvey Green for support, and then back to Stephens. When she continued, her voice was soft, even gentle, as she tried to explain.

"It's enough that my brother is missing. That, alone, gives me the right to look for him, and to try and help him. I can't just count on you, or anyone else. That isn't possible anymore. Rob, Jim and I lost our parents because I counted on other people to lock up someone who liked to drive half drunk. My parents weren't even the first people he had killed. I lost a husband I loved more than anything on this earth. He had thousands, just as committed as you, '. . . standing right behind him.' They didn't do any good. Now Jim is all I have left. I'll be damned if I'll lose him too. And if he is dead, then I have to find the person who killed him. I have to. I can't back away from an obligation like that. Surely, Rob, you of all people can understand such an obligation?"

Stephens did understand, and he could not answer right away. Green, though just three years older than Stephens, looked and sounded more like the gentle father than the hardened agent when he tried to continue. "Cynthia," he reasoned, "Rob and I do understand. But we're pros. We know the price. You don't. You can't possibly do more, or do anything but get hurt."

"We're here until this is over," said Stephens. "It just doesn't make sense for you . . ."

His sentence ended abruptly. Had it not been for the faint glint of metal, Stephens might have missed the shadow that had formed at the very edge of the light that formed a small, glowing shell outside of the eastern bank of windows. Ever since he was surprised in the shed he had accepted the fact that the old habits and procedures were now called for. When he had first arrived at the house, even with the ghost of the Falconer hanging over him, he had not associated the possibility of wetwork with the hills of New Hampshire that meant so much to him. That had changed when he walked into the shed and had been cornered by Cynthia Lebart.

When he saw the dim reflection of metal move slowly upward, about the distance when a hand moves from down at the hips to waist level, he knew they were trapped. They were bathed in the light, in the center of the room, with a row of windows on each side and whoever was outside was covered in darkness.

Stephens flung his body off the end of the couch and towards Cynthia. He was halfway across, arms outstretched towards her like a diver, before the yell of "Down!" started to escape from him. Harvey Green, from too many years with Stephens to doubt his actions, had already begun to move before the first pane of the western windows shattered and exploded in a rain of glass on the floor. The terrible sound ATQ agents called the "Cat Lisp" came from outside the window. It was the sound a bullet makes when cushioned by a silencer. It sounds like a cat that starts to hiss, and then stops abruptly as though a hand had covered its mouth.

Stephens' right arm caught her shoulder and began to pull her off the couch. He saw her mouth had start to open and eyes widen in the classical comic expression that is half question and half surprise. Even before their two bodies had reached the floor, his left hand was reaching for the edge of the slate table in front of them. Green was already most of the way to the floor, and he too was reaching for the other side of the table. The instant search for cover was not a lesson from a training manual, but rather a reflection of the instincts honed by too many times and places in the past when unexpected wetwork had sprung upon them. "Only in the movies," Green would explain to new class twos, "does the hero reach for his gun and turn to blast away his surprise opponent. In the real world, first you jump, duck, dive, or do whatever in hell it takes to avoid being killed. Then, you can think about pulling your gun."

"They're on both sides," said Green with no wasted explanation. His observation was confirmed, almost before he completed the sentence, by a rain of glass from the western row of windows behind the couch.

As soon as they both had leverage, they shoved the slate up and over to provide a shield against the fire from the exposed eastern window. It took only seconds, despite the weight of the table. They left it on a slant, wedged with cushions pulled from the couch, so that the shots from the window could not hit straight on and crack the slate. The couch and the drop-leaf table, in back of them, provided some shelter against the western window.

"I only saw one on my side," said Stephens when he could finally reach inside his jacket for his gun. He lay on the floor, resting full length against Cynthia who was pressed between him and the base of the couch.

"I only saw one, but there could easily be more," added Green.

"What's going on here? Who are they? How did they find us here?" Cynthia's voice behind him was level, but Stephens knew that she was masking the fear inside. He could feel the deep rise and fall of her breathing against his back, and the beating of her heart through her sweater.

Stephens did not answer her. He looked at Green "We've got to do something about these lights. We're sitting ducks in here, and they're hidden in the dark."

"Also, old buddy, I don't want to have to trust this slate forever. And that sofa is going to be the first problem. If they get a little higher for a better angle, or break through the two sides of the drop-leaf, it won't stop a hi-cal."

"Can we move the slate and couch at the same time?"

"I doubt it," said Green. "The slate will take two of us and I'll let you be the one whose fingers are showing. Even if we could, once you pull the couch away from the table it's going to be a sieve."

As they talked, the soft whispers of the cat lisps continued. Only occasionally there was the sound of more glass breaking. Both Stephens and Green recognized the method of pros who avoided making extra noise by aiming through the already broken windows. Both noticed that the person on the eastern side, facing the slate table, was now very slow and deliberate with his shots. Neither needed to point out that he was now aiming at just one spot on the slate, where he hoped to create a stress fracture that would break the slate and leave them helpless. On the other side, the shots were spaced much farther apart. The person on that side was not wasting useless shots. But he was also making sure that Green and Stephens remained pinned where they were.

"We've got to take out the lights, Harvey. How did these things go on?"

"The two near that wall are by the wall switch," said Green, pointing to the northern wall by the den. "The other one is solo."

"Can you get the switch from there?"

"Just," said Green with his usual economy of words.

"You take it first. The lamp's easier. I'll nail it after you hit. Then you take the east window," he said, pointing. "I'll cover west, and we'll let Cynthia rabbit."

"Front or back," asked Green.

"I'm leery about the whole front. There are two doors, front and kitchen. I don't trust it. No doors in back. Just that one over there on the side."

"Upstairs? No porches or doors. Might be a tree or something?"

"None. I walked the yard. I don't think they're inside yet. There may be more than two of them. Too many windows down here for her. Let's send her up the back stairs."

"Got it."

The sound of the bullet hitting the slate had a different tone to it. Both Green and Stephens snapped their head towards the sound, and saw a hairline crack from the middle to the upper edge of the slate.

"Shit," said Green. "One or two more there and it's gone."

Stephens pulled away from Cynthia, until there were a few inches between them. He glanced back at her and was pleased to see she was under control. There was fear in her eyes, but she was calm, and would listen. He realized, as he looked, just how much he liked those eyes.

"Damn," he said as he glanced down at her. "You're wearing that white sweater. Even in the dark it'll be a beacon." He worked his way out of the dark blue suit jacket he was wearing. "Wear this. Don't get up even an inch as you put it on."

While she slipped into the jacket, he explained what would come next. She listened carefully.

"We're going to kill the lights. Harvey will shoot at the switch. As soon as he shorts it out, I'll get the other lamp. You'll have perhaps five seconds while they get used to the dark in here. They'll just shoot wildly until they do. Harvey and I will pin them down. You crawl, just as fast and low to the ground as you can go, to the back stairs."

He pointed towards the back. "Do you know where the stairs are?"

She nodded.

"Head up the back stairs and find a place to hide."

"Is there a phone up there?" she asked. "Should I call the police, or someone?"

Stephens was impressed with the coolness and reasoning behind the question. But by now he had no doubt about the quality of the people outside. "Good thought," he said. "But the phones will be dead. It's up to us. The cavalry's still in Dodge."

He looked at her, and smiled. She smiled back as their eyes met. Both of them were very aware of the warmth from where their bodies had lain against one another. "Ready? Now comes the hard part," he said. "Take good care of my suit. Try not to get any holes in it."

Cynthia didn't answer at first. She continued to look at Stephens. Then she carefully reached up and snaked one arm over to where her purse lay on the couch. She pulled it down and removed the small handgun that was inside. She started to close the purse, but then stopped and looked back at Stephens with a half-smile. "I guess I can come back for this later," she said as she tossed it back on the couch.

Stephens turned back to Green. It was all business now. "Give me just a second, Harvey," he said as he moved towards the right end of the couch so that he could peer around the edge of it to where the lamp glowed against the opposite wall.

"Do it," he snapped.

Green carefully lined up his aim at the wall switch about twelve feet away beside the door to the den. Very slowly he pulled back the trigger. He didn't need a second try. After a small shower of sparks and a bright flash from the switch, the two lights in the room died. At the same time, a light in the kitchen and one in the den faded and died as a fuse, overloaded by the short circuit, gave way in the basement below. Less than a second after the lights dimmed, Stephens took the much easier shot at the lamp that still glowed brightly against the wall. It shattered and the room was plunged into darkness.

Stephens moved with one smooth motion to the right end of the couch where he could now sight the western window. He began to fire spaced, measured shots at the darkness outside. With a parallel movement Green was at the left edge of the slate and began to fire through the eastern window.

"Go. Now!" said Stephens to Cynthia. She began her painful race across the hardwood floors on her elbows and knees. For the first ten or twelve seconds, there was no firing from outside as the advantage changed dramatically against the attackers. Now the interior of the house was dark. The attackers outside were visible even in the dim light of the clouded, nearly moonless sky. The attackers had to dive for cover, and then work towards new, better-protected positions.

It took a few more seconds than Stephens had expected before the attackers renewed their firing. From outside of both windows came a steady rain of fire. There was the sound of glass breaking as the attackers had to make new paths for the bullets from their new positions. The insidious sound of the cat lisps could again be heard outside the windows. Inside, the house echoed with the dull thwack of a slug hitting wood, the plumpf of a shell burying itself in furniture, and the crack of a shell careening off the slate and then into the ceiling.

From the front of the house they heard the tinkle of glass breaking as someone did not waste time trying to pick the front door lock. Immediately Stephens and Green knew that there were at least three attackers—one outside each set of windows and one that would soon be inside.

"You take the back, I'll get the front," said Stephens, and with one smooth movement he rolled across the floor to the base of the wall that separated the den from the great room. As soon as he was there, he quickly removed his tie and stripped off his white dress shirt, and undershirt. He knew that the pale cream of his skin would be at least a small improvement to the bright white of the shirts in the night action. Even such small improvements in the odds could make a difference. Far to his right he heard the faint sounds of Green rolling to the back wall opposite him. Then there was no further sound from Green as Harvey silently worked his way along the base of the far wall and past the stairway beyond.

Behind him in the great room, the sounds of firing had ceased. As soon as Stephens and Green had stopped firing, there was no longer a visible target for the attackers. They would be moving into better positions and waiting for an error by those inside. Since delay worked to the advantage of those inside, they would regroup and develop a new plan of attack. As yet, they had not attracted the attention of anyone passing, or in any of the houses several hundred feet to either side. In the night wind the light sound from the silencers would not carry far. No one had yet heard the breaking glass, and the un-silenced gunfire from Green and Stephens was muffled and contained inside the house. It was only a matter of time before the attackers would have to try either a more direct assault, or use fire or explosives.

Stephens carefully worked his way the few feet needed, until his head was a few inches from the bottom of the doorway to the den. He used the practiced silence that had taken him years to develop. It was a matter of how you placed your weight and how you breathed. Dragging a limb across the floor would make the small sounds that were enough to spell death among professionals. You had to lift yourself on your palms and toes, move forward a few inches, and then rest fully on your chest again before repositioning your hands and feet for the next move. At the same time, you had to control your breathing. No matter what the adrenaline was trying to do to the chemistry of your body it was vital to maintain light, measured breathing, preferably through your nose. The hardest part of the effort, and the last to be mastered, was to control the often overpowering impulse to swallow. In a quiet room, you might be no more aware of your own swallowing than you are of your own heart beat. Yet, the sound of saliva moving in your mouth, or down your throat, stands out from all other sounds as distinctly human and makes it easy to pinpoint your location.

When you are finally able to achieve that degree of silence, the sounds around you seem to grow and become far easier to identify. It was for that reason that, as he lay near the base of the doorway, he heard the faint sound of a swallow within the den. Now Stephens was at the point where, in the movies, the brave hero would get up, roll across the opening, spring up on one knee, and fire a deadly shot straight through the heart of the villain who had been given away by the sound. But in the real world the hero would die long before getting off a shot. The schoolyard tricks of throwing a pebble or showing a hat on a stick didn't work when dealing with pros. Usually, the only thing that mattered was silence and waiting. It was a matter of mistakes. Among the very best, the person who made the first mistake would be the one to die that day. Among the very best, you could never really win such fights. You had to wait for the other person to lose.

From the back of the house Stephens heard a single shot. It was not from a silenced gun and was accompanied by the sound of breaking glass from one of the rear bedroom windows. He knew that one of the attackers had made a mistake, and had been unfortunate to make that mistake in the sight of Harvey Green. The odds would now be closer by at least one.

As he lay there, Stephens knew that such situations gave you a brief window to change the facts before you lost the chance forever. Soon the attackers were likely to resort to explosives. Or, if there were enough of them, they would enter simultaneously from too many directions to be resisted. The presence of one attacker already inside the house would be the beginning of the end if not soon countered. Right now, there was a small window of time where the attackers were not yet fully reorganized for the new conditions. Stephens and Green had to become the aggressors, or to lose the window. When it closed, they would be trapped.

Stephens knew that he would have to make a move very soon, and therefore his only choice was to make a rookie's move. He needed to force the action before he ran out of time. The one factor that might work in his favor was that all actions by the attackers showed they knew the caliber of the two men inside the house. It was clear from the careful and well-planned attack that the attackers knew they faced Green and Stephens. If the person lying wait in the den knew that he was up against a class six, then Stephens knew he would expect only the actions of a class six.

Carefully, slowly, he inched his way back towards the couch. When he got close, he switched his gun to his left hand and reached out with his right for one of the cushions lying on the floor. He never took his eyes away from the two doors. Most of the time he stared at the den door. Occasionally he would glance at the open kitchen door in the corner of the room. He counted on Green have closed off the far end of the great room. When he had the cushion, the return was even slower. He had both hands full and could not allow any sound to betray his actions.

When he once again reached the base of the wall near the door, he switched the gun back to his right hand and the cushion to the left. He turned onto his right side, and then lifted the pillow up against the wall as high as he could reach, until it was just to the right of the door opening. He inched slightly forward, until his right elbow was two inches from the base of the door and his right hand, with the gun, was pointing straight up along the side of the doorway. Finally he was ready. He held the pillow on a slant, and then moved it carefully up the wall, making sure that there was just the tiniest bit of noise from the fabric against the wall. When it was about four feet up the wall, he let the corner of the pillow peek around the edge of the doorway. It was the distance off the ground that the head or shoulder of a crouching person would be.

The intruder inside the room did not even wait a full second before firing two shells directly through the center of the dim shadow. The two shots were precise, entering the cushion less than three quarters of an inch from each other. Although Stephens could not yet know how accurate his judgment had been, the intruder knew more than just the caliber of the two people inside the house. He also knew he faced Rob Stephens and Harvey Green. The last thing that he anticipated from a Green or a Stephens would be a rookie scam.

Both rounds entered the pillow with a deep thump that is much like the sound of a bullet entering flesh. The intruder saw the dim shadow of what he thought to be a shoulder, or perhaps a head, stagger and drop slightly. Then he saw it start to rise again as his target must have been trying to stand up. The intruder began to squeeze off another round to finish the job. He smiled as he pictured his reward as the killer of either Green or Stephens. Just as the trigger reached the last sixteenth of an inch before the slug would be fired, the intruder saw a quick movement at the very base of the door as the arm and head of Stephens glided into the doorway. He saw the two flashes, and heard the sound of the two shots. He felt the first slug enter his chest, and the second rip into the side of his head. He heard the rude, loud clatter of his gun falling to the ground. He heard the rush of a tornado or hurricane, and strangely, the sound of crows calling. The last thought the intruder had was to wonder how someone could hold a gun in his foot, and kill him with it.

Stephens knew better than to rush into the room. For a full minute after he heard the body crumple to the ground, he concentrated on all of the sounds in the room. He knew that there was at least a small chance that there was a second person in there. He had stopped like this dozens of times over the years, and for all but a handful of those times the wait had been a fruitless waste of time. But, on that handful of occasions, the patience had saved his life. When finally he was convinced that the room was empty, he slipped into the room. It took only a few moments to confirm the death. He worked past the body, over to the other door, and carefully waited again to hear any sounds from the dining room or the stairs beyond. He could see the front door, slightly open, with broken glass from a side window on the floor.

When he was sure there was no one else there, he edged his way back to the body on the floor. Stephens was not at all surprised to find that in the dark he found nothing on the body. There was no watch, jewelry, wallet, or any other item that might identify the man. He removed the black sweatshirt and black knitted hat the man had been wearing. He put them on. He could feel the blood around the small hole on the left side of the shirt against his skin. Because of the dark shirt and hat, now only his face would be revealed in the darkness. Stephens reached over and found the gun the man had dropped. He rested it on the chest of the man, and never taking his eyes away from scanning the two doorways he used his left hand to remove the clip. When he determined that the clip had nearly a full load, he returned it to the gun, and slipped his own into his belt. He pulled an extra clip from the man's pants pocket. From that point on he, too, would have the use of a silencer-equipped weapon.

Stephens crept down the small hallway, next to the front stairs that led to the kitchen. The den was on his right and the dining room to his left. He looked up the stairs and at the kitchen door ahead. Finally, he realized what the rest of his plan would be.

When he came to the doorway to the kitchen, he again stopped again and listened. Once he entered the kitchen he would be an easy target should anyone be watching from outside. There was another door, leading to the outside, in the opposite corner of the kitchen. The whole left end of the kitchen was a bay window. If he were to go into the kitchen and turn right, the door to the great room would be four feet ahead. Just to his right would be the stairs down to the basement.

He waited and listened intently at the kitchen door. Stephens did not think that there was anyone else in the house, but knew far better than to rely upon such an assumption. Even if the room was empty, that would be small consolation. The windows and the outside door meant that the room would almost certainly be under observation. Whoever had been firing through the eastern window at the slate, if not the victim of Green's shot ten minutes earlier, could easily watch both areas.

He remembered from his earlier search of the house that the basement door opened towards the great room. Thus, it would not be possible to sneak in from the great room. The basement door was partly open. He waited no more than thirty seconds while he analyzed the possibilities. The easiest thing might have been to use a flash of light to destroy the night vision of the watching attackers. But the kitchen lights were dead. They had died with the same fuse overload that had saved them in the great room. He could always use a piece of furniture as a shield. However, the plan he had in mind required surprise, so even if the shield protected him it would be clear to anyone watching that he was now in the basement. He realized that he faced a no-win situation. To protect himself as he went around the corner could cost him the critical commodity of surprise.

The only logical action was clear to him. He slipped the silenced weapon into his belt next to his own gun. Next, he tugged the sleeves of the sweatshirt down over his hands, until he had covered all possible skin that might act as a pale beacon to anyone watching. He crouched down on the balls of his feet with his right foot next to the base of the door and his right fingers wrapped around the door jamb. He pulled the knit hat down to completely cover the white skin of his face, even though, for the moment, it would cover his eyes and blind him. Finally, he shifted all of his weight to his right foot, leaned back a bit, and then smoothly pivoted forward on his right foot. He swung silently around the door jamb, his left shoulder just ducking inside the partially open basement door, until his left foot reached the top of the basement stairs. In the same smooth motion he reached out with his left hand to brace himself against the wall of the stairwell, lifted his right foot, loosened his right hand, and swung the rest of himself through the open door.

At the top of the stairs he froze, just inside the door, crouching blindly on the balls of his feet, just a few inches inside the doorway facing the kitchen. He froze in that exposed position. Finally, when he was certain that anyone watching would be satisfied by the lack of any follow-up motion should the first movement have caught an eye, he leaned back and moved down two more steps.

When he was no longer exposed, he readjusted the knitted hat and listened carefully for any sounds. He was thankful that the move had worked. He had not been spotted. But, he did not waste time congratulating himself. He knew that all you could do sometimes, was take the path with the best chances. You could not change luck, and could not take credit for it. He would need more luck before he was done.

With wide-spread legs, and a rocking motion like a penguin, he walked down the stairs. He placed his left foot next to the far left edge of each step, and his right foot by the opposite edge, so that he stepped on the portion of the stairs best supported by the beams underneath. There was very little noise from his steps. At the bottom of the stairs he took a few steps to the left and waited for his eyes to adjust to the darkness of the basement. After a while, he could begin to see the faint outline of the narrow windows at the top of the basement walls.

When he could see well enough to avoid obstacles, he started towards the first of the windows. One by one he walked to each of the windows, in turn. At each he would stop and carefully look out. At the third, down in the rear corner near the garage, he was rewarded for his plan. As he approached, a small dark shadow moved slightly in one corner of the window. It was the outline of a foot from someone crouching near the wall of the house. He stepped back from the window, and investigated the remaining two windows before he returned to the foot. He went to the far side of the window so that he would be directly behind the person outside when he reached the window. When he was in position, like a snake out of a pit he rose up until he could see the back of the person outside.

Without taking his eyes off the man outside, and with his gun pointed directly at the man, he reached out his left hand to the lever on the window. If it was at all possible, he did not want the sound of breaking glass to give away his actions. Should the man hear him and begin to turn, he would have no compulsion about shooting him in the back, through the window. At least there would be one less attacker, and he still might be able to sneak out of the basement. The window was the old fashioned type held at the top by a lever and with two metal tongues on the bottom that fitted into matching grooves. The view through the window was clear. Stephens recognized the signs of recent cleaning. He hoped that, when cleaned, the window had been opened.

With infinite patience he opened the lever. The whole action took more than fifteen seconds, but the time dragged on as though it took minutes. He made no sound as he turned the lever. Finally, he felt the lever clear the top, and the window was ready to be opened. Stephens did not even consider trying to open the window in the same slow manner. Under the best of conditions he did not expect silence. All he wanted was much less noise, and much less identifiable a sound, than would be made by breaking glass. The window made a soft grinding sound from the dirt caught between it and the sill as he swiftly pulled it open. Before it was halfway down, hinging forward on the bottom two pieces of metal, he fired twice into the left side of the turning man's back just below where he knew the angel wing to be. The sound of the two successive cat lisps echoed in the basement, but were not heard outside. The body, as it slumped to the ground, made almost no noise as it fell from its crouching position to the garden bed a few inches below.

Stephens reached up and gave three soft knocks on the ceiling above him. The raps were for Green to hear upstairs. They would not be heard outside. It would be very clear to Green as to who had made them, and why. If there were others now inside who heard the knocks, then it really didn't matter. That could only happen if Green was dead, and then it would already be too late for anything Stephens might try to do.

He lifted the window up, and inward. It easily lifted out of the frame. He placed it onto the floor, listened carefully, and then pulled himself up and out of the window. He lay close to the ground near the body, until he was sure that no one else was nearby. He reached down for some of the dirt and rubbed it into the skin of his face and hands. The dirt eliminated the last distinction that prevented him from becoming just another shadow in the darkness around him. He felt a small measure of satisfaction. He was pleased to see that the old abilities and habits had come back, and that his instincts were still sound. Most of all, he was pleased that three of the attackers were dead, that he was outside, and that the tides that controlled that night had changed. Those tides now bore inexorably against whoever he might find in the night.

"Harvey," he thought, "the odds have shifted."

He began to move towards the back of the house.

Chapter Eight

Harvey Green did not have to hear Stephen's silent comment to know that things had changed a great deal. He had been moving from one room to another, edging up to a window, and observing the grounds outside. Since the time earlier when an undisciplined and unwise attacker had raised his head up to look inside a darkened window, no one had made such a mistake again. When Green heard the three light taps near the western side of the house, he knew Stephens was in the basement. On silent cat's feet, as silent as the Sandburg poem, he crept to that side of the house and waited next to one of the side windows. A few moments later he saw a figure rise up from where it could easily have remained hidden, and then move towards the rear of the house. Despite the change in clothes, he knew that it was Stephens. He tapped, ever so lightly, on the glass of the window. He saw Stephens, below, turn and give a brief nod before the shape melted into the darkness and out of sight again.

Having Stephens outside told Green a lot about what had happened with the intruder in the front of the house, and about the course of events still to come. It meant that there were at least two attackers dead, counting the one he had killed earlier and the one he assumed was now in the front rooms. Although he had not been able to see the body near the basement window, he could guess that a third might have died during Stephens' exit from the house. For certain he knew that with Stephens outside, silently among them, the attackers had become the attacked. His job was now clear. He would continue to move, and would give the impression to those watching that both he and Stephens were still trapped inside the house. He would give them solid reasons to keep their attention focused on the inside, not out.

Green returned to the rear corner room on the opposite side of the house from where Stephens had exited the basement. He worked his way to the window that faced the east yard of the house. He ducked down and turned his head on a 45 degree angle. He moved his head until only the right eye appeared in the lower left corner of the window. Carefully he looked outside for any sign of an attacker. In a way it wasn't important if the attacker was exposed or not, just that he was in an identifiable position. Green's hope was to find any target to shoot at, so that those outside would know where he was for the moment. If the target was in the open and could be hit, it would be a nice bonus. But it was not essential.

If he saw no one, he could not just aimlessly fire through the window to get their attention. Those outside would see immediately that he was firing at nothing, and would know just as quickly that it had to be a red herring. Whatever he did would have to be done very well, and would have to appear to be a logical move for a class six. Green decided that one such move would be to open a window as though to make a listening post to monitor the events outside. He pulled back from the window and studied the room, looking for something that would let him open the window without exposing himself. He crawled over to the frame bed against the far wall, and felt underneath to test one possibility. To his satisfaction, he found that the old bed used wooden slats to support the mattress.

When he returned to the window, he first stood well to one side and used the board to trip the latch that locked the window. He held the slat with the flat side facing to the outside so that the smallest possible profile showed. He made sure that he did not hit the window or cause any noise. When it was unlocked, he crouched down beside the window. He used the slat to slowly push up against the trim dividing the panes of the bottom window to silently raise the window three inches. He did not need to make any noise to accomplish his goal. Those outside would be waiting, and intently watching, for just such a move. It was very unlikely that they would miss the action of the window opening. If somehow they did at first miss it, they would soon spot the newly opened window.

When he was done there was no reaction. Green did not expect those outside to shoot at shadows or at a piece of wood. He kept the board in his left hand as he moved out of the room. He worked his way along the base of the wall in the great room towards the den. It took three minutes to travel the forty feet over to the den. When he reached the door, he waited another two minutes to be sure that the black form he could just make out on the floor was the dead intruder he expected to find. Four years before, in small hotel just west of Cairo, Green had lost a friend when a "dead body" turned out to be a live substitute who lay in wait for someone to return and take it for granted.

Once inside the den he used the slat again. Here he did not open a window. He used the board to cause the curtain on the front window to move slightly, as though brushed by someone passing. Then, at the side window that faced to the west, he used it to pull one edge of the curtain back an inch as though by someone inspecting the outside. This time he expected a reaction from outside. At first he was surprised when there was no shot directed towards the curtain movement. Then he smiled in appreciation.

"You must have taken this one out, old buddy," he thought. "Nobody's home over here anymore. That makes three. Very good. Very good, indeed."

When that was done, Green headed towards the dining room. It was time let any attackers on that side of the house know he and Stephens were still moving around inside.

Stephens was crouching at the rear corner of the house at the same time that Green was opening the window on the far side. He had no idea that it had been opened. Yet, while he could not know the specific actions that Green would be taking inside, he had a pretty good idea of the general plan that Harvey would use. The two of them had been together on enough assignments that they could predict each other's moves with a fair degree of accuracy. It was perhaps even more important that they could rule out, with near certainty, a whole series of possibilities. In their work it was actually more important to know those things your partner would not do than the ones he or she might do. Stephens knew that Green would be taking steps to establish their presence inside to those watching outside. Green would create the illusion of two people inside, and find some way to make one of those outside people become a target. The whole idea would be well understood by a David Copperfield or a Doug Henning. To create an illusion you need to create plausible explanations for what does happen, and have your audience spend a great deal of their time watching what does not really happen.

The key, as always, would be patience and stealth. He would have to wait for the attackers to make another mistake. But this time that mistake would be helped along by Green inside, and by the powerful tool of surprise in the hands of Stephens outside.

Three of the attackers were dead now. Stephens did not know how many were left. His intuition told him there had to be at least two more. First of all, the enemy would know about the Green kill, and would suspect that a second had died after hearing the two un-silenced shots inside the house. A single remaining attacker would not have stayed to face two live sixes. Second, Stephens did not think it likely that only three people would be sent to attack a pair like Stephens and Green no matter what value had been placed on the element of surprise.

Finally, it was the position of the attacker by the basement window that convinced him that there were at least two more attackers. Attackers of their level would have every side of the house covered. The man killed by the basement window was close to the middle of the western wall. From that position he would be able to see only one side of the house. If the attackers were short-handed, they would have placed their people on the corners where they could see two sides at once.

Stephens considered the places he had seen during his earlier walk around the house. He thought about possible cover where the attackers might be positioned. The stone wall along the whole edge of the back yard was one. A woodpile was at the eastern edge of the yard in a key position that would oversee both the back and east yards. Twenty feet outside the great room windows on the east side of the house was an old New England root cellar. The cellar was roughly eight feet square and was recessed into the ground with the top two feet showing. The top was covered with sod that sloped down on two sides and the back. In front, steps led down to a small door into the cellar. While he doubted anyone would be inside the cellar, the mound would provide excellent concealment and cover to someone observing the kitchen and great room. The front side of the house had no real places to hide. While there were trees and a large stand of bushes on the front corner of the lot, a person there would be much more exposed than on any other side of the house. Whoever was stationed out front would have the very limited role of watching and waiting. Little movement would be possible.

Stephens looked around the corner to the back side of the house. A few feet in front of him was the black shape of a body on the lawn.

There were no other signs of the attackers. The body was lying on its back, face towards Stephens, eyes wide open and unmoving. Both hands were visible, out at the side, and empty. No gun was in sight. There were broken shards of glass on the ground around the body with two small pieces reflecting dully on his chest. Stephens did not have to look up to know that the window in the wall above the body would be broken, and that he had found Green's earlier kill.

Stephens watched the eyes intently for any sign of movement. When he had confirmed that the body was no immediate threat, he intently scanned the stone wall sixty feet away behind the house. He did not really expect to see anyone there. Along the far eastern side of the lawn he could see the darker shape of the woodpile. He studied it as he had the stone wall, but saw nothing except the smallest trace of a man's shadow at the corner of the pile. Whoever was stationed there was very good and very quiet.

Stephens waited for a full minute before he decided to return to the body beside the open basement window in order to verify a plan that was forming. He stretched out the body to see if the size and build was roughly like his. The man was smaller than Stephens, but it would be a close match when seen at a distance. He searched the body to see if those outside had any means of communication. Like the body inside in the den, there was none. The body was wearing the same black sweatshirt and knitted cap as he had taken from the body inside and was now wearing. He pulled off one of the shoes, and tried to squeeze it over his own foot. The shoe was much too small to fit. He knew that his shoes would be different, but in the darkness they were not likely to be seen. "Damn," he said to himself, shaking his head in the night.

Stephens moved back to the rear corner and searched one last time for anything revealing motion the location of another attacker. The shadow by the woodpile had not moved. Finally, in plain sight of anyone watching he crouched, and then crept along under the windows to the opposite corner. He had no doubt at all that at least one pair of eyes outside was following his every movement. His plan to get that watcher to show himself was based upon two factors. One was that the surprise and darkness would let him pass for being one of them. The second was that Green had by now given him some something to work with.

When he got to the far corner, Stephens found the window that had been partially opened by Green a few minutes before. As soon as he saw it he knew how to proceed. He turned and signaled the woodpile and the stone wall where he knew at least one of the attackers would have to be. Crouching below and just to the side of the window, he pointed to the opening, and then raised one finger in the universal sign to ". . . wait a moment." He moved back to the corner, and then along the rear of the house, until he was just below and to the right of a second window on the back wall of the same room. When he was in position, he began a simple pantomime to indicate that as soon as the watcher would shoot through the open window, he would fire through the side window and catch whoever was inside in a deadly crossfire. Finally, he signaled that he was ready.

As he crouched by the window, he saw the slight change in the shadows at the end of the woodpile. The person there was very good. Had Stephens not been staring at that area, he would have missed the small movement of an arm and head moving into position to fire. Stephens raised his arm in the universal sign of a policeman saying "stop" or of an assassin saying "wait." He stood up with his back tight to the side of the building and his weapon just under the window. He pressed his ear against the wall as though listening to sounds inside. He then pulled back, and nodded to show that he was ready.

The person behind the woodpile, without leaving the protection it afforded, fired three rounds into the window Green had partially opened. Stephens waited until the last shot, and then swung up and fired two deadly shots through the window into the room beyond. The window shattered in front of him as the slugs lodged harmlessly in the bed against the far wall. Stephens looked through the window, and after a few moments raised one clenched fist over his head in triumph over the death of the imaginary person inside the room. Then he crouched down again, and raised one finger to show the woodpile that he had gotten one of those inside. He stood up briefly and studied the interior of the room as though to verify the kill. Then, still facing away from the woodpile, Stephens signaled for the attacker at the woodpile to come over to the side of the house to help finish the assault.

The figure behind the woodpile hesitated for no more than a few seconds before he started to move. He was the leader of the attackers and a veteran of many such campaigns. He knew instantly that Henri, the person he thought was crouched under the window, had a plan to enter the house now that either Green or Stephens had been killed. The leader was bothered that Henri had left his post on the far side of the building. "There is no discipline in these idiots they gave me," the leader thought. "This fool will crow at his success and forget all about the risk he took in moving." He looked down to his right where he could see the small depression where Abman still watched the front of the house. "Even if Stannik was ignorant enough to get himself killed, there are still three of us against one," he thought. "And now Henri has a way for us to get inside the house." As prepared to move to help Henri, he had one final thought. "What if it was Stephens he killed? Oh please let it be Green, not Stephens. Leave Stephens for me!"

The leader scanned the windows to see if he had been seen by those inside the house. He saw no one, but knew that was no guarantee he was safe. He also knew that the longer he waited, the more the temporary advantage gained by Henri would slip away. He rose, and crept around the woodpile to the side of the kitchen, and stayed low to the ground until he was just beneath the window Green had opened. He listened for any noise, but heard none. Finally, he moved to the next window where Henri waited.

"Which one?" the leader whispered intensely to the form in front of him.

There was no answer at first, just Henri's left hand signaling to wait. Then, the hand signaled the leader to move around to the other side of the window. The leader edged past Stephens to take up the post. At first, he did not even look at Stephens. He knew that his first responsibility in his new position would be to scan the corners of the room that were in his field of fire. While he did that, he tried once again. "Henri," the whisper was a bit more insistent. "Which one did you get? Was it Stephens or Green?"

When there was no answer and when his scan of the room was complete, the leader took a quick glance at "Henri." As he started to turn back to the room, he stopped abruptly and turned back to study the eyes that he found coolly looking back at him. At the edge of his vision he saw the weapon aimed directly at his chest, while his own gun pointed uselessly into the room. He was every bit as good as Stephens had guessed. The shock of recognizing the face of Stephens two feet in front of him, where Henri should have been, delayed his reactions less than a second. But even as he begun to swing his own gun down the leader knew it was too late.

In the stretched and warped timeframe that controls such moments, the next half second seemed to stretch into minutes for the attacker from the woodpile. He knew with total certainty that he could not move quickly enough. He knew that even the short delay in his reactions had made no difference. A part of him felt nothing but respect, and a trace of awe, at the knowledge that there was another who could kill him. Until this moment, he had not believed that was possible. In the five months he had worked with the Falconer preparing for Boston, he had first been afraid of the Falconer, then just respectful, and finally had begun to believe that ". . . The Falconer is good, but I think he gets old now. Maybe the old stories of him and Stephens are just old stories. Maybe it is time for a new leader here."

The leader had been angry at the last instructions from the Falconer before he left to lead the attack at the Robbins place. He had started to walk away with a curt ". . . Don't worry. I'll get them . . ." when the Falconer had reached out, and with surprising force spun him around with a hand clamped onto his arm.

"You're good, my young friend," the Falconer had said with an intensity that for a moment shook the team leader. "But you now face Stephens and Green. Either one of them could kill you in a room full of your friends. Stephens might just be able to kill all five of you in that same room. So don't be a hero. You will have surprise. Use it. You will have little time. Don't waste it. And most of all, don't forget that it is Stephens who will be in the shadows. Have the sense, little boy, to be afraid. If you do, you might live this night."

In his anger the leader had not listened. When he was the first to drop his eyes from the confrontation, deep inside himself he realized that he was still very much afraid of the Falconer. "Maybe," the small voice in him had said, "I *could* gain from more time with him." But he did not even consider Falconer's warning about Stephens and Green. Now, as the bullet ripped through his heart, he recognized the truth. He felt strangely glad that it had happened this way. "Falconer, I failed tonight. This one is left to you to finish. You were right. *But, and you let everyone know it took nothing less than Rob Stephens to kill me."*

Stephens reached down and took the silencer-equipped weapon from the body lying beneath the window. He stood back up and handed the weapon through the shattered window. In a few seconds the gun was pulled from his hand by Green inside. Now Green would also have the advantage of a silencer. Stephens held up three fingers. Green held up one. Stephens motioned for Green to go to the left, and that he would head to the right. Green nodded once in reply. Stephens stooped down and once again dissolved into the darkness.

In the real world that Stephens and Green faced each time they went into the field, one of the most difficult parts of an assignment was knowing when it was over. Over the years they had shared many jokes about the simple, clear-cut endings in the movies or on the television thrillers. They could never understand how the good guys always know the precise time when they had won, when the last bad guys were all down, and when it was time to stand up and ". . . walk over to kiss the girl." In their world, it never worked that way. When you were in the middle of wetwork and decided that it was now time to stand up, that was exactly the time you should be most careful. It was rare that you knew how many opponents had started the battle, and could also be certain no others had been added later.

It took nearly three hours after Stephens had handed the gun through the window before they were reasonably certain that there were no more attackers on the site. With the phones out they could not immediately call for help from the Agency. Neither would leave the other alone, and possibly greatly outnumbered, until the area was secured. Diversions, like a fake fire alarm or an explosion would never help. The confusion and turmoil only would aid the attackers who would be using silencers, and who would not have any particular regard for innocent bystanders. Such a diversion would also destroy any chance they might have to uncover evidence from the area, and would certainly lead to some difficult questions about the four bodies, broken windows, and slug craters that would be the irrefutable sign of a firefight.

Slowly, and very carefully, both continued the search. They looked for people first, and then for traps or explosives that might have been left behind. All of this had to be done with exactly the same degree of care and patience that both Green and Stephens had exhibited from the first shot through the window. No director stood just out of camera range to signal ". . . it's a wrap."

Twenty five minutes into the search outside the house both heard a car start on the road in front of the house. Green was the closest to it. He was standing beside the shed doors when a light sound of the door opening, seventy-five feet away on the road, gave him a small warning before the ignition caught on the first turn of the starter. Stephens was on the opposite side of the house near the woodpile. Before either could get safely to that side of the house, the car pulled away from the road near the entrance to the driveway and sped towards the center of New Ipswich. Had either run fast enough they could have easily reached the front yard in time to fire at the retreating automobile, but neither Green nor Stephens gave even a moment's thought to following. You do not get many second chances if you make a practice of running across exposed and unknown areas when other class fives, or sixes, might hide in the darkness. Nor do you impulsively jump into a car and give chase. First of all, that would draw your own people away from the scene of a known danger to achieve an unknown gain. And, even if the area was known to be safe, it would still be a sucker's bet until they had searched their own car very thoroughly.

While Green thought it very unlikely that anyone would be able to get back into the house during their search, he did not ignored that possibility. Before he had left the house to join Stephens in the search outside, he went up the back stairs, and, at the top called softly for Cynthia Lebart. There had been no answer. Once again he found himself crawling near the base of the walls as he searched the top floor of the house. Ten minutes later, outside the door of a bathroom, the small telltale sights and sounds that very few other than he or Stephens would have seen let him know she was inside in the darkness.

"Cynthia, this is Harvey Green," he whispered. He was pleased to see that there was no answer from inside and felt great respect for the control she showed. She didn't know him well enough to be certain it was his voice when whispering.

"Cynthia, you're wearing Rob's jacket. I shot the switch, he shot the lamp. You caught him collecting rocks for a son he doesn't have."

"Come in, hands first please." The voice was level.

"Cynthia, I'm not going to drop my gun, but I'll hold it out in plain sight. I'm staying low, on my knees."

Green did exactly that as he entered the darkness of the bathroom. He could barely see a shadow against the porcelain of the bathtub on the far side of the room. Cynthia Lebart lay on her left side in the bottom of the tub. Her knees were drawn up in the fetal position. Only a shoulder, the side of her head, and the gun in her right hand showed above the edge. She looked carefully at Green framed in the dim light of the doorway, and then stood up.

Green reached out a hand and helped her out of the tub. The hand was warm and moist. Inwardly, Green admired the control of her voice that had not shown the fear indicated by the dampness of her hand. "I see why Rob likes you," he said. "Very good choice. The tub would have helped protect you, and you had a good view. But I want to make sure that you understand something. As good as it was, I knew where you were. I could have killed you. This is not a game, Cynthia. There were at least four nasties outside who could have found you."

She thought about the words for a few moments. "Four? Did you two kill four people? I heard two shots."

Green avoided a direct answer to her question. "We've stopped four so far. We're pretty sure there are more, so you have to stay up here a while longer." He started out the door. "Let's get you settled somewhere even better."

Green chose a position in a recess that had been filled with bookshelves in the upper hall. From there Cynthia Lebart would be able to see the tops of both stairways. He removed the books, and then the bookshelves from their brackets. Next he pulled a bureau out of one of the upper rooms and placed it so that it was in front of the recess. Finally, after Cynthia had moved into place, he slid the bureau to the wall and piled books to cover any cracks or openings that remained. When he was finished, she had as good protection as he could fashion, and had an outside chance that she could kill someone attacking her before she was killed.

"Cynthia," said Green as he prepared to leave, "we may be quite some time. The worst that can happen is that you'll be stuck here until help arrives for us in the morning."

"What if someone comes up? How will I know if it's you or Rob?"

"If you see anything move, shoot it. Don't think about it, don't wait, and don't have any doubts. You'll know for certain if it's Rob or me. We'll make sure. Besides, you wouldn't see either one of us unless we wanted to be seen."

Green started towards the back stairs. He had gone just a few feet when he heard her softly call his name. "Harvey," she said, the voice muted and questioning, "why did you say he likes me?" It was the first time she had called Green by his first name.

Green had started outside the door, but stopped at the question. He didn't know why he had said that, or for that matter, what specific things had led him to the conclusion. He and Stephens had worked together for parts of seventeen years. In all of that time he could not remember Stephens liking any woman other than Joyce Patterson. And with Joyce, it was different. She and Stephens would never be anything more than very close friends. Once, perhaps ten or twelve years ago, he could remember Rob speaking of a young girl from back in his college days. He knew little of that, only that it had not worked out, and the girl had slipped into that special, quiet place in Stephens' memories where the most cherished times were stored.

"I'm sorry. It wasn't my place to say that," he said. "I guess when two people have known each other as long as I've known Rob, you just sort of know things." Then he tried to change the tone. He remembered the jacket Stephens had given her. "Besides, this is the first time I've seen him give away his clothes on a first date."

Chapter Nine

It was just past midnight when Green and Stephens finished the sweep outside the house and stood just inside the door to the boat shed.

"We were lucky, Harvey," said Stephens. "You and I should both be dead, now. They were careless, or we would be."

"How did you pick up on them, anyway?" asked Green.

"One of them was stupid. He got too close to the window. Another two feet farther away and I never would've seen him start to aim his weapon."

"What now? The field team isn't due until six or seven in the morning. They won't be prepared for anything like this." Green looked down at his watch, "That gives us at least six hours to kill."

"One of us should watch this place while the other finds somewhere to make a call."

"What about Cynthia?"

"Well, if nothing else maybe she finally got the message she's way over her head," said Stephens. "We've got to get her out of here before she sees even more."

"There are four bodies for her to stumble over. Let's get her out of the way tonight."

"Did you check out our car?" asked Stephens.

"A quick look, but I wouldn't trust it until the lab boys run over it in the light." They both knew that crawling around underneath it in the dark with a penlight wouldn't accomplish much of value.

"What about her car? Do you think there's any chance they knew about it?"

"I don't see how. That would mean they were here when we showed. If so, they would have picked you off while you were alone outside and I was upstairs."

"That's our best bet, Harvey," said Stephens. "You walk down and pick it up, and then find a phone. I'll watch her and the house while you call for a full wipe team, and they better include some extra cover, too. When you get back, we'll get her out of here."

"I'm not all that sure she'll quit that easily. I'd feel a lot better if we could have one of the boys keep an eye on her for a few days."

"That means keeping her around until they arrive," said Stephens. "She's going to be tripping over bodies until they do. I think we're better off if she leaves as soon as you get back."

"You let her go and she's got a six hour lead on any tail. I wouldn't bet a lot of money that she'll go right home and be easy to find later."

"I don't think we have a choice, Harvey," answered Stephens after a long wait. He looked directly at Green in the dim light in the shed. He crossed his arms in front of himself and pressed his lips together as he considered what to say next. "And I'm not all that sure a tail is a good idea."

Stephens let the comment hang there without explanation. Green knew exactly what Stephens was thinking. It had been foremost in his own mind since the first shots were fired that night.

"You think she'd be in danger, don't you?" said Green, bringing into the open the questions that had been hanging over both of them. "Calling for a tail would tip off whoever told the Falconer we were here."

"We've got a mole, Harvey. A pretty highly placed one at that. By now half the Agency knows about the Falconer and about us. But damn few knew where we were going this morning. One of those people set us up."

Neither wanted to be the next to speak. In the hours searching the outside of the house after the attack, both had run over the same list of names and faces searching for any clue that would identify the traitor. Finally Stephens spoke. "There are only seven prime names, Harvey. You, me, Joyce, Bill, John, Lowe, and Jacobi. Add Miller and some of the deputies. Maybe Harrington, or Chambers. As many as ten or twelve at ATQ. I don't know how many up the line over John, or in 4th or Treasury, have been briefed."

Harvey chose to state the obvious conclusion to be drawn from Stephens' list of names. In a way, he was making up for making Stephens be the first to have to name their friends.

"If we request a tail, she's probably dead. One of our friends is a traitor."

Stephens' voice was very soft when he finally answered.

"And you and I, old friend, are alone out in the cold again."

When they entered the front hall again, Green took the lead and made sure to make a great deal of noise opening the door. He stood well out of sight at the bottom of the stairs and called to Cynthia Lebart.

"Cynthia! It's me and Rob. We're back inside. Rob, say something."

"Something," answered Stephens, the weak vaudeville pun covering the tired sound of his voice.

There was the sound of moving furniture and of falling books, followed by quiet footsteps. Green and Stephens moved to the base of the stairs and arrived there at the same time Cynthia Lebart arrived at the top of the stairs, smiled at the two below, and started down.

"'Something?' Is that all he can say? Good lord," she said, apparently unbothered by the eyes of the two men watching her descend the stairs. "I'm being saved by Alphonse and Gaston, or maybe it's Larry and Moe. Does that make me Curley?"

When she reached the bottom of the stairs, she began to remove the jacket she had borrowed from Stephens.

"When you're done, grab your things and give me your keys," said Green. "We're going to need your car for a few minutes."

"What happened to yours? Did they . . ." She stopped in mid sentence as she saw the small hole and matted blood that was centered directly over the heart in the Stephens' sweatshirt. She reached out her hand impulsively towards the apparent wound.

"My God, you're shot!"

For the first time since the events had started, her voice betrayed her apparent calm. Small explosions of forced breath mixed in with the words. She stared at the wound, resting her hand lightly on his chest. The caring and intense concern changed slowly to a question when she looked up and saw a slight twinkle in the eyes looking back at her. Slowly she realized that he seemed quite healthy for someone who had just been shot through the heart. Stephens raised his hand up to where hers rested next to the hole. He slipped his thumb under her palm and gently, warmly, cupped her hand in his.

"We agreed," he said, touched by her concern. "No bullet holes. I'm okay. And I'm very glad to see my jacket, and what was in it, is okay as well."

She began to smile, but did not complete it as she finished putting together what his answer must have meant. She drew her hand away, and then stepped back from him. Her reaction was that all too human switch from relief to anger that often happens when a crisis ends. It was shaped by all the fears and the thoughts about her brother that had dominated this night. They had all been controlled, and kept inside. Now all the feelings exploded in the air between them.

"It was someone else then," she said, with indictment in her voice. "You killed someone, and then you took the shirt off a dead man? You're wearing a dead man's clothes? What are you?"

Both Stephens and Cynthia Lebart stood opposite each other, poised like children in a school yard quarrel. The brief glimpse of tenderness and affection that had been on her face was gone. Stephens briefly closed his eyes before pushing the personal aside and tried to get back to business. A small part deep inside him had to accept that this would be just another example, yet another time, when circumstances and reality would find it all too easy to overcome possibilities and hopes.

"Ms. Lebart," he said, resigned to the change between them. "There were five people here tonight who tried very hard to kill all three of us, including you. They were very good, and very persistent. I didn't ask for what happened. With such people, sometimes the only way to save a life is to take theirs first."

He reached out and snatched the jacket that she still held, partially outstretched, in her left hand. "And I think it's about time you wake up to what you're into."

"What I'm into?" she retorted. "Apparently I'm *into* killing. And robbing dead bodies in the night. How many did you kill?"

"Would you have killed me in the shed?" he asked.

"If I thought you had murdered my brother!"

"Then are we so different? I didn't have to *think* I faced a murderer. Maybe you forget the sound of all those slugs tearing up the living room while you and I played huggy-body by the couch. But I don't. That gave me a pretty good indication that they weren't very nice people!"

The sparks were back in her eyes. She said nothing more. She spun on the ball of her right foot and walked down the hallway, through the kitchen, and into the great room beyond.

"Don't let it bother you," said Harvey after she had left the hall. "Neither of you are making any sense. You'll both figure it out eventually."

Stephens didn't answer at first. He stared down the hall where Cynthia had disappeared. When the sound of her footsteps died away, he turned back to Green. "Figure what out?" he asked.

"Sometimes, old friend, for someone who is very, very bright you can be very, very dumb. Why, that you two like each other. What the hell else could cause such sparks?"

Stephens had a trace of pride in his voice when he answered. "She did do all right tonight, didn't she? She was scared silly, and still did okay."

"She needed a target just now, Rob. You were the dog she needed to kick."

"I do understand, Harvey." He gave the rueful half-smile that was so characteristic of himself when he was introspective. "I just usually don't have a dog of my own to kick. Except for you, old friend. I guess that you and I will always have each other to dump on."

—w—

When Cynthia returned from the great room with the car keys, it was Stephens, instead of Green, who ended up walking to get her car. Stephens had reached out to intercept the keys she tried to hand to Green and had muttered "I'll get the car. *You* stay with her" as he opened the door and stepped into the darkness. He would make the call to Virginia before returning. It would summons an immediate sterilization team and would move up the arrival of the lab team that had been scheduled to pull into New Ipswich around dawn. The team would provide immediate support and backup, and would free Green and Stephens from the site. Within hours after their arrival there would be no sign outside of the firefight that had occurred during the night. Within two days at the most, it would take very close inspection inside to find any traces of the action.

Cynthia Lebart and Green stood there a few moments after the door had closed. Green turned back to her and his voice was very gentle. "Another half hour and you'll be away from all of this." He motioned over towards the den. "The best place for you is in there. I need to keep moving around. Don't turn on any lights."

She took a few steps towards the den, and was part way through the door when she stopped suddenly. She jumped back a step, startled, when she saw the body lying there. She paused in the doorway for several seconds, thinking about what must have happened there in the dark, before she turned back to Green.

"Rob did that, didn't he," she stated calmly.

"He had to. There was no other choice."

"Is there ever another choice, Harvey? If I try to find my brother, will I have to become like him?"

"You're dead wrong about him, you know. He is nothing like what you seem to imagine. Perhaps someday you'll understand why he is so special."

"How can someone who kills for a living be special?" she asked. Her voice was quiet, and sad, as she tried to understand. "He went outside tonight, didn't he? How many did he kill out there?"

"He did what he had to do."

"You do the same things, Harvey. Why is he any different, then?"

Green thought about his answer for a long time before he responded. Even to himself he had never before put into words the answer to that question. "You know, it has nothing to do with how good he is at what he does. Nothing at all. There might even be a few people in the world as good as he is at all this. I could probably find you a dozen more who, at least on paper, should be much better. But the difference?" Green shook his head gently. "It's why he does it, and what it costs him every time he does."

"I don't understand," said Cynthia.

"You see, he does it because he feels he has no choice. Rob looks at things a very different way than you or I. He can't walk away from things when they hang there. If it's something important, something that must be done that no one else can do, then the things that drive him leave him no choice but to do it. That's the key Cynthia. That's where it all starts. When Rob knows that something is right thing to do, that's enough for him, no matter the risk."

"But many people make hard choices, Harvey," she said. "You do. You're here."

"Oh, don't compare me to Rob," he said with a slight self-depreciating laugh. "I'm good. Very good, even. But if I know I'm way over my head, *I walk away*. I get help, or let the moment slip aside. And I can live with that. Rob can't. He never could. His curse is that he knows he's the best, and there are times that for him to walk away would mean those he left behind would be hurt. Or killed. And yet, if he stays, then often others must die by his hand. What you don't see is that he hates what he does. To him, killing is killing, no matter what the final gain. He can't accept that he must sometimes choose to trade one life for another. Can't you see the dilemma? Think of all the snakes battling in his mind."

Cynthia concentrated on everything Green was saying. He pointed to the door that Stephens had just closed. "When he walked out that door, don't you think inside he wanted to keep walking? Maybe even to take you with him? Maybe to go back to teaching, and the children that are so important to him? But he can't. There are too many obligations that he's unable to ignore. Your brother is one. The face in the picture I showed you is another. Cynthia, this thing with your brother is part of something terrible. Something that, unless stopped, will cost a great many lives. Rob is cursed to know that if he walks away, it *will* make a difference in the number of people who will die."

"How can he live with the things he does?" she asked, her voice almost in a whisper. "How can he sleep at night?"

There was compassion in his voice when Green answered. "He can't. The rest of us can accept the price. 'The end justifies the means' can cover just about anything for most people. But Rob can't make that distinction, that rationalization. The 'means' he has to use chew him up inside. When I have to kill someone, I can accept it. To me it's just something that had to be done."

Cynthia did not say anything. All of Green's word were churning and blending in her thoughts. She was trying very hard to understand Rob Stephens.

"Cynthia, have you ever seen one of the old war movies when the 'hero' throws himself on the grenade to save his friends?"

"Yes," she said very softly, nodding slightly.

"Well that's the difference between Rob and the rest of us. I wouldn't throw myself on that grenade. I'd dive for cover. And I could live with that choice without a problem. It would be bad luck, a terrible thing, but something I would know was out of my control. Rob would not hesitate to dive on the grenade. And he would not be thinking of being a hero, or even of his friends. He wouldn't even have to know the people he saved. It's just that the cost to him if he did *not* do it, later, would be worse than the cost of his life. He would never be able to live with not taking what, to him, was the right action."

Cynthia didn't answer when she realized that Green had finished. She looked down and slowly shook her head. She walked back into the den, stepped over the body as though it were just a throw rug, removed the magazine lying open on the leather easy chair in the far corner, and lowered herself slowly into the cushions. She pulled her legs up underneath herself, hunched her shoulders forward, and tightly hugged herself with arms crossed in front of herself. For the next half hour, she too fought the snakes in her mind. All the images of that night battled in her thoughts as she relived all that had happened, what might have happened to her brother, the dark shape of the body on the floor in front of her, the sound the bullets made whipping around them in the great room, and the horrible waiting upstairs for the battle to end.

Most of all, she tried to deal with the two Rob Stephens who battled in her thoughts. One was a black wraith, terrible and avenging, sweeping down on a field of battle to sever the heads of those aligned on the battlements against him. The other had gentle, caring eyes, and had been able to press her hand in a way that pushed away the fears, and had touched those places deep inside her in a way that she had forgotten could be done.

Chapter Ten

There were faint traces of light in the early morning sky when Stephens and Green heard the automobile pull into the driveway of the Robbins home. The weak light could not yet give any definition to the day. It could only cast dim shadows, etched one against another in the most beautiful of nature's efforts. The patterns intertwined, and stood against the quietude that always precedes the dawn. There are gentle sounds, and soft callings of the few animals that are part of this special time. This is the time the loons will, and of those who would revel in the dance. This is a time when hushed murmurs still claimed ascendancy over the coming strident calls of daylight.

It has always been one of the cruelest of life's ironies that the morning sky is seen by so very few. While evening will share her gentle winds with all that care to wait and watch, the treasures of dawn are hidden from all but a handful. Aaron Copland, who could capture such mysteries and somehow weave them into musical themes worthy of such mornings, understood the irony. "It's comical," he told a young admirer after one of the first performances of *Appalachian Spring*. "The best of these themes sprang from the morning skies and the haunting effect they had on me. Yet had I not worked through the night, trying in vain to craft a feeling that eluded me, I would never have found the answer. I wonder. Look at Van Gogh's *Starry Night* and what he could do with the magic of evening. Did he ever bask in the pre-dawning? What might he have created had he done so?"

The time was nearly 4:30 a.m. when four people stepped out of the light green Chevy sedan. All were very careful to keep their hands well exposed at their sides and to stand away from the car. For the first ten seconds or so the car doors were left wide open so that the light from inside the car, combined with the headlights, would bathe them and the area nearby. The light would let anyone watching see who they were, and see inside the cars. Every step the new arrivals took was with the certain knowledge that they were being observed by two class six agents, and that it would be a very good idea to be sure there was no doubt at all about their identity.

To the four of them, the ten seconds in the light seemed to drag on into hours. Nothing in their training could let them totally control the terrible feeling of exposure to whatever was around them. The most junior of the four had a dozen years of field experience. Even had they known the area to be clean their instincts still would have cried for them to douse the lights. But this was not a clean area. They were exposed by the light, in a known wet zone, with the specter of the Falconer nearby.

Three of them were men wearing jeans, old shirts and ankle-high work boots. The front seat passenger was a woman. While the other three stood near the front of the car she walked through the headlights, past an outdoor lamp, towards the lighted side door to the house. The three by the car waited in the light until the woman was half way up the walk, before one of them reached inside the car to switch off the headlamps. Then they softly closed the car doors and moved away to blend into the darkness. Each moved in a different direction. They had waited long enough to insure identification by the two inside the house. More time was not needed. Could you have probed the instincts of the three men that screamed at them to move out of the light, you would have found that standing there longer was not possible.

Upstairs Stephens watched the scene unfold from his watch post of the past few minutes. Cynthia Lebart had driven away three hours ago. Since then, Stephens and Green had been constantly moving and watching as they waited for the help to arrive from Virginia. Stephens covered the front and west side of the house. Green had the east and back. Neither stayed at one position for more than a short time before moving to another vantage point. When the woman began to walk towards the house, neither she nor the three men saw any hint of Stephens as he pulled back from the edge of the darkened window that had been his watch post for the past few minutes. He smiled as he recognized the "Receptionist" who had so professionally guarded the entrance to the underground maze at Folkes farm.

"Harvey," he called softly, "we have friendly visitors."

"I heard the car. Who? How many?" was the equally muted reply from a room at the far end of the hall.

"Four. I only know one. The screen outside the Folkes elevator."

"Pat Waters. She's very good. They sent the first team."

Stephens made no sound as he went down the back stairs, through the great room, and then to the side door. As he approached, he saw Waters waiting coolly and patiently on the other side of the door. There was no doubt in Stephen's mind that the strength he had sensed in her at their first meeting was very real. Waters was totally in control of the situation as though nothing around her was at all out of the ordinary. Three of the six panes of glass in the door before her had been shot out, and to the side of the house a few feet to her left she could see the dim shape of the dead attacker lying near the basement window. She glanced towards the destroyed windows farther to her left and two obvious slug craters in the nearest wood clapboards. Yet, her expression would indicate she was doing nothing more unusual than visiting a "messy old friend."

She was neither surprised nor startled when Stephens face emerged from the darkness, without warning, a few inches from the door. There was a slight trace of amusement on her face when she recognized him and thought back to their first meeting.

"Status?" she asked as soon as she recognized him.

"Clear, I think. Four unfriendlies dead. Nothing since just after midnight. No ID other than a guess they were probably class five equivalents. One got out clean."

"Harvey?"

"Upstairs."

There were two sixes on site, both she and Stephens knew that she would be the sole site control officer. He and Green would take direction from her unless there was an active firefight. She turned and signaled the men in the yard. As she stepped past Stephens, he switched off both the light over the door and the light on the pole lamp a few feet down the walkway. Immediately the men dissolved into dim shapes that made very little sound as they started about the work of unloading cartons and supplies that filled the trunk and every available space in the interior of the car.

"You appear to have been busy," she said motioning down as her feet crunched on the broken glass around the door. "Mind if my friends join the party?"

"Tell you what," he answered as he thought back to their first meeting, "this time I'll even be the one to fetch the coffee."

Pat Waters offered a wry smile in response. Once inside, she avoided the easy temptation to begin the full debriefing process with Stephens. She knew that it would be daylight soon, and that only the cloudy night sky prevented a passing car from seeing the clear signs of a firefight from the road. In the short time left before dawn they had to accomplish all the cosmetic changes that would buy time for the full scrub team when it arrived. What was needed now was to pin down the essentials.

"Rob, I'm Pat Waters. I'm a five, and head up this team. I've handled these before. On short notice I've only got two threes and a four outside, so we'll need your help for a while longer yet."

Stephens knew as well as Waters that the three men outside would be badly overmatched against a team the caliber of those that had attacked them the night before. He moved to the base of the stairwell and called softly up to Green. "Harvey. Take one sweep of my sides while I brief Waters. We still own cover until the big boys arrive."

Waters waited for the acknowledgment from Green, and then began to cover the critical points. "You appear to have a world-class mess here. The rest of the team is at least an hour behind us, maybe two. We flew ahead to do a quick mop before dawn. What's out front that can be seen from the road?"

"I think it's clean, but Harvey and I swept it last night when it was still dark, and quite unfriendly so it would be easy to have missed something. All I recall is a pane of glass out by the front door." Stephens motioned towards the great room. "Most of the action centered here. There used to be two long banks of windows on both sides of this room. Both sides were destroyed. Crossfire. The west side where you came in will show up easily from the road. The east side of the house can't be seen from the road. The kitchen blocks it. There are a couple shattered windows out back."

"What about the rest of the inside?"

"Other than this room, and one in the back, it's pretty mild."

"Bodies?"

"One on the west side near the door as you came in. One in the front corner room and two out in back next to the house. Neither of the two in back can be seen, unless someone drives all the way into the yard. The backyard might be just visible to the house on the east. There was at least one more, but we lost him at the end. He got to his car untouched. No other cars, so doubtful the total was more than five or six."

Despite all her experience, for a moment Waters could not shake the image of what must have happened in the home. She looked around the battle-scarred room, considered the bodies of four very skilled enemies on the scene, and pictured the survivors being forced to flee from Stephens and Green. For the first time, she believed the stories told about Rob Stephens. As she heard the calm tone of his description despite what she knew must have happened, the events seemed totally believable. She now understood why stories about Rob Stephens were always told in such quiet tones.

It took a few seconds before she asked her next question. "Any locals know you're here? Any signs of interest yet?"

"None. A few we met yesterday know we're here, but most of the wetwork was silenced."

"Have we got lights in here?"

"The front part of the house is blown. There's a fuse box at the bottom of the basement stairs. The plug under that window is okay, but the lamp's shot."

Pat Waters walked slowly towards the destroyed west side windows. Even in the dim light she could see that cosmetic fixes were impossible without major carpentry. Each of her steps was punctuated by the sound of crackling glass.

"Is the other side as bad as this?"

"At least."

She needed only a few seconds before she knew the next steps to take. "All right," she said with a bit of resignation in her voice. "A fix is out. Not enough time. We're going to have to play hide and seek."

She turned back towards Stephens. "I'm afraid you and Harvey are going to have to handle cover for a while longer. I'm going to need all my people to clean up the obvious garbage outside. I'd say we have about 15-20 minutes before it gets light enough to be seen from the road. We'll stick to fixing the west side windows and moving the bodies. What's in that garage near our car?"

"It's a boat shed. There's plenty of room around the boat if you need it. If it helps, you'll find the old man had a lot of tools."

"We'll put the bodies in the front room with the other for now."

Over the next twenty minutes the four members of the preliminary field scrub team solved the immediate problems in a deceptively simple manner. The key was to use the few items they were able to bring with them along with those "props" that could be found at hand. One item in the trunk was a collapsible sawhorse equipped with a sign reading "Shaeffer's Roofing and Remodeling." Another was half dozen large sheets of canvas. A soon as the bodies were moved out-of-sight into the house, two "workmen" took a ladder they found in the garage and leaned it up against the west side of the house. Two large sheets of canvas were used to cover the shattered windows. As soon as it was in place, one of the two men climbed to the roof and began removing shingles and tossing them over the edge to the ground below. Next the ladder was moved to the less visible east side of the house and the windows there were covered. Finally, since there was only one ladder, it was returned to the west side so that it would be quite visible from the road. The illusion was simple. To anyone passing it would be clear that "real professionals with an early start" had been hired to reroof the Robbins home and ". . . are even so careful that they're using canvas to protect the side of the house from falling debris." If anyone did pull in, Pat Waters represented the Robbins estate and was getting the home ready for sale.

As soon as the two windows were covered, Pat Waters and the two remaining workmen began addressing other areas that were visible from outside. Any pieces of glass were picked up before they would catch the glint of the morning sun. Next, they used the most important items they had brought with them. Over the years, time and experience had taught the scrub teams that gallons of putty and a dozen tubes of latex artist paints were the most effective of all the quick-fix tools. Once the colors were mixed with the putty to approximate the color of the house, a half dozen slug craters visible around the edge of the canvas could be scraped smooth and filled. During all of this time Stephens and Green patrolled the upstairs windows to ensure there would be no surprise visitors.

In less than half an hour anyone in a passing car would not be able to tell from the road that a firefight had occurred. Even a person standing in the driveway would suspect nothing but a remodeling job. By the time the two vans full of additional "workmen, gardeners, and equipment" arrived just after dawn, Waters and one worker had replaced the telltale broken glass in the side door with panes taken from rear rooms in the home. A small section of the house near the front corner had patches of paint and a worker was carefully scraping loose paint from the clapboards. About a third of the west roof had been removed. The Robbins home would actually have a new roof by the end of the day. A truck had already been dispatched from Nashua to pick up a load of shingles.

When the rest of the scrub team arrived, nearly half of the new people concentrated only on repair. The remainder had far more specialized skills. "Gardeners" were able to sweep the outside of the house. The den was turned into a small laboratory for investigation of the four bodies. By ten that morning the windows in the great room had been repaired and painted. By noontime, had it been absolutely necessary, an outsider could have been brought inside the great room with a reasonable degree of confidence. Such a visitor would have found many pieces of furniture "protected from damage" by sheets during the "remodeling," and would see a great deal of plastering and touch up work in progress.

Even to those involved, the most remarkable sight was still thirty hours away. By the end of the following day the house itself would show no signs of the night's events. Except for a few pieces of furniture "out for cleaning," the house would be more than just back to normal. It actually would be quite a bit better than it had been a week before. Some five years earlier, an astonished deputy director of the Agency on assignment in Madrid had his first opportunity to see both the 'before' and the 'after' of a full field scrub. "My God!" he had exclaimed, "It's a blooming value-added operation." Company legend insists that he promptly volunteered to have his personal home used for a training firefight and scrub effort in order to raise the selling price.

Stephens and Green left the Robbins home a half hour after the follow-up vans arrived. Among the contingent in the vans were class fours and class fives whose sole responsibility would be the security of the scrub team. Throughout the long vigil during the previous night, sleep was a most distant concern for either Stephens or Green. But now that there were fulltime people there to pick up the duties, and the immediate needs had passed, the impact of the past eleven hours of high intensity action hit both of them. The first shots had come through the windows at 7:00 the previous night. It was 6:30 the next morning when three of the class fives escorted Stephens and Green back to the Quiet Pines Motel.

Stephens had provided only the briefest summary of the night's activities to Pat Waters and her team before leaving. The detail would come later. The scrub team would spend the next few hours concentrating on the most vital cosmetic changes needed to disguise the night's events should an unexpected visitor arrive. At the same time, lab specialists would gather data from the area. Fingerprints of the bodies would be faxed to Virginia. On-site lab work and analysis would be accomplished using a highly sophisticated portable field laboratory. All of the grounds, especially in the woods where Stephens had taken the blood samples, would be swept.

Stephens and Green would return to the motel and be well guarded so they could catch four or five hours sleep before returning for a full debriefing. Three of the class fives would accompany them back to the motel to ensure their safety. Two of them would follow in the sedan that brought Waters to the site. The other would drive with Green and Stephens now that their car had been swept and cleared. When they arrived at the motel, Stephens pulled up near their rooms and then walked down to the motel office. The second car pulled in to the Silver Ranch parking lot down the road.

"Morning Mr. Jones! You were certainly up early. Your car was gone when I got up at six, and I didn't even hear you drive out," observed the owner while motioning towards the car with Green and the other two waiting outside. "I assume you found a place to get breakfast."

"Yes, thought just a quick bite," replied Stephens with a genuine friendliness and manner that could only indicate that he and was eager to face the new day after a restful night's sleep. "We had to run up to Peterborough very early to pick up some people. I'd appreciate it if you could hold off on cleaning the rooms until later this afternoon. Mr. Kelleher and I will be having separate conferences for the next few hours and would like to extend the rooms for another night."

"Oh that's hardly a problem! I appreciate the business," said the owner with pleasure at his good luck. "When you're ready, just poke your head in and I'll clean up the rooms."

When Stephens returned to the car and prepared to enter the motel room, there was no trace of the previous day's casual approach. He would not again take things lightly or for granted. Like a long forgotten old coat that is rediscovered in an attic and found to be once again very comfortable, he found he had slipped back into the old role easily and completely. There was very little trace of the quiet country school teacher left in him. Guards or not, he would be absolutely certain that the rooms were clean before he would sleep in them.

Before he approached the door he walked around to the backside of the motel and studied the rear, the bathroom windows, and the area beneath them. When he was satisfied that neither window had been disturbed for years, he returned to the front to study the large windows, the two flanking crank-open windows, and the doors. The two fives stood with their backs to the windows facing Green and Stephens, gesturing with their hands and nodding, making it clear to anyone watching that an animated conversation was in progress. Only someone very observant would realize that Green and Stephens were looking beyond the fives to study the building, and that the fives, in turn, were constantly scanning the area. Meanwhile, fifty yards away the third guard sat in his car. To anyone watching, the driver seemed to be very bored as he looked around and occasionally glanced at his roadmap.

When they were confident that the doors could be opened safely, they entered the rooms. Once inside the next minute was spent making sure that there was no one hiding in the room. Stephens left his guard standing just inside the now closed door. He slowly worked his way around the room to the closet, the bathroom, and the shower. When it was clear that they had no visitors, a more detailed look at the room was begun.

The guard carefully swept the room looking for any bugs, using a small electronic device not much larger than a pack of cigarettes. The sweep with the portable electronics would be just a first pass. A careful manual search for a bug would follow. Later, when freed of their duties at the Robbins home, the scrub team would bring in the full equipment that would let them complete the search. One of the most incredible ironies of the high-tech revolution was that a physical search had once again become the best way to find the most sophisticated of bugs. Variable frequencies, voice-activated transmission, and delayed transmission in data-compressed bursts made electronic discovery a fifty-fifty affair. The new rules of the game had become deceptively simple—if you're in doubt, then don't say anything you don't want overheard. Stephens and the guard didn't really care if there was a bug. They had no intention of speaking about sensitive matters within the room, but instead were attempting to determine just how far the Falconer and his people might have gone.

While the guard searched the front room, Stephens carefully studied the folds and wrinkles in the bedspread and in the clothing within the suitcase. One of the clearest indications of entry would be if his suitcase had been searched. All of the folds were exactly as he had left them. The toilet kit was at the same angle he expected. When he carefully lifted a neat pile of undershirts to expose the strap holding a suit in place beneath them, the clasp on the end of the strap was at the correct position. Finally, he lifted the left corner of the toilet kit half an inch.

"Hold it, Harry," he stated softly to the guard then in the process of searching the opposite wall. Harry stopped exactly where he was and turned towards the bed. For a moment or two Stephens also remained frozen in his position, leaning over the bed while lifting the edge of the toilet kit with one finger. Then he slowly lowered the kit. It had been the smallest of signs, the slightest of mistakes on the part of whoever had been in the room earlier. But, now Stephens was certain that a very top professional had been in the room and had searched the suitcase.

When he had lifted the edge of the toilet kit, there had been no sound from within it. He had left a tube of Chapstick carefully balanced in the kit. Any movement would gently dislodge the tube. The sound would be so slight as to be almost unnoticed unless you were expressly waiting for it. Even if you did hear it fall, it would be very difficult to identify the cause of the sound. But if the suitcase had been untouched, the tube would still be in place. The fact that there had been no other signs at all meant that no other explanation was possible. A cleaning person, someone dropping off towels, or the owner primping the bed would have left other signs in the room.

"We had a visitor," said Stephens as he straightened back up. "From what I see whoever was here was among the best I've ever seen. He bypassed every little trap I left without leaving a sign. I don't know many people who could have done that."

"What did he miss?"

"Just one small fold was wrong," Stephens lied easily without hesitation. "It was under the toilet kit and he missed it."

The tiredness that had started to creep into his chest and thoughts passed as quickly and as simply as though it had never been there.

"Wait here. Our visitor was very good. Please don't search further until I return. I suggest you avoid the chairs or anything else until we comb the room," he said as he walked towards the door.

"You going to warn Green and John?" asked the guard.

"Yup."

"Good. I can use the break to take a piss," stated the guard with a half chuckle. "I must have killed a pot of coffee so far this morning!"

Stephens paused at the door and turned back towards the guard. While his voice was quiet as though he were offering only an offhand idea, his eyes were deadly serious. "Harry, if I were you I wouldn't touch a thing until this room is swept. When I get back, you can take a leak out back of the motel."

Harry waited patiently while Stephens went next door to Green's room. A moment after Stephens' light knock, the door opened cautiously. Stephens slipped inside.

"Hold it, John," he said softly to the agent who was in the process of feeling the curtains for any small bumps. "The room is hot. Let's hold for our friends." The guard gently let the curtain flow back into position and pulled his hands away. For a few seconds he stood there with his hands in front of himself, palms out and forward in the classic position a child takes when saying ". . . I didn't touch it mommy." Then he slowly let his hands fall to his side.

Stephens turned back to Green. "I had a visitor, Harvey."

Green did not even think of asking Stephens if he was certain. After all the years working together, he knew that such a statement would only be made if Stephens knew it to be correct. "John," he said, holding his hand cupped to his ear to make remind him of the possibility that the room might be bugged, "we're going to step outside where it's a bit cooler."

Once outside and a few feet away from the building, Green and Stephens took positions where they could face each other and yet see all approaches to their position.

"Rob, there wasn't a trace in my room, and we've covered most of it. We have more to do, but I did finish all my own stuff."

"From what I saw, this one is not likely to have left any traces."

"Our friend, himself?" asked Green, referring to the Falconer.

"That would be my guess."

"You must show me your trick. All my bait caught nothing," said Green as he nodded slightly in appreciation. "What actions?"

"I don't know yet. Maybe it's just a search. Perhaps a bug. But it might be an insurance policy left by our friend. I suggest we ask Waters to send over an SMC team. I'm sure she has a bomb specialist in her team. Our visitor might have left a little present in case his plans at the house didn't work."

Stephens and Green had too much respect for the Falconer to conduct an SMC, Search with Maximum Caution, when there were fully equipped experts available to do it. They would leave two guards in the rooms to make sure there were no unexpected visitors before the SMC arrived. Green and Stephens would return to the Robbins home after advising the motel owner about a "conference of associates" to be held in the two rooms.

Stephens and Green drove back to the Robbins home. The third agent followed in the car behind. Neither Green nor Stephens said anything for the first few miles. Both spent the time carefully reviewing and cataloging the events of the past few days. There were few hard facts and even fewer solid inferences they could draw, but there was one inevitable conclusion. No matter how much they each tried to develop alternative explanations, neither could escape the conviction that they had been set up.

"If there were any doubts before, Harvey, I'd say it's pretty clear that we were made long before we got here. Someone knew where we were staying, and that we'd be tied up at the Robbins place long enough to search the place."

"Why keep the search so clean if they knew we'd be blown away the same night?"

"It only means they knew for certain it was us. The Falconer would not take the two of us lightly. He'd hope we would be taken out, but would have a backup plan. My guess is that both rooms are quite hot."

"If so, it was done well. I saw nothing on the first pass."

"Neither did I, Harvey. But with Falconer, I don't expect to. We're lucky he left the one small sign that he did."

"Then we're in deeper shit than we thought, old friend. If I buy what you say, then every move we made last night was known well in advance. They knew who we were, where we were staying, and where we were going. They even knew our timing. Someone gave them a bloody roadmap, and an agenda, to boot."

"It's our friend the mole again, Harvey," said Stephens as they pulled into the Robbins driveway. "Christ. Whoever it is, he's high up. Folkes, and maybe even Langley, has a hole the size of a house. Who the hell is minding the store back there? The Company's been blown at high levels and no one seemed to have a clue when we were back there."

Green looked up and saw Pat Waters as she walked towards the car. Both knew that they would say nothing of their suspicions to her, or to anyone else until they had answers instead of just questions.

"Rob, it looks as though it's up to us to mind the store without counting on any help. Problem is, we've got a bit of a chicken and egg situation here. We have to solve this one before we can take the time to chase after the mole. Meanwhile, of course, the mole will be doing everything possible to help the Falconer get us first."

Stephens reached to open the door as Waters reached the side of the car. He looked back over his shoulder at Green. "Catch 22, old friend."

Chapter Eleven

It was 12:30 that afternoon when, as planned, Green and Stephens were awakened from their shared bed in the front upstairs bedroom in the Robbins home. They had been asleep for about four hours and none of the sounds of the carpentry, the confusion, nor the talking in the house below had been able to intrude upon their sleep.

Green, as always, slept soundly. He had the remarkable ability, envied by all of his associates, to sleep as though dead to the world when the moment called for it. It was as though there were some special ability, some special sensor in his mind that controlled his degree of sleep. When the situation called for caution, he too, like Stephens, could spring up at the slightest foreign sound that encroached upon his subconscious. Those mental controls knew that this was not such a time. At that moment, the Robbins home had a level of security that might rival the White House. Green knew that anything powerful enough to break through such security would find his wakefulness of little extra deterrent.

For Stephens, sleep was always a far different thing than it was for Green. He could never turn off the vigilance. He always slept lightly, awakening a half a dozen times each night. Sometimes he awoke to a small sound that had to be identified and categorized as "safe" before he could return to sleep. Most often he woke up because something that had been percolating in the back of his mind—the answer to a problem, or the reason that something did not seem right to him—had suddenly come into focus while he slept. His mind had decided it was far too important to wait until morning.

Only rarely did Stephens wake up because of a dream. His dreams usually followed no pattern. They were disjointed scenes that only rarely involved himself. Sometimes they were of places or friends in his past, sometimes pure fiction from books or movies, and sometimes that kind of intermixed nonsense that only dreams can be.

This night, however, the dreams were different. Throughout the night there was only one dream. It was centered on the vision of Cynthia Lebart. He could feel the softness of her body next to his as they lay against the couch. Then the couch would blend and mix to become a different place, where the softness of her body was a thing to be treasured and shared. He dreamed of holding her naked against to him, sheltered and cupped next to his body with her head lying nestled on his shoulder. He could see the shadows of the night rippling across the softness of her skin, and could feel his hand pass softly over the smooth curve of her side.

He heard his own words as they spoke of many things that had lain hidden in him for a lifetime. He could feel the gentle kindness in her eyes as she listened and understood. He felt the warmth of her breath on his neck, the touch of a hand on his chest, and the smell of her hair next to his face. Even though her face was nestled, hidden against his shoulder and neck, it was somehow her eyes that dominated the dream. They seemed to speak, and to understand all that he said. He realized that he was able to explain things, and find words that he had never been able to find before. For the first time, he could define and shape his fears and shadows. After a while, the thoughts he had never been able to share before became something she could understand. She was able to reach out to touch the same shadows with him. And with another to help hold them, he felt them melt and become less important than ever before.

When finally the shadows had dissolved, he was at peace as he had never been before. There was nothing left except the smell of her hair, and the warmth of her body next to his. He saw her head lean back from the safety of his shoulder and watched her eyes met his. And then, at that precise moment of his dream, he thought he understood what love might be. He knew it was that force that could make you smile with just the thought of another, and that it was also the feeling that could sweep all words away to make you silent, with awe. He knew that it was a force that could make holding more vital than touching, and that made touching, when the time was just right, more powerful than life. Her mouth was open slightly as she leaned towards him, and her hand reached out for the back of his neck to pull him towards her.

But the hand that had just moments before been that of Cynthia Lebart blended into the hand of Pat Waters reaching down to awaken him.

Before the professionalism born of what seemed like decades of experience took control, he resented the day, and wished for nothing more than to continue that night and the dream that had shaped it.

"We gave you an extra half hour," he heard the voice of Pat Waters say. He closed his eyes again and tried to blank out the sounds and the reality around him. But nothing he could do could bring back the dream.

When they came downstairs for the main debriefing session, even Stephens and Green were impressed with all of the progress the scrub team had made. Neither had before seen a "before-and-after" in person, and both could now understand the old story about the deputy director who volunteered to let his house get destroyed. Stephens recognized some of the furniture from the night before, and some new items, as well. All of the mangled pieces were now hidden in the basement. From elsewhere in the house furniture had been found to partially replace the missing items. A couch from the master suite, end tables from two of the bedrooms, and one of the chairs from the den had been moved here to add to the illusion. All of the furniture in the great room had been pushed up against the front wall of the room and was partially covered with drop cloths. The rest of the room was filled with tarpaulins and paint buckets. Three master carpenters were still working to finish the total rebuild of the room. The only thing left to be done was repainting before the room could pass a very close inspection.

Outside was the muted drone of a pair of lawnmowers going over the grounds. Neither Stephens nor Green knew if that was part of the routine, or if they were there just to create noise to mask out any eavesdropping that might occur. Outside both banks of windows they could see "gardeners" at the distant edges of the lawn carefully raking the edge of the lawn and the flower beds. Only a very trained eye would notice that their eyes only rarely looked down at their work, and that they were always facing outwards towards the forest, the roads, or the yards beyond. No one passing on the road saw them long enough to notice that they spent a great deal of time in the same area, and that all wore loose jackets that were open at the front.

There were four of them who met in the basement. Joining Pat Waters, Stephens, and Green was Herb Greenberg. Greenberg was a short, thin person who looked very out of place in his workman's clothing. He had a worn red flannel shirt, frayed khakis complete with patches and the effects of age, and boots that were carefully scratched and worn. Despite all of the effort used to create the illusion of normalcy, Greenberg looked as though he had just put them on for the first time. Part of the incongruity was the wire-rimmed glasses he wore. Greenberg had been on dozens of field efforts before, including a handful nearly of the magnitude of the Robbins home. Yet, he could never escape the look of a stereotypical professor, more at home in library stacks reviewing research material than poised over the bodies he was so often called to investigate.

The first part of the session was devoted to a detailed review by Green and Stephens of the night's events. The four sat huddled at a card table in the basement. There was a portable recorder on the table. A few feet away, bracketing the table, were two boom boxes playing tapes at moderate volume. The output of one could be clearly identified. It continuously played the classic tapes from the group *Boston* doctored only to eliminate most of the pause between the tracks. The output from the second recorder could not so easily be identified. It was a carefully selected mix of random sounds chosen to disrupt any effort to monitor the conversation.

It took Stephens and Green thirty minutes to relate the critical points of the previous night. They took turns, carefully describing the action with remarkable recollection and accuracy. They described their visit, the ambush, and the ensuing firefight. The provided their assessment of the facts and their own conjecture about any gray areas. They were careful to account for every key moment, and that one attacker had escaped. They could even recall specific sounds, and could account for the exact interplay of events. Oddly, during the entire discussion, neither appeared to recall that there was a third party named Cynthia Lebart on the site. It was as though she never existed.

Stephens and Green had worked together long enough so that their stories blended and matched instinctively, without conscious effort. They didn't need review or rehearsal to understand what needed to be said, or how to ensure that their two versions dovetailed without gaps. Each would embellish the other's lies, when necessary.

When they finally completed their summary, Waters and Greenberg brought them up to date on the lab and scrub team findings.

"We have nothing on the four bodies," said Greenberg with the clinical precision that totally belied his workman's clothing. "They were steam cleaned before coming to the site. The slugs in two of them, front room and west side, match your gun Stephens. The one in back is a match on Green. The one in the back corner was killed by the second gun you were carrying, Stephens."

"There's next to nothing on the IDs," said Waters. "We faxed the prints to Langley several hours ago. So far, the only data is that the left index finger on one of the Stephens' kills matches a partial found in the pilots cabin of the TWA plane in Beirut. There's no name or face attached to it. It's still in the A-U file."

"A-U?" asked Stephens. "What the hell is that?"

"Sorry. Active-Unknown," said Waters.

"Garden-variety clothes," said Greenberg. "There are probably a hundred places they could have bought them. The labels indicate they all used different stores. We have some fiber traces on the leg of the Green kill that appears interesting, but I doubt anything will ever come of it. It's some kind of standard canvas and could have come from anywhere."

"There's canvas in the shed," offered Waters.

"I know. That's the problem," he said before turning back towards Green and Stephens. "Chalk that up as an incidental note in the file, at best."

"What do you have on the weapons?" asked Green. "I suppose they're clean, too."

"Squeaky clean," answered Waters. "No markings. Serial numbers were filed clean. Standard Italian Berettas, post-fitted silencers. There must be a few thousand that would meet that description."

"An early look makes me suspect that they went too deep for even acid-etch testing," said Greenberg. "We'll give it a try back at Folkes, but I don't expect anything."

"By the way, there were two who were missing theirs. Which of your pick-ups went with which body?" asked Waters.

"I took the one from the body in the front room," stated Stephens. "Green has the one missing from in back of the house."

"Anything on the car?" asked Green.

"No tracks at all," said Greenberg. "They spun the wheels when they pulled out. It was a front wheel drive. Midsize, based upon spacing."

"By the time you called, they were long gone," said Waters. "We've notified local PDs to be on the lookout for an abandoned car and to approach it with care. The cover is that it might contain missing blood samples that could be contaminated with AIDS."

"Then our fifth visitor escaped," stated Green.

"If it's only five," said Waters, after a pause. "We think you were up against seven."

Neither Green nor Stephens even glanced at each other. Both calmly looked at Waters.

"I can account for only five," said Stephens, without any hesitation.

"The prints are pretty clear," said Greenberg. "We have three sets of foot impressions we can't match. Four other sets match the bodies. Plus we have yours. One of the unknowns was next to the car, and appears to have stayed pretty much in the same place for a long time. Our guess is that he was there guarding the car and was not part of the action. There is another set near the front of the house, and another in and around the shed. The one in front is a man, over 200 pounds, in the six to six-three area. A couple tracks we found indicate he was probably the one you heard get to the car and leave. The one near the shed was small, maybe 100-140 pounds and with a small foot more like a woman's."

"Could they have been from earlier in the day?" asked Green, smoothly.

"No," answered Waters. "They're all fresh. The ones in front seem to go with an indentation under the brush and a spent shell casing we found there. The ones near the shed actually step on your prints at one point."

"Think back carefully," asked Greenberg. "Was there any indication of another intruder?"

"None," said Stephens. He turned to Green. "I don't even remember the shed door being opened after we checked it out. Do you?"

"It wasn't. There's no way I could miss such . . ." Green stopped short as though he had suddenly remembered something critical. "Wait a moment. Just before I made the first kill, he was looking back over his shoulder towards the shed."

"Could it have been a control? A nonparticipant in the wetwork sent just to verify the results?" suggested Stephens.

"That could make sense," offered Greenberg. "We found slugs from only seven weapons. The one at the car and the one in the shed didn't fire anything we could find."

"I'm certain there was no one outside when we made the final sweep," said Green. "All three must have been in the car when they took off."

"Have you run this past Langley yet?" asked Stephens. "They couldn't miss this many if they all entered the country together."

"Washington came up dry," answered Waters. "There's no record of five or more knowns entering all at once. Anyway, if it were anyone we were tracking we'd have a print match by now. None of these came in through open channels. We seem to have missed at least half dozen major riders on the midnight express. Someone was sleeping."

"We all were sleeping," mused Stephens, introspectively. "Harvey and I were caught like school girls."

"Asleep or not, you made it and they didn't," said Waters with pragmatic logic. "I'd say you did reasonably well against the odds."

Greenberg looked over to Waters and nodded briefly before turning back towards Stephens. "You did even better than you might think back at the motel."

Stephens immediately recognized by the change in Greenberg's tone that the follow-up team must have discovered more at the motel than simply a bug, or confirmation that it had been searched. He looked intently at Greenberg.

"The place was hot," continued Greenberg. "There was enough plastic explosive in there to take out the entire motel."

"We swept most of it and there was nothing obvious," said Green. "What did you find?"

"Let's put it this way," said Pat Waters with a trace of amusement. "The trap would never have gotten me. Only you or Green would have bought the big one from it."

"Hmmm, this a 'girls are smarter than boys' thing?" asked Green, with a quizzical smile, as he sensed the teasing in her voice.

"Your friends left a present that would only catch someone who lifts the seat to pee," she answered. "Picture two pounds of plastique on the bottom of the seat rigged with a reed switch detonator."

"Shit," said Green. "I guess there is a certain crude artistry to that."

"By the way, Harry damn near passed out cold when they found it," said Waters, referring to the guard who had accompanied Stephens back to his room. "He says that he was on the way to use the John when you discovered that the room had been canvassed. He claims that he'll never lift a toilet seat again, even if it takes a sex change to make sure."

The rest of the debriefing took less than a half hour more before the four at the table were confident that all the key ground had been covered. By the end of the day more would be known as additional tests were completed and some of the samples arrived at Folkes Farm for full analysis.

Green and Stephens knew that, to a large extent, they had come to a dead end. It was reasonably clear that the Falconer was based somewhere in the general vicinity of New Ipswich, but there was no way to pin down a specific location any finer than that. The only lead still open, and that a questionable one at best, was the vague tie to the 11:55 group in Boston. There was also the nagging certainty in both Green's and Stephens' mind that Cynthia Lebart somehow knew a great deal more than she had let on.

"What's your next move?" asked Waters as they got up from the table. "I don't see much left here."

"It's not at all clear yet," answered Stephens. "We were hoping you people would come up with hard information."

"We're at least a couple days away from anything solid," offered Greenberg. "Without a match on the prints from Langley, we'll have to do it the hard way."

"Bradford called while you were sleeping," said Waters. "He asked that you call when we were finished with the debriefing."

"Have you got a clean phone set up yet?" asked Stephens.

"Upstairs. Master bedroom. Series Red."

When they walked back upstairs, there was no one in the great room. The tarpaulins and ladders were gone. The smell of fresh paint permeated the air. All of the furniture was back in position. Green and Stephens could recognize pieces of furniture that had come from other parts of the house, yet the room made sense. They were both astounded by its appearance. Stephens walked over to the western bank of windows that only hours before had been a twisted, shattered mass of wood and broken glass. He reached up and had to run his finger over the sash and the mullions to confirm that they were solid. He turned to look back at Green and shook his head, side to side, with respect.

Before he went upstairs, he stepped out the side door to look at the side of the house and the nearby grounds. The side of the house was smooth and in the process of being painted. There was no sign anywhere, even knowing where to look, of slug craters. Above him he could hear the continual hammering of the roofers, and an occasional 'thwack' as a new strip of shingles was laid in place.

When he came back inside, he found Green crouched next to the east wall of the great room. He had his cheek pressed close to the now dry paint and was sighting along the wall. This section of wall had been directly opposite the western bank of windows and had been the home of dozens of slugs from the previous night. Even with close inspection the wall seemed smooth and clean.

As he pulled back from the wall, he let out a small whistle. "Damn," he said respectfully. "What have we got here? Six, maybe seven hours since the full team arrived? You could let a bloody realtor show the house this afternoon."

In the upstairs bedroom there was a small box the size of a paperback sitting on the corner of a night stand by the bed. It was plugged into the phone wall jack. The phone was plugged into the box. Stephens glanced at the box for a few moments before picking up the phone. He dialed one of the 800 numbers into Folkes that would leave no record on the Robbins phone bill.

"Good day. May I help you?" answered the pleasant male voice on the phone.

"Yes. Mr. Red please," he said and reached out to flick one switch on the box near the phone.

The line immediately developed a hollow hum, and then the faint trace of what had been the man's voice on the other end became a garbled mix of clicks and wheezes. A few moments later the line cleared and the man's voice returned. "Series red in place," he said. "Do you confirm?"

"Confirmed," he answered. "This is Stephens. Please get Bradford."

In two or three minutes John Bradford's voice came over the phone.

"I have the earlies on my desk from Waters. It looks as though things were pretty messy there."

"We were lucky, John. I'd say we came within two seconds of being statistics in her reports. We should have been nailed. One of them made a small mistake."

"Your enemies always seem to make small mistakes."

"You might wait for the full reports before you chalk this one up to some kind of false modesty, John."

"The count still at four?"

"Yes. Plus one that escaped. Waters and Greenberg are sure there was a sixth, and maybe even a seventh that Green and I never saw."

"Anything more on the IDs from your end?"

"Greenberg has nothing. None of the four was Falconer. He wasn't one of the ones who escaped, either," Stephens said with absolute conviction. "We would know if he had been on site."

"You've heard that we came up dry at this end?"

"How the hell could that happen, John? You can't just miss a half dozen like these?"

"No answers yet. It makes no sense at all. We're tracking forty-three visitors right now. None of them match the prints we were faxed. Christ, even if they all sneaked in on midnight express I can't believe that our sources gave us nothing on them." There was a pause before he continued. "Rob, Joyce thinks they must have had a friend high in Langley or Folkes."

Stephens looked out the window at the Gardeners still working in the yard below. It was his turn to pause while he considered the paths he might take. He had intended to keep silent on his theories, but had not expected Bradford to take the lead with such a direct accusation.

"You know we were blown here, John."

"I know."

"There aren't many who knew the details and timing."

"Could *you* have slipped?" asked Bradford.

"Maybe, but I don't see it. Green and I have gone back over everything and can't see any mistakes."

"What's next?"

"We haven't decided. John, this is big. Whatever it is, we've left the minor leagues far behind. No one sends a six man wipe team in to take out two people, unless we were very close, or unless they could take no chances. I don't think we *were* close. It must be something so sensitive that they couldn't even take a small risk that we might stumble on to part of it. Anything more on the President?"

"No. He's going. The damn fool insists on being in Boston in two days. He won't even listen to me."

"Who's going with him? Standard treasury?"

"At least we won a small concession there. We have two of ours in the team. Your old friend Hogan will be one of them." Hogan was one of the dozen sixes in the agency.

"Hogan will make a difference, but I don't think it'll be enough. John, if they sent a full team just to take Green and me out, what the hell are they going to throw at the President?"

"We'll have backup."

"Will that help if they know the plan, in advance?" asked Stephens.

"It's all that's open to us. The President won't budge."

"John, do you think Green and I should go rogue? Maybe the best move is to play this without any more ties to Folkes or Langley?"

There was another long pause on the line. Stephens could hear a muted sigh before Bradford continued. "Rob, that might not be enough this time. There's one more point I have to pass on to you." Stephens heard the change in Bradford's voice. There was an undertone of sadness there. "The ciphers Lowe was working on were altered."

"While at Folkes? For certain?"

"No question. Lowe's woman Dickenson was there the day it was received, and then left on vacation for the past week. She came back this morning. There was no doubt in her mind that the numbers were different than she remembered."

Jennifer Dickenson had a both a photographic memory and an uncanny gift with ciphers. She had first become a code-breaker during World War Two and had personally scored some of the most critical code breaks of the cold war period. Years before the war, as a teenager, she held a job in Chicago railroad switching yards. She was one of the last of the number readers—that rare breed who would simply watch a train pass through the yard and could memorize, for later recording, all of the serial numbers from dozens of freight cars.

"We went to verify it and found the original was gone," Bradford continued. "About twenty percent of the code was changed. We wasted the entire past week chasing shadows."

"Any chance she's wrong this time?" asked Stephens with little hope that she was. "What about the backups on the computer? Don't they archive everything each night?"

"This one was clever. The changes were made within two hours after Jenny first entered the cipher into the computer. The first backup that night was of the altered version."

"What now?"

"We're starting over again based upon Jenny's version. Christ! We have eleventy jillion dollars worth of computers and security, and we still have to rely on the memory of a seventy-three year old!"

"John, that would seem to confirm it. We should go rogue. The leak is back at Folkes."

There was silence again on the phone. Stephens realized that Bradford had more to say.

"John? You might as well give me the rest of it. It's clear they're one step ahead of us on every turn, so far."

"Rob, the only hard evidence we have on the cipher switch is that they used Green's access code to enter the computer and make the changes."

"Green?" Now it was Stephens who hesitated before continuing. "Any validation of location?"

"Green was in the building. He checked in about fifteen minutes before the change, and left the building less than an hour after."

Outside the "gardeners" were still at work. The lawn had been mown in crossing patterns that gave the backyard the look, from above, of a plaid patchwork quilt. Stephens could see the bow of the sailboat through the open shed doors. For several seconds he stared intently at the faded gold lettering of the word "Susan" on the bow.

"You're wrong, John. It makes no sense."

"We, too, want to believe that. We've been over it and over it here. Joyce, Bill and I spent the past few hours reviewing everything." Again the slight pause. "Rob, I had to order a full internal an hour ago. Sanders is cross checking everything over the past few years against Green. Joyce will handle the background checks. We don't like even saying this, but we feel you have to be careful."

Stephens looked out the second floor window. From that vantage point he could easily see Mount Monadnock standing proudly against the clear blue afternoon sky. The location of Emerson's Chair, three-quarters of the way up the eastern face, was clearly visible. He closed his eyes and in his mind was sitting in his favorite place on the side of the mountain. He could feel the wind against his shirt, and the warmth of the sun on his face. He could feel the hard granite against his back, and could hear the calming sounds of the mountain. As always, as though he were actually there, things simplified for him and he could sort through the conflicts and confusion to an answer. This time, the answers were not clear, but the path to be taken was.

"John, I'll call you from Boston."

"What about Green? Do you want us to take the action here?"

Just as clearly as though he were in the room, Stephens could picture Green's face, with the lines of age etched into it, exuding a sense of trust and wisdom that had always been important to Stephens. He could recall the tone of Green's voice, and a host of quiet times in the past. He could remember times when the two of them were all that stood between death and the other.

"No. No action at all," he said, his voice soft. "Let it be business as usual. This one has to be mine."

Stephens did not wait for an answer. He very gently, and slowly, placed the phone in the cradle. He stood and took one last look at the mountain in the distance. He felt very old.

Chapter Twelve

Massachusetts has always posed an immense problem to those who chose to live there, and even more of a problem to those who would try to understand it. The deeper you delved into the makeup of the state, the more you would find just another, deeper level of riddles to be answered. It was boxes within other boxes within even more boxes. No one has ever gotten within the innermost, tiny box to find out what lay at the heart of the Massachusetts culture and society. Indeed, only a handful of the very best scholars and political scientists had ever achieved the insight to realize that there was no innermost box. It goes on forever, layer after layer.

Even the political experts that flocked to the state every four years, despite all of their experience in other states, considered Massachusetts a form of crapshoot. It was a place where certain things were sure to happen, but those same things defied the demographics and common wisdom. They happened, despite a host of factors that elsewhere would have guaranteed just about any outcome than the one that would occur.

Here, in the heart of the technology belt that surrounded Boston, are many of the most creative and brilliant minds in the country. At all levels, the average person in the state is different from the rest of the country. There is an odd blend of common sense, practicality, and reserve mixed in with the abilities of those who sit in the board rooms, or design computers, or pack circuit boards or work the shipping docks. The old New England work ethic is still in favor. There is a measure of awareness, commitment, and understanding that is the real basis for the Massachusetts claim to its high tech throne.

Yet, these very same people defy any logic when it came to the politics of the state. Year after year they seem to be led like sheep through the political process to elect, often by landslide margins, those people whose manner and record had the least in common with them. Glitz and glamour is always very important to a people who would find such attitudes silly in the normal course of events. Here, in the home of the men and women who two hundred years ago set integrity and honor above all else is perhaps the most routinely corrupt and feather-bedding political structure in the country. In the state where Adams and Revere dedicated their lives to freedoms and liberty is the most one-party state in the nation.

In all, perhaps an obscure treatise by a Harvard professor more than eighty years ago provided the greatest insight into Massachusetts.

> You must remember the roots of the first families to arrive here. They were fleeing from the impact of aristocracy in Europe. Aristocracy had always been, for them, something both hated and envied deeply. Yet, when they got here, their first step was to create a new aristocracy. It was one that matched their needs, for sure, but an aristocracy nonetheless. The huge difference was that this was an aristocracy *they could control*, and therefore, there was no longer a need for envy. Well under the surface you might find that envy had been replaced by a measure of disdain. More than any other commonwealth (and just that term 'commonwealth' says a lot!), the residents of Massachusetts would dearly love to elect a king. Had we not the Cabots and the Lodges, we would have been forced to invent them.

The skyline of Boston was magnificent when Stephens and Green drove over the crest of the hill on Route 2 in Belmont. It was one of those days when it would be special to be in downtown Boston, to stand somewhere near the base of the Hancock Tower, and to watch the interplay of images reflected in its sides. You would see the wavering reflections of the slightly distorted clouds, the planes departing from Logan Airport, and the endless parade of gulls from Boston Harbor.

The legendary 'falling windows' of the Hancock Tower were solid now. At least they were under control. Every year or two one of the huge panes would still break loose, without warning, and plummet to crash on the streets and sidewalks below. But, it was far different from the days of the early Seventies when scaffolds and protected ramps had to be erected to cover the sidewalks from the near daily falling of the glass. Now the differences in air pressure and the winds off the harbor that were underestimated in the initial architectural plan had been recognized and understood. Specially trained guards toured the building each day, looking for the telltale slight discoloration in the glass that had been identified as the inevitable precursor to a pane about to take flight. And, two or three times each month the suction cups would be called in, and then be clamped against the suspect pane so that it could be removed and replaced before it could begin its long tumble to earth.

If you were on the west side of the reflecting green glass tower, you would see the full mirrored image of the old Hancock Tower, somehow the perfect counterpoint to its modern replacement. Perhaps no other single image, the old reflected in the new, more symbolized the dichotomy that was Massachusetts.

Standing less than a thousand feet away was the Prudential Tower. So much of what the Hancock Tower had become was due to the Prudential Tower, and to a side of corporate America little recognized by most. It had been built as much due to personal factors as to any clinical need for space. The old Hancock Tower, now lost in the western shadow of the new, had held sway in that section of Boston for years until the Prudential Tower had been erected to stand dominant just a few hundred yards away. A new Hancock Building was predestined as soon as the Prudential Tower was just an ugly skeleton of girders. There was no possible way the board of directors at Hancock could sit around the venerable, thick, maple table that dated from colonial days, look out their window, and accept the Prudential Towers' claim to the high ground.

When the new Hancock building was finally completed, there were many who fully expected the Prudential to retaliate in kind. They would not have been surprised to see the Prudential add a story or two, or something equally impressive, had it been possible. There is a recurring rumor among the Boston inner circle, shared by the tight knit Brahmins of the financial community, that the directors of Prudential spent just over a quarter of a million dollars in the late Seventies to commission an architectural study to look at just such a move.

When Stephens and Green pulled into the Embassy Suites Hotel in Alston, overlooking the Charles River and the old Polaroid Building on the opposite side, it was nearly six o'clock. They had made just one stop along the way, at an Army and Navy store in Leominster. The plastic bags in the back seat now held a suitable collection of clothing for two people who were about to join the 11:55 group. Some had the appearance of the Vietnam era, and others were just old. Thanks to the insight of the retail clothing industry, always sensitive to trends and the needs of the public, the clothing was prewashed, prewrinkled, and even preworn. The clothing manufacturers had finally found a way to raise the old concept of planned obsolescence to an art form. They had enticed young consumers to demand clothing that had most of its life used up long before being shipped to the stores.

When Stephens and Green quietly left the hotel at about eight that evening, they bore little resemblance to the two who had checked in two hours before. Stephens was someone carved out of the turmoil that was Vietnam. He didn't wear full fatigues, and yet he somehow looked as though he had just stepped out of a Huey gunship near the western landing pad at Chu Lai. The boots and blue jeans were matched with a green fatigue top. There had been sergeant stripes on the sleeves when he purchased them, but Stephen had carefully ripped them off. He had spent close to a half hour brushing the sleeves so that the patches looked as though they had been removed years before. On both shoulders he had black, camouflaged field patches. One was the MACV patch. The other was First Air Cavalry. He had smiled when he first saw the patches among the collection available at the store. When he first picked them up, his days back with 1st Cav seemed close. It was the first good luck of the assignment. Should he happen to meet another ranger from his 'Nam days, it would be an easy, natural cover.

Green was the other side of the Stephens coin. He had the fatigue pants to match Stephens' top, and wore an open shirt. Green had not been in Vietnam. But perhaps Grenada was not very much different. Both were little more than honorable efforts, perhaps Quixotic, where honor and taking a stand were as important as what the stand accomplished.

The two would be able to mix with the 11:55 group. Perhaps the greatest irony of the meeting would be that there was so little difference between them and the 11:55ers. They shared the same goals and hopes. The only difference was that Green and Stephens could never escape the reality of the bonds between cause and effect. They had both paid their dues far too often to expect countries to 'unite in noble causes.' In the real world, countries, like people, inevitably took those actions that led to advantage. Stephens and Green, if asked, would not hesitate to admit their respect for the goals of the 11:55 group. But they both knew, as with idealists of any generation, the means chosen by the group were little more than honorable efforts, perhaps Quixotic, where honor and taking a stand were as important as what the stand accomplished.

—~—

When they walked into the back of the assembly hall that had been confirmed by Virginia as the main public meeting location for the 11:55 clan, there were only four people there. Three were up at the far end of the hall, engaged in a quiet conversation. Nearer at hand, a young man was picking up unused handouts from the folding chairs that filled the center of the hall. There were perhaps fifty chairs set up in precise rows that seemed more appropriate for a military gathering than to a more informal, unstructured group like the 11:55ers. It was evident that few people had turned out for the meeting that evening. Most of the chairs had handouts, still in their original position, on the seat.

"Evening," said the young man, pleasantly, as he looked up at the entry of Stephens and Green. "You're a bit late! We just finished up."

"I'm sorry to hear that," answered Stephens. "We don't get to Boston that often and both hoped to catch tonight's meeting."

"Where are you from?" the young man asked as he continued down the rows, collecting the pamphlets.

"The City. New York. We escaped there for a week up here on business."

"Well, if you're going to be here for a while, we'll be doing it again in a few days. I'm not sure just when, yet," he said, turning to motion towards the three people still talking at the front of the hall, "but you can check with the 'Spoon.' She'll tell you."

"The Spoon?" asked Green.

"Oh yes, you're new," he chuckled. "The Spoon, Witherspoon. Amy Witherspoon. She's the girl on the left, up there."

"Thanks."

When they approached the front, the ongoing conversation was anything but the zeal and enthusiasm that might be expected from a group with the zeal and aspirations of the 11:55 clan. The tone, and the faces with it, showed deep disappointment.

"Did we get *any* publicity?" asked the young woman who had been identified as Amy Witherspoon.

"Nothing. EEI wouldn't broadcast anything I gave them," answered the other woman. "I tried to call RKO and got bumped after about a minute or so. Williams said the show was only covering the Pakistan hijacking."

"The Globe?"

"Nothing. Local papers, nothing."

"We put up posters in all the usual places," added the young man. "That was the only thing that pulled at all."

"Shit. Seven people for something like this. Seven people."

"Make that five," said the other young woman, bitterly. "Two of them were street people. They were only looking for food. They're the ones who left half way through the meeting when they realized we wouldn't have any."

None of the three spoke for a few moments. Underneath the disappointment was a genuine lack of understanding for not seeing a packed hall. The three stood silently, not noticing Green and Stephens nearby. The only sounds were the soft steps of the young man still picking up pamphlets, and the ever present background drone of the traffic in the street.

It was Stephens who broke the silence. There was genuine sympathy in his voice. "Sounds as though you're going through the same things we did back in the sixties. It's not easy."

The three looked up at the newcomers.

"Ever listen to Dylan?" Stephens continued. "Maybe you'd now understand what his songs meant to us."

"Dillon? You're putting me on," The young man was the first to reply. His eyebrows were raised quizzically and there was a slight look of disdain on his face. "Even I know Dillon wasn't around in the sixties."

The other young woman's face went through a series of expressions. It started with annoyance at the interruption, and then progressed to the same quizzical disdain. However, the look abruptly changed and became one of amusement followed by laughter. "Doug, you're such a turkey! You're thinking of Matt Dillon, the actor. He's talking about Bob Dylan!" Within a few seconds, all three of them were laughing.

"Hey, I know Dylan's stuff. He's good," said Amy Witherspoon to Stephens. "My folks have his records."

"Don't feel bad," said Green, smiling at the young man. "A friend of mine has a kid who thinks the Beatles were Paul McCartney's old backup band."

"Which Dylan song should we be playing?" asked the other young woman.

"Oh I was thinking of *The times they are a-changing,*" answered Stephens. "When we started, it was all so important. A hall like this would be mobbed. Seats filled, and they'd be standing all around the edges," he said, motioning around the room. "But then things changed. It became less and less important. I guess it became common, ordinary. People stopped coming. And Dylan stopped selling."

"I know what you mean," said the other young woman, with sadness in her voice.

"It got so that when it was a nice day, or the Yankees were playing, or there was a party, or a good show on the tube—that was all it took to kill turnout. The meetings took second place. They weren't new enough, or fun enough. When people started going to a 'meeting,' rather than to a 'happening,' it became work."

"At the end, we used to wait for the weather report before making plans," added Green. "We would try to schedule everything for overcast or cold days. You had to be careful, and lucky. If the weather was too bad, then they'd stay home. If it was too nice, they'd go somewhere else. Lord help you if it was a night like this," he said motioning outside. "This will be one of the last nights like this of the year. It's a night for lovers, not for commitments."

Amy Witherspoon offered her hand to Green. "Well, at least we got you two, even though late. I'm Amy Witherspoon. But I think you'll find I've been nailed with the nickname of 'The Spoon.' This gentleman and obvious music expert," she said, pointing to the young man, "is Doug Marsden. And over here is Kathy Whitworth."

Green and Stephens introduced themselves using the lawyer names of Walter Jones and Ken Kelleher. After the round of helloes, handshakes and nods, Amy Witherspoon came right to the point. "What can we do for you? You certainly missed our 'big show' and huge crowds."

"Well, we were hoping to get here in time to hear you," answered Green. "An old friend of ours was very impressed by what you were doing. He said that you were the key factor in that nuclear referendum here in Cambridge."

"Yea," replied Doug Marsden. "That one surprised just about everybody."

"After hearing so much about you, we both decided that the next time we came up here to visit Raytheon, we'd have to stop in. Usually, we just visit friends."

"Who told you about us?" asked Amy Witherspoon.

Before Stephens could answer, Kathy Whitworth broke in.

"Raytheon?" she asked with a voice that had quickly hardened from the friendly tones of just moments before. "What do you do there?"

"My company subcontracts with them on some of their government business," Stephens answered, noting the change in tone.

Kathy Whitworth's face tightened with anger. "Then why do you do it? How can you work for a company like that? Every dollar they make is from a missile or a gun or something that kills other people."

"Now Kathy," Amy Witherspoon started to explain, "You've got to . . ."

"No, no," interjected Stephens. "She's not far from the truth. Most of it may be pretty tame stuff, but there are parts that have got to change. But that's also why I'm still there." He turned to face Kathy Witherspoon. His eyes were filled with understanding, because what he was inventing about a mythical assignment with Raytheon was very close to his feelings about his work with the Company. In all the years of questioning what he did, and all the long walks at Wendlandt trying to explain it to himself, his words to Kathy Whitworth were the first time the motives and the words all came together.

"Kathy, it would be easy to leave. I could go tomorrow and be glad of it. But that would leave it all in the hands of people who have no questions at all about what they do. Should we just turn it over to them?" he asked softly, pausing only briefly before continuing without waiting for an answer. "I know it doesn't change things, but it *does* temper things. It does make sure questions are asked. Maybe it's the only difference we can make?"

The last sentence, which had started out as a statement, had turned into a question. Stephens found himself looking at Green as he asked it. Both of them realized that the words were about the years with the Company, and with ATQ. "That's why the two of us continue, isn't it?" he asked as he watched the understanding in Green's eyes. Green nodded his head slightly in return. Neither said anything for a moment, and then Stephens turned back to Kathy Whitworth.

"All I can tell you is that I feel better knowing we're inside. It's much better than standing alone outside, watching and knowing that there would be no checks and balances at all that way."

"You know," said Doug Marsden, looking at them with renewed interest, "I'd never have thought of it that way."

"Oh, I don't claim that we can change it much," said Green to Marsden while still looking at Stephens. "You never change something that size. The best you can do is maybe change its course a tenth of a degree or so every so often. The hope is that those tenths add up, and that the overall direction really does change." He was looking intently at Stephens now. "And you have to hope the others change, too. If Raytheon changes, but the other *companies* don't, it would all be for nothing."

Only Stephens noted the slight emphasis on the word 'company.'

"Do you think you can give it a conscience?" asked Doug. "Is it working?"

"Shit Doug. That's a lot of bull," Kathy Whitworth interrupted. "Wake up! You look under the surface of all that melodrama they just dished out and you'll find their hundred grand salaries are just about all the 'conscience' they need."

Kathy Whitworth stood there with her hands tightly balled at her sides. She had plainly drawn the lines. There was no doubt to any of them, including the young man from the back of the hall who had now joined them, that there would be no budging from her position. The new arrival reached out his hand.

"Hi, I'm Tom Curtis," he said. "Kathy's *our* conscience. Like any conscience, a bit strident at times, but we need that to bring us back to earth every so often."

"Every movement of any value needs one," answered Green. "Dylan was ours."

"At least there's one big gain from all this," said Amy Witherspoon, trying to change the mood. "If you two *do* pull down the big bucks, then a sizable donation might be in order here."

It was exactly the type of comment needed to defuse the situation.

"Shit," answered Green. "We don't get close to that if you add the two of us together!"

"So you were in all this back in the sixties," mused Curtis. "That had to be an awesome time. Can you join us in a few minutes? We've got to fold up the chairs first, but then we're going to grab a bite down at the

Square. It won't be fancy, but you can see," he said, motioning around the old hall, "that we don't live in the high-rent district."

"Sure, might be fun comparing stories," said Stephens before turning towards Kathy Whitworth. "What about you, Kathy? Can you handle a couple capitalistic warmongers like Ken and me at the same table?"

Kathy gave a half smile in return. But the eyes did not match the smile. Regardless of the look, she had made her judgment about Stephens and Green.

"Come on, then," she said. "Might as well get some amusement out of the evening."

The short walk from the assembly hall to the public cafeteria on the edge of Harvard Square was made special for Stephens by the warmth of the night, and the company of the young members of the 11:55 clan. It was almost as though he were back in school himself, back with friends, arguing Nixon or Johnson or whatever else was the focus at that particular time. He found it so easy to remember similar nights from so many years ago. All that was missing was the gentle touch of a girl's hand in his. As he walked he was surprised to find himself remembering the sounds of Chad and Jeremy, slightly distorted when played by a cheap portable radio, from a summer night back in 1966.

Stephens liked the 11:55ers. The friction didn't bother him. Every group from the sixties had its Kathy Whitworth. All had the nights when nobody came, and the rare highs when it all went right. Most of all, he still respect what the 11:55ers were trying to do, no matter how foolish he thought their means to be.

The cafeteria at one end of Harvard Square opposite the Coop and the subway entrance has changed little over the last fifteen years. It was still filled with that peculiar mix of people that can be found only in a handful of places in the world, like Cambridge or San Francisco or London or Paris. It was a combination that made no particular sense, and was only possible when the character of a place included the college students, the street people, and all in between—mixed well with an odd blend of honesty before being dropped into one location. It was like mixing a rainbow of paint colors. In all other places, the colors would immediately blend to a muddy shade of gray that leaves nothing of the original beauty. In places like Cambridge the colors weaved and intertwined, but never blended. The colors would dance and mate, but they would never disappear into grayness.

There was always a small portion from Harvard or Radcliffe in the cafeteria. They would be the ones who couldn't afford full Harvard board, or had to wait for the next check from home, or were just caught in the middle class tuition squeeze. They would studiously try to look as though their visit were no more than a course assignment, 'required eating,' or a chance to view the human condition. Their demeanor would be carefully chosen and controlled to make sure all knew that this was not their 'normal' type of place.

Perhaps the largest group of patrons was the townies, the kids in high school or just out of high school, who chased the irrational grail of belonging to the Harvard community. They would be the same kids who would wander the aisles of the Harvard Coop or dare a walk through 'the Yard.' The hope was that somehow all they sought would rub off on them, and that the ultimate might occur—they would be mistaken for a Harvard student.

There were no representatives of the street people there this night. They were usually the smallest group, perhaps three of four people on a heavy night. Years ago they would stand out in stark contrast to the image of colleges or the mansions of Brattle Street. But now they were so common that they blended in, a gray presence in the back of the scene. After a while, they had become invisible. There are a host of unwritten rules in Cambridge that cover how the residents handle the street people. All are carefully crafted to ensure that the street people can be safely ignored while giving the appearance the city is helping them. The rules all have in common the goal of making certain that the city did not actually do anything that made a difference in the long term, while also making absolutely sure that there was no 'smoking gun' that could ever be seen as a sign of this planned neglect. The rules saw no problem in shooing away the street people from the Harvard warm air vents, where they would sleep and huddle in the sleet of winter. But the same rules would have the city officials rise in anger if grates were placed over those same vents that might ". . . drive some poor wretched sole to the death of a freezing New England blizzard." The street people would only enter the diner for warmth, or shelter, on the very worst of nights. They knew that there were only so many times each year that they would be tolerated in the diner, and they carefully husbanded those few chances. They knew better than to squander one of the few chips they had on a warm November night.

The final group was the old people of Cambridge. They always stood out in stark contrast to all the others. They were quiet couples and lined old men who came there because there was a blue plate dinner at a price that could not be matched anywhere else within walking distance. The special would be filling and warm, and if you didn't mind settling for just a glass of water with it, the cost was less than three dollars.

The old and the Harvard students shared a common though strongly denied bond. If you watched long enough, you would suddenly realize that these were the only two of the groups that would never make eye contact with each other. The Harvard students would contact all of the others to show their superiority to the townies and the street people. The old people *had* to make contact with all the rest. It was their only bond to those things they tried so hard to remember. But the old, and the Harvard students, would never lock eyes. They had an instinctive, silent agreement about it. To do so would force them to admit how similar were their fears, and how much eating at this cafeteria was a sign of those fears. To the old, they had to eat there, and being there was an admission of what their lives had become. For the Harvard student, the place represented the fears of what could happen, of what a life might someday be.

They both knew that if they did lock eyes with one another, they would be unable to back away from how much alike they were. Their fears, one of what might have been lost in the past, the other of what might still be lurking in the future, would surface to dominate the illusions they both worked so hard to craft.

Chapter Thirteen

It was towards the end of the meal when they finally got back to the discussion of Jim Peterson. For more than an hour they had shared stories of their two efforts, alternating between times nearly two decades apart. Kent State was compared to Three Mile Island. Woodstock played counterpoint to Chernobyl. And most of all, the conversation seemed to center around Richard Milhous Nixon. The members of the 11:55 clan, all in their early twenties, wanted to understand about Nixon more than any other thing.

They had grown up well after the Nixon years. At first Stephens was astounded by the intensity of their questions. They kept pushing and probing. Only late in the conversation did he finally understand that they were simply trying to reach back and become a part of that time. To their generation, the whole decade of the sixties was a legend that they needed to reach out and touch. Their childhood had been spent just beyond the era of Nixon, the Kennedys, King, Woodstock, and even the Beatles. These were the stories their parents had passed down. But unlike ancient stories by the campfire, where the legends were lost far back in history, these stories were almost near enough to touch. The four of them would be ever relegated to being just on the edge, but never a part, of one of America's most sweeping times. For the past three hundred years, each century's decade of the sixties had marked a time of mighty upheaval. Like the revolution, or the civil war, they would have to read of this time in textbooks. They could only fantasize about being there, and try to understand the meaning hidden in the eyes of those who had been a part of it all.

From their vantage near the front of the diner they could easily watch the people passing by on the Square. Even late at night there was endless activity. Window shoppers at the closed Harvard Coop, passengers entering and leaving the stairs down into the MBTA subway station, students and old people and street people were all out in force tonight. Inside, a jukebox blared in the far corner. The sound of John Cougar Mellencamp was a long way from that of Chad and Jeremy.

"Well," said Amy Witherspoon, "are we anything like what your friend led you to expect?"

"Oh, I think Tony was pretty accurate," said Stephens, easily using the name Jim Peterson had used during his time with the group. "No big surprises at all. At least, not yet."

Kathy Whitworth looked up suddenly from where she had been idly drawing in ketchup on her plate with a cold French fry. "Tony? Was your friend Tony Cope?"

"Yes. In fact, we hoped we might run into him here."

"How'd you know Tony?" asked Kathy Whitworth. There was a marked change in her tone with the question. Much of the tone of accusation had been forgotten. Stephens and Green glanced briefly at each other as both realized that there was a clear link between Peterson and the young woman.

"I got to know him a couple years back when he was in school. We did a research project and he helped out a couple of professors on the team."

"You know Tony, then?" asked Green. He could see that all of them were hesitant to talk about Jim Peterson, and that they all pointedly avoided glancing towards Kathy Whitworth.

"We all knew Tony," answered Doug Marsden for her. The statement hung there for a few moments before anyone followed up on it.

"Where is he, anyway?" asked Amy Witherspoon. "None of us have seen him for a couple of weeks. He was pretty active with us for a while there. I thought he was going to join us full time."

"I'm not sure myself," answered Stephens. "When I talked to him a couple weeks back, he was all hot to have us meet you. He even thought he might be able to meet us here."

There was an awkward silence. Kathy Whitworth had resumed drawing with a French fry. The others had suddenly become intent on studying those passing by in the street and pointing out various clothing or habits they saw. For the next few minutes the only conversation was ". . . oh look at the turkey in the . . ." or ". . . how old do you think she really is . . ." Two or three people entered the diner during the period and started through the line. There was one loud crash from the direction of the kitchen.

Finally, Amy Witherspoon decided to explain. "Look, your friend isn't exactly on best standing here. He walked out on Kathy two weeks ago without even a goodbye."

"Kathy, did you ever hear anything back from him?" asked Doug Marsden, gently.

"No," came the quiet reply. "Nothing yet."

"Creep!" said Amy Witherspoon.

"That doesn't sound at all like Tony," said Green. "I don't understand it. Tony's pretty solid."

"Maybe you should ask your friend about it," said Tom Curtis. "Seems to me that he's not quite as solid as you think."

"Please don't say that Tom," said Kathy Whitworth, gently. "It isn't fair. Tony didn't try to hurt anyone."

"Then why haven't you heard anything for two weeks?"

"I don't know," she answered. "I just don't know." Kathy Whitworth looked up at Green and Stephens. "Do you?"

"There has got to be more to this," answered Stephens. "Did you two fight or something?"

"No. Nothing like that," she answered. "He said he'd be gone for a day or two, and then just disappeared."

"Where was he going?"

"I'm not sure. I've thought about that every day since he left, and I just don't know. None of it makes sense."

"You said you thought it had something to do with Henri?" said Amy Witherspoon.

"That was my only idea," shrugged Kathy Whitworth, "but it doesn't help."

"Who was Henri?" asked Stephens.

"I don't think any of us really know," answered Kathy Whitworth. "For someone who spent a few days here, he never talked much about anything."

"He hung around for about a week when he first arrived from France," added Doug Marsden. "He was waiting for some kind of a job to open up. He stayed with us for a few days until things worked out."

"Tony and he got to know each other a bit," said Kathy Whitworth.

"Where did Henri go?" asked Green.

"I don't know that either," answered Kathy Whitworth.

"He went to Peterborough, up in New Hampshire," said Tom Curtis, with a measure of surprise in his voice. "I thought you all knew that."

"I didn't," answered Amy Witherspoon.

"Me neither," said Doug Marsden.

"Sure. He told me on the day he left that he was going to Peterborough. Made a big joke of it. He said he was going to live on a rabbit farm. Henri kept saying that he was going '. . . to be taught by a rabbit to do it like a rabbit.' That was his big joke."

"You think Tony had something to do with him?" asked Stephens.

"I don't see how," answered Tom Curtis. "Tony didn't know him before he showed up. Henri just sort of drifted in."

"He never did make much sense," added Amy Witherspoon. "He was just marking time. Tony was pretty interested in him, though. Towards the end they talked quite a bit. Tony was there the day they came to pick Henri up."

"Who was that?" asked Green.

"Just someone in a car. I didn't see who was inside. The car had that tinted stuff on the windows that keeps the car cooler in the summer."

Stephens glanced briefly at Green. "Did Tony meet them?"

"He might have. He was there."

"Kathy, did you two talk after that?" asked Green.

Kathy Whitworth did not answer at first. She was staring at Stephens. There was no longer any trace of accusation in her face. The look, instead, was more that of someone reasoning out the last parts of a puzzle. Without realizing it, she had folded her hands as though praying, and then pointed her two index fingers upward into the kid's "church and steeple" position. She repeatedly pushed her index fingers against the bottom of her front teeth as she thought.

"That was the same day, wasn't it Kathy?" asked Tom Curtis.

Kathy Whitworth did not even glance at the source of the question. Her response, when it came, was very soft and was directed only to Stephens.

"I know who you are."

The table went silent. Her three friends were trying to understand what had happened that had so changed the tone at the table. They felt as though they had now become outsiders. Both Stephens and Green understood exactly.

"Raytheon, you said," she said quietly.

"Yes, Kathy," answered Stephens. No one else at the table spoke.

"We should talk you know," she said.

Stephens only nodded.

"Hey, what's the big secret?" asked Amy Witherspoon. "You guys can't get away with trying to spoon-feed the old 'spoon.'"

"Yeah," added Tom Curtis, "this is getting pretty heavy. You guys going to let us in on the game?"

It was Kathy Whitworth that answered first, even before Stephens could begin something to change the direction of the conversation. "Oh, Tony left some papers with me that might belong to these guys. It was some stuff from a project he was working on."

"Ooooooo," said Tom Curtis, smiling. "Top secret stuff, huh. We're in the big time now, eh Kathy?"

"Oh shut up, Turkey. It's just some lousy papers." She turned back to Stephens. Her voice now was back to normal. "Why not follow me back to my place when we dump these turkeys? You can take a quick look and see if the papers are yours?"

The six began to collect their plates and clean up the table. Kathy Whitworth's comments had restored the enjoyment of earlier in the evening. Outside, the Square was still filled with activity. Inside, there were still about a dozen people in the diner. As they started towards the trash cans against the back wall, one of the people who had entered the diner part way through their meal put down his coffee and walked to the door. As the man stepped through the door, Stephens found himself staring at the man's back. He was not surprised to see that Green, too, was watching the man leave.

As they left the diner, Rob Stephens didn't know exactly what had triggered his awareness of the man who he now knew had been watching them. A part of his subconscious had been aware for several minutes that something was wrong. He had thought that his uneasiness was due to the case in general. Yet, when he saw the person leave a table that was just a few feet away, and then walk out the door, he knew that the uneasiness had been due to something far more specific. As Bill Robbins had understood in his last moments, there are patterns in hard men everywhere that set them apart. The calm and control of the person leaving matched those patterns. They had somehow registered on Stephens when the man had first entered. Now the vague impression had been qualified and confirmed.

Their years working together made communication possible with just the slightest of a nod from Stephens when combined with a quick movement of his eyes towards the door. "Why don't you walk ahead and get the car, Ken," said Stephens to Green as the group walked out into the evening. "I'll walk over with them to the MTA stop and get directions to Kathy's. You can pick me up here in just a few minutes."

"Why don't I just ride with you two?" asked Kathy Whitworth.

"That would be easier, but we have to make a couple stops first," Stephens answered. Then he turned back to Green. "Tell you what, Ken, if she gets me lost I'll take a cab back to the hotel." Green would now understand the basic plan should they be separated.

After exchanging goodbyes, Green started down Brattle Street back towards the auditorium as the rest of the group headed towards the stairs that led down into the MTA station. The man who had watched them was nowhere in sight. Down on the T platform there was the usual Saturday night traffic. There was fresh graffiti on the far wall opposite where the group waited for the train's arrival. Despite the situation, Stephens had to appreciate the dry wit of the person who had dared to cross the tracks and stand there with a paint can. In bold, flowing script it was easy to read that "The average person is well below average."

As the sound of the train approached, Stephens saw the man start down the stairs into the subway. He had obviously waited somewhere nearby and had also listened for the noise from the train. Stephens took another quick look around the platform, and confirmed his fears that the conditions were all stacked the wrong way. There would be little he could do should the follower wish to initiate action. There was even less he could do to stop the group from being followed. All the man would have to do would be to get on the same train, and wait for the right opportunity. Stephens would be tied down with a group of amateurs who had no idea of what was happening, or that time always favors the seeker when there are innocents involved.

"Look, I'm going to run," he announced when he had decided what action to take. "Kathy, the directions sound easy. If I get a move on, we should be done with our stops in an hour or so. We'll see you at your place then."

Stephens started walking directly towards the man. He knew that was the only approach to change the focus away from the platform. He made sure that he locked eyes with the follower. Stephens wanted to be certain that the man knew he had been spotted. The man stopped halfway down the stairs, looked quickly to each side, and then back at Stephens. He was wearing a green, lightweight jacket that was open except for the bottom snap. His right hand slipped into the pocket. Stephens was certain that the lining had been removed from that pocket so that there was easy access to a weapon underneath.

The man turned casually and started back up the stairs. He did not even glance over his shoulder as he disappeared back into the night above. Stephens carefully followed less than fifty feet behind. At the top of the steps, he could see the man just reaching the other side of Peabody Street. The man headed north to walk along the Harvard dormitories towards Peabody Square. Stephens stepped out of the MTA entrance, and crossed the street to follow. Once across, he saw Green appear out of a darkened doorway on the opposite side of the street and begin to parallel their movements.

For the next ten minutes, the man led them aimlessly around the Peabody Square area. He was very good. He changed his direction often enough that Green was never able to work his way into a position to cut him off. Every time that Green positioned himself ahead of the target the man would change sides of the street, or cut through a side street. Occasionally he would make an effort to lose Stephens. Both Stephens and Green could see that he was not very concerned about being forced to act. He was a professional and was waiting for the right moment.

Near the entrance to the Harvard Law School just such an opportunity finally came. The man walked up to a Cambridge policeman who was resting one foot on the bumper of a vintage white Mercedes 180SL convertible as he wrote a ticket for a parking violation. Stephens saw him stop, and immediately knew that the man had chosen his place. He quickly gave a brief signal to Green, and turned to walk in the opposite direction.

"Hey you!" yelled the officer. Stephens continued to walk. "Freeze mister. Now!"

Stephens turned immediately. "Me officer?" he asked as he watched the man walking into the yard of the Harvard Law School. Stephens saw the slight smile, even in the darkness, on the man's face. He also saw Green ambling across the street to continue the chase. The officer's hand was on the handle of his sidearm.

"Against the fence, please," he said in a voice that made it clear that the word 'please' was rhetorical.

It took half an hour, and a few calls back to the station before Stephens could leave. His right to carry a weapon was easily verified. Stephens jumped right to what those in the Agency called MSC, or "Maximum Scenario Corroboration." This was the top level of cover when an agent had been picked up by local police forces or other agencies. It was designed to provide the speediest possible release. It was based upon a phone call initially routed through the main US Treasury phone number, but then rerouted as necessary. The person back at Langley, Virginia, who answered Stephen's call punched in the name Walter Jones into the agency MSC computer, and responded that Jones was ". . . a member of Treasury actively investigating counterfeit cigarette stamps."

It was a bit harder to confirm that the story the police officer had been given about a liquor store holdup was an invention. He had been told that the man he saw the start of a robbery, and that Stephens, knowing he had been spotted, had followed the 'witness.' A separate squad car was dispatched to the site where the man had claimed to have seen the robbery. Finally, as it approached 10:00 p.m., Stephens was released with full apologies for ". . . a nasty practical joke."

When Stephens finally walked out of Cambridge precinct 4, there was still plenty of activity on the streets. It took only fifteen minutes before he was able to hail a cab back to the Embassy Suites Hotel. Whenever Green finally returned, they might still have time to visit Kathy Whitworth. If not, they would have plenty of time the next morning. As he started the drive back, he hoped that Green had been more successful than he had been.

It was just before 11:00 p.m. when Stephens entered his hotel room. Green was not yet there. He looked at the empty hotel room, and thought about what seemed to be an endless stream of such rooms over the years. In the quiet, broken only by the soft hum of the heating fan, he thought of Cynthia Lebart. As he walked towards the phone to call back to Folkes Farm, he gave half-serious consideration to trying to call her.

He sat on the side of the bed and considered where she might be just then. 'Damn,' he thought, 'I miss her.' He was no longer surprised by his feelings about her. The room seemed very empty as he thought of her. He turned on the television, with the volume down low so that it broke the silence, but not enough to intrude on his thoughts. Finally, he picked up the phone and called Virginia.

"We were made again," he said, simply, when John Bradford got on the line that was protected by the same device that he had used up in New Ipswich. "Harvey is still out there somewhere." Stephens summarized the key points if a few short sentences.

"Any ideas?"

"Listen. Even though we didn't fill anyone in on the specifics, you people at the farm were the only ones who had any idea what we had in mind. It wouldn't take much to figure out that we were going to Boston. From there our next steps would be pretty obvious."

"Rob, even I didn't know for sure. Why are you so sure you were made? Maybe it was just a fluke?"

"This guy was top level. He set up that cop as calmly as you or I might order a cheeseburger."

"Again, any chance it was a coincidence?"

"I don't believe it. Neither do you."

"We had full controls on this one. There are just seven people who are cleared for this. There's no way in hell anyone back here blew you, Rob."

"They blew both of us," answered Rob Stephens pointedly. "Harvey was set up, too."

There was a long delay on the line.

"Rob, we've got more on Green. We had to run all the standard checks on him because of the code leak. Joyce, herself, handled the reports."

In the background Stephens heard the slight scrape of a key entering the lock. He rested one hand on his weapon and stared at the door as he waited for Bradford to continue. The door opened, and Harvey Green carefully edged into the room. When he saw Rob Stephens he smiled, dropped his hands to his sides, and then stepped fully inside and closed the door.

"I lost him," said Green as he removed his Jacket and ran his fingers through his thin, receding hair. "That Virginia?"

"Yup. Bradford."

"Is that Green with you," asked Bradford on the other end of the phone.

"Yes."

"Listen Rob," Bradford continued on the phone. "I've being trying for about three hours now, since I heard, to figure out how to say this nicely. But I can't. Joyce found some joint bank accounts in Green and his mother's name. They total more than $800,000. The latest deposit was $50,000, just two weeks ago."

Stephens looked up as Green removed his gun and stretched his arms. Green looked back and smiled again. "I must be getting old," said Green. "He ducked right into one of the dormitories. Cool as can be." Green flopped down into one of the two chairs in the room. "They got anything back there?"

"Nothing much. Bradford says they've fallen flat, so far."

"What do you want from here?" asked John Bradford. "We all talked it over. We still think that Green should be pulled."

Stephens looked towards Green. Green was no longer watching him. Instead, he was staring at the television. His mouth had fallen slightly open in surprise. Then Green turned to look intently back at Stephens.

"What the hell is this?" Green's voice was incredulous.

Stephens looked at the TV and saw his own face as the lead item on the WBZ 11:00 p.m. news.

"I'll handle it," said Stephens. "Wait until I call in before taking any action."

He gently replaced the handset in the telephone cradle. His voice was calm and controlled. "Can you turn that up?"

The announcer was in the middle of a report on the killing of a young woman in Somerville. ". . . police suspect that this man, identified as Walter Jones, might be involved in the brutal murder of activist Kathy Whitworth, daughter of noted Boston lawyer Henry Whitworth, earlier this evening. Several of her friends confirmed that Jones had planned to meet her at her apartment tonight. Jones was last seen having dinner with Whitworth and her friends at a Cambridge restaurant just hours ago."

The photograph was obviously taken in the diner in Harvard Square with a telephoto lens. Green was just discernible in the background. "This photograph was anonymously provided to Captain Reichart of the Cambridge PD earlier this evening. It has since been recognized by Officer Gerald Hall of the 4th precinct who . . ."

Stephens did not even listen to the rest of the words. His eyes were fixed upon the upper right-hand corner of the photo. While others would think it a strange defect in the film emulsion that had no significance, Stephens saw the crude outline of the letter 'F' that had been etched into the film during development. He stared at the letter and the clear message that had been addressed directly to him. He thought of the warning from John Bradford.

Then he thought briefly, oddly, of Cynthia Lebart. She seemed a long, long way away.

Chapter Fourteen

As soon as the television news story ended, Stephens called Amy Witherspoon. He knew that by now the police were monitoring her phone. But the time spent at the 11:55 assembly hall, and later at the diner, had allowed a surprising bond to build with her. He saw parallels between himself and the young woman. She was an odd reflection of who he had been a decade or two before. Despite knowing that it would not be likely he would see her again, Stephens knew she deserved a call, despite the risk. The call would be traced if he were foolish enough to stay on long enough, but he had to tell her that he was not the killer of her friend.

When the phone was answered, after four rings, the two handsets had been lifted almost simultaneously. Stephens could picture whoever was at the other end with Amy, counting beats like a conductor so that they both picked up the phone extensions at the same time. It was done very well, indeed. Few people would have been able to detect the slight echo of the second set being lifted.

"Amy, this is Walter," he had said into the waiting line. Stephens didn't give her time to answer before continuing. "Please listen, I don't have much time. I just saw the news about Kathy."

"They say you killed her. The police came. They say they have proof."

"Amy, I'm sorry. In a way they're right. It is my fault. But Amy, I didn't kill her. I never got to her place tonight."

There was a small delay before she answered. Her voice was very soft, and was almost hidden by the laughter of a man and a woman walking by in the hall outside Stephens and Green's room. "Then why is it your fault?"

"She was seen with me, Amy." There was a trace of bitterness in his voice. "That's all she did. She was killed because someone thought Kathy might know something." He shook his head slowly. "She died because she met me. Nothing more than that."

"The rest of my friends? Are they in danger, too?" Stephens could tell by the calmness of her voice that he had been right about the start of a bond.

"No, Amy. I don't think so." He thought about the unseen person on the other end of the phone. "By now all of your friends have someone nearby to watch out for them. The person who killed Kathy got what he wanted. A message was sent, a line closed. No more, no less."

The line was silent for several seconds that seemed to stretch into minutes. Stephens glanced at his watch as he carefully monitored the elapsed time of the call.

"Walter, be careful. Remember what you said over your spaghetti at dinner. 'It's a tough world out there.'"

Stephens had to allow the slightest of smiles to surface at the comment. He had made no such comment at dinner, and had eaten a cheeseburger. Despite all of the 'proof,' Amy had believed him. In her own way, she was trying to warn him about the person on the other end of the line. For a moment, he wished to continue to talk and share more time with Amy. Her voice sounded so young and, at the same time so aged. It was a voice that carried echoes of the sixties, or of any of the countless times before that a generation began to question life. It was the timeless voice where certainty has faded to merely hope, and hope could only inspire tales to make up in fantasy what was lacking in fact. It was the angst that created the tales Camelot, or Quixote, or countless stories around countless tribal fires. Legends had to provide what life could not.

It was the voice that always marked the ending of real childhood, and the start of understanding. Stephens could remember when he had made the terrifying transition from protest and involvement, to awareness of what was really happening. He could picture his sixth day in Vietnam when he helped to pack his first body bag. The protest marches all at once seemed silly when faced with the all-too-real magnitude of the war. On that day his voice, too, had sounded like Amy's. It mixed the timbre of a child with the words and phrasing of adulthood. It was a voice that would never again be able to cradle the gentle echoes of innocence.

In a way, he regretted that his last contact with her would be a lie to give a red herring to the eavesdropper. He needed to buy time to begin the search in Peterborough.

"Thanks, kid. Too bad you weren't there with Dylan and the rest of us. We wasted a lot of time back then, and I guess we didn't accomplish much. It doesn't seem to matter now. Makes no difference that it turned out we were right. I think you would have understood it all." Stephens pulled the conversation back to the present. "Amy, Kathy's friend came from the Worcester area. The answer's there. Peace, my friend."

He started to hang up the phone, but stopped with his arm half way down to the desk beside the bed. He looked out at the darkened sky with the Polaroid sign just across the river. He glanced at his watch to confirm that there still hadn't been enough time to trace the call. He had another fifteen seconds of safety. He put the phone back to his ear.

"Amy?"

"I'm still here."

"I'll get him. Whoever killed Kathy."

"I know."

Stephens thought a great deal about the events of the past few days during the drive towards Peterborough the next morning. At the Embassy Suites they had been seen only by a bored registration clerk earlier in the evening. Stephens knew that even the most observant person is not likely to equate a well-dressed Boston lawyer with the ex-soldier murderer of a young woman. By remaining they were able to blend with the morning hotel checkout and join hundreds of thousands of others in the constricted streets of the Boston rush hour.

As well, they had both needed sleep. New Ipswich was starting to take its toll. With the President's visit to Boston only two days away, there would be few opportunities for rest like this again. It had not been a sound sleep for Stephens.

The New Hampshire town was the only remaining lead. Neither he nor Green spoke much in the car. Both were reviewing what seemed like an endless succession of dead ends, both looking for a pattern amidst the confusion. Both were looking at exactly the same facts, but from very different perspectives.

Inevitably, no matter how much Stephens wrestled with the facts, the television news report the previous night could only indicate betrayal. Someone had clearly known where they were, and about their contact with the 11:55ers. Someone had realized the sensitivity of the lead they had been following, and had killed a young woman to create another dead end. All this had been done with remarkable speed and efficiency, complete with "photos at eleven." It had to have been orchestrated by someone who knew their movements. Yet, other than Green, no one in the Company had known their specific plans.

As Stephens drove north, he sifted through all the information Folkes had provided about Green. The discovery of the large bank account in Green's name and the use of Green's access codes to destroy the crypto files were damning enough. Added to that was Green's rare failure to track and catch his prey during the chase through Harvard. But intermixed as well were times over more than a decade he and Green had worked together. He remembered places they had been, and the hard times they had shared. And the one fact that stood out more than any other amidst the news from Virginia was that Stephens trusted Green.

It was a terrible contradiction. The conclusions, and the facts, simply didn't mesh. It was times like these that he would remember a phrase from Ayn Rand. "There is no such thing as a contradiction," she had her protagonist in *Atlas Shrugged* proclaim. "If you think you have one, then one of your facts is wrong." From years of experience, he knew Rand's observation was accurate. Many times he had revisited a contradiction, and re-examined his facts. This time, however, he could not see an error. The conclusion was that Green was the traitor. The contradiction was that Stephens was certain he could trust Green with his life. The test of Ayn Rand's premise would have to wait.

Stephens thought also about Kathy Whitworth. For the nth time he reviewed the events of the previous day, looking for the mistake he had made, or the missed sign that would have prevented the killing. He thought a great deal about the fire in her eyes as she had spoken about her beliefs.

The once beautiful, peaceful town of Peterborough was in its own way much like Cambridge. The image differed a great deal from the reality of the place. Perhaps, it is just another version of a common mold for all towns. The veneer of a town is different from place to place, but it is inevitably just a veneer. Once you can strip it away, you find the same patterns that exist everywhere.

The view west up Main Street in Peterborough encompassed many layers in the history of the town. At first, it was the idyllic setting for a postcard view of quaint New Hampshire. Next, it was a setting that helped inspire the writing of *Our Town.* Then, it was the scene that opened the old television series version of *Peyton Place.* At the top of the hill at the East end of Main Street was a house that had deteriorated from graceful old home, to nursing home, and then to apartments over just a few years time. Along the street you could see new buildings and growth that had profited the insiders who had then changed the laws to make sure they restricted future profit to themselves. The artist colony had receded in the face of industry. Peterborough had become the hub of the computer publishing industry. "Our Town" had grown up. Perhaps it had always been grown up, but had before been better able to hide the chips and cracks that lay beneath the veneer.

Stephens and Green had just hours to retrace Jim Peterson's steps. There were three obvious starting points. Stephens and Green would start with the Peterborough Police Department, and then would split up to cover the real estate records at the town hall and the clippings up at the Peterborough Transcript. On short notice, there had been little choice except to use the Walter Jones and Ken Kelleher aliases once again. The risk was significant that the two names had been broadcast to police departments in the Northeast after the Kathy Whitworth murder. But it would be impossible, without help from Folkes Farm, to create the supporting collateral for a new cover. To Stephens, contacting the people in Virginia seemed to be a very poor bet. They could only hope for local police inefficiency—that their descriptions were on an unread teletypewriter printout tacked on a crowded bulletin board.

"Chief Meltzer, thanks for seeing us," said Stephens as he and Green were shown into office in the back corner of the station. "We are concerned enough about Jim Peterson that we think we might have to file a missing persons warning."

Meltzer pointed at the phone. "You want me to get the forms?"

"Maybe later," answered Stephens, flowing easily to the explanation he had planned that would allow him to ask questions without starting formal procedures that might backfire when the police started to look at names. "One of the people back at B-G thinks he might have finally tracked Jim down. We'll know later this afternoon and can always file then, if still needed." Stephens saw the slight puzzlement he had expected to see on the chief's face. Over the years he had learned that the natural use of informality infused lies with more authority and credibility than any other artifice. "Oh, sorry. When you work for a mouthful like Bannik, Warren and Graves, you find B-G at lot easier to handle!"

"I can imagine," said Meltzer. "Now, as I understand from Sergeant Wilson, no one at your place has seen Peterson in the past three weeks. Why suspect trouble? Why not just a vacation, or an affair, or something a little less exciting?"

"That's what we all thought, at first. But a guy like Jim doesn't just disappear. He's too serious about his job."

"I remember Peterson," said the chief, looking into the distance. "I always thought he was a reporter, or something. Never would have guessed he was a lawyer."

"Why?" asked Green.

"Well, he asked about as many questions as a lawyer, but I swear that he said he was with the *Globe*."

"He was involved in some pretty secret corporate stuff," offered Green. "A Japanese company you'd recognize, if we were allowed to say the name, is looking at buying a company near here. We all had to sign nondisclosure agreements that allow them to cut off the portion of our anatomy of their choice if we discuss it with anyone. Maybe Jim figured that pretending to be a reporter was the easiest way to do his background checks and run bona fides on the company."

"Could be, but I don't remember any of his questions being about companies. You know, he must have spent a few hours right in this police station. Just about all of his questions were about the Jackson killing. A couple of us even took him to the site once."

"Jackson?" Stephens remembered the Jackson murder well. It was the lead story in the Transcript for several weeks, and a hot topic at Wendlandt Academy. But it would be difficult to explain how a lawyer from Boston knew so much about a local matter.

"Tom Jackson was a cop here for more than twenty years. Someone killed him. It was a pretty messy job, too."

"No suspects yet?"

"We still don't know." The chief's eyes tightened and his face hardened. He and Jackson had always been from the area. They had gone to school together in Peterborough. Both used to meet, as kids, to sit on the small porch of the old MacDowell cabin not far from the school. Both had set their hearts on the same girl, Janet Worcester, who had lived in the house just a few hundred feet from the cabin. Both had laughed together many times.

"Tom was a good man." Meltzer shook his head slowly. "Some bastard just killed him. We don't know any more than when it happened. Some hop-head, probably. Just blew off the side of his face. Then threw his body, like so much trash, into a rain ditch next to the road."

Stephens and Green kept silent after the chief's voice trailed off. After nearly a minute, when the chief turned back towards them, Stephens continued.

"I'm sorry, chief. It isn't hard to see that you and Officer Jackson must have been friends."

"Good friends. The best."

"Could there be a tie with our friend, Jim? It doesn't make much sense, but nothing in this does, so far."

Chief Meltzer nodded in agreement as he thought about the question. "Must say, you might be right. I don't see the connection, but Peterson sure spent a lot of time looking into the case. A friend of mine up at the Transcript said he read through just about all of the back issues going back a year or so."

"What was his reason?"

"Like I said, he just seemed to appear and fit in. After a few, days you just sort of got used to him being around and asking questions. He was an easy guy to get used to."

"We know," answered Green.

"The last day I did see him, now that I think about it, he was higher than a kite. Claimed that he was on the verge of something unreal. 'This will blow the socks off everyone back at my Company' was what he told me."

"What was he on to?"

"What was he *on* might be better! Not sure why I had a feeling your friend could help us somehow, but we took him up Sand Hill Road, where it turns off to Monadnock General, to see where we found the body. I was explaining that we found the body there, but Tom's empty car down on 202. Suddenly Peterson turned around and stared back at the road. 'Sand

Hill Road? Sand Hill Road?' He must have repeated it four or five times, like a question. Then his eyes opened wide, and he shouted it out. 'Sand Hill Road!' That's when he told me he would blow your socks off."

"Nothing more than that?"

"Nope. Nothing more, period. Said he was really sorry, and then ran over to his car and blew back down towards town. Christ, if half the Peterborough PD hadn't been on the site, at least one of us would have ticketed him somewhere along the way back for driving to endanger. Never saw him again." He looked over to the calendar. "That was three weeks ago, tomorrow."

"Any idea where he was going," asked Green.

"Matter of fact, I know exactly where he went. The Transcript. Scared the shit out of old Mary Webster in archives. She said he raced in like a crazy man, looked up some of the old issues he had been studying, and then raced back out. Don't know what happened from then, though."

Stephens and Green looked at each other. Stephens saw the almost imperceptible nod of Green's head. Chief Meltzer caught it as well.

"You know, for business lawyers, you two ask as many questions as your friend did. I get the distinct impression you both know more about the Jackson case than you let on."

"You're probably right," Stephens was the first to reply. "Both Ken and I started in criminal law. It's tough to put all the old suspicions and habits aside when you leave burglars for boardrooms," he said with an easy smile. "Even after ten years in mergers and acquisitions, I guess it's never far below the surface."

"One thing for certain, "Green added, "Walter and I will keep you informed. We'll give a call back to B-G and make sure they know we're going to have to fill you in on the Japanese, and anything else we discover."

"Frankly Ken," said Stephens, turning to Green, "I'm beginning to think the best bet is to turn this all over to the police. When we get out of here, let's find a quiet phone and call back. If they have nothing new, and we don't tumble onto anything with an afternoon's work, then let's submit a missing persons and head back to Boston."

"I think you may be right, Walter," said Green.

Both turned back towards the Chief and rose out of their chairs. The Chief remained seated, and stared at both of them. He crossed his arms and leaned back in his chair. Finally, he leaned forward and rested both forearms on the old wooden desk in from of him.

"Gentlemen, Tom Jackson was my friend. It's not easy sleeping nights with no answers for his wife and kids. And you guys leave me with an itchy feeling. Something with this Peterson, and with the two of you doesn't add up. Now I can't stop you from poking around a bit, but I can book you for obstruction in a minute. You find something, anything, you bring it right to me. No. Better than that, don't even wait that long. Call first to give me the basics, and then come over with the details. I'd hate to see you two disappear on me, like Peterson."

Outside the Police Building the sun was shining brightly. It was another warm, Indian summer day.

"Sand Hill Road mean anything to you, Harvey?"

"Nothing."

"Me neither. Not even a glimmer."

"You going to take the Transcript?"

"Yeah. Seems the best shot. At least it appears we *have* a shot, again. I thought everything was a dead end in this gig."

"I know," said Green. "I'll work through the records at the town hall. Real estate is probably the best bet. There might be something in permits."

"I'll drive down if I find something. Why don't you walk down to the Transcript if you finish first?"

"Deal."

Stephens had no trouble finding Mary Webster at the Transcript. He had even less trouble getting information about Jim Peterson. Mary enjoyed people, and talking to or about people. She was a fitting guardian of all the words stored in the archive section of the Peterborough Transcript.

"A computer? A Computer!" She laughed as she answered one of Stephens' first questions. "Why no. We're not that big yet. Not like the Sentinel over in Keene. Why they put a computer into their archives just last year. Bill Solo, Bill's the head of their archives. Well Bill told me it never worked right. He can remember things faster than the computer can find them. Most of the good stuff was never loaded. Well Bill . . ."

"Mary," Stephens interrupted, "I've got to come back and talk more with you. This is all so fascinating. But today I'm in a big rush. My boss, a real turkey, wants me to finish up all I've got to do by this evening. I need days here, and he expects me to do all this in hours."

"My boss is just like yours. They're all the same," Mary commiserated as she walked towards the drawers filled with microfilm. "You want the rolls from this summer," she said. "That was the stuff Jim wanted. Why, he spent days looking through must of been two hundred issues. All that time I don't think he found a thing."

She pulled out one drawer part way, stopped, pushed it back in and reached for another.

"Nope. It was this one. This is the one he was looking through when he let out that whoop."

"What was that all about?"

"Well, he came back here a couple days after Tom Jackson was found. Poor Tom. Always such a nice guy. About the only person who didn't think he was the greatest was Janet Worcester. Old Tom couldn't get anywhere with her." She placed the drawer next to the Kodak microfilm reader. "Anyway, after all that work he gave up. Then, a few days later he comes crashing through the door and runs right down here into archives. He didn't even stop at reception. Gail says he didn't even answer her. Just shouted 'Mary!' at the top of his lungs. I was over there in the utility room, so he didn't see me at first. Went right on yelling my name, and pulling drawers out to carry them over here to the Kodak. It took about an hour before he said anything again. He kept putting rolls on the Kodak, spinning them through, and tossing them aside to look at another. I got to tell you, when he was done, it took me most of the next day rewinding and organizing his mess."

"Did he tell you what he was looking for?"

"No. Not a thing. Just kept spinning rolls like a crazy person. Then he let out a whoop, wrote down some notes, and ran out as fast as he had come in. Never so much as a thank you! Never came back either."

"Why do you think it was this drawer?"

"It was the one out when he left. Most of the rolls were still in it. Just the first half dozen or so had been checked."

Each drawer contained forty rolls in two rows of twenty each. "My guess is that it was one of these," she said waving her finger over three or four rolls.

It took until just after four that afternoon, more than five hours after he had started, before Stephens realized that he had found what he was looking for. All through the afternoon he had looked at hundreds of articles, stories, obituaries, school notices, and even advertisements. It was a slice through the fabric of the town. Each of the rolls contained more than 800 frames, each frame representing a single page from the transcript. The four rolls Mary Webster had identified represented nearly six months of issues.

It was quiet in the archives that afternoon. The only regular sound was of Mary as she busied herself with an endless succession of disorganized tasks. She would flit to one bank of film to another, back to recent issues in paper format, and then to the camera. On those few occasions when Rob Stephens would pause to rub his eyes and stretch from the constant reading, he could see no method to her effort. No single task ever occupied more than a few minutes. Every task was attended to, and later re-attended to, many times during the day. All the while she would hum softly and intermittently. Throughout the day the tune was rarely other than the Beatles "Lonely Hearts Club Band."

Shortly before Stephens discovered the one key clipping that snapped all the random facts into a vital answer, he realized that there was a logical purpose to Mary's effort. In a job that rarely varied, where all was manual and by rote, she had found a way to give the illusion of variety to her work. She would never stay at any one task long enough for it to become boring. It infused a sense of purpose and control into a job that had neither characteristic on its own. In her own way, she had become a manager. She managed a phantom team of people throughout the day by making endless "decisions" as to what now had the top priority of all the assignments before her. The result at the end of a week might be a little less efficiency, but it made the sameness of the job bearable.

It was a small comment in the weekly "Our Town" column that provided the missing factor. It was a small thing, easily missed. But it linked all the random facts he had accumulated over the past days.

> It was a busy week for Beth Hogan up at Chambers Realty. According to Ken Chambers, "Beth might have some kind of sales record for Peterborough." Seems that Beth managed to sell five properties by Thursday, and still have a 7 pound 5 ounce baby son on Friday Morning! Ken seemed to be a bit

> surprised when she didn't show up for work again Saturday. "After all," said Ken, "The properties represented more than $1,750,000 in sales. I can't afford to have her lie around for the rest of the week!"
>
> For those of you who don't know Ken, he *is* kidding! Beth has worked up at Chambers for nearly fifteen years now. Some think Ken should long ago have given her a piece of the action. Beth doesn't seem so worried. "I make enough in commissions. I'd hate to have to take a pay cut if I became an owner."
>
> The biggest sale was the Patrick Building on Main Street. This is the fourth time Beth has sold this same property. In fact, her first sale as a realtor back in 1964 was the Patrick Building. She sold it to two local women who started a ladies fashion store. How many remember who were the first co-owners of the "Saltbox" store?
>
> She also sold the beautiful old Sand Hill Farm up on Pack Monadnock, complete with its forty acres, four buildings, pond, and countless white rabbits. The new Sterns Lane development saw three of their new homes sold. Two of these were side-by-side, sold the same day, on back-to-back visits! Her final sale was the Peterborough Lanes. Beth sold that to our own Ben Farnwald. Since Ben owns the Stearns Lane Development, Beth might have cashed three checks from Ben in one week.

As soon as he had finished the article, he knew it was important. He didn't yet know *why* it was important, but he knew for certain that the final piece of the puzzle was lying there in front of him. As was almost always the case, it was not some obvious new clue that did it. This time, as so often in the past, it would be a small thing, a trivial thing, or perhaps just a feeling that flagged that portion of his mind that had been silently trying to fit the pieces of the puzzle together. Invariably some invisible trigger would force him to stop, gaze into the distance, and then he would listen ever so carefully as though the answer would ultimately be heard rather than thought.

He reread the article again, slowly, trying to determine what was triggering those signals. He knew for certain that the pattern was about to snap into focus, but for several minutes it eluded him. Finally, as unexpectedly as the signal had come, he knew where the Falconer could be found. The pieces fit together. He understood Jim Peterson's last days and could appreciate the spycraft in the boy that had allowed him to find the Falconer, and that had led to his death.

"You did good, Jim," said Stephens silently, as he softly nodded his head in respect. "Damn good."

Over in the corner, Mary Webster had been watching him since he first had stopped. She too spoke silently to herself, but the thoughts were not of respect and admiration. "This one is as loony as they come," she thought. "Spends all afternoon going crazy with the Kodak, then goes into a trance. Dumb flatlanders!"

Chapter Fifteen

Within five minutes Stephens was back at the Town Hall. He parked in the lumber store lot across from the old movie theater, and walked the couple hundred yards to the Town Hall. He passed the drug store, with the old felt sign and white plastic letters in the window showing the lunch menu. He saw the "8OUP . . . $1.00" on the sign where so many years before a frugal, but clever, store owner had made up for a missing "S." Even the sign was subconsciously filed away in the back of Stephen's mind, perhaps to become part of some other puzzle, until dismissed and forgotten over time.

The town hall was small, and most of the upstairs was an open assembly area for town meetings and an occasional high school dance. In the basement were the town records and archives. Most of the planning and deeds offices were on the main floor. It was clear, after one pass through the old brick building, that Green was not inside.

"I'm looking for my partner," said Stephens to Royce Berry. The sign on Berry's old, scarred wooden desk identified him as Commissioner of Deeds for the town. He passed his calling card over the small wooden rail. "His name's Ken Kelleher, and I thought he'd be here looking through the old records."

"He left," answered Berry without looking up. He continued to leaf through a stack of old papers and paid no attention to Stephens' outstretched hand. Finally, when it was clear that the commissioner was unlikely to volunteer much, Stephens pulled back his hand and slipped the business card back into the side pocket of his jacket.

"He left?"

"Yup."

Again the conversation died.

"Mr. Berry?"

This time Royce Berry did look up. His lips were pursed together and he exhaled strongly through his nose to make certain that the stranger saw the annoyance. 'Too many new people in this damn town,' Berry thought. 'What does *this* one want?'

"What?"

"Mr. Kelleher?"

"I told you, he left." Berry motioned towards the door to the street with his head. "Took off with his two friends."

"Friends?"

"Yeah. The two guys that met him here."

"Met him?" One of the most effective probing techniques, when you had little to go on, was to repeat back a small part of the person's last sentence. That would prompt them into continuing while you looked for a pattern to better lead the questions.

"We'll, your friend was a bit surprised. They came in while he was reading through the transactions file. Didn't say much. Kelling just joined them."

"Did you hear where they were going? I was supposed to meet Ken here."

Berry shook his head side to side with irritation. "Mister, I never met Kelder before today. I don't know his friends. All I know is that one guy seemed more interested in me than in talking. Just stood by the door trying to peek at my work while the other walked over and met your friend. Now it wasn't my business then, isn't now, and frankly it's not likely to become my business."

Berry shook his head once again, and let out one final snort before returning to his records. The room seemed very quiet. Late afternoon sunlight streamed through the huge window on the far wall and outlined the dust on the wooden shadowbox around it. In a far room, there was the intermittent staccato of a typewriter. Stephens looked up at the clock on the wall. 4:06. It was late. Tomorrow the President would visit Boston. Stephens knew where the Falconer might be, but now Green was gone. As he pulled his eyes away from the clock and started towards the door, Stephens wondered just how late it really was. For the first time, he had the cold feeling that it was too late.

—~—

Outside the town hall there were six or seven cars backed up at the light where Route 202 intersected with Main Street. Even "little" Peterborough was starting to have signs of growth. Stephens stood on the wide granite steps and looked up and down the street. Instinctively he glanced at his watch. 4:11. 'No surprise,' he thought, remembering the clock back in the deeds room. As he stood there rapidly piecing together his ideas for the next steps to take, he almost missed the car as it passed him heading south towards route 101. Had the tinted passenger window been up, he would not have seen the long brown hair that lightly whipped against the outside of the car by the wind as Cynthia passed. She never looked his way.

Incredibly, despite standing there in the open, Stephens was certain she had not seen him. He almost called out, but even the shock at seeing Cynthia in the car did not overcome years of experience. Automatically he first took a quick look at the driver. The half-formed shout stopped instantly in his chest. He felt a part of his mind issue a succession of conflicting orders to squat down, or to freeze, or to run. He had ignored all those instincts, and was standing perfectly still, only turning slightly so that his full face was not easily seen. Above him, the town bells began to ring four times. Another part of his mind, like so many times before, was able to process the ridiculously incongruous thought that the town clock was two or three minutes late.

Stephens followed the progress of the car as it headed slowly away. It turned left towards the same place where Stephens had parked his own vehicle. As it turned, perhaps two hundred yards away, the side profile of the Falconer in the driver's seat was clear. Falconer looked straight ahead as he turned. His signal was on and he even stopped to let a child cross in front of the car. In back of him another car honked impatiently.

Stephens started down the right side of the street looking for a break in the cars that had started moving again once the light had changed. Half way to the turn he cut across, carefully dodging between cars, and walked quickly towards the corner. He slowed as he approached it the corner, looked down the street, and saw no trace of the gray Buick he was following. He knew that the street looped back up past the A&P and movie theater, and then past an old diner, until it came back to Main Street. It was clear that the Falconer must be parked in one of the two lots that lay within the next hundred yards.

Just past a bakery was the first of the two lots. It was the same one, opposite the old theater, where Stephens had parked. He walked slowly, carefully assessing the territory ahead and the few people walking in the area. He smiled and said "Hello" to the two ladies standing in the doorway of the bakery as he passed, never letting the words interfere with his total alertness. When he reached the end of the bakery, and the first parking lot started to pan into view, he saw the Buick parked on the far side of the lot in front of the lumber store. He could see the shadows of two people in the front seat of the car. They were facing each other and gesturing occasionally. He felt the coldness return. As he started down the side of the lot, screened by parked cars and the narrow row of decorative scrub pines, the cold was replaced by sadness. Stephens knew the hope that had been building about Cynthia Lebart had just died.

There were a dozen cars in the lot, and people would pass through the lot every minute or so on their way to one errand or another. He stood behind a row of trees that lined the right and left side of the lot. The lot had room for four rows of cars, two down the middle and one on each side. The Falconer had parked in the far left corner of the lot. Stephens would have to cross over the lot to reach him.

In the middle rows four vans were parked almost side by side. They were the only possible cover on the approach to the car. He worked his way up the right side of the lot, until the vans were directly between him and the Falconer. Then he stepped out from the trees and moved quickly past the first line of cars. He stopped when he was safely hidden between the two vans and could look through them to the car just thirty feet away. The silhouettes were still there, gesturing and talking.

"Damn you Cynthia," he thought as he reached inside his jacket for his weapon. "Damn you."

When he heard the sound of the electric window going down just inches from his side, and immediately after it the sound of a second, and then a third, he stopped with his hand just inside his jacket. He did not have to wait for a voice. Stephens stood perfectly still for several seconds looking straight at the ground. He dropped his empty hands to his side. He closed his eyes. Then he raised his head, opened his eyes, and looked almost straight up at the sky. He took in a deep breath, held it for a second, and then let it all out in a gush with his lips pursed like a half kiss. He heard the side door of the van to his right open, and only then did he turn towards the vehicle.

Stephens ignored the hard faces he saw in the van windows, with silenced weapons pointed directly at him. He didn't have to look inside to know they would be there. He ignored the sound of the car door opening, and then closing, thirty feet away. He ignored the sound of people walking through the parking lot with no idea that death was so nearby. He glanced only briefly inside the darkened van, and ignored the shadow of a man beckoning Stephens to enter. Despite all the noise of the town in the background, Stephens heard nothing else but the steps coming slowly up behind him from the direction of the car. Even in this wide open parking lot, with nothing to fear and only years of habit guiding the person approaching behind him, Stephens found the softness of the steps remarkable.

"In a way, I'm sorry," said the voice behind Stephens. It was a hard voice. There was no breath to it, just the words clipped and sharp. The silent figures within the van could not help looking at one another when they heard the undertone of respect in the voice. It was a tone they had never heard in the months of working for him. "You and I should have ended with honor, perhaps in some great endeavor. Not in this place. Not like this."

Stephens turned slowly around to face the Falconer. He had never been this close before. The eyes and the hooded look that so marked the man were clear. Yet, as Stephens studied his adversary of so many years, such trivial things seemed to surface. He saw that he was two or three inches taller than the Falconer, and was perhaps thirty pounds heavier. Falconer was lean, with a hardness of body to match his voice. He still had the baby face that had served him so well for so many years. There were the first threads of gray in Falconers hair, and lines around the eyes. Even at thirty-five life was hard on those like Falconer and Stephens.

"You expected me," Stephens said simply.

"Yes."

"This was simple, effective." Stephens gestured towards the surrounding vans. "There was just one way I could come. You knew that and planned well."

"Yes, old friend. You had just the one option."

Beyond Falconer Stephens could see the shape of Cynthia Lebart in the car. He wanted so much to call out to her, to understand what she had done. He thought of her, and Green, and all the false ends over the past few weeks. He thought how senseless all the past years now became, because of this one place and time. All the pluses added up to little, and this one big minus would offset them all. The Falconer would live, and the balancing factor of Stephens would be lost. Boys like Jim Peterson would have to become men too fast. And even while a part of his mind was examining and discarding endless possible schemes to change the facts, the rest of his thoughts were filled with bitterness. Stephens felt drained and tired. Inside it hurt very much.

"You had no chance, you know," said the Falconer. He alone of the ten people involved in the scene could understand exactly what Stephens had been thinking. "There is no one else who could have come this far, Stephens. I always knew where you were, and what you were doing. You should have died three times by now."

"New Ipswich was very close."

"What you did at New Ipswich should be taught to every new trainee at Folkes. But even they will not understand it. I think that even I might have died at New Ipswich, Stephens," he said simply.

"I assume we go to the Sand Hill house now?"

A small smile crossed Falconer's face. "Good! Very good! I told my lieutenants that you would work that one out. We were just in time here, then?"

"Just in time."

"You'd have paid us a little visit then," said the Falconer, nodding slightly as he thought of the prospects. "I would not like to imagine what might have happened had you the advantage of surprise."

"Green?"

"Later." The Falconer pointed towards the van. "Please. I'm sorry for the next part, but these sheep don't understand the wolf they beckon inside."

Stephens stepped up into the van. It normally held three rows of seats, but the middle one had been removed to leave free space. Once inside, while three men held silencer-equipped weapons pointed at him, a fourth pulled out four sets of handcuffs. Stephens was laid face up on the floor of the van. Carefully, never getting in the line-of-sight of the guards, Stephens' left hand was handcuffed to the bottom of the passenger seat and his right hand to the driver seat. Then the legs were tied to opposite ends of the rear bench. Finally, his head was covered with an old canvas sack. Then his weapon was removed, and his body was searched completely. It was not the quick frisk of television shows. The young man doing the search was very thorough. No part of his body was ignored. When complete, here was little chance he carried anything dangerous.

Only when he lay spread-eagled and helpless on the floor of the van did the guards ease up slightly. Even then they made sure that at least three, at all times, concentrated on Stephen's every breath. They had been very carefully briefed on this. "One week ago this man killed Maman, Henri, Stannik and Hochman. Gertmeyer and Mustaf just got away. Six against two in an ambush. Do not blink or this Stephens will disappear. Do not sneeze or he will quell the cough before it leaves your throat. And remember most of all, if there is one man who the Falconer might fear, it would be this Stephens."

Stephens could hear the first van pull out. Then his van drove away. It pulled slowly out of the lot and up to Main Street. At the end of Main Street the old house that opened the "Peyton Place" series looked down from the hill as the van passed below. They passed the stone Episcopal Church and the quiet houses beyond that lined route 202. A mile north of town they bore right, up Sand Hill Road.

As they were passing the site where Officer Jackson had been killed, Stephens was no longer thinking of the Falconer, or of Green, or of the President. He had stopped thinking of the bitterness he felt from betrayal. He no longer ran over the list of those back at Folkes Farm, along with Green, who might have been the one to betray him. He was no longer second guessing with horrible self-incrimination, all of his actions over the past few days.

Instead he pictured the gray Buick that would be just ahead, or just behind, the van. And he pictured, inside, the warmth of Cynthia Lebart. He could feel, again, the touch of her hand in the front hall of the Robbins home after the firefight. He could feel her soft body next to his, and the swell of her breasts as she tried to control her breathing, lying behind him on the floor when the attack first began.

Under the canvas bag his eyes were closed. "Damn you, Cynthia. Damn you."

Chapter Sixteen

At the top of Sand Hill Road, just before it turns east to pass over North Pack Monadnock Mountain and back down the far side towards Greenfield, is the entrance to Sand Hill Farm. It had been more than thirty years since any real attempt at farming had been made there. The place had become, paralleling the growth of Peterborough five miles down in the valley below, a very different place than it had started out to be. After many hard years of effort, attempts at farming had slowly ebbed away, giving in to the even harder realities of economics. The place had become a quiet country home. The rough barn had long ago been converted into a full outbuilding that included garage and work shed under and two big rooms over. A small guest house was built by one of the first families that followed the last of the farmers. Years later, the ramshackle chicken coop was leveled and replaced by a one room artist's studio. Still later, a small gazebo was built in the back of the house. One owner had bought three white rabbits for a daughter's fifth birthday. The rabbits had been let free long before she had celebrated her sixth, and in the thirty years since that time, in the way of all rabbits, the three had become dozens.

Sand Hill Farm had long ago completed its metamorphoses into a remote North Country estate. The fields were wild again. Its forty acres included miles of sheltered trails, endless stone walls, a gentle pond, and countless hidden glades in the pine forest. The main house was drafty, expensive to heat, and always a bit cold on winter nights. But the old farm had a charm and a location that somehow compensated for all that to each generation of new owners. It was perched on the side of North Pack Monadnock some 1500 feet over the valley, overlooking Peterborough and Dublin nestled below, and Mount Monadnock twenty miles to the west. It was a beautiful place, and few could escape its lure. The distance from the town afforded it a graceful seclusion that captivated each new owner. Only later would the price of that distance become apparent. Few realized until well after the purchase that the farm was far from any fire station, and no hydrants were possible at that elevation. The fire insurance surcharges, alone, put the costs of ownership beyond all but a few.

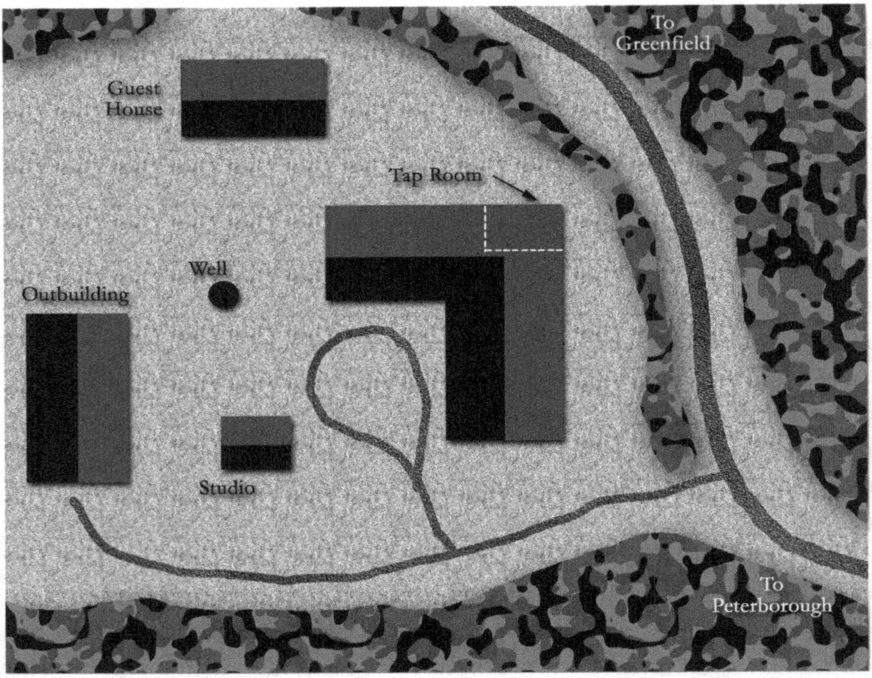

The four buildings that were the heart of the farm were concentrated on a two acre corner of the property a half mile from the road. They were clustered around the old well that provided the water for the home. The main house rambled around a series of fireplaces. In back of it was the small guest house. The outbuilding was to the left of the house.

The studio stood in the middle between the main house and the outbuilding. Any seasoned realtor would immediately recognize it as the selling "hot button." Few people exist anywhere who do not think they have at least the soul of a writer, if not the talent. Just one view of the studio had to stir visions of sitting warmly by the fireside while the cold winds of a long winter night swirled outside. It might be a vision of writing, or of reading in an easy chair, or of making love in front of the entrancing flames—or of whatever was that one vision buried deep in all of us that needs sanctuary and warmth to escape. The vision would inevitably come for anyone looking to purchase Sand Hill Farm. And the realtor would close the sale.

Few owners ever used the studio for long. The book they wanted to write was never found within themselves, or it turned out to be impractical to haul wood to get the fire started, or the long cold walk over was too much. Perhaps the romance was found to be one-sided. The lure of the studio was first relegated to the state of "something I really ought to do," then later ignored, and finally was forgotten. Within a year or so the reality of the financial burden to heat the drafty old house, and the costs for insurance and repair would add up. Pretty soon the house would be back on the market in favor of a more practical home down in the valley. One romance would end and the next realtor would bring up the next dreamer for the start of the next fantasy. It was an endless pattern. The people would flow and change. The house remained the only constant.

When the van pulled in next to the garage Stephens' hands were released from the seats and recuffed behind his back. The hood was removed from his head. Then his feet were released and he was led across the yard, past the studio, towards the main house. As he stepped out of the van, he saw the front door just closing some 200 feet away in front of him. The Falconer and Cynthia Lebart were already inside. It was nearing 5:30 in the early evening. At this time of the year it was already near dusk. On the lawn were tens of white rabbits casting long shadows in the late sunlight. The lawn was close cropped and had large bare areas from all the years of rabbit grazing. It was already cool. Stephens realized that the cold nights of fall were starting.

Inside the house he was led to the second of the two realtor "hot buttons" that usually captured the heart of any prospective buyer not already hooked on the studio. It was a large tap room at the rear of the house. The walls were rough-hewn timbers with small windows looking into the forest beyond. The high, vaulted ceiling had been built decades before the average homeowner had even heard the term "cathedral ceiling." A small balcony overlooked the room. In years past the room would be furnished with leather couches and deep easy chairs. Lamps would cast a warm glow in counterpoint to the glow from a fire. It would be a place to read, and to talk, and to laugh with family or close friends.

Now the furnishings were far more sparse. An inexpensive couch was pushed against the right wall of the room. Next to it was a single chrome floor lamp. In front of the fireplace was a round wooden table with four chairs. The fireplace was cold and empty. In one corner was a large pile of used newspapers. At this time of evening there was even less than the usual light from the small windows to assist the dim offering of the lamp.

There were just two people in the room when he was pushed through the door. He almost stumbled and turned around quickly, not in anger, but as a measured effort to see what level of response he might expect and how well trained were the guards. He was not at all surprised to find that they would have been quite ready for any such move, had he been at all serious. Two people stood behind him, about four feet apart, each with a handgun aimed coolly at his head. Six feet behind them was a third. The person directly behind him, the only one within reach, was unarmed. If he managed to jump the closest guard he would still be unarmed, would be holding a guard who had no weapon to use, while three others waited in perfect position handle any surprises.

Cynthia Lebart sat on the far end of the couch away from the lamp. She did not look up at him as he entered. Instead she sat with legs crossed, calmly using the rounded end of a nail file to push at the cuticles of her left hand. She glanced up only briefly as Stephens walked towards the table. Then, she calmly returned to her task. In the dim light at the end of the room the Falconer stood alone next to the table facing the mortar and fieldstone of the fireplace. When Stephens reached the table, the Falconer turned to face him. He pointed to the chair opposite the fireplace.

"Gertmeyer, please stay for the moment," he said as Stephens lowered himself into the hard wooden chair. "The rest of you may leave."

Hans Gertmeyer stood ten feet behind, and to the left of Stephens, intently watching the back of Stephens' neck. He was a huge man, with the look of an oversized football linebacker. His hand dwarfed the gun he held as he instinctively chose a position that left the Falconer out of the direct line of fire. Gertmeyer did not even think of asking for one of the vacant chairs.

The Falconer turned to where Cynthia Lebart sat on the couch. "Cynthia, my dear, why don't you go and make sure that we have arranged an appropriate place for Mr. Stephens. I would like a few minutes alone with him."

Cynthia Lebart looked up at the Falconer, and tightened her eyebrows as she formed a question. "Perhaps I could . . ."

"Not this time, my dear," Falconer interrupted. "Not this time. Maybe later. Please do as I requested."

Cynthia nodded twice and rose from the couch. Stephens turned at the start of the motion and looked directly at her. Her movements seemed so graceful to him. As she turned towards the back of the tap room her eyes swept past him, and then returned. For a handful of seconds, she locked her gaze to his. There were traces of anger, sadness, and what Stephens could only read as hurt intermixed in her eyes, but he could not decipher the message hidden there. Finally, she slowly closed her eyes, and then looked down and continued her way out the room. The faint trace of her perfume remained in the air after she passed.

When she had left, Falconer walked around to the back of the chair where Stephens sat, being careful to motion Gertmeyer to move so that he always had an unobstructed line to Stephens. He pulled a second set of handcuffs out of his rear pocket and connected one end to the cuffs holding Stephens' hands together behind his back. He attached the other end to the rail that joined the rear two legs of the chair.

"I'm sorry, Stephens. This is not good enough to hold one such as you. But it is enough to give one such as me enough time to be secure."

"I understand," said Stephens simply.

When the second set of cuffs was secure and Falconer was on the far side of the table, Gertmeyer left the room. The door at the far end closed with a solid thump. The room was very quiet. The scraping sound of the Falconer's chair, as he pulled it across the wide planks of the flooring up to the far side of the table, seemed unnaturally loud to both of them. The Falconer leaned forward, placing his elbows on the table in front of him, formed his hands into a position of prayer with his thumbs resting under his chin and his two index fingers on the bridge of his nose. The echo from the obtrusive sound of the chair faded away and was replaced by silence. Only the faint sound of the wind outside broke the quiet. Both men in the room studied the other. Neither had ever been this close before in all the years they had stood at opposite ends of the same events.

Stephens was the first to speak. "Where is Green?"

"He is fine."

"Fine?"

The Falconer ignored the question. "You know, I didn't expect to ever meet you again Stephens."

"Many of us thought you were dead."

"And you?"

"I hoped, but I was never sure."

"London?"

"Even Harvey was certain you died there. Back at ATQ they went so far as to close the files." A clear vein of irony entered his voice as he recalled the old Mark Twain line. "It appears reports of your death were somewhat exaggerated."

"Not by much. I should have died. I almost died. Instead I took a foolish risk."

"It worked."

"But, old friend, it's a risk I would no longer take," said the Falconer. "You did have me, you know. Had it happened today, then the ending might have been far different. I am older, and perhaps wiser. I would have just given in. There was no way out. Why die when there might always be a chance to change things later?"

"How did you get out? A part of me always knew you had, and in the past years I never found the answer."

The Falconer laughed gently and looked for a moment over Stephen's head and far into the past. Then he returned to the present. "I did a thing only a madman, or maybe one like you or I might do. Do you remember that jeweler's safe in the building?"

Stephens thought for a few moments. "No."

"There was a large floor safe, just big enough for someone my size to squeeze inside. I placed it near the window on the first floor. I used half a roll of tape to make sure the dial would not turn, and a piece of rope to hold the handle in the open position. Then I set the charge. I ran back to the window, saw Green outside and took a few shots at him, and then ducked inside and pulled the door shut. I could barely move. The blast blew me through the wall and two or three feet into the yard." He shook his head as he remembered the time. "I still find it hard to believe what I did. It was a desperate act. Do you have any conception of the number of ways it could fail? Since that time I must have thought of hundreds! The most obvious? What if it had fallen with the door down? How would I have ever lifted it open?"

Stephens did not answer at first. He could remember times when he, too, had been caught with only such an act of desperation between him and failure. "I have been inside your safe. Twice. My odds were the same as yours." He found himself asking the same question he had asked himself so many times in the years that followed. "Why did we live through them?" He looked up at Falconer. "Why are we always saved?"

"I don't know. Luck, perhaps. Or destiny. Fools and Englishmen. Or maybe that should now be changed to 'Falconer and Stephens.'"

The Falconer's voice had softened when he continued. He leaned back in his chair, and his eyes were half closed as he looked back to that time. "You know that Green still might have caught me. Before the explosion he was behind a trash bin about twenty yards from the house. The safe ended up a few feet away from the base of the house. When I first peeked out, half unconscious, there was Green right in front of me. He had moved up next to the building and was crouched part way up in the rubble of the destroyed wall. The safe had tipped over. It stood on its top with the door facing back towards the house. I was so groggy I could barely see straight. He never looked back my way."

The Falconer rose from his chair and walked over to one of the small windows. He looked outside at the darkening sky. The clouds were swirling and building, and the winds blowing from the northeast had increased over the course of the afternoon. The clouds were laden with the moisture they had picked up over the ocean just fifty miles away. It would be a hard night. Rain was almost certain.

"I almost killed Green then, you know," he said softly. He felt a bond with the angry night skies outside the window. "I had the door slightly open and had him in my sights. It would have been so easy. I remember it so well. I remember knowing, really *knowing* that I could take him out, and maybe even you. God, what a feeling." He turned away from the window and pointed with his right hand at Stephens. The other hand was clenched tightly at his side with the intensity of the memory. "Do you have any idea what that was like? Can you imagine how close I was to doing it?"

Stephens did not answer immediately. The dark silhouette of the Falconer against the window dominated the room. He remembered how he had felt back then, being so close. In his own mind he could see the same scene, but in his the person in the safe was himself, and the broad back of the Falconer was the easy target a few feet away.

"Yes. I can. Why didn't you?"

"I almost did. I swear the trigger was half way back. But then I realized that I had an incredible opportunity. I could die! I could disappear. All that I wanted to do would now be possible. Finally, I would have the chance to achieve this thing, tomorrow!"

The Falconer moved close to Stephens. He leaned slightly over him, his eyes wide with the intensity of his feelings. "You see, I knew even back then about tomorrow. I didn't know the time, or the place, but I knew this time would come. And then, right then, I knew it was finally possible. I could disappear, and wait, and prepare! I could . . ."

The Falconer had both fists clenched by his own face. He stopped in mid sentence, slowly let the air back out of his lungs, and dropped his hands. His features softened. "I'm sorry. I got going there, didn't I?" He stepped back and returned to his chair, letting out a small laugh as he sat down. "When this is over perhaps there are things I might share with you. But this isn't the time."

Stephens pulled slightly at the cuffs. He wanted to see if there was any play or give in them. The basic idea of a simple plan was forming. If there was some play in the cuffs, and if he could get the Falconer as agitated once again, there might be a small chance. The Falconer caught the slight movement. He smiled slightly and gently shook his head side-to-side twice. Stephens discarded the half-formed idea.

"So I didn't shoot," continued the Falconer. "If you were to find Green with a bullet in the back after the blast, it would not have escaped you that I must be alive. So, when Green moved into the mess to investigate, I crept away. No one was looking my way. By the time you were in the middle of searching the area, and long before any help arrived, I was well on the way out of the city."

"You just disappeared? Nothing since then?"

"Nothing. I waited all those years for the right time and place. No one, not any of those few who used to know me, had any idea I was alive. Not even your 'Kingmaker,' because Arafat himself did not know!"

Stephen's face showed nothing of the reaction churning inside when he realized that the Falconer not only knew of the ATQ's most secret asset, but also the mole's internal code name. There were less than a dozen people in the entire Agency who even knew the name Kingmaker. Only five were cleared for any of the details. If the Kingmaker was not a secret, then anything within the Folkes Farm complex would be an open book to the Falconer. The reason for all of the dead ends and failures over the past days became just a little more clear. The brief slip by Falconer shortened the list of potential moles back at ATQ considerably. The traitor had to be one of the five. In his mind, the list was altered. Only the names of Bradford, Green, Patterson, Sanders and Jacobi remained.

"It's pretty clear that at least one person knew about you," Stephens said, masking the bitterness that had sprung up again at the futility of his efforts to retrace Jim Peterson's steps. "You obviously had help the past few days. How long have you had someone inside ATQ? Years? As far back as London?"

Falconer laughed. It was genuine laughter, shared with Stephens. "Once again I underestimate you, Stephens. A simple slip and you start to put things together. I must be more careful, then!"

"Does it matter anymore?" Stephens pointedly looked down over his shoulder in the direction of the cuffs. "I don't seem to be much of a danger anymore to whatever you're planning."

"Perhaps, but I'd like to learn a bit from you before I answer your questions."

"Just one question, then. How did you know about the girl, Kathy Whitworth? Why did she have to die?"

"She might have been able to point you to this place. I don't think she had any idea what she knew, or how important her knowledge was, but she did. I managed to learn that from Peterson before he died."

"I had little hope he was alive. By the large maple at the Robbins place?"

"Very good! Very good, indeed." There was a great deal of respect in the Falconer's voice. "That one would not be easy to piece together from the facts. But yes."

"Peterson did well. I never met him."

"You should have, Stephens. You should have. If that boy had become a man, he would have been the equal of you and me. He somehow put it all together, tracked me down, found me, and even escaped. He was a worthy adversary, a remembrance of me years ago."

"But you still had no problem killing him."

"There was little pleasure in that one. I did what I had to do. The boy had already spent time with Gertmeyer, and Hans had gone too far too fast in trying to find out what the boy knew. He must have been half dead already when he jumped out of a car at better than 50 miles per hour. The fall ripped up his body even more. Still, he found the strength to jump, and the courage to lead us through the woods. Stephens, the boy lost the rest of them. What did he have? Two or three years? A class one? Two? He eluded all three of us for more than an hour. He almost made it. When I finally did track him down, the life was out of him. And the old man had found him."

"So Robbins had to die, too."

"In a strange way those two were intertwined that day. They were much alike, you know. Each was a slice of the same person at different times in their lives. Both were worthy of us, Stephens. Such deaths might be necessary, but they should never be taken lightly."

"Perhaps like the death of one of us, by the other?"

The Falconer did not have to answer. Both he and Stephens knew how the scene between them had to end. The room seemed cold. The last rays of the late afternoon light had disappeared. Only the single lamp partially opened the darkness of the room. Both faces were partly in shadows, accentuating the hard lines, and the soft caves around their eyes.

"The girl, Whitworth? Only Green and I knew we planned to see her."

"Oh yes, Green again. He certainly is at the heart of these things, isn't he?"

"Did he tell you about the girl?"

"He didn't have to. You did. I always knew every step you took."

The Falconer looked towards the back of the room. "Gertmeyer!" he called. The door opened instantly and the big man swung quickly into the room in a crouch, with his weapon pointed directly at Stephens. Behind him could be seen the edge of a second face, and the barrel of another weapon, peeking past the door frame. Only when he saw the Falconer's hand upraised, and saw for himself that Stephens' hands were still handcuffed to the chair, did he straighten up. He did not lower the weapon.

"Yes, sir?"

"Please have Brinks bring Stephens' gun."

When the weapon arrived, the Falconer removed the magazine and insured that there was no shell in the barrel. Then he removed the shells from the magazine. He handed the shells to Brinks.

"You see, Stephens, your weapon is empty." He turned to the two men. "Please leave again. This weapon is of no danger here."

They were alone in the room again. The Falconer walked around the table to Stephens, holding the gun's magazine in his hand. "I only had to know roughly where you were. When I needed an exact location, I just asked this where you were!"

The Falconer noted with satisfaction the quizzical look on Stephens. He held the magazine out and turned it from side to side so that Stephens could easily examine all parts of it. "Nice, huh?"

"It always served me well."

"This one served *me* well!"

"You lost me."

"Your magazines were all replaced, Stephens. These are just like yours, except for one small detail. These let me trace you. Even you would not find the difference."

"A bug?"

"A homing signal."

Stephens stared at the magazine. He thought back to the time at New Ipswich, and realized that he had carried the weapon during the middle of at least two sophisticated bug sweeps. It was next to impossible that the caliber of equipment available to a full field sweep team would miss a homing transmitter. "Unless," he thought, "it was only on when demanded."

"Triggered?" he asked, testing the one possible explanation.

"Yes."

The transmitter used an incredibly simple, but effective concept. It was designed to never transmit unless it first received a signal. Based upon the signal it received, if the first pattern exactly matched a preset code series, and then it would send out a single brief pulse on any of 256 frequencies indicated by the second part of the message. It was almost undetectable. In receive mode, it operated at such little power drain that the battery could last for more than a year. Transmitting used much more power, but it was usually good for at least a few dozen transmissions. In the hands of someone like the Falconer that was more than enough to do the job.

Stephens felt the bitterness churn upward in his stomach again. "I made it easy, didn't I," he asked softly.

The Falconer looked at Stephens. When he answered, there was a measure of gentleness in his voice. "No, Stephens, another made it easy. Only you could have gotten as far as you did. One such as you deserves better friends. But there are those, perhaps most, who measure friendship only in terms of gains and losses. Their measure of friendship is always in terms of the *future*. They can only ask, 'does what I expect in the future justify my effort in the present?'" He sat back in his chair. "But you and I measure friendship only in terms of the past. The future is irrelevant. A friendship, once earned from the past, can never be changed by events, real or anticipated, in the future. It is a commitment that, once made, knows no deadline."

The room was quiet. Even the wind outside had died down. For that moment, the two inside the room had put all of the present and past aside. Each recognized the cruel irony that, for each of them, the enemy on the other side of the table might be the only person capable of understanding the snakes in each other's mind, and the forces that drove them. What counted, briefly, were only the shared paths they had chosen in their lives. Each could look back over two decades and see so many of the same visions. Each could remember the same fears, and once, the same hopes. As they looked into each other's eyes, they both saw reflected there the same emptiness that they each knew inside.

"Have you had friends, Falconer?"

"Some. No," he corrected himself. "Few. Some might have been so, had times been different."

"You and I have seen so many die over the years. Perhaps it was better to have not made them than to have to bear their death."

"You killed some who might have been mine."

"And you, mine."

"But, Stephens, we did what we had to do. Did you ever doubt that we were right?"

"The times were different. We were so young. Dying seemed more noble, back then."

A genuine smile crossed the Falconer's face. "I was right, all these years. You and I are much the same, Stephens. You understand that, don't you?"

"Yes, I always did," Stephens answered, with a portion of the same smile forming. "Now we are both older, and the things we did as children seem so foolish." The smile turned into a quiet laugh. "I don't suppose you ever knew about Star Trek?"

"No. When did that happen? Beirut?"

Stephens laughed again, longer this time. "No, see how hard it is for you and me to leave behind what we are? You try to remember a code word, or a place from our past. I am asking about a television show, nothing more."

"Star Trek?"

"Well, perhaps you know about our westerns then? Good guys, bad guys, shoot-em-ups." He saw the Falconer's nod. "Good. Well I remember one show when the two enemies have a showdown. Only it was in space instead of the street outside the saloon. It was a great battle, and the two captains fought heroically, and gradually earned the respect of each other. Then the good guy finally won. The bad guy is about to die, and he looks at the good guy. 'We are alike, you and I' he said. 'In a different reality, we might have been friends.'"

The Falconer did not answer. He looked back at Stephens, his head tilted slightly to one side, his lips pursed together. The wind had picked up again and the rain had started. There was the gentle drone of raindrops on the roof of the tap room, and every so often a gust would blow the rain against a row of windows in an insistent plea to enter the room.

"There is only this reality," he finally answered, with sadness clear in his voice. "No amount of wanting can change that."

"I know."

"Stephens, old foe, you know I need to find out what you know."

"I figured that," answered Stephens simply. "That is part of this reality."

"I don't suppose you would simply tell me?"

Stephens only shook his head.

"No. Of course not. You know, I'm not sure which answer I would have preferred. With a 'yes' I would have been disappointed. It would have meant you were other than I thought." He motioned to the door. "But, a 'no' means I must send you out with Gertmeyer, there. You know what that means? We have little time. I do not have the luxury of friendly persuasion."

"We both knew that when I entered this room."

The Falconer stood up slowly and started towards the door at the back of the room. He stopped half way around the table. At first, he just looked down at the dusty floor. Then he turned back to Stephens. "You know, I knew you were at Wendlandt," he said very softly. "I even came there once and saw you. You were talking to some school kids. I had come to kill you. You were a potential danger, a risk I could not afford."

Stephens' face did not change. "I envied what I saw, Stephens. You seemed to be at peace. For the only time in my life I walked away from a killing. That could not be the place. Do you understand?"

"Yes, I do Falconer," he answered. Then even Stephens was surprised with his next question. "Falconer, what is your name? None of us ever knew."

"None did. It has been so long since I used it that there are none left who know it. The last name no longer has any meaning. It is dead with ties to no one living. The Falconer is good enough now. But I will tell you my first. It was Lehar. For other than you that does not exist, either."

"Lehar," Stephens repeated. "Lehar. I'll share one thing. I do not believe that name appeared anywhere in any of your files."

"I know."

"You've seen your file?"

"Yes."

The rain was coming down hard now. It was easy to hear the rushing sound of the water flowing in the down spouts.

"Before you go for Gertmeyer, can I ask you one thing, Falconer?"

"Of course."

"I think that maybe I finally know what you and I were all about. Do you think we were put here as a counterbalance? Could it be that all we were meant to accomplish was to cancel each other out?"

"Like good and evil? Yin and Yang?"

"Yes."

"I don't know."

Chapter Seventeen

It was cold on the walk back across the yard to the outbuilding. The two guards followed on either side of Gertmeyer and Stephens. Gertmeyer held Stephens roughly by the arm. It was not for guidance. Stephens now needed support to be able to walk. Gertmeyer had set the tone for the rest of the night as soon as they had stepped outside the front door. Without warning he had violently kicked Stephens on the side of the right knee with the hard point of his boot. The knee immediately buckled, and Stephens twisted and collapsed on the lawn. Without waiting, Gertmeyer immediately launched another vicious kick to Stephen's left side. The sound of a rib cracking was clear in the night air.

"That is for New Ipswich, asshole. And the second just for general principles, because I don't like you."

Gertmeyer reached down, grabbed each side of Stephens' jacket, and then easily lifted him up until Stephens' face was an inch from his. Stephens' feet were dangling a few inches over the ground. Gertmeyer did not even have to strain to lift the half-unconscious body. When the two noses were nearly touching, with Gertmeyer's eyes wide open with rage and Stephens half closed with pain, Gertmeyer spat into Stephens' face. The spittle was foul smelling, of cheap chewing tobacco, and the bits of food ever between his teeth.

"That is just a down payment. Here's a bit more, on account. A preview of what is to come."

Gertmeyer lowered Stephens slightly before bringing his knee up with all the force he could gather, aiming above the groin to land in the abdomen. He dropped Stephens, letting the body fall limply to the ground. Stephens' mouth was wide open, gasping, trying to suck air into his starved lungs. He tried to fight back the fingers of fire that were running through his body. The small part of his mind that he still mastered let him fight for control of his body. He knew that he had to fight the terrible vacuum in his lungs by willing himself *not* to breathe, so that the muscles in his abdomen would stop their spasms. Then, in small steps, he would be able to take in air. At first a teaspoon, then a tablespoon, then a slight breath, and then finally a gasp until he was back in control of his lungs. The cold night air was his ally. It could not stop the fire in his side or give strength back to his leg. But the cold's bite came through the other sensations, and gradually helped him claim wider and wider portions of his mind.

It took nearly a minute before he was able to painfully roll up onto his hands and knees. He remained there with his head hanging down. Stephens knew that if another kick were to come, whether it be now or later, there was nothing in him left to stop it. All he had been able to do was turn as he got up so that the side with the broken rib was opposite the huge man towering over him.

The kick did not come. Gertmeyer reached down, and with one big hand grabbed the back of Stephens' jacket and pulled him to his feet. "You can walk, or I can kick you across the yard." Stephens, facing the opposite way, could not see the twisted smile on Gertmeyer's face. "I would rather you walk. I'd like to save a little of you for the real fun."

At the end of their walk the four men entered the door in the center of the outbuilding. Once inside, you could turn left through a door into the garage, go right into a large work shed, or go up the set of stairs that split the building. At the top, a landing led to two rooms on either side. Stephens was led, half dragged, up the stairs into the room on the left over the garage. Inside, a steel chair was waiting along with a small pile of rope and pieces of lamp cord. Against the wall was a row of black fifty-gallon chemical drums with yellow tops. Despite all around him, Stephens instinctively filed away the contents of the blue and white label in his memory.

While the two guards watched, Gertmeyer removed Stephens' jacket, shirt, shoes, and pants. Gertmeyer handled Stephens with no more effort than if he were playing with a limp rag doll. At one point, he easily lifted Stephens up on his shoulder so that he could pull off Stephens' pants. Finally, when Stephens was down to undershirt and shorts, he was thrown onto the chair. The chair was solid steel, made years ago by one of the prior farm owners. The gutted seat of an old tractor had been bolted to a piece of steel plate for a base. It was a frugal, typically Yankee use of an inoperative old tractor to build a sturdy chair for the shop downstairs. The cold, hard metal cut into Stephens back and shoulder blades and his head whipped back with the force of the fall.

Gertmeyer picked up a handful of the lamp cords and tossed them to the base of the chair. He squatted down on the right side of the chair, reached out his hand, and clamped it around Stephens' neck with the thumb just a bit off center on the esophagus, and the other four fingers at the back of the neck. Stephens knew that the power of those hands would be enough to crush his throat.

"Try. Just once. Please try," said Gertmeyer as he used the other hand to make a slipknot in the cord around Stephens' right wrist. "Maybe you could get away. Maybe I wouldn't be fast enough. A swift kick would surprise me, maybe?" He laughed as he finished wrapping the cord around the arm of the chair. Then he repeated the process, after switching hands, on the other. When both hands were secure, he let go of the neck and completed the job. First he tied both legs to the bottom of the chair, taking pleasure in pulling the cords until he saw the pain just beneath the surface of Stephens' control. Then he took another loop and tied it around the top of Stephens' neck. He walked around behind the chair, and without warning yanked the cord back and down, tightening it at the same time. He pulled the cord taught and slipped it through a hole at the base of the chair. He then pulled it even more, until Stephens' head was stretched back, staring at the ceiling, stomach pulled out away from the chair.

Finally, he took one last cord and looped it around Stephens' waist. "This is my own special touch. Enjoy breathing? Well, just watch how these two cords fight each other. If either is loose, all is fine. But if I tighten both, then even the mighty Stephens must fall. The one on your neck is already tight. Let's play with the stomach one."

Gertmeyer pulled the cord to force the stomach back into the chair, fighting the opposite pull of the cord around Stephens' neck. Now Stephens could barely breathe. Either the cord around his neck or the effect of the cord constricting his stomach would have been enough to make breathing difficult. The combination of both nearly stopped his breathing, and made only rapid shallow breaths possible.

"The Falconer has a couple questions for you." Gertmeyer stood behind the chair, looking down at Stephens' face. "I don't suppose you'd like to volunteer anything before we start?" Stephens did not answer. He concentrated on shallow breaths that never seemed to satisfy his lung's need for air.

"No? I didn't think so. So, now it's time to explain this chair." Gertmeyer's face seemed unreal to Stephens. It was leaning over his, but facing the opposite direction. He was looking straight up at the man's mouth. "Well, about now you should be finding that breathing is not so easy. You can breathe, but can't seem to get ahead. Your body needs air more than anything else." He laughed. "You can go for weeks without food, and even days without water. You can lose your eyes, your ears, or most anything else. But lose the ability to breathe for more than a few seconds and your body goes crazy. Every muscle does whatever it can to get air. The brain goes a bit crazy. You see and hear things that aren't there. It invents terrors you cannot believe just to make you gasp for air."

Gertmeyer reached his hand down and placed it over Stephens' mouth. He waited that way for more than a minute, saying nothing. Stephens knew what was happening. Despite his crudity, Stephens saw that Gertmeyer was good at this. He was delaying for much the same reason they never show you the monster until late in a horror film. The viewer's mind is always able to create a demon far scarier than the film version that ultimately surfaces. Stephens found himself thinking about Jim Peterson, and wondering if Jim had preceded him in this chair.

Gertmeyer smiled, and shifted his hand slightly so that his thumb and index finger could close off Stephen' nose.

"The beautiful thing about this is that your body can recover faster, once it gets air again, than from loss of food or water," said Gertmeyer. Even though Stephens had closed his eyes, Gertmeyer had no doubts about the reaction starting in the body on the chair. "Why, we can do this again and again. I can let your own body try to destroy you, then just remove my hand, wait a few minutes while you recover, and then start it all over again."

Stephens' body was already starting to move under the control of the motor reflexes that control living. His abdominal muscles began to shake as they desperately tried to suck air into his starved lungs. His upper chest began to ache and press as it tried to extract more oxygen from air already exhausted. The tightness spread slowly up into his neck, then his head, until it seemed his sinuses would explode. His shifted his body right and left, trying to break the grip. The cord on his neck pulled tighter with each movement, cutting into the side of his neck where the knot pressed against the skin. His wrists began to bleed from the force of his movements. The cord in his stomach pulled so tight that even with Stephens' lean body the skin on each side of the cord enveloped it. Finally, he could see nothing except incredibly bright flashes of light, and could hear the screaming sound of what seemed like thousands of mad eagles. There were no heroic thoughts as he passed out. His only thought was that if the hand would leave his mouth he would be able to breathe. There was no other feeling, except the pressure of that hand covering his face, and the roar of the train crashing through the walls of his skull.

Gertmeyer, from all the experience gained over years of using this approach, knew exactly when Stephens passed out. He immediately removed his hand. Then he quickly reached down and loosened the cord around Stephens' middle, and began to give mouth-to-mouth resuscitation. When Stephens came to a few moments later, his first sensation was of the foul smell of Gertmeyer's breath entering his own body.

"Well, looks like you made it," said Gertmeyer as he pulled away. "This might not be good news, but I assure you I've never lost a guest doing this. Some might've wanted to die, but I always bring 'em back." He leaned forward until his face was just over Stephens. There was a condescending smile plastered on his face. "You see, asshole, we can do this for hours. I can put you into hell, and then bring you back out, as often as I like. What do you think? Anything clever pop to your mind?"

When there was no answer, Stephens saw the smile of genuine enjoyment on Gertmeyer's face. Gertmeyer squatted down and tightened the cord around his middle again. Then he asked the two guards to leave.

"You know, there are endless combinations of this idea. Let's try a personal favorite." He reached into his shirt and pulled out a package of Camels. He pulled on out, lit it, and spoke through the gap to the left of the cigarette. "Breathing is hard, but can you imagine coughing? Coughing with no breath, and little room to move?"

Gertmeyer pulled the cigarette out of his mouth and held it next to Stephens' nose. The hot ashes fell off and burned his upper lip. Gertmeyer smiled, and touched the end of the cigarette to the small spot where the ashes had fallen. Stephens jerked his head violently to the side with the pain, only to rip the cord into his neck. Gertmeyer smiled again with satisfaction, and then reached out his other hand to cover Stephens' mouth. Now the purpose of the cigarette became clear to Stephens. With all of his breathing concentrated through his nose, it was easy for Gertmeyer to channel all the smoke into his lungs. The impact was far worse than before. His lungs, just barely holding their own to start with, couldn't handle the smoke. Between the smoke and the slight ashes drawn into his nostrils, he began to cough, vainly trying to discharge air when there was not enough in his lungs for a cough. His body arched and fought the cords, and the pain of the cords played counterpoint to the cry of his body for clean air. Despite constant heaving, the muscles of his chest lost the ability to draw air. The lights came, and the screaming sounds, and mercifully the darkness.

It took longer this time for his eyes to re-open. Again the first sensation was the foul smell of Gertmeyer's breath. "Well, welcome back Stephens. The great one, Stephens. Well, you don't seem quite so great to me. You're just a naked little man tied to a chair. Still don't want to talk? Well, time for a new game."

During the next hour, Gertmeyer tried all of the variations of the basic concept he had ever used before. At one point he almost lost Stephens. Gertmeyer had to untie him, lay him on the floor, and work for more than five minutes before he was certain that Stephens would recover. After he retied him in the chair, he went outside to where the two guards waited.

"This one is a devil," he had said, spitting onto the grass. "The little shithead is a hard one, I'll grant him that. I've never had anyone go this long. Shit, I may have to use the battery bit. 'F' will kill me if I don't get the crap he wants out of Stephens, and he'll kill me if I screw up and kill him. Asshole."

"Calling Falconer an asshole can be hazardous to your health," said one of the guards.

There was real fear in Gertmeyer's voice when he instantly answered. "No! No! I meant Stephens. I didn't mean the Falconer. You wouldn't say I meant 'F,' would you?"

"No, of course not," answered the other guard with pleasure. Gertmeyer was now the Falconer's right arm since Maman had died in New Ipswich. He was the one Falconer would send to enforce discipline, when needed. "Just remember, you owe us. Keep that in mind next time Falconer asks you to handle a problem with us."

When Gertmeyer returned to the room, Stephens was partially alert in the chair. The cords around his middle and his neck had been removed. He was secure in the chair, but now he could breathe. Stephens knew that he was on the verge of either talking, or dying. His whole body ached with stabs of pain. His head hurt terribly from the lack of oxygen to his brain.

Both wrists and ankles were bleeding freely now. His stomach was raw, and the side of his neck burned fiercely from where the knot had been.

He knew that he was at the end of his ability to survive. Even if he wanted to talk, he knew next to nothing about the Falconer's plan. He knew it would happen tomorrow, would involve the President, and that was about all. The President would arrive early in the morning, just after rush hour traffic. He would be out of the city by noon. About all Stephens knew for certain was that something would happen involving the President between 9:00 and 12:00 the next morning. He had lost all track of time while in that room. He had no idea it was just after 10:30 p.m., and the President's arrival was less than eleven hours away.

With black humor Stephens was able to appreciate the irony of the situation. The Falconer wanted to find out how much he knew. He actually knew nothing. But he couldn't let even that out. If the Falconer knew that his plans were unopposed, then nothing would stop him. The one small hope was to convince Falconer that he was protecting vital information so that Falconer might delay his plans. It was a tiny possibility, but the only one left. It meant several more hours with Gertmeyer, unless he could goad Gertmeyer into a mistake that ended the session. The trick was to end it, without ending it permanently.

"That's hardly any hope at all," he thought. "Hardly any hope at all."

Stephens had no false illusions that he could hold out "until dying a brave death." That was the stuff of stories. With professionals who know the darker side of spycraft, there is no possibility of holding on to secrets anymore. There are chemicals, or ways of producing degrees of pain that the mind cannot fathom, that eventually break through any barriers. You could only stall for time, and trade off pieces of your body, or of your mind, for the precious time you bought. The real masters of spycraft did not learn to withstand pain, they learned to avoid it.

"Welcome back," Stephens said to Gertmeyer as the man walked back into the room. "Time to dance again?"

Gertmeyer stopped by the door. His forehead tightened. "Dance? You call this dancing?"

"This is something new, at least. It's even worth a brief write-up in my report," he said with disdain, beginning his plan to bait Gertmeyer. "Something for the boys back at Virginia to add to rookie orientation lessons."

Gertmeyer threw the cigarette down and violently crushed it into the tile floor of the room. "You ain't gonna be writing reports anymore, shithead," he snarled, as he strode over towards one corner of the room. "You won't be writing, reading, or even thinking all that clearly when I finish."

When Gertmeyer returned to the chair, he had a large automobile battery held under one arm. The smile of triumph had returned. "That kid didn't take well to this. This is when we learned just about everything we needed from him." He rested the battery on the floor next to the chair. Then he picked up another loose piece of lamp cord, and carefully attached one end to the two terminals of the battery. The cord was about four feet long. Gertmeyer stood up and held the two ends out if front of him. He leaned towards Stephens, and quickly brushed the two ends together. The electricity from the battery arced across the gap with a bright flash and the hot snap of the miniature lightning. The smile on Gertmeyer's face became a grin. He let one of the leads dangle safely to the side so that his left hand was free. Then he reached out, and with one quick pull ripped the undershorts off Stephens.

"Yup, this generally gets your attention. You know the old saying, don't you Stephens?" he said, leaning forward, nose-to-nose to gloat. "People come around when you've got them by the balls!"

This was the small opportunity Stephens had been waiting for. "Shit, here goes," Stephens thought. "Hell of a way to stop this."

The roar of laughter was choked off immediately when Stephens spat directly into the face gloating so near his own. Gertmeyer's face became red and his eyes bulged with rage. He took one fast, deep breath before his free left hand swung in a vicious hook to crash into the unprotected side of Stephens' face. Stephens never had the opportunity to take satisfaction in the success of his idea before he was knocked unconscious. He never knew the Falconer had run over to the outbuilding immediately after getting Gertmeyer's report. He would have been the only one there who would understand why the Falconer did not even bother to punish Gertmeyer.

"You fool, Stephens," he would have heard the Falconer say to the form slumped in the chair. "You damn fool. You'll be out cold until it's too late. Gertmeyer didn't have a chance. He had no idea the price you'd pay to keep silent."

There were clouds and mist in his dream. He could feel the wind gently caressing his cheek, and could smell the wildflowers that he so loved on Mount Monadnock. The view from Emerson's Chair was transformed into one of the loons dancing on the lake at dawn. Then it changed into another place, a welcoming place, where all he could see was the ghost of Cynthia Lebart floating gracefully before him.

"I love you, you know," Stephens said to her in his dream. "I never had the chance to say that to you."

The vision reached out a hand, and he could see traces of tears in the vision's eyes. "Sshhhh," she said. "Don't talk. Don't try to talk."

"But I have to, Cynthia. How can I let this, like so many other things, be left unsaid. Too many things unsaid. Too many lost years." In his dream he smiled, and was at peace. "I've known since New Ipswich. But I never thought I would be able to say it. I love you."

The vision leaned forward towards him. Through the gossamer of her ghostly gown he could see the soft curves of her body. He reached out and held her, drawing her into his arms. She seemed to flow into him, filling the nooks and corners and all the emptiness inside him. He felt her breath on his face, and then the soft touch of her lips on his. When he felt her body against his, and the power of her touch sweep through him, all the pain in his past seemed different. He could remember all the years of forcing tears and emotions back out of sight. Now he felt safe as he saw those same tears, this time of happiness, waiting just a small distance behind his eyes.

In the dream, for a moment he remembered the last time a woman had said she loved him, and the terrible pain and questions that had followed when she had gone. All the strength that had helped insulate him in the following years from the chance at more pain, no longer seemed important. The defenses no longer seemed needed. All the doubts that had taken over in the years since were now distant, vague. There were still questions, but he sensed a difference. Stephens knew she would be part of the answers this time.

"Are you real?" he asked. "Will you ever be real?"

"I loved you before I met you, Rob," the vision whispered back to him. "You turned out to be just the person my Jim always felt you were. The one he spoke about so often. I started to know even then. I shall always love you."

The vision's body melted and blended into his. He felt the gentle hand resting on his face, and the softness of her chest rising and falling from her breathing next to him. Stephens so wanted to make love to the vision. But even more, he wanted to lie in the shelter of her warmth and know the peace of her arms.

The vision gently pulled away. In the dim light of the room, he could see the full shape of her body through the gown as she walked to the end of the cot where he was tied. He felt light tugs on his feet as she loosened the cords. The she freed his wrists. He tried to pull himself up, but could not. There was no strength left in him.

The vision touched the side of his face again. "Sshhhh. Lie down. Wait. Morning will come. When it comes, you'll be free." The vision flowed into the corner of the room and lifted a book from behind one of the steel drums. "Here. I left this for you. It's all I could find to bring over. I think it's important." She returned it to its hiding place.

"Cynthia, why Falconer. Why? How?"

The vision returned and knelt next to the bed. She placed her right arm on his chest and her head on his arm. He was able to lift his other arm to rest on her shoulder.

"He killed Jim. I knew that. I also knew from Jim he was in Peterborough. I just didn't know what he looked like."

Stephens could remember back to another dream. He could see Green showing her the photograph of the Falconer while back at the Robbins home.

"You gave me the face. I just had to come and wait. He likes pretty women."

"Cynthia, he is death," he said to the vision. "He can kill you with a glance."

"No, dear Rob. As much as I love you, you're wrong this time. I *will* kill him. One night while that pig is on me in bed, I will kill him. A time will come."

Stephens felt the pride for her grow, and swell, until it nearly swept all else away. The pride mixed well with love. His last vision before he slipped back into darkness, was of her face close to his, love in her eyes, and the gentle touch of her hand on his face.

Chapter Eighteen

The sounds of the vans pulling out just before dawn awakened Stephens. From the cot he could hear the quiet voices of ten or twelve men as they loaded the last of their equipment and then climbed inside. When his eyes adjusted to the dim light that came under the door, he could see that no one else was in the room. After listening carefully, he decided that no one was outside the door. "They must be at the bottom of the stairs," he thought. He started to raise his arm to see how tightly the bonds held him to his bed, but was stopped short by the excruciating pain of his muscles resisting any movement. He was raw and bloody, and his side ached with a constant sharp throbbing.

Stephens began the long process of regaining the ability to move. He clenched and reclenched his fists dozens of times, until he felt the circulation begin and some flexibility return. Then he concentrated on one arm at a time, moving it a fraction of an inch in either direction, then inches, then side to side. Whenever he moved his left arm, the whole side of his body was racked by fingers of fire as the arm muscles pulled against the broken ribcage. It was only when he was able to raise both arms straight up that it dawned on him he was not tied up. "Damn fools," he thought. "They count on the door locks and guards?"

For the next fifteen minutes, Stephens worked at forcing his reluctant body to respond to his commands. It seemed like a major triumph when he was able to painfully swing his legs over the side of the cot and sit up. Later, when he had managed to stand and stretch and some degree of mobility had returned, he could understand the feelings of those who finished a marathon.

His clothing was nearby, in a clump on the floor. Stephens ripped up the undershirt to fashion a crude support bandage for his ribs. He took the white shirt, and crept around the room looking for anything to darken it. The only choice was to rub it through the dust and dirt on the floor. In the dim light of the room the shirt shifted well towards the black end of the color spectrum. Stephens smiled as he realized that the darkness would now be used to his advantage. He carefully opened one of the drums of chemicals he had seen against the far wall. It smelled a bit like transmission oil. The label called it "Texo 127 HD." To him it appeared to be nothing more than an industrial chemical of some kind. He searched the room looking for anything to use as a weapon. There was nothing, except the rope used to tie him up. He looped one end of the rope around each hand, and headed for the door.

Just before he reached the door, he stopped as the dream came back to him. His eyes tightened quizzically as he remembered the vision of Cynthia. He looked back at the cot, and then without realizing it, absently touched the side of his face where her hand had rested. He looked down in the darkness at his wrist, and then back at the cot again. Recollection of the dream flooded back. He went back to the chemical drums against the side wall. He crept over to the nearest drum, the same one he had tested moments earlier, and reached behind it. His hand touched something solid, and even before he had it in front of him, he knew it was a book. And he knew that the vision from the night before was real.

As he held the book and thought of Cynthia Lebart, some of the fatigue that had dominated his thoughts faded away. He realized that he might just have all the time he needed, after all. It was a volume of Robert Frost poetry. In the dim light he could see the strip of paper marking a page near the back of the book. He only had to make out the first few words when he recognized the poem. It had always touched him more than any of the other gentle musings of Frost. His eyes were closed and there was a slight smile on his lips as Stephens pictured the last stanza that had always seemed to be written just for him—Frost's deep understanding of the obligations that so shaped his life, and the commitments that always seemed to come before a life of his own.

The woods are lovely, dark and deep,
but I have promises to keep
and miles to go, before I sleep,
and miles to go, before I sleep.

And then he realized something else. He knew that the Falconer did not suspect Cynthia Lebart, and that Green knew all about her. The snap of another puzzle piece into place was almost audible. His instincts had been right about his old friend. Green was off the list. Five suspect names had become just four.

"You were real," he whispered softly into the night. Then he started back towards the door.

—w—

There was no one outside the door or near the outbuilding when he looked outside the door at the bottom of the stairs. Full dawn was close. In the far eastern sky the glow that precedes the sun had started to chase the night ever westward. In the house across the yard many of the lights were on. There was no sign of movement in the house during the minutes he carefully scanned every window. He guessed that the Falconer and all his men had left for Boston. Stephens guessed it was about 6:00 a.m. He would need to search the area, and then find a way to Boston himself.

Stephens left the doorway and entered the work shed that was at the bottom of the stairs. The early light was just enough for him to see that it was nearly empty. The previous owner had cleaned it out when he sold the house. Stephens searched the room for a better weapon. He found an ax handle, and tucked the rope into his back pocket. In a crack between two planks of a workbench he found a large forty-penny common nail. It was rusted, and five inches long. Instinctively he tucked the nail into his belt.

As he was about to leave the work shed, he heard a slight noise above him in the second room upstairs that was opposite the one where he had been held. It was just a light scrape of something hard on the floor. Stephens froze in the darkness and listened. There was no repeat of the noise. His eyes narrowed as he envisioned Gertmeyer sleeping in the room above. He forgot about the pains searing his side.

Stephens blended into the night, and became one with all predators as he climbed the stairs. His feet never made a noise. At the top of the stairs he listened for any repeat of the sound, and then carefully peeked through the slightly open door. The room was almost a mirror image of his, with no furniture along any of the walls. In the middle of the room he could see the outline of someone slumped on a chair.

"Shit," Stephens said to himself as the shape assumed identity. "I should have known."

Stephens swung the door open and walked over to the chair. Green was unconscious. There was blood dripping from open wounds on his face and chest. There were burn marks on both arms. Twin trickles of blood flowed from his mouth and his left ear. Stephens laid down the ax handle and held his ear to Green's chest. The heartbeat was there, but weak. Stephens lifted one of Green's eyelids. The blank pupil behind it gave no response. "I'm sorry, my old friend. I let you down."

It was then, as his eyes swept the room looking for anything that could help, that he saw the large dark shadow behind the door. Even before he saw the darkness at the top of the shadow split to become an evil grin of yellowed teeth in the dim light, and even before he heard the wicked laugh, he knew the origin of the shape.

"So, Stephens, you've found your friend. A bit too late, perhaps?" Gertmeyer stepped into the open. He held an ugly, stubby gun aimed directly at Stephens. "Take a good look at him. You and I have a whole day to play here, before you catch up with Green. After the crap I took last night from Falconer because of you, you owe me."

"You did this?" Stephens asked, stalling for time. He felt the churn of bitterness again at his own failure to anticipate Gertmeyer had been left to guard him. "Where are your guards to help you?"

"There's no one else here now, asshole. They all left. Just me."

"Just you, and your little friend there," said Stephens, pointing at the gun. No plan had yet formed. He needed more time. He held out his empty hands. "Guess you need that against someone unarmed."

"What about your little toothpick there?" said Gertmeyer, nodding at the ax handle.

Stephens reached down and picked up the ax handle. He hefted it and turned his head sideways to look up at Gertmeyer. The plan had come. It always did.

"This ax is far more use to me than that little gun is to you." Stephens smiled calmly. The assurance on Gertmeyer's face faded as he saw the genuine confidence on the face across from him.

"You see," Stephens continued, "I can use this. Yours is useless. How would you explain shooting me to the Falconer? Did I escape while you were responsible? Did you get the information first? Did you lose your cool again?"

Gertmeyer's hand dropped to his side.

"Seems to me that if you shoot me, the Falconer is more dangerous to you than I am."

Gertmeyer's concern slowly gave way to assurance again. "But I could always shoot your friend, couldn't I? And you don't want that, do you?" He aimed the gun at the limp body of Green.

"He's almost dead anyway," Stephens lied easily. "It's too late to save him now. And anyway, shoot him and you're still faced with me. You gain nothing."

Gertmeyer stared at Stephens. His left hand, the one without the gun, opened and closed compulsively. His eyes darted from Stephens to Green to the ax handle, and then back to Stephens. Finally, the hard smile returned. "You're right! Very good. So I can't use this." He pulled the door open, backed into the hall, opened the opposite door and tossed the handgun inside. "This will be better anyway. Much more fun."

Gertmeyer crouched with both hands in front of him and entered the room. He carefully watched the ax handle in Stephens' right hand. He kept circling to the right to keep away from it. With every step he closed the distance a little. Stephens was forced to circle, keeping between the chair and Gertmeyer. As he neared, the huge German would feint to test Stephens' reactions. With each movement, the fingers of fire reappeared in Stephens' side. His knee was almost useless. He could move only as long as he was careful, but no sudden movements were possible. A sharp cut, or an attempt to kick out, and the knee would probably collapse under him. Stephens recognized the makings of a very short fight. He did not like his own odds.

"You don't move very well, asshole," said Gertmeyer as he closed to within four feet. "Perhaps you should just give in. Maybe I would forgive you and let you go." Stephens did not answer. The grin on Gertmeyer's face made clear the value of the offer.

Stephens was not ready for the move Gertmeyer made. He had expected a bull-like charge straight at him. But Gertmeyer showed remarkable agility for so large a man. Before Stephens could react, Gertmeyer fired out his right foot in a sweeping side kick that connected squarely with the left arm hanging limply by his side. The arm was driven into the cracked ribs, and the fire and flames tore though his body. Before he could clear his vision from the pain, Gertmeyer spun gracefully around on that same right foot, and swept his left foot out to crash into Stephens' right knee. It collapsed immediately. As Stephens fell, Gertmeyer reached out and easily plucked the ax handle from his hand. He tossed it into the corner with a chuckle. Then Gertmeyer squatted down and turned Stephens onto his back. He grabbed Stephens by the collar and pulled his head up to face him.

"You will watch your friend die," said Gertmeyer. "It will happen very slowly, and with a great deal of pain. Then you'll die, even more slowly. I will tell Falconer that you knew nothing, and died from the interrogation."

Buried somewhere in all people are instincts and patterns that stretch back into times past remembering. They lie dormant, lost in the convolutions of more educated thoughts. Most people pass a lifetime without touching them. Only when nothing else is left, and all nobility and reason is stripped from a man will they be the last possible way to survive. Stephens was almost beyond knowing what was happening around him. He was moments from falling unconscious. Yet, the small corner of his mind that was still functioning ordered his right hand to slip down towards the nail in his belt. The room was spinning around him, and nothing made sense. He felt his fingers close on the nail.

At that moment, he could focus on just one thought. Stephens used all of his remaining control to force open his eyes. He only knew that he had to be able to look Gertmeyer in the eye. "This is for Green . . ."

The right hand flashed up from the belt. When it reached its goal, there was no strength left in Stephens' body. Gertmeyer saw the motion out of the corner of one eye, and then that same eye did not seem to work properly. He could not seem to hold Stephens any longer. Stephens fell in a clump, unconscious, on the floor at Green's feet. Gertmeyer looked down at the body, and then reached up to touch the nail buried deep into his temple.

"Shit," he said, trying to pull it out. "Shit."

His last sight through his right eye was of Stephens and Green. Then the vision faded, and clouded, and was replaced by the vague face of someone from years before. He did not have time to recognize the face before he died.

When Stephens came back to consciousness hours later, sun was streaming into the room. It was already mid morning. The weight of

Gertmeyer's body on his made it hard to breathe. It was not easy to get up. With every movement, new sources of pain in his body became evident.

Green was still unconscious. His heartbeat seemed a bit stronger than Stephens remembered from the night before, but he was still not far from death. Stephens reviewed the options. He had to get Green to safety, but there were few places he could be taken nearby where Stephens was certain he would be safe. Green was not exactly the type of package he could drop off at Monadnock General Hospital. Plus, he had no assurance that the Falconer's men would not find Green there. Even the Peterborough Police were a risk. There was too much of a chance that the Falconer bought an informant inside Chief Meltzer's operation.

Even Stephens was surprised at the answer that came to him. It took only fifteen minutes to confirm that the farm was empty. Gertmeyer had been the only one left behind. Once he was certain, he used the phone in the main house to call Myrna Glover.

"Myrna, this is Rob Stephens from the school. I need your help."

There was not even the slightest hesitation in her answer. Her voice was calm and controlled. "Where are you, Rob?"

He told her the location. "Please bring some blankets, and some bandages. I have a friend who is in trouble."

"I'll be there in about twenty minutes."

When the old Volkswagen Beetle pulled up, she had missed her estimate by less than three minutes. Myrna helped as Stephens carefully placed Green in the front passenger seat. He sat in the back for the ride to Dublin. He was half asleep during the ride, and no one spoke. Myrna never asked about Green or about the condition of her two passengers.

When they arrived, Stephens carried Green into the house. Between them, they dressed his wounds as much as could be done with the medicines at hand. Then, using old Ace bandages, Myrna helped wrap Stephens' side. When she saw the ugly purples and swelling of the broken rib, she just looked up at him, and then went back to her task.

"Myrna," he asked when she had finished, "I need to find out what's happening. Do you have a television?"

There was no television in the old home. It had been one of those things that had never been necessary when evenings were so filled with her books, or friends, or music, or just quiet knitting.

There was no need to search long for a news report on the radio. Most of the stations were hooked to their network affiliates for constant, live broadcasts from Boston. The news was all the same. There was little detail yet available. The reports all carried little more than a couple minutes worth of hard news sandwiched between commentary, interviews, or pure speculation.

But the hard facts were consistent across all channels. The President and several cars in his motorcade had been captured on the way from Logan Airport. No demands had yet been made public, and no one had any idea what the demands might be. All that was known was that the cars were trapped in the Sumner Tunnel under Boston Harbor. There was no indication in any of the reports about the identity of the terrorists. Stephens realized that he was the only one who knew that answer. There would be those from ATQ who would suspect, but they could do little until demands were made, and terms discussed.

At this stage, as always, almost all factors favored the terrorists. If they had taken even the most basic preparations, they could hold out for days, even weeks. Stephens knew that there was rarely anything that could alter the balance after the first few minutes had passed. Whoever ATQ had in Boston would be at the start of the long waiting period that began all such battles, while the factors were analyzed and the equations calculated. The outcome would be inevitable, and depended only upon the strength of the terrorists' plan, and the skill of its execution.

"Myrna, I need your car," Stephens said aloud as he finished wrapping his side. It was already 11:00 in the morning.

"Might I expect to get it back?"

"I think so."

"You're part of that thing with the President, aren't you? You're going to go to Boston?"

"I have to," he answered simply.

She gestured up towards the academy, just a mile up the road. "Wendlandt? What was that? How was that a part of all this?"

"It wasn't, Myrna. It was supposed to be the end of it."

"We called you the 'quiet one.'" She thought back over the past four years. "That must have been funny."

"It was the best, Myrna, of all the names I've had. It was the first of which I was proud."

"And can you make a difference down there?" Myrna Glover did not expect an answer. Instead she looked deep inside Stephens. Those few who might remember the night at the town hall so many years earlier would recognize the look. John Hardy and Bill Parsons would know it instantly.

"I guess you might, maybe you might." She quietly answered her own question. "I hope you're not too late."

"Too late?" he muttered, looking past Myrna with the answer. "Too late *again*? I should have been able to stop it from even starting. But I couldn't save a boy, or my friend here, or even a young girl. Yes, for what it will be worth, I must go to Boston."

"And will I see you back, Rob?"

"I'm not sure of that, Myrna."

"I suppose that you don't want anyone to get near your friend."

"No one, Myrna. No one at all. I'll make sure the right people call first. There will be two of them, one a woman. They will give you the number 1231. That's my birthday Myrna. Maybe it should be April Fool's Day instead, the way I've done so far, but it isn't."

After he left, Myrna Glover walked over to the wall where Walter's shotgun had remained for the ten years since she had lost him. She reached up and gently pulled it off of the pegs holding it against the wall. It was warm from the hearth below, and felt for a moment as though her dear Walter's hands had just left it. She went over to the cupboard and found the box of shells. Then she walked over to where Green lay and covered him over with an Afghan that had taken three winters to complete, a square at a time, looking for exactly the right combination of patterns and colors. She pulled her rocker over next to the bed and sat down. She carefully removed her blue scarf, folded it, and placed it on the edge of the bed beside her before she loaded the shotgun.

Myrna Glover was eighty-one years old. A person she trusted had asked her to watch his friend. She did not know why. But she understood the commitments of trust. None would pass there save she chose to let them.

Chapter Nineteen

The trip down to Boston in Myrna Glover's Volkswagen was painful. The old car was fine for short trips putting here and there around Dublin. But it had long since passed the time when it should have been retired to any of the hundreds of fields full of rusted cars that are tucked behind the idyllic forests and hills of New Hampshire. The shock absorbers had needed replacement thousands of miles ago, well before the odometer had been reborn at all zeros. At fifty miles an hour, which was about as fast as Stephens felt he could safely drive, every small bump, pothole, or rough surface would shake and bounce the car in a constant vibration that seemed to claw at everything that hurt in his body. The tape around his side did little to help the searing flashes from the broken ribs as they shifted and poked at his insides.

Stephens was glad for the time spent in Boston years ago. Only that made him realize the foolishness of trying a direct route to the Sumner Tunnel. Traffic, normally a mess at this time of day, would be a disaster with the tunnel blocked off. All of the expressways into the downtown area would be backed up for miles. It would be what the local news radio station, WEEI, would call a "snail trail" on its hourly traffic reports. He doubted that he could get within four or five miles of his destination. Instead, he would take Memorial Drive through Cambridge into Chelsea, and then down Eastern Avenue to the back way into the airport that led between the freight terminals. Once at the airport, he knew he would still have to walk the last mile or so, but at least he could get far closer than would be possible by any other route.

The radio had offered little on the way down. It was clear from the reports that the President's motorcade had been trapped inside the tunnel when explosives had collapsed both ends. At least four cars from the motorcade were thought to be buried in the rubble at the two ends. The

President's limo was believed to have been well into the tunnel, away from the ends, when the blast had occurred. There was no report of demands, and no indication as to what would happen next.

Since there was so little hard news, the radio reports were speculative and often contradictory. Some questioned whether the President was actually in the tunnel. Some reports had terrorists inside the tunnel while others reported a Mexican Standoff just outside it. The police could not get in and those in the tunnel could not get out. There were vague reports of gunfire at one point. The bulk of the time was spent in speculative interviews with one politician after another. The Washington bureaus would report on the location of the Vice-President. Someone would give a capsule summary of some past act of terrorism. Another live report would say little more than ". . . there's little apparent activity here at the scene." Commentators would switch back to Washington for empty comments from another congressional press aid.

The Presidential candidates, with the elections so close, were having a field day with the opportunity for press coverage. A black Presidential candidate offered to help negotiate the situation. Another candidate, more known for his role as a television evangelist, volunteered to be swapped for the President.

As Stephens entered the outskirts of the airport, he focused what little hard information was available. He could draw only three tentative conclusions. First, the explosions must been professionally set to completely block the ends of the tunnel against a wide-open assault. Next, since traffic would be a nightmare and since cars could be too easily traced even if movement were possible, then helicopters would be the only possible means of escape. Finally, there must be a threat of further terrorist action that was stopping the use of explosives to clear the rubble. Only by such a threat could the terrorists ensure an assault on the tunnel would be seen as far too risky. Their entire plan would be based upon that threat. As long as it existed, there was very little that could be done. Remove the threat and the Falconer's plan would collapse. As usual in such events, the major ideas were very simple. But the execution of those plans, and the endless chain of countermeasures to be considered, was far from simple.

It would become a massive chess game with both the Falconer and Stephens trying to look many moves ahead, anticipating each other's moves, and knowing that the players were very evenly balanced. But here, instead of playing wooden pieces to the side of the board when captured, it would be real people who would die. And in this chess game Stephens started out without his strongest piece, Green, and with the Falconer holding the tunnel. It was like playing down a rook against a grandmaster.

When he finally approached the ramp to the Sumner Tunnel, Stephens' whole body ached. He had hobbled nearly a mile after abandoning the old Volkswagen by the side of the road when the traffic jam made further driving impossible. Perhaps reacting to his haggard and tired look, and to the anger and embarrassment at what was happening on "their beat," the policemen conducted their search of him with a healthy dose of extra vigor. The "pat down" was more of a "slap down," and Stephen's knees had buckled the first time the police officer had pushed against his broken ribs.

Finally, a senior officer had believed the look in Stephens' eyes just enough to radio down to the ATQ checkpoint already established near the toll booths outside the tunnel. That same officer realized he had been right when Joyce Patterson herself showed up to escort Stephens back to the scene. The officer had been in on the initial briefing just two hours earlier. He had seen the power Joyce Patterson represented, and the strength in her and in those around her. From all too many years on the force, he could read people. He could cut through the layers quickly to judge the person underneath. Within a few seconds he knew Joyce Patterson had earned her position. From the moment she arrived on the site she had commanded the respect of all the local Boston Police Department people who had been rushed to the scene. Most BPD officers were old-time cops, and for them women were never really accepted, especially in positions of authority. "But this one sure as hell is accepted," he had thought early into the first briefing. "I'd like to see the one who can back her down."

As the officer watched Patterson lead Stephens back to the entrance, supporting him gently with one arm as she did, somehow the officer was not surprised when he realized that the ragged, bruised individual who called himself Rob Stephens was someone who Patterson clearly respected.

"Where are they?" asked Stephens as soon as they arrived, scanning the buildings that overlooked the site. He glanced only briefly at the pile of rubble that could be seen twenty yards inside the entrance to the tunnel. Instead, he concentrated on the surrounding area where he knew the Falconer would have at least one observation point. For most of the two dozen police officers helping cordon off the area, the debris was like a magnet. Their eyes continually were drawn back to the jagged pieces of concrete and dirt, as though they could somehow look straight through it to the President's motorcade beyond. A small patch of black, decorated with a still intact set of tail lights, was clearly visible next to what used to be the right wall of the tunnel. The weight and size of the cave-in on top of the car had crushed the taillights to within a couple inches of the ground.

The Sumner Tunnel is one of two parallel tunnels that cross diagonally under Boston's Inner Harbor connecting East Boston, including Logan Airport, with the North End. The Sumner travels southwest towards Boston, while the companion Callahan Tunnel heads northeast out of Boston. Eight toll booths at the Sumner entrance converge into the tunnel's two lanes in a distance of less than 100 feet. Entering the tunnel during rush hour is a mix of bumper cars, chicken, and demolition derby.

The pie-shaped entry ramp slopes down into the tunnel about a half mile from the edge of the inner harbor. Even from the toll booths you are already too low to see any part of the harbor through the maze of buildings and houses in between. Because the entry was depressed well below ground level, Stephens knew that none of the buildings on the harbor side could offer a view of the tunnel entrance. Even the closest buildings on either side of the entrance ramp would have blind spots that the Falconer would find unacceptable as anything more than a backup vantage point.

"I assume your people are ignoring the buildings on the harbor side. They don't have a clear view," he said matter-of-factly, as he turned and looked back at the houses and buildings that were some 100 yards to the northeast. "What about them? Some of them can see everything that goes on down here."

"We don't know yet. We can't send locals in without making it quite obvious, and our people aren't here in quantity yet. If they see anything, they've made it clear they'll retaliate."

"How many ATQ on site?"

"Seven, with more coming. Langley will add to that."

"Level?"

"Two fives and a four. Not much to go with yet."

"What's on route?"

"Mainly fives. We do have Jacobi and Sanders on the way up. They're in the air already."

"Field-ready sixes?"

"Not before early evening, at the best. We kind of counted on you and Harvey."

Stephens looked away from the buildings and back at Joyce Patterson. "Harvey won't be with us. At least not for a while."

"Later?"

"Maybe, but it's not clear," he answered, without explanation. He turned back towards the buildings. "Do you know who's out there, Joyce?" he asked quietly.

She didn't answer him. She stared intently at Stephens, knowing that an answer wasn't required. She nodded slowly. "The Falconer. I felt it somehow," she stated softly. "I hoped the feeling was wrong."

"No doubt at all. I sat across a table from him yesterday."

"His people?"

"Good. Very Good. Trained and disciplined. They won't make mistakes."

"Do you know what his plan is?"

"No clue yet."

"It was eerie. There was something about the voice, even through a scratchy radio link. It could only be Falconer." She nodded back towards the houses to the Northeast. "There's no way to search through there without him knowing what we're doing. Until we know a little more, that wouldn't be much of an idea. He's already told us there are more charges in the tunnel."

"What's his comm-link?"

"Moving matched pairs. I think he has at least three, maybe four."

Stephens tightened his expression and shook his head side to side. "Nothing there for us. By the time we chase down all the links this will all be over."

"I know. We've got full monitoring equipment being set up, anyway."

This was, as are many things in tradecraft, a very simple yet effective idea. The Falconer had set up a network of phone lines from a carefully hidden central point. Each line connected to a transmitter. Meanwhile, three or four pairs of radios were in the hands of runners who kept moving at all times. The Falconer would keep switching both the active transmitter, and the transmission frequency used. Depending upon the frequency used, only one of the runners would receive the signal. The second of the two radios carried by the runner would then retransmit the signal on the frequency that was intended to be heard. Since the runners kept moving, and since the active radio changed every few seconds each time the Falconer switched frequencies, triangulation was impossible. The Falconer could employ dozens of frequencies in a prearranged pattern. Finding and tracing his signal was nearly impossible. Even if a runner was caught, there were three others until he was replaced.

"Anything at all to the reports some of them are inside?"

"Nothing solid. Just typical of some of the rumors flying around. They were reporting a full firefight when I first came in." Patterson grimaced. "Most is just press hype and the usual overactive imaginations."

"And up to four cars crushed?"

"Some truth. There might be two, but we currently think just one," said Patterson. "Let me fill you in on what little we *do* know. We had explosions in both ends of the tunnel. There are at least nine cars in the tunnel at this time, and maybe a tenth. Two are Boston PD, two are Secret Service, one is the President, two are President's staff, and one is the Mayor's vehicle. Added to that are four motorcycles. That gives us a total of twelve police officers potentially inside. We're waiting for verification, but we think there are ten more from Treasury." She pointed towards the car buried under the pile of concrete and dirt. "There might be two cars under there. We had two press vehicles trailing the motorcade. One you can see. No chance of survivors. Our friend was very precise when he instructed us to keep well away from the rubble, 'or else.'"

"So that makes more than twenty professionals of one sort or another. What's the civilian count other than the President and mayor?"

"Seven or eight, and that includes the first lady. Plus the six possibles in the press car. No one knows for sure who was with the Mayor."

"How long before the entry was the tunnel sealed off?"

"Thirty minutes."

"Any chance that someone was inside all along?"

"None. The tunnel was clear."

"Service points? Storage rooms?"

"There's some kind of a crawl space the length of the tunnel, but every door to it was padlocked."

"Any police on position in the tunnel?"

"None. Just the normal MDC person at the watch booth in the middle."

"Any possibility of a switch."

"Treasury is pretty thorough on these things. I think not."

Stephens turned away from the buildings, and grimaced in pain as the movement put pressure on his broken ribs. "Shit," he said, both at the pain and the facts. "What contact with the Falconer, or his people, so far?"

"He never identified himself as Falconer. Just a voice. Within a couple minutes of the explosions he was on the police band with instructions on his choice of frequency. He's using the police reserve band."

"Nice choice," Stephens interrupted. "It's easy to pick up, and most civilians with scanners ignore it."

"He warned that both sides of the tunnel are under observation and that there are more charges inside. He'll set them off if anyone approaches either the ends, or approaches the nearby buildings. He thinks ahead." Patterson shook her head in frustration. "We're 22'd. We have to assume he really does have more explosives in there. Any move, and he lights them off. Even if we find and cut his wires, we're still frozen. The moment we make a hole, he now has line of sight to punch through a radio signal. Boom if we do. Blam if we don't. Catch-22 in spades."

"What communication so far with the cars inside. Treasury will have radios in all cars."

"Nothing. This one's a bit of a mystery, Rob. There's no wideband jamming, and even if there were, treasury insists their people inside have equipment that can punch through anything. Still, we've had nothing since the equipment got here and was set up about an hour after the explosion."

"That doesn't make sense. Not even the raw carrier frequency? Even garbage?"

"I guess there could have been something earlier before we set up, but there hasn't been a whisper for the past three hours." Her eyes tightened with uncertainty. "I don't think they're sending."

"Dead?" he asked softly. "Is there any chance they've been flooded? More explosions deeper inside?"

"Rob, we just don't know. We're all guessing here. We've tried to aim sound detection at the tunnel. But from this distance, and with all the background crap, no one can hear a thing."

"We've got to know what we're working with," Stephens said. "Does Falconer give any idea? Any demands yet?"

"Not a word. Just warnings to keep back. But we may have something going for us. Did you ever do much with the group at NSA?"

"No. They were always pretty weird. Pretty much played their own game."

"They have some amazing stuff using computers to analyze sounds. It's the same stuff they developed for the Navy to use when trolling for 'Titanium Whales.'"

Stephens looked at the woman as though she had lost her mind. "What the hell are you talking about, Joyce?"

Patterson had to let a small smile escape through the reality of the moment. "That's right. You've been out of it for a while! Titanium whales are a rare breed, have their breeding grounds near Vladivostock, usually carry nuclear missiles, and tend to be considered very unfriendly by the good guys. We like to know where they are at all times."

"Titanium whales," he repeated as understanding dawned on him. "What does that have to do with us?"

"NSA uses computers tied to microphones, radio receivers, and even sonar equipment. They feed it through special artificial intelligence software to do pattern recognition. They can filter out the gudge, and identify things by the sounds they make." She nodded towards the tunnel where the President was trapped. "Remember when he was on the air right after the KAL-007 airliner was shot down, and identified the pilot who did it to the press?"

Stephens nodded.

"NSA had recorded the microwave bands in real time, caught the transmission from the Russian pilot who fired the missile, screened out the static and background sounds, and fed the voice into their computer. They had him identified right down to his squadron number even before the plane hit the water."

Stephens considered the possibilities that would arise if he could hear what was happening inside the tunnel. "They're on the way here with some of that stuff? Is it that easy to move in?"

"No. You and I got lucky for a change. Not only is the company that makes the computer just twenty or thirty miles west of us, but there's also a delegation of spooks there today looking at new equipment. They heard about this mess, put two and two together, and called us. They're having the people at the computer company pull together all the hardware and will fly it over by helicopter by the end of the day. They're flying the rest of the software and sound equipment into Hanscom Field from Ft. Meade. According to what little I've been told, if there are people alive in that tunnel NSA will know it, and will identify them."

"What about the tunnel itself?"

"There's a man on the way over from Boston Mass Transit. He'll give us all the details."

"The explosives?"

Patterson did not have the chance to answer. Both she and Stephens turned when they heard the shout of a police officer who was now running towards them. He was carrying a radio, and was slightly out of breath when he pulled up next to them.

"They're back on, Ma'am," he said to Patterson before shifting to face Stephens, "but they want to speak to him."

Both Stephens and Patterson looked at each other before turning back towards the officer.

"They asked for me?"

"Yes, sir. You are Rob Stephens?"

Stephens looked down at the ground for a few moments before turning back to look at the buildings to the Northeast. "He knows I'm here," he said softly. "He's watching us right now."

"He asked for you, sir, by name," said the officer, holding out the radio.

The radio felt strange and heavy in Stephens' hand. He stared at the buildings in the distance. Hundreds of windows reflected the blank sky back at him. Dozens of vacant rooftops stretched spiny antennas towards the clouds. Scores of empty doorways hid their secrets from him.

He raised the radio and depressed the talk button. "Stephens here."

"I underestimated you." The hard voice came over the radio with no preliminary greetings. "That's the second time I've done that."

"Perhaps not. I was able to do nothing to prevent *this*."

"But, at least you can still prevent many deaths. Stephens, you and I are professionals. We can look calmly at the facts, no matter what we feel about them. Neither of us will do anything foolish. My people know their duties. They will not do something stupid. Can you say the same for your people?"

"Not for all of them. These police officers are good, but you can't expect any of them to have our kind of experience."

"But you are there, Stephens. And, unless I've made another mistake, you should be able to control events. Is that not so?"

"I hope so, but there are people here who've never worked anything close to this kind of thing. Amateurs make mistakes."

"Perhaps they need a bit of a lesson? Am I correct that there is a man in the toll booth nearest the airport?"

Stephens looked towards the toll booth. There was no one visible. He turned towards Patterson. "Is there someone inside?" he asked with the switch turned off.

"Yes. He's one of ours."

Stephens raised the radio. "Yes, I believe that there is." He knew that there would be no value in lying. The Falconer would not have asked the question, unless he was certain of the answer. The statement was carefully crafted to tell Patterson and Stephens that they had no secrets from him.

"Then I am sorry you had to hide him there. My instructions were very clear about letting anyone close to the tunnel."

"Robinson!" Patterson screamed as she instantly realized what would happen next. "Get out of there! Now! Run!"

A head slowly appeared peeking around the corner of the booth.

"Run!" she screamed again.

Robinson had taken no more than two frantic strides before the explosion ripped apart the toll booth. The sides bulged, and then split in a dozen places, peeling down in strips like a flower's petals. The roof of the booth careened back towards the airport to crash on the roofs of the abandoned cars now packed into the ramp leading to the tunnel. Glass from the windows showered the area, glinting in the sunlight like a summer shower. Robinson was caught from behind and thrown down and along the ground, as though a giant hand had swatted him. Before it finally smeared to a stop on the concrete, it was obvious that there was no life left in the body. When the echoes of the blast had faded, Robinson's body lay crumpled and twisted in a spreading puddle of red.

"Bastard!" Stephens spat into the phone. "I didn't need that message. I know what is expected."

"But Stephens, others there did not. Now they do. It is nothing more than that."

Two police officers had started to move towards the body. "Stop them, Stephens."

"Don't go near," Stephens called out. Instinctively almost all of those close to Robinson crouched down.

"Leave him there, Stephens. It is too late to help him, and he will be a good reminder to the rest."

"He was just a kid," Stephens said bitterly into the radio as he looked at the shattered body of the young man crumpled on the concrete.

"No. He became an adult when he chose this path. And that choice was his alone."

"What do you want?" Stephens' voice was now as hard as the Falconer's. "What does it take to end this?"

"You and I will have to change history, Stephens. We'll have to make up for the past. This will end when you and I forge an agreement that's a new beginning."

"Delusions, Lehar?" Stephens did not want to use the name Falconer over the radio. "Events like this have a way of fading, and being half forgotten with time."

"But we will change more than just events. We will change the way people think. Why Stephens, we will alter their very perceptions of themselves."

"That has been tried many, many times before. You, after Beirut, must know that."

"Ah yes, Stephens. But that was so far away. This is *here*." The final word was thrown over the airwaves. "This will happen *at home* for you Americans!"

"What do you want?"

"Not yet, Stephens. Not yet. I'm not yet ready to make my demands. It won't make any difference to you, but for others it will be better for me if they think for a while about all this. I'd like them to be as receptive as possible to my 'requests' when I make them."

"And in the meantime? How do we know the President is still alive?"

"You don't. But let me work on it. Perhaps I can let you speak to him later today."

Stephens' eyes tightened as he considered the implications of the offer. "Just how do you propose to do that?"

There was a brief return of the humor in the voice. "I can do it, Stephens. Count on it."

"Let me check with the people here."

"Fine, Stephens." The voice was again cold. "But not too long, please."

"Joyce, you've got to work the intruder issue. Hard and fast," he said with the mike off. "We've got to be sure about whether or not he has a plant inside the tunnel."

"I've got to believe none. But we're still running a full check." She stared into the distance as she analyzed the known facts. "The tunnel was clear. That leaves the cars. The only chance might be the Mayor's car. Or maybe the lead press car, if it cleared the explosion. Both should be pretty easy to check out. But my take is 'no way.'"

"They've got to have some kind of radio link inside."

"I don't see it."

"The only way we could talk to the President without them losing control is by radio. But the rubble cuts off all radio communication. They can't be looking to us to dig through to send a person inside to verify he's alive, or to dig enough to drop in an antenna. The risk we would do something more is far too high. The only safe way is a radio conversation. That means they *already* have communication inside. They must have a link *even* with the ends collapsed."

"But anything they have powerful enough to punch through that rockslide would be traceable in a second."

"There's a direct link inside. I'm certain of it. A wire or an antenna we don't know about. It bypasses the rubble."

"Okay? But why not just walk someone right up here to the edge of the rubble, bold as brass."

"If they did that, it would blow their whole hand. It would prove that they had to be close to get a signal inside to talk. Therefore, they'd have to be just as close to set off another explosion. All we'd have to do is keep them away and the President would be totally safe in there."

"Why not just force us to bring up the equipment for him?" Patterson and Stephens had always been very effective whenever working together, because each could assume the role of 'devil's advocate' when reviewing options.

"Aha. Catch-22 again. To do that he needs a threat. The threat would have to be another explosive inside. Then he'd have to prove he could set it off by a small demonstration inside. But he can't do that if he needs us to bring up the equipment."

Stephens brought the mike back up to his face again. He was on the verge of allowing too long a silence. "When can we speak to him?"

"I will decide," answered the Falconer.

Stephens barely listened to the reply. He had already turned back towards Patterson. "They've got an antenna," he announced. "We've got to get the plans to the tunnel. They've got a wire inside, somewhere. And Joyce, despite what you think, he's got someone in there, too!"

"Damn. I'll get our people looking," she answered. She motioned towards the van and immediately the door opened and one of the agents on site stepped out.

"Who just left your van?" asked the Falconer almost immediately. "I have a report of people moving out of your communications base."

Stephens appreciated that question also served to warn Stephens that the site was under observation. "He's only warning the others to keep clear of the entrance."

"Stephens, no more than that, please." The voice was flat and cold. Even over the radio, to those listening in the van it seemed to carry the unmistakable feel of death.

"I understand, Falconer. I fully understand."

"And the others around you?"

"They will not be a problem."

"Very good, Stephens. I knew you would not disappoint me."

"Actually, it's not my call," he answered without hesitation, knowing that he could not be tied to the location. "This is not my site. But the one in charge will have no trouble with these people."

"Ah. Then I was right about the woman. It must be none other than the renowned Joyce Patterson. I did not expect they would send her to the scene. No one has seen her in the field since a year or so after London. I expected someone lesser, perhaps Bradford or Sanders."

Stephens did not respond to the bait.

"Well, it matters little, Stephens. For now, let's all remain calm. Later today I will allow you a brief conversation with your dear President. Perhaps we can let the first lady speak, as well."

"When?"

"I told you, I will decide when you may talk to them Stephens."

"That is not necessary. Others here will be the ones to speak to him."

"But I would be far more comfortable with you, Stephens. There would be far fewer chances for foolishness with you there. And far less need for additional demonstrations to convince the others."

Stephens easily saw the trap he had expected all along. If he were the contact, then he would be tied to the radio, and to a specific location. More importantly, he would be forced to respond instantly to any request, and thus would lose all freedom of action.

"That's not possible, Falconer. Your friend Gertmeyer was not a gentle person. I am of little use to these people, and am barely able to even stand here."

"Ah yes, Gertmeyer. I assume that Hans paid the price for his mistakes?"

"If he's watching from wherever he is now, he will have a measure of satisfaction in the price he extracted, first." Stephens coughed wetly into the radio. "I'm still coughing up blood." Stephens had to smile wryly as he realized how little exaggeration there was in his words.

"I could insist, Stephens. Perhaps another demonstration?"

Stephens' voice was very controlled when he answered. "You could. But that would not change anything."

There was a long silence on the radio. Finally, when the Falconer spoke again, Stephens could swear that he heard the faint trace of amusement in the Falconer's voice, and could almost see the thin smile on the face somewhere nearby.

"Stephens, I understand. I told you last night that you and I are much alike, no matter how little you wish to accept that. The obligations always come first, long before you and I can enjoy the final chance to sleep we each await with such hope." The voice was soft. "Maybe it is better this way. Fitting perhaps. Do what you must do."

Chapter Twenty

"Animals! Nothing but animals." You could see the anger in the face of the short, old man who stood with gnarled fists shaking slightly at his sides, near the entrance to the tunnel. His eyes were half closed and the words just barely escaped through his lips. Angelo Cuomo shook his head side to side with dismay, his thin white hair shifting slightly as he did. "Look what they did to my tunnel."

Angelo Cuomo had been part of the Boston DPW for more than fifty-two years, long past mandatory pension age. In order to get around retirement rules, the last three city councils had each hired Cuomo as a "special consultant to the city" so that he could continue to oversee tunnel operations. Every time it happened, the Boston Globe ran a series on corruption and featherbedding among council members. But Cuomo had been able to withstand the pressure. His father was part of the crew that built the tunnel, and his uncle had died while building it. To Angelo Cuomo, these were *his* tunnels. He would hover over the periodic sandblasting, or cleaning, or painting as though the tunnels were part of his family.

"Mr. Cuomo, they tell me you know just about everything about these tunnels," said Patterson gently, realizing the pain he was feeling from the sight of the pile of rubble. "We need to know exactly what we face here. We need to know about design, construction, entrances, exits, pipes. How close is that rubble to the waterline? Everything. Anything."

At first, Cuomo did not answer or look at Patterson. He just continued to move his head side to side very slowly. Patterson was struck with the realization that Cuomo wasn't even interested in the fact that his President was in danger. She wondered if Cuomo had even given that a thought.

"Lady, I hope you nail those sons of bitches," Cuomo said, pulling himself away from the view of the rubble. "I hope you nail them good."

"We're going to try, Mr. Cuomo."

"Well let's cut through the crap to the main thing. I done heard about the flooding stuff on the radio. It's a bunch of bull. If the other end's like this one, then there ain't no flooding. We got to go another three, four hundred feet into her before that could happen."

"Can it be flooded?" asked Stephens.

"Yup. But it would take a holy mother of an explosion to do it. I'll tell you one thing. Whoever did this knew what they were doing."

"What do you mean?"

"They couldn't have picked a better spot to plug the ends. They're in just far enough. Come another ten yards this way the whole front end of the tunnel would have gone. That overhang would be down here. Maybe that house up there, too. Would have taken heavy stuff *days* to cut through."

"That overhang looks like thirty feet of solid rock," said Stephens. "I wouldn't guess that they could budge it without an A-bomb."

"Does look that way, doesn't it. But it's mostly facing. All the piping to the blowers goes through there. My dad used to say that was the weak link in the design. 'Too much design' he used to say. 'Not enough structure.'"

Both Patterson and Stephens found themselves drawn to stare at the facing, and the five and six story buildings overhanging the end of the tunnel.

"There's not much bedrock near the surface," explained Cuomo. "You've got to get another fifty, sixty feet beyond where that explosion happened before you hit rock. Set the explosion there, or most any place before the flat stretch at the bottom, and you find the granite ledge that drove the crew crazy when they built this thing. Put the blast next to that rock and you'd just scratch the paint, and maybe chip off a few tiles." Again the head shake. "Nope. They done their homework. I suppose the other end's the same, except they blasted down another twenty, thirty yards in?"

Patterson looked resignedly at Stephens. "It is."

"Bedrock again. Just a little different level. Goes farther in. My dad told me that they could have saved six months of digging if they had moved that end of the tunnels over just about a hundred feet. Could have missed the whole ledge over there. But some bunch of politicians who had jockeyed to buy the land blocked it."

"So they knew the layout," said Stephens. "But how did they set the charges? Where?"

"That one bugs me. I've been thinking about that one a lot. There ain't no place obvious. I don't see where you can hide it. I doubt President what's-his-face carried them in with him." Patterson smiled inwardly as her suspicions about Cuomo's level of concern for other than the tunnel were confirmed. "He alive?"

"We think so, but we don't know for sure. No one knows if there were more explosions farther in."

"Well, if they set off big ones way down in, especially just before where it flattens out at the bottom, then they could have some problems. Your President might get a little wet."

"If it started to flood, could they get above the water at this end?" asked Patterson.

Cuomo gave the question a few moments of thought before answering. "Well, maybe. It'd be close. Let me tell you about my tunnel. The water in the harbor is about seventy feet deep. The outer shell of the tunnel lies about thirty feet below the harbor bed. The bed's mainly goop and sludge for the first 10-15 feet before they start to hit solid stuff. The soft bed gave the diggers fits back then. Always worried about cave-ins. Had to make a couple granny chambers and keep air tanks right where the guys were working."

"Granny chambers?" asked Stephens.

"Yeah, escape tubes. So that even your sainted old granny would be safe if she was down there."

Cuomo stooped down to sketch in the dirt on the pavement. "Both ends slope down about thirty degrees for a half mile or so. Then you got a flat spot of maybe another half mile. When they built this thing, they done it right. There's two tunnels, one inside the other. The main driving tunnel is designed to be pretty watertight all by itself. The ventilation shafts and conduits for the telephone cables are between the tunnels. The outside one is completely watertight. My day used to say '. . . the outer tunnel was built first, but built to last.' Point is, would take a pretty good blast to get through all that."

"Seventy feet of water?" said Stephens.

"Yup. The outer is coated inside with an electrolytic paint. A touch of moisture and the paint starts to conduct electricity. We constantly measure humidity in the outer tunnel. Stays a constant range between seventy-eight and eighty-three percent year after year. A leak, and the sucker will set off alarms you wouldn't believe."

"Wait a minute," said Stephens, "how much space between the tunnels?"

"About seven feet."

"Enough space to walk in there?"

"Yup."

"Can you get in there?"

"Sure can, but that's no help. We go in there twice a year for an inspection, ourselves. Pretty smelly and stale, but you can make it. There are six pressure locks, tubes with sealed doors at each end, between the inner and outer tunnels. But all six are well inside the tunnel. When you drive through, you probably seen the steel security doors to them."

"I've seen them, but they don't look like sealed doors."

"Those aren't. They just protect against stupid drivers. The real doors are behind them."

"Damn," Stephens said. "Then there's no way for us to get inside?"

"None. The closest one is a few hundred feet past the explosion. Like I told you, these people knew what they were doing."

"What about the ventilation tubes? I heard they have big fans sucking out the exhaust."

"They do, fellah, but those tubes are eight inches in diameter. They use a lot of smaller ones that could be encased in the concrete of the tunnel, instead of big ones that would have weakened the shell. Even a kid couldn't fit through them."

Stephens was silent as he considered what he had learned. He started to cross his arms in front of himself when the pressure on his ribs sent pain streaking up and down his side. "Mr. Cuomo, if they set off another charge inside, it seems to me that you're saying maybe nothing would happen. There seems to be an awful lot between the tunnel and the water."

"Does seem that way, mister. They designed it well. Pretty safe. But you don't need water to kill all them people. A cave-in could do it, once the skin of the tunnel was split. It's like a mine. The pressure from all that depth can bring the roof down in nothing flat. It's a little like a stone arch. When everything's right, it can hold tons. But, remove just one key brick and it can't hold squat. If they could get between the inner and outer tunnels, it would be easy."

"Could the charge they used at the ends do it?" Patterson asked, pointing towards the entrance.

"Maybe, but I don't think so," Cuomo answered after some thought. "I think it would have to be four, five times this size. For that, you don't just sneak in and hide a stick of dynamite behind a Coke can. You need a couple suitcases of stuff."

"That wouldn't be a big problem," said Stephens to Patterson. They both knew about explosives that would fit *in* a coke can that easily could blow through anything the old Italian had described.

"Remember, all that silt and guck's been packing down for years. There's even a big barge full of granite blocks sunk two years ago and is sitting right over the Sumner. So, you may not get water, but you sure can get a hell of a lot of dirt. If you're going to suffocate, doesn't really matter much whether you're sucking dirt, or water, does it?"

"Mr. Cuomo, I'd appreciate it if you could stay around until the plans arrive," said Stephens. "I don't see much hope from what you've told us, but an idea might come where we'll need your help. I think . . ."

"Don't you worry about that at all," interrupted Cuomo. "I'll be right here. You want help with the shits who done this, then you got it."

Cuomo had walked about a dozen feet when an idea that had been simmering at the back of Stephens' consciousness finally took form. "Mr. Cuomo, what is Butyl Cellosolv?"

The old man stopped short and walked slowly back towards them.

"You do know a little something, after all," said Cuomo when he was back beside Stephens and Patterson. "That's good stuff. We use it to clean the tunnel. How come you know about it?"

"I saw it somewhere. Where do you get it?"

"A company named Texo. They got a rep down on the South Shore, Duxbury I think, who gets it for us. Texo 127-HD is the best stuff for a tunnel like this. Use the Texo stuff to swab it down on a graveyard shift three times a year. All the exhaust and dirt cakes on after a time, and would turn my tunnel black as night if we let it get out of hand."

"When's the last time?"

"Two months ago. Just after Labor Day."

"Same as usual?"

"Yup. Started around 11:00 at night and finished up by 5:00 the next morning before traffic started. Took us two weeks. We close down one lane at a time."

Patterson turned to Stephens. "I don't see the connection. Where did you come up with the link?"

Stephens looked at her for a second, raised his eyebrows briefly as he ducked the question for the moment, and then turned back to the DPW retiree. "Are you sure they've done nothing since then?"

"Certain."

"Anything strange about that time?"

"Not a thing. I was there myself, as usual. I've worked with those guys for a couple dozen years. Why, two of us go back well into the fifties together."

"No one new on the job that night?"

"Well yes, there was. Joe's been with us only three years now."

"I mean, *really* new. Maybe just that night?"

"No one like that, mister."

"Most of the guys from that night still with you?"

Cuomo laughed. "Mister, you don't understand Boston at all. You get into DPW, and you're there forever. Oh sure, the big shots at city hall think they can push us around sometimes, but they never get far. Our local can blow them away!"

"Any chance another crew went there later?"

"None. It just don't work that way. No one goes here unless I'm with them. They won't be back again until after the holidays."

Stephens considered what the old caretaker of the tunnels had told him. He tried to remember everything he could about the barrels at the rabbit farm. He didn't remember whether they were full or empty, although he could surmise that at least some of them were now empty. He tried to picture the kinds of actions Falconer and his people might take. Finally, after two or three minutes of dead silence, he knew with reasonable certainty how explosives had been laid in the tunnel. It now was just a matter of pinning down the details of when.

"The problem is," he said aloud, mainly to himself, "knowing how they did it doesn't help much."

"You know how they planted the explosives?" asked Patterson, recognizing a look in Stephens' eyes that she had not seen in nearly seven years.

"Yes, I do, Joyce," he said, as helplessness swept through him. "For what it's worth, I do. But it eludes me what value the knowledge has." He stared down at the ground, shook his head gently side to side, and let his breath escape slowly. The frustration of the past few days finally settled in and seemed to sap the last of his energy.

Before Cuomo walked away, he glanced back and forth at the two agents. One was a man, tired and haggard, who clearly was in pain from the way he absently stroked his palm up and down his side every so often. The other, one of the most striking women he had ever seen, seemed to be both friendly and casual and yet totally in control of the events whirling around her. Cuomo realized that they were different from any of the people he had known over his seventy-two years. He had met with the politicians, three mayors, union leaders, street people, and a host of others in between. He had known good people, and bad. He could easily distinguish between the endless thousands who worked so hard to present the illusion of power, and the handful who never needed to try. Cuomo would never be able to explain it with any eloquence, but he understood the difference instinctively. There was an inner strength in some people that lay quietly behind all that they did. It was the same strength that had always been inside his father, always there to sweep away the doubts, or hurts, or fears of a child.

"Yup," he thought, as always feeling good inside when he remembered his father. "Dad would have liked these two." Cuomo was not surprised that the two brought back the memories. He knew that the two people standing front of the tunnels he and his Dad had both loved, would do whatever could be done to make things right. That was the thing he most remembered about his Dad. It was not that everything would work out. Sometimes even his dad failed. It was the certainty that whatever his dad *could* do, even if not enough, he *would* do. Cuomo smiled as he remembered, once again, how much he still missed his Dad thirty years after his death. He found he was grateful to the two people standing there, looking so tired and small against the events around them, who were now linked to those memories.

He turned to face Stephens and Patterson. "Who are you two, anyway?" he asked them quietly, not expecting or awaiting an answer. "I hope you are as good as I think you might be. I think you have to be."

"I hope we are too," answered Joyce Patterson, looking past Cuomo to the houses to the Northeast, where at least one pair of eyes had to be on them at that time.

"Tell me about the chemical," asked Patterson after Cuomo had left. "What did you call it again?"

Stephens and Patterson had moved away from the entrance to the tunnel. They were now back on the far side of the toll booths, about 200 feet up Porter Street, the road that leads to the remote parking lots that served the aitport with shuttle buses. They preempted a small convenience store that partially overlooked the site. You could see the toll booths and the van, and part way down the ramp towards the entrance.

"Butyl Cellosolv, HD-127. I ran across it up in Peterborough."

"What happened there?"

Stephens reached instinctively to hold his left side as he answered. "You don't really want to know."

"I can assume this 'Gertmeyer' was at the heart of it?"

"Yes."

"And Green, too?"

At the question Stephens looked long and hard at Joyce Patterson. She understood the questions going through his mind, and waited quietly. Stephens' thoughts, just then, were of times long before the scene at the tunnel. He was remembering London, and Joyce Patterson's last major field assignment. It was a year before his final days with the company. Like so many of the visions etched into his memories, London centered upon a handful of faces, most stark and angry, and one or two like Green that offered hope. Quietly, without fanfare, he knew that she too was of the later.

Stephens could remember many places, and many times with Joyce. London was just one of the times when Joyce had made the difference. He remembered her diving across barrels of soap in the London warehouse, twisting as she fell to get off an impossible shot. She had seen the man who crept, unknown to Stephens, to a clear firing position a few yards behind him. He remembered how she had been shot while laying there exposed after the dive. He remembered waiting for help after the action, while he could only slow her bleeding, and both of them thought she would die. A small smile of satisfaction surfaced as he realized that he trusted her. He searched briefly, one last time, for any traces of doubts, but still found none.

And the list that was five, then four, was now three.

"Green will be okay," he said, he began to tell her about Peterborough He saw a very slight answering smile on her face. She too, he realized, had understood that there was a mole in ATQ. She too must have realized it could not be Green.

"Green was hurt bad," he answered simply.

"This Gertmeyer?"

"Yes. Good guess."

"How bad?"

"Very bad. He's at a safe house." Again he smiled as he thought of Myrna Glover, and her likely mock anger if she ever were to understand what honor was implied by his label for her home. "We need to send help for him."

"Rob, you and I both know that it has to be done right," she said, referring clearly to the mole within the department. "Multiple call?"

"Yes. The only way. Please handpick all three. Make sure one is a woman."

Joyce Patterson looked intently at Stephens for nearly ten seconds, and then nodded slightly as she realized how strong was his trust in her. A multiple call was a proven old method, used whenever there was a severe, life-threatening danger from an unknown mole. At least two people would select three others for a specific assignment. The three would be informed of their assignment at the same time. The goal was to make sure that there were at least two of the selected who were solid. One person would never be allowed to select the three. If only one person made the call, and if that person were also the mole, then the choice could easily include some of the mole's allies within the department. Yet, Stephens had asked her to make all three selections. She understood more than anyone in the company how close Stephens and Green were. They were friends among people who could never take that label lightly. She also knew that people like Stephens did not entrust the lives of those who had earned the label of friend to one who had not.

"Joyce, please make sure that they take care of that old woman. She's different from most, and special to some. She's not ATQ, but won't take her responsibility lightly. Tell them to treat her with deep respect," he added as she turned to summon another messenger from the van. "She's earned it."

"Why send a woman?" asked Patterson.

"I wanted her to be at ease with whoever showed. I told her one would be a woman, and they would identify themselves with the code 1231."

After Stephens described the Glover location to the young agent from the van, he arranged a call to Jim Lowe and Jennifer Dickenson in the ciphers department. Once they were online, Stephens told them about the book of Frost poetry. Lowe's people would be able to tap into the Library of Congress computer to call up all the same edition. By no later than the end of the day they would break the code if, as Stephens was convinced, the volume was the key to the literary progression.

The next step had been to begin a series of calls to verify Stephens' theory about the way the explosives had been set in the tunnel. As he expected, the calls to the Boston Police Department had come up negative, just as had the discussion with Angelo Cuomo earlier. He got the answer when his call to the head of the Mass Transit Authority led him to the night-shift toll booth supervisors. One remembered two nights a week ago when ". . . a special DPW crew experimented with new cleaning procedures . . ." during the graveyard shift. Very little was known about the crew. They had the normal police support to divert traffic around the bright yellow DPW trucks. They had worked, each night, for about two hours. Nothing seemed unusual.

"The problem is, Joyce," Stephens explained after he ended a follow-up call to the police, "there was no such crew. And the Boston PD never assigned officers to the tunnel. Cuomo is certain that there is no such thing as a 'special crew,' or any 'tests' of new procedures."

"What does that buy us?"

"You do get right to the point, Joyce," he answered wryly. "As far as I can figure out, it buys us nothing. We know they used the phony crew to plant the explosives. Five will get you ten they were, are, in the vent slots that line the top and bottom of the tunnel. I guess it does prove that they had the opportunity to plant all they could possibly need in there. Four, five hours is a lot of time if you've planned well."

"He would have planned well," she said softly, knowing that the conclusion was obvious. "At least it does tell us that we can assume that the rest of the tunnel is mined."

"Any luck with the search for the antenna?"

"None yet. There's nothing obvious. But with all the miles of cable in and out of that tunnel, any one of them could have been spliced into an internal antenna of some sort. We're going on the theory that if they have an antenna, it's connected to a cable that exits at the Boston end of the tunnel."

"The explosion less on the far side?"

"At this end most of the cables were cut in the blast. We don't think that Falconer could be sure that any would last. The far end is a little better. Maybe ten or twenty percent at the Boston end were torn out. A good seventy, eighty percent went at this end."

"No cables exit out the top? The middle?"

"None. Remember, the cables are in narrow pipes built into the cement of the inner tunnel. That thing's sealed tight until two cable hatches on each end just above each entrance. Both lead up from the small pipes into a small chamber, and then up into the distribution network in the Boston sewer system. The one at this end will take the best cable splicers weeks to repair. The explosion was quite a bit to the side of the chamber, but when it caved in, everything was torn loose."

"They must have expected that. Falconer would have planned the blast. Why lead us right to the other end? A red herring?"

"We came to the same conclusion. Very fishy. So we're checking out the cables at this end, too. We've got one of the splicers working the main branch points in the sewer system over the entrance. The trouble is, above the chamber or what is left of it, they branch in half a dozen directions."

"How long before we know if any are tied in to an antenna?"

"Hours. But maybe never. Our guys think we are chasing our tail here. Unless we happen upon an obvious transmission, they might not find anything. And even a transmission can be disguised, encoded. We don't have the right equipment yet to monitor anything. They're using just probes and earphones in there. And even if we did get equipment here, and figure out how to get inside, how can we find a transmission that might not be there."

"A snipe hunt, then?"

"That's about it. There are some four hundred various cables passing through there, most holding dozens of wires inside. Our best estimate is we have two or three thousand individual lines to chase."

Stephens looked up at the clouds moving in off the ocean to the northeast. "What if we cut them, instead of splice them?"

"What!"

"Let's cut them."

"Which ones?"

"All of them."

"There's some risk, of course," she said as she considered the impact of the idea. "He might have a way of monitoring the continuity."

"But Joyce, unless we've missed something pretty major, that's the only communication into the tunnel. We've already agreed that he can't punch a signal through that rubble. So, we cut him off from anyone he has inside."

"And we cut him off from any more explosives, too," added Joyce.

"I know."

"I like your idea. If we pull it off, he has no more teeth. It becomes nothing more than a waiting game."

Despite the optimistic sounding assessment, both sensed the feeling of uneasiness lying between them in the room. Neither made any move to call for a messenger to start the cable cutting action. Both wished to wrestle with the idea a bit longer, to identify and understand the warning signals that tugged impatiently at the edge of their thoughts.

Stephens had been sitting on a tall stool behind the counter, leaning forward, resting his forearms on the dirty brown counter in front of him. He stood up and reached one hand behind himself to pull the stool away. It scraped loudly on the wooden floor. The sound seemed to be an echo of the scrape of his chair, when sitting before the Falconer up in Peterborough less than twenty-four hours earlier. He walked over to the windows full of food cans and cartons, and looked through the gray, streaked film to the buildings in the distance.

"You'd like to be out there hunting him, wouldn't you?"

"It's hard to wait." Stephens inclined his head towards the buildings. "He's there. In one of those. The chances are that he's watching me right now."

"Over the years, you and I seem to have spent half a lifetime just waiting. Green, too."

"I know. Still, it's never easy for me."

"So, we wait some more. At least until help comes."

"I wish Green was here. We'd be stronger."

"I know."

Stephens turned back towards where she sat, partly hidden in shadow in the darkened room. "I hate waiting. I remember watching the old Sherlock Holmes movies when I was I kid. No matter what they were doing, the movie always dragged for me until the investigation was complete, and Holmes had worked out the answer that told him what actions to take.

When I knew it was coming to that point, I'd edge forward on my seat waiting for him to say 'Come Watson, the game's afoot.' That was the signal. The wait was finally over. Now, the action was coming." Stephens motioned out through the grimy glass panes to where the buildings that he knew must hold the Falconer reflected the late afternoon sun back towards them. "What is he up to? Why no demands? He knows that the night will even things just a bit. Why wait?"

"Rob, something stinks here. We cut the wires and he has no antenna. No antenna, and no threat. No threat, and the game's over. That's too bloody easy. I can feel Falconer laughing at us right now. We're missing something major."

"I know. I feel it, too." He absently pounded one fist lightly on the frozen foods locker in front of him. "Okay. I know that he has a deep mole in ATQ, but that isn't enough. That only helps in the planning." He turned back from the window to face her. "But that doesn't buy *squat* once the President entered the tunnel. Hell, if he had five moles and the whole ATQ staff, they could still do little now with all the coverage and outsiders here! The Falconer's got to play the rest of this hand by himself."

"Rob, of course this all *would* make sense if we assume he is in total control of the inside of the tunnel."

"All the reports say that can't have happened."

"Maybe the report would have been more objective if they had said that there is no trace of it happening."

"The inner doors were locked. No one was inside at the start other than the one, carefully screened and vetted tunnel monitor. Every passenger in every car was screened by Treasury. Where's the hole?"

"Then, basically we've got an absurd Catch-22 here," said Joyce. "Falconer can only exercise one of two options, and neither is possible. First, he could try to get the President out of there. But once the President is physically in his hands the game is over, so there's no way we would let him march up here and dig through the rockslide at either end. Second, he could blow up the tunnel with the President inside. But a bomb needs to be set off, and he appears to have no way to do that. No antenna to set it off remotely, and no one inside to do it. It all comes down to one of these two, and he hasn't tried the first or done anything to convince of us the second."

"You know," Patterson continued, "I'm beginning to agree with you. Maybe the strongest proof we have that he's got someone in the tunnel—is that there is no proof at all. It's like watching a master magician. He gets us looking at the right hand, and the left runs the show. Look at the left, the right takes over. Illusions and diversions. Everything tell us that no one could be in the tunnel. Therefore, there must be someone."

"Wait a minute." Stephens' voice was almost whispered as the start of an idea formed. He stood in the dusty light with his head tilted to one side, staring at the ground, with the index fingers of both hands pointing out. "We agree that they can't get a signal inside the tunnel. Right?"

Patterson nodded.

"It also means no one inside can get a signal outside."

"So?"

"Damn," he said, shaking his head side to side in frustration. "I don't know where this leads. I'm just grasping. But this is key, somehow."

"We're going over the same old ground, Rob. We're beating this to death, here."

"Anyone talked to the locals about the street lights?" Stephens asked.

"I covered that just before you came. We're doing it even one better than just that. The local Edison people are going to have a brown-out on this section of the grid. What lights do work will be at about forty percent power. It won't be real dark, but it won't be very light, either. At least we'll have some cover. Right now he can see the start of every move we make. That will even things a bit."

"Harvey would call that, at best, a 'very wee bit.' But, it is better than nothing when we go out there."

"Rob," she answered softly, "it always seems to come down to that again, doesn't it? No matter how much we plan and try, someone always has to go 'out there.'"

She did not expect Stephens to answer. Over the years they had each faced many situations when there was no longer any distance between 'cause and effect.' The time for planning and conjecture would be over. Now action would have to be taken, along with the inevitable consequence of those actions. It was these moments that left a burden of fears, or memories, or nightmares that could never be lifted. It was that terrible point in events when a choice had to be made.

The wind off the harbor had picked up a bit. A swirl of old papers and dust swept by in the street outside the glass door. The police officer stationed on the sidewalk just outside the door buried his head into his right shoulder, and tightly pressed his eyes closed as the dust drove against his carefully starched blue uniform. He had been one of the officers on the site, doing traffic duty to hold back the local traffic from the tunnels, when the explosions had occurred. He resented the simple guard duty, and, like most of the other officers he could not understand why no one was taking any action. He wanted to do something, anything, other than wait. "Shit," he thought, "at least they could ask me inside. Probably drinking cold beer and telling dirty jokes."

He caught the tail end of their conversation when Patterson pulled open the door to call for the splicers to cut all lines. What he heard confirmed his suspicions about the joking. "But at least the game will be afoot, eh my dear Stephens?" she had said. Only later did he realize that there was no humor in her voice. He tightened his eyebrows as he tried to understand the message in the tone. At first he remembered it to be resignation, or perhaps pain. But then he found himself thinking it sounded like something out of the Dickens novels he had read as a child. Old Miss Wright, his tenth grade English teacher, had called it 'the cruelest form of irony.'

"Nah," he muttered to himself as Patterson walked down towards the communications van, leaving Stephens alone in the darkened storefront. "They must just be tired. That's it. Tired."

Chapter Twenty-One

By the time the sounds of the helicopter carrying Sanders and Jacobi could first be heard, sweeping in low over the tightly packed old wooden houses to the southeast, the robberies had already started in downtown Boston. The first reports had come in just after noon. This day would be far different from the lunchtime '. . . get out, run errands, and be back before 1:30 . . .' scramble that Boston workers have raised to an art form. The sidewalks were packed. There was no possible way to get a car out into the streets.

The "T" was jammed solid, and for a day made the legendary Tokyo subways look tame. People crammed into the subway cars, bodies pressed full-length against those surrounding on all sides. The spontaneous remark of one middle-aged gentleman, upon leaving the car after having been pressed up against a lovely young woman for more than an hour, was picked up and repeated by hundreds of commuters that day. By evening thousands claimed the witticism as their own. "Ma'am," he had said, "it was a long time ago, but the only major difference I can recall between this and my honeymoon was that I wasn't standing then."

Like dominoes falling, the events at the tunnel had spread throughout Boston and into the surrounding suburbs. When the Tunnels had first been closed by police in anticipation of the President's motorcade, the Southeast Expressway immediately packed solid. When the tunnel was not reopened on schedule, it took less than half an hour for the end of the Massachusetts Turnpike extension into Boston to follow. An hour later found Route 93, Storrow Drive, Memorial Drive, and dozens of less well known arteries into the city equally immobile. Amused shoppers at the Newton Star Market, built on a bridge over the turnpike, stood at the windows and laughed and joked with fellow shoppers as they watched the plight of motorists standing by their cars on the expressway below.

Later, when they went to their own cars, they discovered that the jams had spread up the exit ramps and into the surrounding roads. They, too, were now trapped in the middle of what had been so amusing just minutes before.

By noontime enterprising vendors were scalping sandwiches to drivers on the Southeast Expressway. Many drivers had been in the same place since just after seven that morning. There were lines waiting at any restroom within walking distance of all major roads. Male motorists, caught for hours in the middle of the Tobin Bridge, had little recourse except to add to the pollution of the harbor a hundred feet below. Showing the remarkable pragmatism that always lays beneath the surface of New Englanders, women banded together to provide screens of overcoats over the grating in the middle of the bridge. Despite the inevitable results, the vendors could not keep up with the demand for coffee.

The first robberies had carefully and deliberately built upon all the chaos already occurring. Three separate armored cars, while stalled in the traffic, had been attacked by teams of motorcyclists. The hits were fast, clean, and violent. All were accomplished in exactly the same manner. Horrified motorists, trapped in their cars just a few feet away, could do nothing but gape helplessly while the teams blew out the front windshields of the armored cars with enough explosives to instantly kill all within. It was very clear that there was no interest in negotiation with the drivers. The technique was brute force and speed. The drivers were expendable, irrelevant. Police airwaves were saturated with dozens of fake calls that scattered the already overtaxed police forces. With the highways in and around Boston a huge, endless parking lot, there was no way for police cruisers to approach the robberies. Police officers were left to sputter in helpless rage as they sat immobile in their cars. By the time some of the few available police motorcycles could be dispatched, the robbers were long gone. In the three armored trucks hit, all eight guards had been killed. Horrified onlookers, half in shock, had told of guards being coolly shot through the head after they had dropped their arms and surrendered.

Initially no one saw any connection between the robberies and the events in the Sumner Tunnel, and so the reports were not even considered worth relaying to the ATQ site. To the beleaguered officers manning the overwhelmed dispatch center in the basement of the Boston Police Department, it was bitter frosting on a harsh cake that already included just about everything bad they could imagine. The early theory was that enterprising locals were taking advantage of the total chaos. Enough of the crimes were quick, opportunistic hit-and-run efforts that a pattern did not surface. Reports flooded in about a raid on an electronics store, a holdup of a downtown movie theater, a quick hit at a supermarket, and innumerable robberies at liquor stores. With all the turmoil, two of the three armored car hits were not confirmed until more than an hour after they had occurred. When a police helicopter finally was able to drop a small squad of BPD officers on school yard next to one of the armored cars, they found people sitting, half in shock in their cars. They had been staring at the bodies on the road in front of them, and at the charred shell of the truck, for nearly two hours.

It was well after midday when Captain Weathers of the Boston Police Department realized that beneath the surface of all the reports was a subset that was well planned, and all too effective. There were six that stood out. Three were the armored cars. Two were simultaneous hits at the Bank of New England and Bank of Boston towers, in the financial district just a few hundred yards from the Boston entrance to the tunnels. Another was at the Fidelity Clearing House. The common denominator was cool professionalism and careful organization that could not possibly be a spontaneous plan to take advantage of the complete disorganization.

"The same son-of-a-bitch who did the tunnel had to plan this," snapped the normally controlled Captain Weathers as he stared at the situation map, now dotted with colored pins, in the dispatch center. His hands were clenched in frustration by his side. The massive BPD, in which Weathers had genuine pride, was reduced to near helplessness by the lack of mobility. The only effective resources he had were a small team of mounted officers and a handful of motorcycle police officers. His fleet of squad cars was nearly useless in the massive traffic jams caused by the tunnel. His two police helicopters were preempted by the tunnel shuttling duties. Worcester and Springfield were the only other Massachusetts cities with helicopters. Both had their helicopters in the air heading to assist Boston, along with two from Hartford, one from Providence, and one from Concord, New Hampshire. But Weathers knew that they'd arrive long after the main events were over. And with equal bitterness he remembered his own decision, at interdepartmental meetings just over a year ago, to drastically cut back the size of the BPD motorcycle fleet because of the long periods each winter where they were impractical.

Much later in the day a comment overheard during one of the robberies explained link between the tunnel events and the sudden crime wave. Four men successfully walked off with a half-million in cash from the Fidelity clearinghouse operations. As they started back up the stairs towards the main lobby, one robber had let out an excited whoop. "Shit man. He's worth his cut! This is just as easy as he told us it would be. I can't believe it!" His leader had ordered him to "Shut up," but the robber had added one final gloating comment. "How the hell did he know that the pigs wouldn't be able to move an inch by eleven o'clock?"

Stephens had no such difficulty figuring it out.

"You have to admit, Joyce, it's a brilliant stroke. We could hardly have the city better tied up in knots than it is right now. This is as good as giving BPD the day off."

"Is it just more confusion he's after?" asked Joyce Patterson. "That doesn't quite seem to be enough. I don't see how that can help him here."

"It doesn't have to. But it doesn't hurt. At the very least the Falconer has improved the odds another notch. He's covering his bases. I'd do the same." Stephens glanced down at the summary report that had just been delivered covering all of the robberies so far reported. "If this guy Weathers is correct, then Falconer has done much better than just pad the margin of safety. He has also padded his wallet to the tune of a couple million dollars, perhaps as much as five million. You can cause a good deal of trouble with a five meg bankroll."

At about the same time Jacobi and Sanders touched down at the entrance to the tunnel, the ninth bank robbery of the day had just gotten underway. The first eight had been complete successes for the robbers. This ninth robbery was stopped because Captain Weathers, in desperation, sent officers on foot to begin to stake out banks not yet been hit. Meanwhile, most remaining banks and branches finally had begun to close early as a preventative measure.

"Well, you certainly have things well in control, Stephens," Sanders spat out as he strode through the door to the convenience store. "It seems all hell has broken loose with your little case here."

"Carl, you *could* manage a 'hello' upon occasion, couldn't you?" said Joyce Patterson.

"Hello doesn't seem quite appropriate considering how much your friend has screwed this one up."

Joyce Patterson took a deep breath and then exhaled slowly. "Carl, this hasn't been much of a day so far, and I'd just as soon you don't make it worse. None of us has been particularly effective in making a dent so far."

Sanders stopped a few feet inside the door. Behind him Pete Jacobi stepped quietly into the room, slowly closed the door, and appeared to look helplessly from side to side before wandering over to one corner where he could lean against a bare stretch of counter.

"Besides, if the two of you would stop to look beyond your asinine male hackles, you'd remember that you were always a damn powerful team." She waited a few moments for her words to sink in. "Right?"

"Maybe you're right, Joyce," said Sanders with resignation in his voice.

"I am," she answered forcefully.

"But, it's a bit more accurate to say it was always the *three* of us." He turned to face Stephens. "I suspect that neither of us is very thrilled by working together, but let's get to it anyway."

"Agreed." Stephens nodded once as he answered.

"Where do we stand? I had precious little hard data when I left Virginia, and assume that most of that has changed since. Stephens, is it confirmed the Falconer is back?"

"Confirmed," Stephens answered simply.

Sanders continued to stare at Stephens as though the answer would change if he waited long enough.

"Carl, it's true," said Patterson. "That, at least, *is* a known."

"Is he tied to the report on Green?"

"Yes," answered Stephens.

"You really needed a multiple call to set Green's pickup?" The question hung in the air. Sanders was all too aware that a multiple call could only mean a high level security risk.

"Yes."

"Care to elaborate, Stephens?"

"Not yet, Carl. Not yet. Let's stick to the events here at the tunnel, and I'll cover parts of that later."

Sander's voice became cold and hard. "Then you're suggesting that I'm a security risk?"

"Carl, you know the script on these things. Someone is a security risk. I called for a multiple on Green's pick-up. That's all there is to it. Let it die for now."

"How high is the risk?"

"Let it *die*, Carl," interjected Patterson. "We'll keep to standard scripting on this. When Rob is ready to call a council he will."

"Are you close?"

"Not yet."

"Look Stephens, that's not going to cut it. Just the fact that you're the one who called for the multiple says a lot about this one. If there is a leak, and frankly I think you've been a bit too long in the cold to be reliable judge of that, then it would have to be at our level."

"Damn it, Sanders, we're drifting away from reality here!" Patterson said emphatically as she stood up and walked over to face Sanders. "For god's sake, the President is still trapped out there! Let's stick with the business at hand. You can chase this down a rat hole for as long as you want, and it still won't get us anywhere. So drop it. Now!"

This was a side of Joyce Patterson that Stephens had seen only two or three times over the years they had worked together. She had such a degree of inner strength that few ever questioned her authority. Command and control of a situation came naturally and easily to her. Often Stephens had seen how quickly others would adapt something she suggested, because of the high respect her views had earned. Yet, despite the calm and patience, there was a strong, tough streak within her that most suspected, but few ever saw. In the Company, every senior person inevitably gets a nickname that sticks. Some are kind, and many are not. But they all share a brutal honesty. One of the most fascinating and energetic traditional activities of all the junior staff was to do one's best to steer others towards a nickname of choice. Just as inevitably, such efforts would fail. The final choice would one that summed up what one's peers had deemed to be his or her most significant single trait. Joyce Patterson was known as "Effie." That was a convenient short form of "E. F. Hutton." It had been a natural, and had been applied, and stuck, within days of the first "When E.F. Hutton speaks . . ." advertisements on television.

"Besides, Carl, the most pathetic part of all this is that we still know so little. A five minute briefing is overkill to cover the essentials."

Sanders, like Stephens, had seen this side of Patterson before. He knew the futility of pursuing his questions further and looked for a way to back away from the issue. "Okay, Joyce. We'll wait until later for Mr. Stephens to tell us what ghosts he sees in the shadows."

Patterson's estimate of five minutes was not far off. She covered all of the morning's events at the site, ticking off the key points on her fingers as she spoke. Stephens noted that she never mentioned his previous night in Peterborough. Instead, she covered the assessment of who was in the tunnel, the death of Robinson, a brief summary of Angelo Cuomo's description of the tunnel, and the various facts that indicated the tunnel was under complete observation.

"So, at the risk of stating the obvious, Falconer knows by now we're here," said Sanders.

"How many came in with you?" asked Patterson.

"Four, and there are six on the way. All fours and fives."

"Where'd you park them?"

"Still at Logan Airport. Out of sight. We can deploy them from there."

"You said the spooks were here, Joyce," said Sanders, referring to the NSA contingent from Ft. Meade. "What did they come up with?"

"Too soon to call. Just before you landed I got a report they're coming in with the results. Should be here any minute."

"A bit out of their league, aren't they?"

"It's a long shot, but it could give us something?"

"Pete, you've been closer to NSA than most of us. Have they resources we can call upon?"

"Huh?" answered Jacobi, looking up from where he had been quietly staring at the floor.

"What does NSA have we could use?"

"Oh. Not much. I guess." Jacobi glanced back and forth at the three people across the room from him. When no one followed up the question, he dropped his head back to stare at the patterns in the dry, scratched hardwood floor of the store.

Patterson, Stephens, and Sanders looked carefully at each other. Stephens raised one eyebrow as he looked intently at Sanders. "Burnt?" he asked softly.

The reply did not carry more than a few feet past where the three of them stood. "Toast."

"This?" asked Stephens, gesturing to the tunnel outside.

"The Peterson kid was his personal assignment. Then Green. Now all this."

"He's done, you know," stated Patterson. "He's of no use to us here."

"I didn't know until we were in the air on the way up here. No option then, but to bring him."

"I'll keep him in here with me," said Patterson. "Don't let him near the field team."

"All right then. Let's work this out. You said you had four at Logan and six in the air. Right?" asked Stephens.

"Right."

"That gives us enough. Finally. Falconer has twelve to fifteen. All top pros."

"Plus the woman," added Sanders.

"What woman?" asked Patterson?

"Oh, no big deal, but there was a report Falconer had picked up a groupie. An amateur."

Stephens' expression did not change at all during the exchange. "Where'd we pick that up?"

"I'm not sure. Came up at staff this morning, I think."

"Joyce, anything to add?"

"Not really Rob. I hadn't heard that one."

"Well, I don't know what it means," said Stephens, leading the conversation away from the topic of Cynthia Lebart. "So, let's map out our options."

Joyce was reaching for the blueprints, and both Sanders and Stephens were guardedly glancing at Jacobi when they heard the faint sound of the explosion. Almost immediately the buzzer on the intercom to the communications van blared.

"Patterson here."

"Ma'am, we have our friend again. Patch it through to you, or take it over here in the van?"

"Patch it through, Payson."

The three pulled close to the intercom. Even Jacobi had risen from his counter and shuffled over to stand helplessly, absently shifting his weight from foot to foot, just behind Sanders and Stephens.

"So you have help, Stephens. This is rich. Very rich! I actually have you, Joyce Patterson, and Carl Sanders all together. And Mr. Jacobi is such a nice bonus!"

"Your 'surprise' lacks a bit of authenticity, Falconer. You certainly knew everyone available would all be called in for this one. All but me, of course, had your friend been a bit more adept."

"Well yes, perhaps that is so. But permit me the pleasure of stating it, anyway." The voice lost all traces of amusement. "I presume you heard the explosion."

"Yes. Obviously, since it happened just seconds ago we don't have any details yet. I suspect you plan to fill us in?"

"Yes, indeed I do. If you check with your communications people, you'll find they recorded a signal just over twenty Meg shortly before the blast. I'm sure that they've been doing wideband tracking and caught the trigger."

"I don't know. But if so, they'll report it."

"Stephens, no games please. Of course they're monitoring wideband."

"Continue, Falconer."

"They will report the trigger signal. You have evidenced the result. It is just *one* of the charges we left in the tunnel to discourage hotheads like Sanders from doing something stupid."

Sanders stepped forward and reached for the intercom switch. His face was tight in anger. Just as the hand touched the switch it stopped. Both Stephens and Patterson saw the self control fighting to take over. The hand stayed poised over the switch for several seconds before it was finally pulled back. His lips formed the silent words "Son of a bitch."

Stephens turned back to the intercom. "Falconer, unless the communications people report that you came up with one hell of a transmitter, we don't see how you could get a signal through that rubble."

There was an uncharacteristic silence for nearly five seconds. "Unless you plan ahead, Stephens, so that you have an easier way through. Despite what they might suggest, the explosion *did* occur. 'I explode therefore I am' Stephens? That one was right near the entrance. Unless your President was unfortunate enough to be huddled up near the end, no one was hurt."

"And if they were?"

"Does it matter? You won't know until all this is over. You have to go ahead on the assumption that there's a President in there to be saved."

"So, what's the bottom line?"

"Blunt, as usual. Okay. What I would really want you could not agree to. So, I want Sanders and Jacobi to get a message. You might relay to them the story of your friend in the toll booth. Then you might point out that I can, at will, signal additional explosions in the tunnel. I want you to keep well clear of both ends. Understood?"

"Mr. Stephens?" the voice on the intercom was of Payson, the senior communications leader. He had cut the Falconer out of the conversation momentarily. "We have a trace on one of the master signals. Please keep him on the frequency."

All four people in the room reacted to the news very differently. Patterson raised one fist and pumped it slowly in front of her, as though trying to insure by sheer force of will, that a successful trace occurred. Sanders smiled broadly and muttered "son of a bitch" again under his breath. Jacobi sighed loudly, and reached up both hands to press against his forehead with relief. Stephens just gazed calmly at the three others, and then shook his head side-to-side twice before reaching for the intercom again.

"Clear, but it's not that simple for us. There are a lot of people on site. We have more damn jurisdictions here than I knew existed."

"That's bullshit, Stephens, and you know it."

"Not really. Your activities in downtown Boston have changed things. The local police now are a lot less receptive to our requests for continued patience. They now question whether or not we should be calling the shots at all. Instead of waiting around, they'd much prefer to come in, weapons blazing."

"You'll have to counsel them more effectively."

"You made them look bad today."

"They can blame me as much as they want, but that, too, is bullshit. They looked stupid because they *are* stupid. I didn't put together police plan totally dependent on full cruiser mobility in a city that most days lives on the edge of full immobility. Any of a few hundred thousand commuters could have told them that. Yet, they chose a plan that pushes the edge of the envelope. That's stupid. All I did was push it just a bit farther."

"And all the lives today? That was their stupidity also?"

"Would you have preferred a more 'gentle' confrontation? Perhaps one that resulted in a prolonged gunfight on a packed highway? If it was a handful of 'innocent civilians' now lying dead out there would your demand for fairness be better served?"

"Now *you* are indulging in bullshit, Falconer. To suggest your plan of attack on the Brink's vans was motivated by care for the 'little people' is rather absurd."

There was a small laugh over the airwaves. "Why is it that I find you so fascinating, Stephens? We chat like school children, dancing in and out of grand issues one minute, and trying to kill each other the next. Silly. And yes, of course you are right. The follow-up to today depends upon adequate funding. We now have that. Efficiently and effectively. Nothing more."

"How can we end this?"

"Stephens, please keep Sanders and Jacobi under control." There was clear finality in the voice.

Stephens stepped away from the table.

"Keep him going," pressed Sanders. "Say something."

"He won't be back on. As it was, he knows he was on too long."

"Well, but we do have a trace," offered Jacobi. "Right?"

"Pete, don't expect much there. It'll be another dead end."

"But Payson said they had a trace!" continued Jacobi. "Surely they had enough time to find one lousy transmitter."

Patterson looked intently at Stephens before shaking her head and grimacing. Then she turned towards Jacobi. "Let's wait for the reports, Pete. Meantime," she said as she reached once again for the blueprints. "It's about time we pull a plan together. We have the usual three options. Wait it out, rush in to free the captives, or try to take out the terrorists." She looked up directly at Sanders. "Carl, all my instincts tell me that waiting is the worst possible option."

"Anything solid? Or just gut?"

"Bits and pieces, but mainly gut."

"Stephens, you agree?"

Everyone turned from the counter, where blueprints were now displayed instead of cheese, when there was no answer. Only then did they notice that Stephens had not moved to join them. Instead, Stephens had half turned back to face the intercom and was staring at it.

"Rob?" she called softly.

"Hold one, Joyce," said Stephens. "Something smells here."

She walked over to where he stood and followed his eyes towards the intercom. "He said something?"

"Or *didn't* say something."

"What are you two talking about?"

"Carl," Patterson answered, "I know what Rob is wrestling with. Something in that conversation left a sour feeling for me, too."

"Okay, listen you two. The words were nothing. Standard threats, nothing more. It's got to be tied to something you know that I don't. Or it's something I'm not factoring as heavily as you are. So forget the specifics, and concentrate on comparing what he said to what happened this morning."

Stephens pulled his eyes away from the intercom and stared straight down at the floor. Then a small smile came to his face and he turned to where Sanders stood a few feet behind him. "Carl, that was good." It was one of the rare times when he used Sanders' first name. "Damn, sometimes you have amazing insights."

"Sure. But how about a detail or two so I know what I did?"

"Joyce, it was the silence when I asked him how he punched through the rubble with the trigger signal."

"Yes?"

"He wasn't ready for that one. It was an uncharacteristic slip. Maybe the first!"

"So he has a wire into the tunnel," offered Sanders.

"No Carl," answered Patterson. "You were right; we didn't cover it with you yet. You didn't know we cut all wires into the tunnel hours ago. They will have emergency lighting in there, but nothing from out here."

"That doesn't make sense. Then you must have missed something. Get Payson."

"Right." Patterson signaled to the communications van. "Payson, were we doing broadband monitoring just before the blast?"

"Yes, sir. As soon as I heard his statement, I had Lockmeyer go over the tapes. There was a 20.2 MHz signal just before the explosion."

"Signal strength?" asked Stephens.

"Nominal. Fine for short range transmission."

"Could it get through to trigger a device inside the tunnel?"

"Without an antenna, no way. Not even close."

"Just *before* the blast?" asked Patterson.

"Yup. About three seconds prior."

"Payson, this is Stephens. Please rerun the tapes. Look for a red herring. Another signal that might have been the real one."

"We already thought of that, sir. Nothing."

"What about the trace on the master signal?" asked Jacobi. It was only the second comment so far that afternoon from him.

"We got a solid fix. A team is on the way."

"I'd be willing to bet that the location is far enough from here that there's no line-of-sight to the tunnel," stated Stephens.

There was surprise in Payson's voice. "Sir, I'd like to know how you figured that one, but you're dead on. The blooming thing was a mile from here near the airport!"

"Payson, work the issue, but don't expect much. What you'll find is an antenna with a wire leading into a sewer or cable conduit that will take hours, or days, to trace. Chances are that there are three of four backup sites just like it. You didn't pick it up before, because he kept switching transmitters."

"He had to know we'd find it?"

"Exactly. We chase it, it costs him nothing, and it dissipates our energy and resources."

"Should I pull back the trace team?"

"No. That's the beauty. There's no way we can ignore something that solid in a situation like this."

"Give us a report as soon as it comes in," directed Patterson.

"Yes Ma'am."

When the intercom went dead there was an eerie silence in the room. With all that was going on around them—dozens of reporters covering the scene and hundreds of police officers in the area—the room seemed momentarily divorced from all of that. The only sound was the soft breathing of the four people in the room and the occasional snuffle of Jacobi, who continued to sit alone and apart from the other three.

"Catch 22, again Rob?" Patterson asked softly.

Sanders looked back and forth at the two. "Catch 22?"

"He triggered the bomb with a radio signal. But no radio signal could have gotten in. Therefore, the blast couldn't have been triggered."

Sanders let a small smile surface. "Then, I guess we're saying it didn't happen."

Chapter Twenty-Two

Stephens had no idea what caused the pieces to finally fall into place for him.

"Henry Rourk," he said with a voice little more than a whisper. Both Sanders and Patterson turned to face Stephens when they heard the name. Stephens was now staring into the distance, eyes intently locked on the patterns that were meshing in his thoughts. His head was slightly tilted to one side. Both hands were partially extended, fingers clenched, as though poised to grab the answers when they completed forming.

"Again!" he muttered.

The word made no sense to either Sanders or Patterson. But they saw Stephens' hands pounding the air in slow motion, culminating in one exultant clench that was held a few moments. Stephens let out a rush of breath, and dropped his hands to his sides. The idea was solid now.

"We've been chasing our tail," Stephens finally explained. "We spent the last few hours adding two and two, getting five, and never had it dawn on us that we should have been adding two and three!"

"You going to let me in on this one?" asked Sanders.

"I'm not in on it yet, either," answered Patterson.

"We've got to enter the tunnel. I know how they set off that blast."

"But Rob, we've been through all that. As soon as we open a hole in the rubble, a radio signal can easily set off another charge."

"We don't go in the end. We go in the middle!"

Once again Sanders and Patterson exchanged looks that were a mixture of astonishment and questioning.

"The reason we couldn't find any trace of anyone infiltrating the motorcade is that they were in there all along. *They were already inside the tunnel.*"

Patterson stared at Stephens for several seconds before understanding finally came. "The outer tunnel."

"Excellent." Without knowing it, he had used the same tone that he reserved for his soccer players on those special occasions when there was an extra measure of pride in their accomplishments. "They were waiting all night, or all week, or since whenever they got there. The blasts that sealed the ends *were* triggered from outside. The rest was all done inside. They blew the doors between the tunnels and entered. Based on the radio silence from the treasury cars I'd wager that they had precious little trouble with any opposition."

"How do we get inside?" asked Sanders. "You two earlier spent quite a bit of time proving that there was no way."

"We forgot what Mr. Cuomo told us. We've got to get him back here. The answer is in his 'granny chambers.'"

Patterson walked over to the deli counter that was now covered with blueprints of the tunnel. She quickly scanned the top print. "Damn," she said as she shuffled it aside and began to leaf through the remainder of the pile. "They're not even shown on these. How do we even know if they're still there?"

"What in hell are granny chambers?" Sanders' voice again showed traces of irritation.

"They're escape tunnels that were part of the original construction phase," explained Stephens. "Two of them. It was a way for the workers to have a chance to escape if a disaster hit."

"They go from the tunnel to just above the harbor bed," added Patterson. She turned to Stephens. "Back to my question. How do we know they're still there? Maybe they were filled in after construction?"

"We don't know," answered Stephens. "But Mr. Cuomo does. We need him back."

Patterson walked towards the intercom. "On it."

"I presume that your idea is to enter the tunnel through these chambers of yours."

"It's a shot," answered Stephens. "Frankly, I don't see another."

"Assume that you pull it off and get inside. Even assume you neutralize any opposition. Then what?" Sanders shrugged, arms out in front of him, head tilted to one side with the question. "If they have explosives wired in there, you still can't bring him out. As soon as you open the ends, they can trigger the blast. Stalemate."

Joyce Patterson answered as she returned from the intercom. "If I'm right about where Rob's going with this, then the idea is for us to rescue the president, and then to bring him out through the chambers into the harbor."

Sanders looked back and forth between the two. At first his expression was skeptical. The expression slowly softened, and then finally became a half smile of appreciation. "I wonder if the old coot can swim?"

"Depending upon Mr. Cuomo, we may just get a chance to find out," answered Stephens.

"He's on his way," answered Patterson. "As I expected, they tell me he's nearby. Didn't really think he could leave his tunnels during this."

"Are there better prints of the tunnel?" asked Sanders.

"Your 'copter has already been dispatched to get them," answered Patterson. "And when I called over I got the NSA report. Nothing of much use. Twice they believed they heard faint footsteps up at this end. There were more footsteps at the far end, but nothing they could make out. No voices at all."

"Their take on it?" asked Sanders.

"A guard at each end and everyone else tied and silent in the middle of the tunnel. They're only confident they can pick up activity for the first few hundred feet at each end. Anything past there is out of range."

"So, sounds like everyone is down in the middle, flat section of the tunnel?" Stephens thought aloud. "That puts the President right between four sets of doors connecting the inner and outer tunnels. We get inside through the escape tubes, enter the outer tunnel, move to the doors, and come at them from four sides."

Patterson grimaced. "Unless the doors are locked, or they have people in the outer tunnel, or he anticipated this one, or the chambers are sealed, or . . . or . . . or . . ."

"Joyce, at least it's a shot," said Stephens. "It's better than we had twenty minutes ago."

"You know," said Sanders, putting together more of the puzzle, "that means that the blast we just heard could have been set off from the inside."

Stephens smiled as he answered. "You've figured it out, Carl. It *was* set off from inside. It was a timed blast."

"Timed?" asked Patterson.

"The radio signal was a red herring," explained Stephens. "It was just to make us think it was triggered from outside. The three seconds were a safety margin to make sure the signal occurred *before* the preset explosion time."

"Try me again," said Sanders.

"Carl, we cut the wires into the tunnel. There is no antenna. And they didn't have a signal that could get through. That fox had scheduled his people to set off the charge at this precise moment. The signal was just a dummy."

"Five minutes after we arrived?" asked Sanders doubtfully.

"Bullshit luck," answered Stephens. "The son-of-a-bitch got lucky. No wonder he was so damn amused when he first got on. If it hadn't been you, then he would have had another reason. Some cop would have 'gotten too close' or some reporter would have said 'something unacceptable.' But the blast would have occurred exactly when it did."

Sanders nodded his appreciation. Then he smiled and gave a half laugh. "Okay. I buy it all. But I do have one last question. Who the hell is Henry Rourk?"

This time it was Joyce Patterson who laughed. "Let me answer that one. The 'Fountainhead.' Ayn Rand. Right?"

"Right."

"It's Rob's favorite quote. By now I should know the page number in the blooming book! Let's see, '. . . there's no such thing as a coincidence. If you think you have one, check your premises. One of them is wrong.'"

"Ah yes. The wrong one was that the tunnel was empty before the motorcade entered."

"Exactly."

"And, for once we might even have the element of surprise," said Patterson. "If Falconer is using the same set of blueprints we have, then he doesn't know about the granny chambers. They were just there for construction, and don't show on any of the current prints."

"Then let me finally contribute something to this mess," said Sanders. "There's a major naval facility up in Portsmouth that includes a training base for SEALs. It occurs to me that they would be particularly useful if we're going for a swim."

"Not us, Carl. Just me." Stephens' voice was firm. "You can't disappear from the site. Neither can Joyce. He'd see that immediately. I can. With what he knows Gertmeyer did, a short absence would be expected."

"You're still holding your side, Rob," said Joyce gently. "I've seen a couple times when you just turned slightly and it clearly hurt a lot. How are you going to swim like that?"

"Joyce, there's no choice. I've got to do it."

The two looked intently at each other for several seconds. Finally Joyce nodded slightly. It was the same nod a few of those at the Dublin town hall, years before, had seen Myrna Glover award to Stephens. She instinctively reached out one hand and lightly touched him on the right arm. "Then go for it, but carefully, please."

Stephens swung his left hand over to rest briefly on hers. "Thanks."

The mood in the old boathouse was quiet and professional. Stephens and the small squad of Navy SEALs climbed into their wet suits and checked their gear, as though they were nothing more than business people on their way to work. The rubber satchels were their briefcases, and the tools and weapons were their obligatory Cross pens and pencils. Every few seconds the quiet rustling was broken by the "thwap" of stretched rubber slapping against skin, or the metallic "chwunk" of a magazine being inserted, or the deadly hammer-fall of another weapon being checked. One-by-one the various pieces of equipment were being examined before being stored in the waterproof pouches that would be strapped to their chests. In the time honored way of the SEALs, there was little talk. The banter and bravado that Stephens knew would have been nearly incessant on the drive down from the naval station in Portsmouth had disappeared once the equipment started coming out of the travel bags.

The boathouse was a half mile southwest of the entrance to the Sumner tunnel. It was old, and sorely in need of painting and minor repairs. Unless repainted soon, serious deterioration of the wood would begin from exposure to the elements. It stood alone some forty feet from the back of the old Victorian house. The house showed a similar, but lesser degree of disrepair. By the back door to the wooden porch, a large patch of clapboards was bare and weathered where months earlier the paint had been scraped off, and then the repair abandoned.

While the squad checked out its equipment, the startled owner of the home was sitting wide-eyed on the old plaid couch in the front sitting room of the house. He would glance back and forth to the television coverage of the tunnel events, and the two armed men sitting in the chairs nearby. One had identified himself simply as "Foster, FBI." The other, the one clearly in charge, said nothing. The answer to any question from the homeowner was invariably the same. "Mr. Kirk, I'm truly sorry, but we cannot discuss any of this." Norman Kirk was quite certain that 'this' had something to do with the President, but beyond that had little idea of what 'this' was. He had seen two dark blue vans pull to the rear of the house when he answered the door to meet "Mr. Foster" and his companion. He was pretty sure the shadows just visible through the tinted side windows indicated each van was full of passengers.

"Why go back there?" he had thought. "Can't see anything from there. Damn boathouse blocks any decent view. Should have torn it down years ago."

But the very worst part of sitting there was the sight of the phone, half on and half off the yellowed lace doily, on the table between the two agents. The more he thought of all the people he wanted to call to tell of the early afternoon's events, the bigger the phone seemed to get. There was little doubt in his mind that the phone was strictly "off limits." Kirk didn't even have to ask. He wondered what would happen if someone tried to call him.

Kirk was right about the vans. Stephens, fourteen SEALs, and all their equipment had been squeezed into them. When they had pulled up in back of the house, the doors had opened quietly, and all of the people and equipment disappeared into the boathouse in less than forty seconds. Once inside the squad had calmly and methodically begun to unpack and assemble the gear.

Stephens picked up the folder filled with diagrams, schematics, and maps that Cuomo had pulled together from the MDC files. He walked over next to the single window on the northwest side of the boathouse. Using three old nails he found lying on the dusty sill he tacked two sheets of paper onto the wall. The first was a profile of the tunnel itself. The second was a survey map of Boston Harbor.

"Gentlemen," he said, slipping easily back into the soft, measured tone that the classes at Wendlandt, or the soccer players at half-time, would recognize. "Gather round and I'll fill you in on what we face."

Stephens waited for the squad to pull over next to the window before he pointed to the map of the harbor. "This is the part that scares me. I can swim, and I can even read a map like this one. But I sincerely doubt that I can do both at the same time. And I'm damn sure I couldn't find the Titanic down there, let alone a small escape tube about four feet in diameter and probably no more than four to six feet above the bottom." He looked around at the young faces in the shed. "So, which one of you is going to get us there?"

"I'll be the one doing that, sir," answered Ned Eaglestone, the only member of the group over forty. The next oldest SEAL was in his late twenties. "However, you'll find that any of my boys can handle that if need be."

"Good," answered Stephens. "As far as I can figure, we need to go about a mile in the harbor, fighting strong currents. There will be next to no visibility. Then we need to find the proverbial needle buried in 200 years of Boston sewage."

"Sir, we do have a present for you that will help on that score," said Eaglestone, nodding towards one of the youngest in the group. "Jim, there, has a cute little item called a P-S-T-S. That stands for Passive Sonar Tracking System and officially it doesn't even exist. We just call it 'Trapper John.' It'll find your needle for you."

"How much of a briefing have you all had?"

"Sir, we know the President's in there, and that there are terrorists in the tunnel. We know you're in charge of this little effort, and have clearance well above even the 'Trapper John' level." Eaglestone looked up and directly into Stephens eyes. "Also, it seems you can handle this sort of dance, sir."

Stephens appreciated the directness of the man. "Sounds like you checked me out, Eaglestone."

Eaglestone did not skirt the question. "I did that, sir. My boys deserved a straight answer when they asked what they were getting into. Rear Admiral Gale sends his regards, sir."

The name brought back a smile, despite the eight years since he had last seen the then-Commander Gale. He had known Gale for just four days, but during that time the two had come to know each other well. Gale's destroyer had provided transport for Stephens, and had waited off shore more than a week after his night raft landing on the southern coast of France. When Stephens had returned with the freed wives of two young navy pilots, Gales never once asked anything about the mission. But during the return passage, he spent many hours with Gale. Many times over the past years he had recalled the insight Gale had offered very late one night over a glass of brandy on the fantail of the ship. "There is no elegance in war, my friend. There is only hurt, and pain, and the baser side of humanity. The elegance is invented in the fantasy of the telling. The only good in war is when honor is drawn out of the best of us."

"Let's continue with those straight answers, Eaglestone," said Stephens, shaking his head slightly, "though I doubt you'll like all of them. One thing all of you have to understand—key parts of what I'm going to tell you are no better than educated guesses."

"Then let's hear them," said Eaglestone. "You might point out which are the facts, and which the guesses."

Stephens pointed at the side view of the tunnel. "The President is in here. There are total blockages at both ends about fifty feet inside each entrance. Based on what we can piece together, the President's car should have been already on the upslope to the Boston side of the tunnel when the explosions sealed it off. Now, all the facts are against this, but I'm convinced that there are terrorists in the tunnel. At the least, they have both ends under tight observations. They've made that real clear. We're also going on the assumption that there are more charges set inside the tunnel, and that they can be externally triggered."

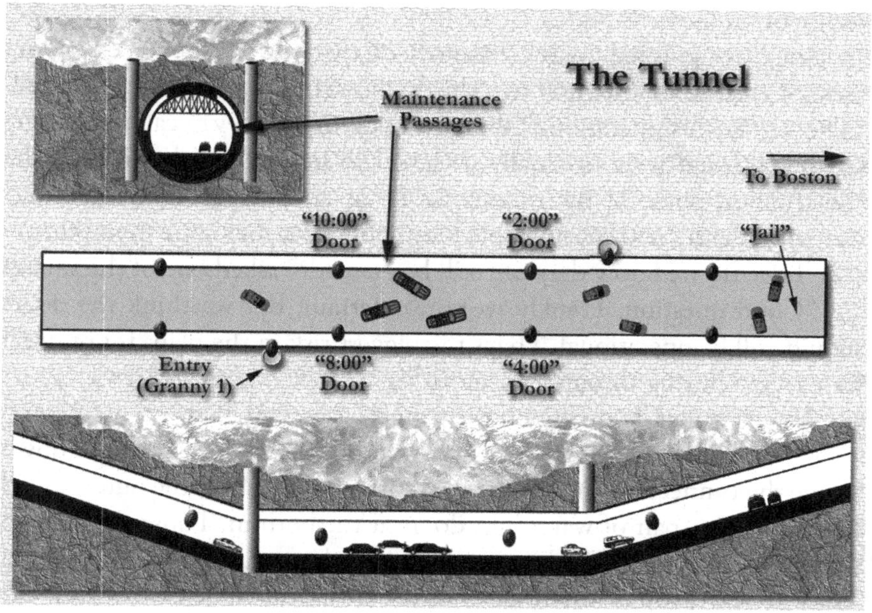

"So the obvious point is that we can't enter from the surface," said Eaglestone, "right?"

"Right. Now if there's one message I've got to make sure you all appreciate, it's that we're dealing with pros here. Don't make the mistake of lumping them in with any stereotype you might have for terrorists. They're headed by a man known as the Falconer. That's a name that should keep you awake at night." Stephens slowly swept his eyes around the intent faces. "Gentlemen, the Falconer is the best. Not second best. Not very good. He's the best there is, and will eat us up if we take him lightly. Anyone have any problem accepting that?"

Stephens swept his eyes over the group once again. He was impressed by what he saw. There was a great deal of quiet confidence and assurance in the room, but no measurable cockiness. "They will do just fine," he thought.

"Okay. Let's get down to it. Like most plans, this one starts out with a fairly simple concept. We're going in there and sneak the President out. There's an underwater entrance to the tunnel that should allow us secrecy. We're simply going to swim to that entrance, take along all that extra gear you guys brought along with you, take the tunnel, and lead the hostages back out through the harbor to safety. Simple, huh?" Stephens did not wait for an answer to the rhetorical question. "Now let's take a look at the reality of pulling this off."

Stephens pointed to the leftmost of two towers shown extending upward at the one-third and two-thirds points in the profile of the tunnel. "The key to this operation is these two columns. They're called 'Granny Chambers,' and were originally designed to be escape tubes during the construction phase of the tunnel. As far as anyone can determine they were never used, and most people long ago forgot they were even there."

"How do we know they can still be opened?" asked one of the squad.

"Good question. Frankly we're not certain, but we think the doors should still be operational. That's the biggest risk in the plan. If not, we'll have to try cutting through the metal."

"I take it that doesn't flood the tunnel," stated Eaglestone.

"Right. This side view doesn't show it, but the shafts go straight down beside the tunnel and are joined by a short lateral shaft to the outer tunnel itself. There's a pair of watertight doors at the bottom. Those are the two that are critical to us. If they both work without cutting, then we're in. The one at the top is watertight, but is not critical. When we open it the shaft will fill with water, anyway."

"The bottom connecting tube?" asked one of the men.

"Double doors. The connecting chamber is about ten feet long, circular, and nearly fifteen feet high. The doors are at the bottom of each side so that there's always a fairly sizable air pocket trapped in the top. Every time we open the inner door we'll get a few thousand gallons flowing into the space between the inner and outer tunnels. After a few transfers it will be pretty messy in there, but that's a problem for the clean-up crew, not us. Any questions?"

"Any idea how much noise that rushing water will make inside the tunnel?"

"What's your name?"

"Dardinski, sir."

"Dardinski, you've done this sort of thing before?"

"No sir."

Stephens gave a small nod of respect to the young SEAL. Dardinski was, at most, in his mid-twenties. "You thought of that potential problem a good deal quicker than I did, Dardinski. According to a couple of the MDC engineers, nothing will be heard inside the inner tunnel. The inner shell is a few feet thick. But your guess was right on. It would have set off a real loud alarm system if we hadn't taken care of it."

"Leakage to the inner tunnel?" asked another of the young men.

"Can't happen, even if one of the inner watertight pairs of doors is open. There's enough space between the tunnels so that we'll be walking in a couple inches of water. The doors into the inner tunnel are fourteen inches above the walkway."

"Once inside, what can we expect?" asked Eaglestone.

"We'll get all of us inside, and in position, before we enter the inner tunnel." Stephens indicated a series of oval shapes on the diagram. "These are the entrances we'll use. There are watertight doors between the inner and outer tunnels. Inside we'll break into four groups. I'll leave it up to you, Eaglestone, to set the assignments."

Stephens pulled out a pencil and sketched a small top view of the tunnel on one corner of the harbor map. Then he indicated the four doors, and drew a circle connecting the four marked doors. "Picture a clock face and the door assignments will be easy to remember. The two at this end will be 'eight' and 'ten' while the far end will be 'two' and 'four.' Clear?"

There were brief nods of understanding.

"The four group leaders will call in when in place. I'll be with team four down across from where we think the President is held. When all teams are ready, the single word 'Boston' is your signal to enter."

"Stephens," said Eaglestone carefully, "how do the friendlies know we're friendlies?"

Once again Stephens felt his initial respect for Eaglestone had been confirmed. He turned to the rest of the group. "Commander Eaglestone hits a key point. Inside the tunnel will be a couple dozen armed men who are probably feeling a bit feisty by now. I want you to go in assuming that the place is full of Idi Amin, Adolph Hitler, and whoever else is your personal bogeyman. But if you enter and are convinced that the tunnel contains good guys, then the word is 'Archangel.'"

"How will they know the code word?"

"The secret service is well trained for such things. They set a series of code words each day for just such a series of contingencies. Archangel just happens to be today's word. They will have gotten the word to the others in there."

"If the tunnel is full of bad guys?"

"Then it will be too late to go back and try diplomacy. Our job will be to eliminate any opposition."

Eaglestone asked the next question. "Is it safe to assume that we are speaking of very permanent elimination?"

"Yes."

"Rules of engagement?" asked Eaglestone.

"Against those you will be facing you should expect no quarter. Expect fierce opposition from fighters every bit your equal, or better. Assume no opportunities to take prisoners, and that you'll need to kill every enemy in there. It probably will be dark in there. The only limit on your action is to do whatever is practical to avoid killing the friendlies. No matter how careful we are, friendlies will be killed in the crossfire."

Stephens waited a few moments for that to sink in. He looked carefully to see if the youth in the room would be a problem. None of the squad, other than Eaglestone, looked old enough to him to have had any battle experience. Almost all more experienced SEAL teams were stationed overseas. Stephens looked intently around the room looking for anything to indicate that they could not handle the assignment.

"Sir," said Eaglestone, reading the thoughts, "kids grow up a lot faster these days than we did. The newest guy here has six years under his belt.

Most of my team spent the better part of last year in the Mediterranean. They've cleared mines, done underwater mapping, and set up electronic surveillance. John there," he said, gesturing towards a quiet seaman at the back of the row of faces, "did a one-on-one water dance with a couple Iranians in the Persian gulf three months ago. It's the kind of thing that we make sure doesn't hit the papers. But one of those Iranians reached heaven a few years earlier than anticipated, and the other was trailing a good deal of red in the water when he turned tail. Stephens, they're young by the standards of our time, but they're old by the standards of theirs."

"I hope you're right." Stephens' voice was soft. "Yet in a way, I wish you were wrong."

"Admiral Gale said that I'd not find you to be a simple person, sir, but that I could put my life in your hands if that became necessary. I took that on faith and am beginning to understand his feelings. You have no such reference check about us, but I still ask you to trust that these SEALs are not children playing games. When the time comes, if it comes, you will have solid men behind you."

"Commander Eaglestone, I do trust that. No more doubts. Now let's get to it. Can you get us to the entrance to the granny chambers?"

"Jim, with help from 'Trapper John,' can get you within a couple dozen feet." He pointed to the chart of Boston Harbor. "Is the entrance positioned accurately on that map?"

"I believe so."

"Then we can get you there. Jim, show Mr. Stephens what Trapper John can do."

The PSTS was contained in a small, flat box not much bigger than a large dictionary. It looked remarkably like a child's *Etch-a-Sketch* drawing toy. The top half of the surface had a flat screen with a thin black grid etched on the glass. Below it to the left was a dial meter that indicated signal strength. To the right was an LED readout that displayed two lines of data. At the bottom were two large knobs for X and Y positioning. In the bottom right was a keypad encapsulated in a waterproof covering. On each side were handles. A pair of telescoping antennas extended less than a foot.

The concept behind Trapper John was simple, but effective. Using the keypad and knobs, the user could enter the coordinates of the target and two known noise sources. The SEALs would leave a beacon at the end of the dock to provide one of the two necessary noise sources. A second beacon had already been placed half a mile away. With two points known and marked with sonar beacons, finding the third point, the entrance to the tunnel, was a matter of simple triangulation.

The last few minutes were spent preparing the watertight bundles of equipment that each diver would carry to the tunnel. They contained both their weapons, and the additional scuba gear and wet suits that would be used to secret the President and the rest of those in the tunnel outside to safety.

"Mr. Stephens," asked Eaglestone, "what if the barge on that chart is right on top of the shaft. Couldn't that do a lot more than just block our entrance? It might also have caused enough damage to have flooded the outer tunnel?"

"If it's on top, we'll just divert to the second entrance. I assume Jim can easily program that one in as well. As for flooding, that hasn't happened. According to a delightful old Italian who briefed me on this, the sensors would have sent off alarms if someone did no more than spill a cup of coffee in there. By the way, I had to make sure they disabled the sensors or our entrance would have set them off."

"Then the entrance must be clear?"

"Unfortunately that doesn't follow quite as solidly as we'd like. The design is quite clever in the tubes. The shaft does not directly connect with the tunnel. It stands beside the tunnel with a connector between them. The connection is planned to shear off if too much force is applied. If the barge is right on top of the shaft it probably just flattened the top and flooded the shaft, still leaving the connector intact. The worst that could happen is that the connector is flooded, too."

Eaglestone reached out, placed his hand on Stephens' shoulder and turned him around so that he could inspect Stephens' diving gear. When it checked out, he slapped twice on the air tank. "Mr. Stephens, it's time to move out."

Chapter Twenty-Three

After a while, the cold in the water started to combat the fire that had started again to claw at Stephens' body. He was the only one of the dim shapes moving through the murky water who did not carry supplies and equipment in packs strapped to his back, or towed behind in waterproof satchels. He would not have had the strength. Even as the cold began to numb the pain in his side, he could not escape the fear that he would be unable to make the half-hour swim from the dock to where they hoped to find the entrance to the granny chamber.

The shapes all around him were blurred, and were often little more than shadows. None of the torches were yet in use. They could benefit from some of the late afternoon light that made it through the layers of dirty water in the harbor to where they swam some twenty feet below the surface. It was deep enough so that they would escape accidental detection from any stray news helicopter, yet not so deep as to lose all benefits of the sunlight. In the lead was Eaglestone. At his side was Jim, holding the 'Trapper John.' The rest of the SEALs formed a Vee behind Jim and Eaglestone. Stephens was directly in the middle of the Vee.

Even with the small torpedo-like vehicles to pull them through the water, Stephens found the strain to be nearly unbearable until the cold finally began to have its inevitable numbing effect. The position of his arms, stretched out in front of him, tightened all the muscles in his side up against his ribs. He was buffeted by the strong currents in the harbor. His right leg found it increasingly difficult to help act as a rudder and stabilizer. With only the left leg working he had a natural tendency to rotate slowly clockwise. Every few minutes, when he was in particular trouble, two SEALs would move next to him and help stabilize his path until he would motion them off.

It seemed to be hours later when he saw Jim point downward and Stephens saw the tip of the Vee start to swoop downward, an aquatic flock of geese searching for land. A few seconds later, almost in unison, the torches were all turned on. If the calculations were correct, they were now near to the entrance of the granny chamber. Stephens glanced instinctively at his watch, but lacked the strength to pull himself forward enough to read it.

"Realistically," Eaglestone had explained just before they had left the dock, "you can liken this to looking for a manhole cover on a snow-covered football field. We can be pretty certain that we'll land somewhere on the field. But plan on a lot of digging in the muck for the cover unless we're awful lucky."

In the dim light as they approached the bottom of the harbor seventy feet down, Stephens saw the looming shape of the sunken ore barge. Despite all of his experience, the eerie shadows of the barge startled him. For a moment he felt like a kid again, swimming in Big Saint Martin's Bay in Michigan's Upper Peninsula. He remembered the first time he had dared dive down and touch the deck of the old logging boat that had burned and sank decades before. A part of his thoughts relived the child's fears and terror from that summer nearly thirty years before.

The barge sat upright, tilted at roughly a twenty degree angle from side to side, partially buried in the gunk and grit of the harbor bed. Even before the divers began to stir up the silt, it was nearly impossible to make out clear shapes beyond the first few feet of the envelope of light from the underwater torches. The water was thick with debris and silt. It looked a bit like watered-down soup, with bits and pieces of things not quite recognizable floating in the suspension. When Stephens reached the bottom he found it even worse than the basin of the Charles River he had known from sailing there back in his college days. It would be easy to sink two or three feet into the gunk. The taste of the water, edging past his tightly clenched mouthpiece, was worse than the look and feel of the water. The thought flashed in his mind that he was swimming through four hundred years of Boston history. Yet, all he could think of was the smell of the fetid, gross pools by the side of the tank trails just west of DaNang.

Eaglestone swam over to him and guided him to a location on the deck of the ore barge away from the harbor bed. He made an exaggerated shrugging motion, before leaving Stephens to direct the search of the area.

Some forty feet to the east of the barge Stephens could just make out the torch of Jim who was marking the center of the target area. All of the other divers had started at that point and, following invisible lines of a compass had begun to search outward.

The first search of the area found nothing. Each diver terminated his outward swim when about seventy-five yards distant from Jim's beacon. They then rotated a few degrees in a clockwise direction, and began to swim back towards the center of the circle. When the whole group had reconvened around Jim, Eaglestone sent them in a new formation to repeat the search. This time they formed two lines, one behind the other like spokes on a wheel centered on Jim. They swam around the circle, slowly getting farther and farther from the center as they went. While slower and more efficient, the result was the same.

Eaglestone swam over to where Stephens waited. He pulled out his underwater slate.

"Certain still here?" he wrote.

"Yes. Silt depth?"

Eaglestone nodded once and swam back to the nearby group. Stephens could just make out a series of gestures that were the SEALs own way of signing underwater. Four of the SEALs opened their bags and pulled out what appeared from the distance to be dark colored sticks. When one of them got closer, later, Stephens saw that the pieces had been screwed together to form five-foot poles with a hook on one end and a deadly sharp point on the other. The pole was long enough to be useful in a wide range of activities, and short enough to be easy to handle if one of those activities happened to be hand-to-hand combat. All three spread out, swam to the harbor bed, and started to probe the silt and muck that dated from the days of Revere and Tremain.

"3-4 ft. max," wrote Eaglestone after his return.

"Use probes?"

"Yes. Will take too long?"

Stephens swam over to the side of the barge and looked down. He motioned to Eaglestone to come over, and pulled out his slate.

"Under us?"

"Don't know."

Stephens thought about the short distance the granny chamber was supposed to extend above the bed. "3-4 high will show?"

Eaglestone just shrugged.

"The ridge?"

Eaglestone looked at the message on the slate, and answered with a lone question mark on his own slate.

Stephens pointed as he showed the slate to Eaglestone. "Ridge from barge."

Over the side of the barge Eaglestone could follow Stephens' outstretched arm, and see the ridge of mud that had been pushed out from under the barge when it sank. The barge was loaded with ore, and had compressed the mud and gunk underneath it as it settled down. All around the side of the barge there was a ridge of debris rising three or four feet above the rest of the bed.

"Good idea!" Eaglestone wrote.

Ned Eaglestone once more swam over to the center of the search circle. With economy of motion and time the SEALs had been continuing the search. The discipline of the troop became readily apparent when every SEAL turned to swim back to the center within a few seconds of the central light being extinguished. Stephens could not help but recognize the source of Eaglestone's pride in his men. "They're your equal, Ned. You done good," Stephens thought.

When the gathering had been completed, Eaglestone dispatched the entire team to probe the ridge around the side of the sunken barge facing the center of the search circle. All of the team assembled their probes, and methodically checked every inch of the ridge. Within less than three minutes the painful flash of an underwater flare indicated success. One of the SEALs, almost directly below where Stephens waited, had struck something large and solid a few inches below the surface. As soon as he swept aside enough mud to see that it was a flat expanse of metal, he lighted a flare.

Despite technology, despite the ability to fly to the moon and beyond Pluto, the effort to uncover the granny chamber was more Neanderthal than 20th century. Like a hive of worker ants, the SEALs swarmed around the entrance and scooped away all the silt and mud by hand. Mud filled the water and made it impossible to see anyone more than a couple feet away.

It took two dozen hands more than five minutes to expose the top few feet of the entrance to the tunnel. It took another five minutes for the current to carry away the muddy water enough to see the result. The tube was roughly six feet in diameter. The door was small, an oval less than three feet high, set on one side two feet below the top of the tube. The door was positioned so that there would be a small air pocket above it when it was opened. Dead in the center, now pockmarked with the corrosion of the past fifty years, was the heavy steel wheel that opened the door.

"Opens out. Go!" wrote Stephens when he joined the SEALs now hovering around the cylinder.

Eaglestone was the first to try to turn the wheel. After a few moments effort, with no apparent movement, he motioned for additional help. Two more SEALs locked their hands onto the wheel, and the rest of the troop looked for ways to brace the three who would attempt to turn the wheel. They anchored their own bodies to the rest of the chamber, the side of the barge, or any other possible source of support. Even with the concerted teamwork, there was no appreciable movement of the wheel.

Once more Stephens saw the gestures and movements between the SEALs that were their own form of signing. One of the team swam away from the group to where their satchels were tied to the railing of the barge. He looked briefly at the splashes of dull colors that identified ownership before picking out his, the largest. He began to open it during the swim back, swimming easily on his side while holding his light and loosening the drawstrings. By the time he was back at the cylinder, he had two tubes of gasses that would feed his underwater torch under one arm, and was starting to screw together the hoses to the mixing valve.

The diver didn't have to look to Eaglestone for direction. Well before entering the water they had discussed the options that they had if they needed to burn through the housing. The most obvious path, burning the hinges, would fail. The door used the three-lever mechanism that is used in ship watertight doors. When the wheel turned, three thick shafts of steel were rotated outward to enter holes on the edge of the housing. They were on the inside edge of a door that opened outward. Even without hinges, the door would not open until the steel shafts had been severed as well. Thus, the only alternative was to make a new door. The diver moved to the side of the door and began the ten-minute job to cut a new opening into the chamber. He would burn an oval a bit larger than the SEALs would normally require in order to accommodate the amateurs in the tunnel.

When the torch first pierced the steel shaft at the start of the cut the result was spectacular. Air shot through the initial pinhole, and then the lengthening cut, in glorious plumes driven outward and reflecting the glow of the lamps and cutting torch. Hues of ice blue and orange blended in the swirling patterns of the escaping air. The magnificent display meant that the granny chamber was flooding, but it would have flooded anyway had the door worked. Even the hardened SEALs floating nearby were entranced by the beauty of the display. One of the divers, who had spent many July 4th evenings on the Charles watching the fireworks bursting overhead, smiled behind his mask as he watched this underwater accompaniment to the glorious echoes of past 1812 Overtures.

Just as the rush of air stopped, signaling that the tube was fully flooded, the diver with the cutting torch stopped with about a foot to go. He moved back to the top of the oval and carefully cut away two holes, each the size of a silver dollar, spaced two inches apart. When they were complete and the area cooled, one of the other divers threaded the end of a strong nylon rope through the holes and tied the ends together. He then tied off the other end of the rope to the railing on the oil barge. The nearby barge offered a much easier method of strain relief than the planned string of divers playing tug-o-war with the cutout piece. A few minutes late the last of the cut was completed. The metal swung easily away from the new hole, instead of falling into the shaft, avoiding the danger alerting those inside by the noise.

Before the divers entered the tunnel, there was one last task. Using long strips of the rubber molding designed for truck edges, two divers crafted a grommet around the outside edge of the tunnel. It was the type of attention to detail and preplanning that sets the SEALs apart. While it is likely that they would have had no trouble with the rough sometimes jagged edges of the hole, the rubber grommet eliminated the possibility of an accident. They would have used the rubber pieces even if there had been no civilians to be shuttled through the hole.

Finally, it was time to enter the shaft. Eaglestone and two others entered first. Stephens and the rest of the troop hovered beside the side of the ore barge, while the SEALs examined the inner doors. The rush of air, earlier, had been good news. It had indicated that the inner doors had been dry and probably operational. Less than three minutes later one of the two divers who had accompanied Eaglestone poked his head out of the new hole, and raised his right thumb to confirm that guess. At the bottom of the tube, a small chamber connected the granny tube and the outer tunnel. The chamber, large enough to hold three or four people at a time, had watertight doors on each side.

As he started down the granny chamber shaft towards the cross shaft at the bottom, Stephens felt the first measure of confidence in events since he had left Wendlandt. Even the pain had left him for the moment.

"Now we remove your fangs, Falconer," he thought. "Without the President there will be only you and me left." He remembered the night at the rabbit farm, and Falconer's question of Yin and Yang. "But that's no surprise, is it my old friend. That's what this whole thing has been leading up to all along."

The feeling of confidence that had filled Stephens just before entering the outer tunnel lasted less than five minutes before reality set in yet another time. That was all the time it took for the four groups to move into their positions at the four entrances to the inner tunnel, and to discover that once again the Falconer had been a step ahead of their plans. They crept along the side of the tunnel, in the small, musty crawlway between the inner and outer tunnels. It took great care to avoid loud splashing in the water that was now up to their calves from the repeated opening of the double door to the outside. Two of the four groups had to crawl silently up the side of the inner tunnel, cross over the top, and slide gently down the other side in order to get to the far-side doors.

There had been no problem establishing radio contact with Patterson back at the base. Boston harbor now had what appeared to be just one more lobster pot with its colorful flag waving and bobbing in the late afternoon tide. Without getting right up next to it, no one would see the wire that provided a radio link between Stephens and the shore. Another part of the plan had started when they left the boathouse—the lights in the tunnel had started to flicker and slowly dim so that there would be little light in the tunnel buy the time the SEALs reached their target. Now Stephens could radio back and ensure the tunnel was dark and the water alarms had been disabled.

It was only when Stephens reached his assigned position at the right-hand door on the Boston end of the tunnel, and took one glance into the tube connecting the inner and outer tunnels, that he understood the Falconer's plan. When Stephens looked through the tube towards the automobile tunnel beyond, he could see that the inner doors had been blown off their hinges. As his eyes became accustomed to the dim light in the tunnel, he could see the door on the far side of the tunnel was equally blown. Stephens could just barely make out the pale faces of the SEALs inside the doorway across the tunnel.

"Shit," he muttered softly, before turning to face the young SEAL directly behind him. "If these two are blown, then I'd be willing to bet that more are as well. That means a lot of enemy entered, entered fast, and without a whole hell of a lot of gentleness."

"You think the tunnel's full, then?"

"Yes. Damn. Signal 'Boston-B.'"

The "B" plan was to have been called only if there was certainly that terrorists were in the tunnel. The "A" plan assumed an empty tunnel. Plan "C" would be called if they lost the element of surprise.

Within seconds, quiet two-word replies were received. Each group added the letter "B" to their clock position. Stephens couldn't help noticing the quiet confidence in the voices. When he heard the "10-B" from Ned Eaglestone, for just a moment he felt a trace of the earlier confidence return.

Behind him he heard the soft rustle of equipment as the SEALs set all unnecessary equipment to the side of the crawlspace and took one last look at their weapons. The same scene was repeated at each of the other three locations. When a full minute had gone by and Stephens was certain that all groups would be ready, he turned to the young seal with the radio.

"Time to dance, Fred. Give the signal."

The SEAL lifted the radio and sent the engage signal. The code word Stephens and Eaglestone had chosen to use was a small joke on the old-time western films.

"Cavalry. Repeat, Calvary."

At all four entrances to the tunnel the SEALs slipped quietly into the tunnel. They were just dark shapes in the dim light, slinking along the tiled sides of the tunnel to glide to the nearest cover. Fifteen seconds later, at a single command radioed back to the command center near the toll booths, the lights in the tunnel came back up brightly. The SEALs were ready, each wearing dark glasses to allow their eyes to handle the sudden harsh glare. The rest of the people in the tunnel had no such preparation. They were instantly blinded, and exposed.

The whole bottom flat section of the tunnel looked like a war zone in the light. Almost at the exact halfway point Stephens could see the

President's limousine with cars pulled sideways, across the tunnel, on either side of it. Two terrorists standing just in front of the cars, one holding an outstretched cigarette being passed to the other, died instantly without knowing who was behind the painful glare of the light. The cigarette fell and rolled into a puddle of radiator fluid from one of the shot-up nearby cars. Even forty feet away the SEALs could hear the sharp hiss of the ember being extinguished, just as the life was extinguished from the body that slumped to the pavement a few inches away.

In the distance Stephens could hear additional shots. It was not a free-for-all. The shots were rare, measured, and deadly. Seven terrorists died during the first fifteen seconds of the encounter. All seven were in the area surrounding the President's car. Only when SEALs began to move towards the limo, did the remaining terrorists began to fight back. The bullet-proof front passenger window of the limo was lowered slightly so that a single shot could be fired at the advancing SEALs. A moment later shots rang out again, but this time unexpectedly behind Stephens at the Boston end of the tunnel. Before the SEALs could react to the ambush behind them, two SEALs were killed. Jim, who had led them to the opening outside with his 'Trapper John' device, pitched forward from where he had knelt examining the two bodies who had been exchanging cigarettes. He ended up slumped over the same person he had killed only thirty seconds earlier. For the second SEAL there was no irony, just the permanence of death.

Stephens pulled out the small radio each SEAL carried for local communication. "Eaglestone, we're sandwiched. Sweep your end, up to the exit. As soon as you know your backside is clear, I need help over here."

"Two men already on their way. I think I'm clear."

"Something is behind us. Sounds like three or four."

"What happened in the limo?"

"Someone took a shot. Can't tell more yet. Tinted windows."

"Rush them? How many?"

"Not yet. Clear and contain. The limo's the last target."

"Roger."

The remaining five SEALs at Stephens' end of the tunnel had immediately dropped into defensive positions to minimize their exposure. One was facing the President's limo with his M-16 aimed precisely at the side window that had been lowered moments before. The window was now closed. His job was to protect the exposed backs of the rest of the SEALs who were behind cover with their focus the end of the tunnel. There were cars stretched out all along the flat section of the tunnel. Most were laced with bullet holes from the initial attack on the convoy by the terrorists. The President's car, and the two cars that had been turned sideways to provide a defensive shield, were clustered in the middle of the tunnel. There were two cars on the up-slope towards the Boston end of the tunnel. One was on a slant a few dozen feet from the start. A second was about a hundred yards from the end of the tunnel, turned completely sideways, blocking the tunnel. Behind him, towards the airport end of the tunnel, cars were spaced all the way to where the press car had been trapped under the rubble. From Stephens' vantage point he could see only three bodies from the motorcade other than the terrorists.

The gunfire came from the Boston end of the tunnel, from behind two more cars turned sideways near the rubble left by the blast at that end. There was a twenty foot space between the cars and the rubble. The shots came from terrorists safely behind the two cars. They were well protected and had a long clear expanse in front of them that prevented any successful frontal attack.

"Hold all fire!" The voice came from one of the SEALs closest to the terrorists. He had a pair of binoculars carefully studying the end of the tunnel.

Stephens did not even hesitate to follow the SEAL's order. He was well past questioning the judgment of the young men. "Cease fire, Ned," said Stephens into the radio. "One of your boys sees something."

"Sir," called the SEAL, "there's eight friendlies, clear vision, behind the cars at the end of the tunnel."

"How far from the shooters?"

"Maybe three, four yards."

"In our line of fire?"

"For sure."

"Ned, you getting all this?"

"Got you. Take it we're stopped cold?"

"Seems we've found their jail."

In the light it was now easy to figure out what had happened to the rest of the President's people in the tunnel. In the three minutes since they had entered the tunnel, the main question eating at Stephens had been seeing just the three bodies. Now the answer was clear.

There was bitterness in his voice as he picked up the radio. "Ned, they anticipated this. He knew we'd come in the middle and not through the ends. They were waiting for us."

The terrorists had herded the survivors to one end of the tunnel, and had positioned cars across the lanes to afford protection. They were now in a secure position behind the SEALs, protected both by the cars and the presence of the civilian prisoners. As soon as their eyes had finally adjusted to the light, the terrorists had an easy shot at the unprotected rear of the SEALs advance. Three could concentrate on firing at the SEALs while the fourth kept guard on the hostages.

"Shit Ned, it's even worse," said Stephens, ducking as another volley of shots was fired from the end of the tunnel. "They can fire as long as their ammo holds out. Any shots of ours that miss take out the friendlies behind them."

"What about sharpshooters," suggested Ned?

"I'm not sure it would work. Couldn't get all four at once. Too risky with the human backdrop. How many do you have if we go with that?"

"I hold a rating. Plus Bill here with me, and Jim in your group."

"Ned, Jim went down in the first shots." Stephens was not surprised to hear the degree of sadness in his own voice. He had never had the ability to compartmentalize and accept such things. It was always personal. It always hurt. "I lost two of your boys here. Just a moment." Stephens called to the nearest SEAL to get the name of the second slain SEAL. "The other was Mark Ebbeson."

There was a noticeable delay before Ned Eaglestone finally responded. His voice was much harder than before. "My end is clear, Stephens. The President's car is between me and you. I could send some of my troops back to join you. What do you suggest?"

Stephens knew he did not have to say anything for Ned Eaglestone to know how sorry he felt about the two boys. "Send me two, Ned. Use the rest for a car-by-car search, and search both sides of the outer tunnel to make sure we have no more surprises. By the way, one thought . . . how does a round tunnel have a flat ceiling?"

"Ah!" said Eaglestone. "Got you, Rob. I'll have my boys check it out."

"Make it fast, Ned."

"Done. One of my guys has an interesting idea. There were no keys in the car he just cleared, but he says he knows how to hot-wire them, if necessary. We could drive up to the end and take them out."

"Maybe. I gave a bit of thought to that one earlier, but I think the hostages blow that idea. As soon as we get under way, they'll start throwing bodies out front. So, when you're in position to go for the President's limo, let me know. The best guess is that the President is in the car, though I'm beginning to doubt it. From what we can see, he's probably one of the one's in the jail. I think we can work the limo separately from the fun up at my end of the tunnel."

"You going to take the limo?"

"Not yet. When your boys finish their sweep and we know that end of the tunnel is safe, and the outer tunnel is clear, we can move in on the limo. I'll wait for you. Then we can figure out what to do about the bad guys at my end."

"No line-of-sight to them?"

"No. The slant in the tunnel hides most of the bottom stretch from them. You have to go to where the road starts back up before they can see us. The limo's a good hundred yards past the point."

"Well, they don't have L-O-S on us, but the ricochets are still fun. I just had a round plug the door of the car I'm behind."

"The cars in the middle should catch most of that."

"Great consolation," the voice came back dryly. "We'll only be 'mostly' dead."

Chapter Twenty-Four

It took Eaglestone's group of SEALs fifteen minutes to verify that most of the tunnel was clear. Other than the limo, no terrorists were left in the bottom roadway, nor the road up to the airport end of the tunnel. The outer tunnel was completely empty. The tinted side windows and the security screen between the driver and the back of the limo made it impossible to know how many were inside the limo. Eaglestone was just returning to Stephens when the radio call came in.

"Sir," said the young SEAL to Stephens, "command is on comms for you."

The small transceivers carried by Stephens and each of the SEALs were good only for highly secure local communication. Two of the SEALs also carried radios that used the lobster pot antenna to keep in contact with Joyce Patterson.

"Here, Joyce," said Stephens, taking the handset.

"Falconer's just gave you ten minutes to evacuate the tunnel. Claims the trunk of the President's car is now loaded with plastique. More than enough to bring down the whole thing."

With the statement, all of the quiet alarms in his mind that had been insistently signaling trouble were finally silenced. Instead, the doubts he had felt after Cambridge and the Rabbit farm began to return. He felt like a puppet, with strings being manipulated by a master puppeteer, and that he had never even seen the strings. He felt his stomach tighten, and his chest become heavy. All of a sudden he knew that the President was no longer in the tunnel. And in a flash, he finally knew how it had all been accomplished. "You damn fool," he thought bitterly to himself. "You blooming damn fool."

Patterson's voice was firm. "Rob, I believe him."

"Joyce, I missed it. He had communication into here all along."

"It looks that way. We don't know how, but he knows what you're up to. Gave us a headcount that was only off by two, and even described your equipment. Recognized the SEALs."

The feeling became certainty. "Shit. Joyce, I missed it all."

"We all did. Nine and a half minutes, Rob."

"Joyce, we have friendlies up at the Boston end, and someone's in the President's limo."

"Your people have kept us up to date."

"Is he going to blow his own people, too?"

"Rob, if he has what he wants, then the rest of them don't make much of a difference," came Joyce's voice over the radio. "I think he blows it if you stay, and probably blows it even if you leave."

"Can he flood the place?"

"Cuomo says yes. He didn't think so until we had a little heart-to-heart about the kind of explosives that might be down there."

"Joyce, the people up at the end are okay. I think they're above the water line. Have Cuomo verify that. But I can't leave without resolving the limo. What if I'm wrong and the President is in there?"

"Rob, that's got to be your call."

"How can we get out in that time? He going to let us blow the airport end?"

"Says go out the way you entered. Said go straight up, and he'll spot you on the surface."

Stephens looked at Ned Eaglestone, who was listening to the same conversation. Eaglestone was about ten feet away, and shook his head from side to side in reply to Stephens' glance.

"Joyce, he even knows how we entered."

"I know."

"I couldn't offer much odds that the President's still here. Have someone locate the position of the other granny chamber. Even money you find an antenna there."

"Being done."

"He's been in contact with those inside since the beginning." Stephens shook his head in frustration, and spoke softly. "Crap luck. Fifty-fifty choice, and we chose the wrong chamber. The other one, and we'd probably have caught him leaving."

"Nine minutes, Rob."

"Joyce, have your people sweep the Boston side of the harbor for a site within a half mile to a mile north. They couldn't pick a site that was any farther for the President to swim. Look for a place where people could swim ashore without being seen, and then take a boat to leave the area."

"Wilco. Why north?"

"Later Joyce. That one will have to hold. I think there might be a way out of this mess."

As so often happened, the idea came spontaneously. It was a gift he would never understand, but one that was always there when most desperately needed. "Look Joyce, try for a stall. I doubt it'll work, but even a couple minutes might buy us everything."

"I'll try. But get out of there Rob. That's an order."

Stephens' voice was calm again. "Right. Thanks Joyce. Buy me time. Any time you can."

He returned the handset to the young SEAL and reached for his transceiver. "Ned. Clear the tunnel. Everyone but you and me. Out the chamber and straight up. Tell them they must be seen on the surface in eight minutes or we're all history."

"SEALs, you heard the man. Move it."

The discipline of the SEALs surfaced once again. Immediately they began to disengage from their positions and move back towards the entrances to the outer tunnel.

"SEALs, two things. Leave all your plastique with Ned and me. And when you hit the surface, make sure that it appears there are a few more of you than there are. Take a couple extra bodies with you!"

"I like your style, Stephens," stated Eaglestone, quickly getting the idea. "Let's make that their bodies, boys. Our guys deserve better."

Within two minutes the tunnel was clear of all except Stephens and Eaglestone. Two terrorist bodies had been taken. When the SEALs surfaced, they would support the bodies between two swimmers. From the shore, in choppy waters and the early evening light, it might look like the full complement.

"Ned, I'll take care of the limo. Whoever is in there has been quiet, but I can't afford to assume he's alone. That should take me a couple minutes. You use the time to climb back up into the false ceiling and move to the area just over their front car. They'll have no idea you're there. I think that's the only mistake they made so far. They don't seem to know about the false ceiling. Plant your explosives over them, but forward of the jail. After I clear this, I'll draw their fire and you blow through the ceiling and take them out from above."

"My friend, I do hope you know what you're talking about."

"No choice Ned. Had I half a brain when I planned this, we'd have a few more options. But I didn't, so we don't. I've been outfoxed at every turn, so far. Time for me to pay the piper."

"Why not let me help here first. Much easier with two."

"True, but you have a good half mile to get in place over them, and I figure you have to pull that off, equipment and all, in less than ten minutes. You get there, and blow on my signal. I assure you they'll be watching me."

Eaglestone nodded once, and then touched two fingers to the side of his forehead in a silent salute. He gathered up the explosives that had been left behind for him, and climbed up onto the roof of the auto. As soon as Eaglestone disappeared through the hole Stephens glanced at his watch, saw four and a half minutes left, and stood up to run directly towards the car. The move was so sudden and unexpected that he was able to dive and roll to the front of the car before the front passenger window started its deadly drop. The one shot that rang out missed him by several feet.

One of the most impressive things about plastique is that it is harmless unless exploded with the proper detonator. You can slam it with hammers to your heart's content. Even fire was safe. All that would occur is that a highly acrid smoke would fill the area. That was the idea that had come to Stephens during the radio call to Joyce Patterson. It was the way he would get whoever was in the limo to leave the car.

The President's limo was fully armored. If Stephens stood on the front hood, he would be as safe from those inside as they were to him from small arms fire. It was that sense of security that caused the startled person in the limo to neglect rolling up the window when Stephens suddenly jumped up onto the front bumper, and then leaped onto the hood. By the time he looked past the assault rifle in Stephens' right hand to notice the left hand behind Stephens' back, it was too late to close the window. Stephens threw himself forward to land on the roof of the car, and like a basketball player with a stuff shot, threw the smoldering plastic explosive into the car. Then he jumped up to stand on the roof of the limo, waiting for the doors to open.

The smoke began to curl out of the partially opened window. Even where Stephens stood the acrid smoke was uncomfortable. Inside the car it would already be unbearable.

"I'll kill her!" The voice from inside the car was interspersed with coughs. "Get down now and I'll let her live."

"Ten." Stephens' voice was cold and hard.

"What? Down now! Or she dies!"

"Nine . . . eight . . ."

"You're counting time for me? You should be counting for this lady, here." Despite the bravado in the words, Stephens could hear the terror behind the voice. He realized that the terrorist in the car had figured out who he was. All of the Falconer's men would have been well versed in his appearance and reputation. He also realized it was a fact, a small one, that he could turn to his advantage.

"I do not like threats, my friend. Your friend Gertmeyer tried to threaten me. He is now dead. Do you know who I am?"

"Gertmeyer dead? You got away from Gertmeyer?"

"Come out now and you'll live. I have no more time. Ten seconds is all I can afford. After that, I will have no time to tie you up. You will have to die. Decide. NOW!"

It was five seconds later when the handgun was thrown out of the side window. Then the door opened slowly, and the terrorist stumbled out of the door, hands up and empty. A moment later a second shape appeared in the smoke. As Stephens moved his aim to the back of the emerging head, he recognized the silhouette of the First Lady.

"Ma'am, please step away from him. Stand clear."

Stephens was impressed at how well she responded. She was reputed to be tough, and some felt she was the real backbone behind the President. Despite barely seeing through tearing eyes, and having difficulty breathing, she stepped firmly to the side.

"Any more in there?"

"None. My husband?"

"I don't know."

Stephens jumped down off the roof and stepped behind the terrorist who was now kneeling on the ground retching. Stephens could see the First Lady, a few feet away fighting for control. He could not help feeling pride in her strength.

"I'm sorry. I lied," he said to the terrorist on the ground in front of him.

"Huh?"

"I have no rope to tie you with." With one clean swipe Stephens brought the stock of the assault rifle down against the base of the terrorist's neck. He slumped immediately to the ground and didn't move.

"Necessary, I trust?" The First Lady's right eyebrow was arched slightly. Yet, the words were more of a statement than a question.

"Ma'am, now you must listen to me. Did they do anything to the car?"

"Yes. I think so."

"What?"

"I don't know. They put something inside the trunk."

"Any idea about your husband?"

"No. They took him out of the car hours ago."

"Hours?"

"Why yes," she said looking at her watch. "I'd say more than three hours ago."

"Is he with the rest at the end of the tunnel?"

"I don't know what you mean."

Stephens looked at his own watch. "We have two minutes. Ma'am, they write that you keep yourself in pretty good shape for an old lady. That true?"

One eyebrow arched again, but there was also a thin trace of a smile in the reply. "I'm not sure I know anyone who has dared put it quite that way, young man, but the answer is 'yes.' I'm no athlete, but I don't need a walker, either."

"Then it's about to be tested. We're going to get into one of these cars, wait for a friend to help eliminate a bit of opposition, and then go up the tunnel just as fast as we can. With more than our fair share of luck we'll drive most of the way up. But the last hundred yards might be a run."

"Then time's wasting, young man."

Stephens moved to the car that had been shielding the limo on the Boston side of the tunnel. Hot wiring was not necessary. The keys were still in the ignition. He had the First Lady crouch down on the floor in front of the front passenger seat. Then he turned the key part way to make sure that he had power to start the car.

"Ned, you ready?" Stephens asked into the radio.

"Just about. You?"

"I've got a car. You give me the word and I'll start up at them. Might just distract them a bit."

"What about the President?"

"Not here. Just the First Lady. She's with me now."

"No problem getting her out?"

"Nope. Nothing to speak of."

"Nothing? I'll bet. Give me another minute. I just got here."

"Your friend, I presume," stated the First Lady. "Is he like you?"

"Yes ma'am. Much the same."

She stared intently at Stephens. Even huddled on the floor of the car she maintained a degree of elegance and dignity. The past years as First Lady had given her the chance to meet many people from all walks of life. Few understood that her real skill, the reason she was indeed the power behind the President, was an uncanny ability to read people accurately. She never pretended to judge the policies being suggested to her husband, but she could unerringly point out the motives and character of those making the offer. That was a more valuable skill than any other in the world of politics.

"What's your name?"

"Stephens, ma'am."

"Just Stephens?"

"Rob Stephens, ma'am."

She stared slightly away as she went back through memory to see if she could recall that name. "We've never met before."

"No Ma'am."

"I'm glad you're here, Rob. Please find my husband."

"I will try, ma'am," he answered, seeing in his own mind the tight eyes of the Falconer in place of the First Lady's accepting glance. "I will try."

"Ready, Stephens. Say when."

"Figure about ten seconds. I'll signal."

Stephens turned to the First Lady. "Stay down. We'll have four people shooting at us. Fasten the seatbelt in front of you and link your arms through it. We're going to hit something pretty hard along the way."

"I've been through this once today," she said calmly as she settled deeper into her position. "It's getting to be old hat."

Stephens started the engine and immediately shifted into drive. Without screeching his tires he accelerated along the flat stretch at the bottom until he reached the start of the upward slant to the Boston end. About fifty feet up the slope he could see the first car that nearly blocked the roadway. He pressed the pedal to the floor, warned the First Lady hold on, and accelerated towards the four foot gap at the front end of the car. Half way to the gap he pulled the transceiver up to his mouth. "Ned, NOW!"

Just before reaching the car that blocked most of the tunnel, he pulled next to the left wall until the metal screeched against the tiles, and aligned himself with the narrow gap. The crash threw the parked car over against the far wall. The First Lady was just barely able to hold on. The seatbelt ripped painfully at her arms. Within seconds the shots started coming at the car, and then two explosions occurred, one just a moment after the other.

It took just a handful of seconds before Stephens realized three things. The first was that the firing had stopped. The second was that the sound of the explosion was not going away. The third was that the sound was getting much louder and seemed to be coming from behind them.

Stephens' car was a third of the way up the slope when the wall of water appeared at the bottom of the slope. It splashed a hundred feet up the slope and then flowed back down. In the rearview mirror he could see the bottom of the tunnel begin to flood. As he reached the halfway point of the ramp up towards the Boston end, he saw the water fill the flat section of the tunnel and start to push up the ramp's slope, like a gigantic toilet overflowing.

"Ned, we're flooding. They blew the tunnel!"

"All four dead here, buddy. Floor that sucker!"

Stephens pressed the accelerator to the floor. The car leaped ahead. "Get up. Look behind us."

The First Lady was remarkably calm as she looked at the water rapidly catching up with them. Then she looked ahead to where the final car blocked the tunnel a hundred yards from the end.

"We're not going to get past that one like we did the first one, are we?"

"No ma'am. We're not."

"I guess that means we have a problem."

"Yes ma'am. Unless you can swim. I suggest you drop anything heavy."

When they were twenty feet from the blocking car Stephens slammed on the brakes and skidded to a stop. He threw open his side door and pulled the First Lady out with him. The water was two hundred feet behind them and advancing rapidly. Stephens pulled her left arm over his shoulders so that he could grab her left hand with his and grab her waist with his right arm. Then he began to run with her up the tunnel. The pain from Gertmeyer's efforts clawed at his side with every step.

They had gone less than thirty feet from the car when the rising water hit them. In less than two seconds it swept them off of their feet and began to drive them forward. They tried to keep up with the speed of the water, but with every second they slipped back towards where the back edge of the water hit the roof of the tunnel, and would soon pull them under. Pieces of debris in the water buffeted them. The mixture of salt water, and the exhaust deposits now washed off of the tiles and dissolved to form a dirty film on the surface of the water, stung their eyes.

The water was freezing. For the first minute, both were able to keep up with the rushing water. Then the cold, and the age of the First Lady, and the pain in his sides all started to take their toll. Without his wet suit Stephens was having great difficulty swimming in the cold water. The First Lady had slowed down to almost no motion, just a faint dog paddle. Stephens pulled her arms around his neck and felt them lock together with her last reserves of strength.

Now, he locked out everything else so that he could concentrate on swimming. He forgot the cold. He forgot the pain in his side and the weight of the First Lady. All he allowed to enter his mind was his arms and their necessity to keep stroking the water and pulling him ever forward. He had no idea where he was in the tunnel anymore. All that mattered, other than his arms and his breathing, was a sense of the direction that was up. Those were the only things he allowed to intrude upon his reality. Arms. Breath. Up. When the body of one of the slain motorcycle officers floated next to him he only partly recognized that it was there. Arms. Breath. Up. The First Lady's arms tightened painfully around his neck. A suitcase swept up an smashed into his wounded side. Stephens ignored the pain. Arms. Breath. Up.

When the back edge of the water finally caught up to him and drove him under the water, he knew that the Falconer would be the victor. His arms kept pulling, now in the underwater stroke instead of the crawl, but he knew it was over. Already his lungs had started the terrible clawing for air that he had known with Gertmeyer. He felt the First Lady's grip weakening, and knew that there was nothing he could do about it.

Most of all, he saw the Falconer staring back at him. Arms. Breath. Up. Yin. Yang. He started to see other things, vague understanding of something blossoming at the edge of his vision. He saw pictures of Wendlandt, and of times spent with children. Incongruously he remembered a time hiding in his room as a child, with nothing but a rat-eared copy of an old *Tom Swift* novel for reading. As his arms slowed. He began to see the shape of Cynthia Lebart, ghostly in the nightgown from the night before. But all of these images were swept aside by the specter of the Falconer standing over him. He saw Falconer's hand being offered in mock tribute. He dreamed that he could see the surface, and air, but then he felt the Falconer's hand grasp his shoulder and push him deeper into the water. Arms. Breath. Up.

Then his body didn't hurt anymore. Not his side from the kicks, or his chest from lack of air. Not his neck from the First Lady's death grip there, nor his shoulder where the Falconer's dreadful hand now grasped him. But the pain was replaced by something far worse than anything physical. The hopelessness that tore through his last thoughts was in knowing that there was no counterforce left to hold out against the Falconer. Deep within he felt only traces of the old drive, the strength, the will to fight on. But it was weak, and it faded quickly. And the most bitter thought of all, which finally left him empty and without the purpose that had sustained him for so many years, was that he no longer had the heart to resist.

Chapter Twenty-Five

It was the brightness of the big construction lights, more than the overpowering noise of the earth moving equipment, that was the first external factor Stephens recognized. The blackness had been slowly giving way to strange images and shadows—a crazed chimera weaving and dancing in a *Danse Macabre* only he could hear. The face of the chimera was ever changing and blending to be one person in his life after another. In each case, just as the face started to come into focus, and just as Stephens began to get a glimmer of the message coming from the eyes of those he saw, the face would shift, the message would be lost, and a new face and message would begin. After a while the chimera had disappeared, as chimeras inevitably do. It spread itself upon a wind, and became part of the sky. All that remained in Stephens' dream was the hint of the original gossamer form, just traces of gentle blues and pastel greens, color hiding behind the substance of the sky.

Only when the bright lights first pierced his lids did the noise, smells, and the cold wetness of his body enter his thoughts. For the next minute, awareness crept back in quiet stages. He wondered about the sounds of water and construction he heard, and filed them away for later analysis. Next came a distant awareness of pain in his leg and side. Finally came the feel of wet clothes clinging to his sides, and the dull ache in his shoulders.

Only when the instinctive inventory of body parts was complete did the remembrance of the water return. Then the images flowed quickly to crash one upon one another. In the space of a few seconds he went from sleep to sitting bolt upright. He recalled the water, the swimming, the First Lady, and the absolute conviction that he should have been dead. Then the pain in his leg and side became anything but distant, radiating outward in sharp pangs.

"Whoa, old friend," came the concerned voice of Ned Eaglestone from a few feet away. "Take it easy for a minute or two. Let the cobwebs shake themselves out."

Stephens saw Eaglestone rising from where he had been adjusting a coat around the shoulders of the First Lady. She was awake, sitting on the pavement against the tile of the tunnel wall.

"Welcome back, Mr. Stephens," she said. Stephens was amazed to see that even with mud streaking her face, her hair clotted and matted with filth from the water, and sitting in dirty wet clothes with a man's coat thrown around her, she still maintained all of the dignity and elegance he had seen earlier.

"It appears you and I made it after all?" Stephens asked.

Eaglestone saw his quizzical look. "Afraid she's a lot tougher than either of us. She came to almost immediately. You've been taking an in-place vacation for the past half hour. Took nearly five minutes before I was sure you were breathing on your own."

Stephens scanned the rest of the quiet faces around the perimeter of the spreading circle of light. The faces belonged to the members of the motorcade who, only an hour ago, were hostages in the "jail" at this end of the tunnel. The shock of the events had them all were strangely silent, standing back away from where he sat, seeming to consciously avoid becoming part of the conversation or action. Above him sunlight was flowing through an opening being cut through the rubble. He could catch glimpses of a bright yellow scoop loader as the opening slowly widened. Then the powerful smell of the salt and harbor water in the tunnel drew his attention to where, just seventy-five feet away, he could see the ebony mirror of the water in the tunnel. There was almost no movement on its surface. Only as the envelope of light from the digging grew could he see the flotsam and jetsam floating there.

He turned back to gaze intently at Eaglestone. "I take it you dove in for us," he stated calmly. "I would have been a day late. A dollar short."

"Did look as though you could use a hand, Rob. And I'm paid to do this sort of thing."

Stephens kept his reply soft and even. Anyone else there who might only hear the voice, and could not see the eyes locked on Eaglestone, would have missed the intensity of the sentence. "I'm grateful, Ned. Thank you."

Eaglestone pointed towards the widening hole. "If they'd stop, we could walk up and through there. My guess is they're setting up some form of defensive perimeter, first."

"Hardly seems necessary any more. Nothing much more the Falconer would want here, is there?" asked Stephens. He stood up and began to stretch as he spoke. The bitterness in his voice was there again, but muted. "I let him get the President, and let him flood the tunnel. With all due respect to the First Lady there's not much of value left."

"Rob, there's at least ten people alive and free who might not have been otherwise. We have the First Lady, mayor, and eight from the motorcade. The President and eight others aren't accounted for. Four of those were in the press car buried at the other end."

"I counted three bodies in the tunnel."

"There was another I doubt you saw up at my end."

"Any I.D. yet?"

"One cop and three Treasury, so far."

"Any chance the President was trapped down there?"

"Maybe, but I'd say absolutely no. They got him out."

"Then the dance begins again, doesn't it. We're back at ground zero."

"Not really, old friend," said Eaglestone. "This Falconer of yours has lost most of his men and is running. And you're still alive. My take is that things are finally in our favor. The odds have shifted."

Stephens motioned towards the people standing apart from them. "They wouldn't have made it without you."

"You know, I'm not sure how the brass will tell me to play this, but I'd like to stick this one through. I don't normally dance on dry land. But if you ask, I'd be pleased to give it a try."

"I'd like that, Ned. Normally I'd have help from someone a lot like you. His name's Green. Usually he's nearby when I most need it, except this time."

Stephens looked at the blank faces hovering just within hearing range. They were silent, shifting from foot to foot. He had seen this many times before in the aftermath of an intense action. It was a complete emotional letdown, almost a mild form of shock. He recognized one of the faces as the mayor. "Any clues from them on the President?"

"Just indirect confirmation of your theory. They did take him out of the limo a few hours ago. Took him into the outer tunnel. I lost my radio in all this, so I don't have verification from shore, but my guess is they found the antenna you said would be at the second granny chamber."

The opening at the top of the pile of rubble was now large enough to allow easy passage for those in the tunnel. The yellow of the equipment pulled back from the opening, and the noise abated. A few moments later the sounds of climbing outside stopped just before the associated face would have appeared at the opening.

"Someone in there wish to give me a signal I'd recognize?"

"Sanders, it's me," answered Stephens, recognizing the voice. "You can stick your pretty neck over the top. No one's going to shoot it off."

"You might, just to humor me, tell me the word of the day."

"Archangel."

Sanders pulled himself the rest of the way up until he could peer inside. "Status, Stephens?"

"We have a flooded tunnel, the First Lady alive, nine assorted members of the motorcade including the mayor, no terrorists, and no President. What about you?"

"Nothing. As soon as the tunnel blew, we sent for the Chinooks to fly in the heavy duty stuff we're using to clear this end. No President. No demands. Not a word, since the blast, from your friend."

Sanders worked his way down the pile of rubble to Stephens and Eaglestone. He scanned the survivors and the water beyond. He looked up at the ripped ceiling from Eaglestone's explosion. He started to say something to Stephens, but stopped when he recognized the First Lady sitting off to the side. He took in her wet clothes, and Stephen's condition.

"My god," he asked softly. "What happened here?"

The First Lady nodded towards the water. "We were down there when it flooded. It was very close."

"How? I mean what . . ." Sanders stared at her for a moment before continuing in almost a whisper. "Somehow I suspect that 'very close' is quite an understatement."

"Would you like us out of here now?" asked the First Lady.

"Yes ma'am. All clear. Start them up." He held up one hand. "You wait, Stephens. When clear, I do have some 'new news' to pass on. One of Lowe's assistant, Sullivan, figured out the code based upon the book of poems you found."

At a signal from Sanders, a half dozen senior agents who had been standing by slung their weapons and climbed through the hole to assist the hostages out of the tunnel. Two of them walked over to where the First Lady had begun to rise to her feet.

"Gentlemen, if it's all right with you I'd like to go it on my own," she said calmly. "If I need help, I'd be pleased to try it with Mr. Stephens. If he's staying behind, then Mr. Eaglestone will do just fine." She reached out and placed her hand on Eaglestone's arm. "Just a little support should be enough, don't you think?"

"Yes I do, ma'am," Eaglestone answered. "Based upon what I've seen, even a little might be more than you need, but I'd be pleased to be your escort."

The First Lady walked over to the base of the pile of rubble. She stepped up onto the first block, and then stopped, staring at the crushed rock in front of her. She didn't turn around to face Stephens until enough time had passed that two of the agents started to move towards her thinking she needed help. Eaglestone, fully understanding what was happening, waved them off.

"I need a moment, please," she said to Sanders. "Please let the rest go ahead of me."

The mayor and the rest of the hostages climbed up the rubble and crawled through the opening. The sound of cheering and applause could be heard from outside.

"Mr. Stephens," she said after the tunnel was nearly empty, "can you find my husband?"

"I don't know, Ma'am. I will try, but I don't know anymore. Very little has worked out the way I thought it would, so far."

The First Lady looked gently at Stephens, and then picked her way back down the rubble and stood next to him. She put one hand on his shoulder, and she gave him a quiet smile. "I've loved my husband for what seems like most of my life. Because of that love, I'm deathly afraid of what might happen. But I know something now, with certainty, that I must tell you." She looked deep into him, as though willing the force of her words to blow by any doubts and any walls. "If my husband dies today, it is because there is no force on earth that could have prevented it. But if God's plan is that my husband lives, and there is to be no more death in this, then it's because you are here."

Stephens' thoughts flashed back to the vague awareness, just before he had passed out in the water, of the glimmer of distant answers to so many of the questions in his life. Then he thought hard about her words. He was convinced that the answers were getting closer, but they remained just out of reach. "Thank you, ma'am. I only hope you're right."

When the First Lady had climbed to just below the opening cut into the rubble, she turned to Eaglestone. "If it's all right, Mr. Eaglestone, I'd like to take the next few steps on my own. Those people out there have had enough fear and helplessness. It might be worth little, but let's show them some strength, no matter how false you and I both know it is."

When the First Lady stepped over the top of the rubble, there were few people close enough to notice her. At first she looked just like any in the string of motorcade survivors who had preceded her out of the tunnel. Most of the attention was centered in a wild cluster around the mayor, who held court some fifty yards from the tunnel mouth, under the Southeast Expressway where it crossed sixty feet over the entryway to the tunnel. At the bottom of the pile of rubble was a lone reporter from the Middlesex News, a small suburban paper. The reporter knew that he was far "too unimportant" to compete for attention with the throng of reporters and cameras now surrounding the mayor. For now, he would concentrate on taking background photographs to go with his story.

When he looked up and saw that another figure was now leaving the tunnel, it took a moment before he realized who she was. But then his expression went quickly from open shock to awe. The late afternoon sun bathed just the upper half of the First Lady as she stood there. The dust rising from the rubble acted as a filter, creating streaks of yellow and orange light that painted her in a diffused glow. Her muddied face was hauntingly beautiful as it was starkly outlined against the sky. As he instinctively pulled his camera up to frame the shot, he was stunned by the nobility and majesty in the person who stood there. He found it hard to focus the camera through the tears that formed in his eyes. After the one shot, he just dropped his arms to his side and cried as she worked her way, alone, down the pile of rocks. Only when she was halfway down did one of the other reporters see her, and began the stampede to surround her.

A year later, his photograph had become one of the handful etched in history. Like Kent State, or Jackie with Caroline and John, or the Dallas Motorcade. It was said that his photograph had impacted a whole generation in how they thought about leadership and values. It was an image that filled people with pride. No one was surprised when the Pulitzer Committee confirmed what everyone else already knew.

"So what's the 'new news,' Carl?" asked Stephens when the tunnel had been cleared of the hostages. Eaglestone had returned from his journey with the First Lady, and was leaning comfortably against the tunnel wall a few feet from Stephens and Sanders. He was a couple of feet from where the ceiling was ripped and scarred from the explosion Eaglestone had set off just forty-five minutes earlier. There was rubble at his feet, and fine dust everywhere. He appeared oddly at home there. Only the three of them remained.

Sanders looked back and forth between Stephens and Ned Eaglestone. It was easy to see the concern on Sanders' face about speaking in front of the SEAL.

"It's okay, Carl. Ned can stay. He's good. I'll take the heat on that call."

Sanders looked uncharacteristically confused. "Mr. Eaglestone, I do appreciate all you've done for us today," said Sanders, "and normally I think Rob's opinion might be enough here to change my mind. But this one's a bit different. It's not his call to make."

"Sanders, he can stay." Stephens' voice was matter-of-fact. There was no trace of question in the tone.

"Rob, this is a Presidential grab. Bradford even flew in to be on-site command. The need-to-know on this one is maximum. I can't change that."

"Carl, he earned it." This time it was Stephens' voice that was different. The initial statement had turned into a request. "You took ten out of here who didn't have a chance without him. Eleven if you include me. And we may need him for the next part."

Sanders looked back and forth between the two. Eaglestone just continued to lean against the wall. He appeared totally indifferent to the discussion, and made no effort to enter it or join either side.

Finally, Sanders threw up his hands. "Shit, what the hell. Nothing else has gone to plan on this one. Why change the pattern now?"

"Thanks, Carl." Stephens sat down on the pavement and untied his shoes. He removed each sock and twisted them to squeeze out the water.

"Let's give you the quick-and-dirty. There *was* an antenna just where you said it'd be at the other entrance. Mr. Eaglestone's SEALs reported that the other chamber was flooded and had been used. Joyce has people searching the shore as you requested, but nothing yet. So the President could be anywhere in the Boston North End by now, and might not even be in Massachusetts."

"I'm guessing New Hampshire, by now," said Stephens.

"Ah, okay," said sanders before continuing. "Meanwhile, staff was an adventure this morning. By nine we had three heavies from Treasury telling us this was *our* baby. Swek, himself was there giving us crap. Seems he conveniently 'forgot' how hard we had tried to persuade him to cancel this visit. All of a sudden it was *our* foul-up and he was there to find out what ATQ was going to do about it."

"Same old Tim," said Stephens, draping his socks over the damp shoes and flexing his toes to dry in the air.

"So Swek's playing cover-your-ass, John Bradford is driving half the agency bananas with his search to find out about the woman with Falconer, and Internal is discovering gem after gem about Green. Harvey now has a *third* bank account that now puts him in the megabuck class."

"All that new at staff?" Stephens asked quietly.

"Yup, and that was just the start. Next we find you've got the book that might be the key, the President is definitely trapped, and the Falconer is definitely at the controls. Later Sullivan comes back and tells us the Crays can't find a single match from the book. Obviously it didn't get any better."

"Sullivan? Marilyn Sullivan? I know that name," Stephens mused as he got up and shifted side to side on his bare feet. "She that mousy little librarian who came over from 4th in '78 or '79?"

"The same."

"You said you had the code figured."

"That was Sullivan, too. She tried every other word. She tried reading backwards. Then, somehow she figured that maybe only the first letters of the decoded message mattered. The words themselves could be nonsense. It was what they spelled out that mattered." Sanders reached into his coat for a piece of paper. "She was right. Just about the time you were going into the tunnel they got the match. Your book *was* the key. One of the Frost poems in the book was the start of the literary sequence. Something about a horse in a snowstorm."

"On a snowy evening?" Stephens' voice was intense.

"Yea, I think so. Started part way into it. The Falconer's sequence was based upon the lines that . . ."

Stephens interrupted before Sanders could continue. Another door had opened in the pattern. "The woods are lovely dark and deep, but I have promises to keep, and miles to go before I sleep, and miles to go before I sleep."

"Yup. That's it. How'd you guess?"

"Yin and Yang," Stephens answered almost too softly to hear.

Sanders looked across at Ned Eaglestone. Eaglestone gently shook his head side to side.

"The bottom line is that it's just another dead end. The letter doesn't make any more sense than any of this so far."

Stephens looked up from where he had been staring at the pavement. "How so?"

"Well, at least we know the purpose. A week ago the Boston Phoenix personals had the same code sequence, disguised as a 'puzzle.' It looks like a set of dates and names. We're pretty sure that it was aimed at multiple audiences. The first part is pretty obvious, now." Sanders pulled out a scrap of paper. "Just five phrases."

Rabbit Farm
1021
1472
Willcrest
Pumpelly Cave

Stephens stared at the words on the paper. "Well '1021' is today's date. You think 1472 is some kind of a date or a time?"

"We don't have a clue. The last two don't make any sense yet."

"I can answer one of them, but the answer makes no sense at all. Pumpelly Cave doesn't even exist."

"Huh? You've gotta explain that one."

"There's no such thing. It's the Flying Dutchman. It's the Lost Gold Mine of the Aztecs."

"I've never heard that one."

"Your wouldn't, unless you happened to live up near Dublin. It's a cave that's supposed to be on Mount Monadnock. Everyone knows about it. But it isn't real. Just a story spun by school children," said Stephens. "Local legend."

The Pumpelly Cave had been one of the great fantasy adventures around Dublin and Jaffrey, New Hampshire. There were dozens of stories about it. It was supposed to be somewhere on the west face of the mountain. It was either small and plush, or it was a huge network of caverns under the mountain. Some felt there was a hidden steel door, others a carefully counterbalanced stone that covered the way. Generations of local children and students at Wendlandt had searched in vain for it. But, of course, none ever found it. The plush hideaway built by a millionaire at the turn of the century simply did not exist. It never had.

"Well, that's where the President is," said Sanders. "He's in an imaginary cave. Obviously he didn't mean the cave, so it's a code word for something else. We're going on the assumption that, whatever it really is, it's tied to the mountain. We're pulling together a force to comb it. National Guard will seal the whole area off from civilians. We felt that . . ."

Sanders stopped when he caught the motion of Stephens sharply cocking his head to one side. Both Sanders and Eaglestone saw that Stephens was no longer listening to the conversation. Instead, Stephens was staring blankly down at the pavement, while absently massaging his forehead.

It was happening again. It was the feeling that always came just before understanding. He absently turned away from the other two and instinctively headed down towards where the edge of the water. The dark ripples were the closest thing he could find nearby to one of the quiet places that always had proven the best places to loosen such thoughts. His bare feet made soft slapping sounds as he picked his way down to the water. It was easy to see in the light now, and shell casings that had rolled down from where the terrorists had made their last stand cast long shadows along the roadway.

Stephens stared at the patterns on the surface formed by the dirt and scum and oil of the tunnel. Gasoline leaking from the cars a half mile down under the surface formed a kaleidoscope of colors when triggered by the floodlights that now bathed the inside of the tunnel. He tightened his eyes as he realized that the blues and pinks and rust colors in the pattern were part of the answer forming.

It was the glimpse at one color that had triggered the answer. It was bright royal blue, and it danced on the water just as it had danced in the air when it flowed behind the old woman who had somehow been there, just when needed, at so many critical junctures over the past few years.

"Myrna Glover and her scarf," he whispered as he turned back towards the two men at the top of the tunnel, thought complete.

"Carl, those lines are a sequence. 'Rabbit Farm' is the meeting place for the main assault team. '1021' is the date this would all happen. 'Pumpelly Cave,' whatever that means, is where it will end. '1472 Willcrest' is an address! Get your people looking at maps. See if there is a street named Willcrest on the harbor close to here. Then get an ATQ heavy force there quick. You'll be too late. But that's the next piece of this puzzle."

Joyce watched the medic tape Stephens' side as she listened to the latest bad news to be called into the command post in the deli. Sanders and Stephens had returned to the deli at the airport end of the tunnel. In the hours since Stephens and the SEALs had left to enter the granny chamber, a full communications van and a dozen ATQ staffers had been dropped into place just outside by helicopter. The ATQ team now had secure communications to their headquarters staff and to the forces that were now deployed throughout the Northeast.

John Bradford, from a small table in the corner with two computer consoles, could tap into resources and communications networks wherever needed. It was as easy for him to link with the police force as it was to contact the White House. With a few queries he could receive photos and dossiers from any location on earth.

Both ends of the tunnel had been partially reopened. Ned Eaglestone's SEALs had drawn the ugly job of body removal until a replacement team arrived. Only one body, one of the two senior BPD officers who had motorcycle duty leading the motorcade, had risen to the surface on its own. The police officers had waded into the foul water at the Boston end of the tunnel to retrieve it. One of the most repeated scenes on all the nightly news stations would be of the slowly growing line of bodies, draped in damp canvas, at each end of the tunnel.

Joyce returned the phone to its hook, and turned to Stephens. "Well you called that one. Perkins found 1472 Willcrest. Just as you thought, Falconer is long gone. They found the owners in the basement. Both shot. One bullet, temple."

"Nothing else, I'd bet."

"First pass says squeaky clean. The owners have a boat, but it's still there. The boat was tied to a tree on land, though, and appears like it was moved to leave the dock free for another boat. No one saw anything. The dock is pretty sheltered." She shook her head. "Just perfect for this sort of thing."

"I don't expect it to lead to anything," added Sanders, "but we have people at each of the local stations looking at their TV news film. With all the news helicopters that were in the air we might get a shot of the boat."

The medic was done with the tape. Stephens stood up, felt his side with the flat of his hand, and pulled his shirt back on. "I've been out so long my knowledge is limited to Clancy novels, but is there any kind of satellite coverage that would help?"

"That's actually not so farfetched an idea as you'd think," answered Patterson. "I had ATQ chase that question an hour ago. Nothing was positioned close to here. NSA has something they won't even describe to me that can be repositioned, but not for another half hour."

Jacobi looked up from his phone where he was in nearly constant communication with ATQ headquarters. Since the explosion, he had slowly become more active and involved in the process. "That won't help," said Jacobi. "I doubt he'll still be in the boat by then. He has to assume we'd figure it out by now."

"I agree," answered Stephens. "What about the Phoenix ad?"

"Nothing," answered Bradford from his console. "The ad was delivered in person, and paid for with cash. Total dead end. Lowe says they don't even save the originals for that kind of ad."

"Any idea why the Phoenix?" asked Patterson. "It looks to local to get much coverage."

"A little wider than we thought," said Bradford. "The Phoenix circulation people gave us a list of places outside Boston that take copies of all issues." He looked through a pile of papers until he found a specific one. "Dozens of towns in Massachusetts. Seven in New Hampshire . . . including, by the way, Peterborough. Providence. Three in Connecticut. Three in Vermont. Portland Maine. It does get around."

Stephens walked over to the bank of phones and sat down next to the streaked and dirty window. It was dark now, and the light trying to get through the grime was from the streetlights rather than the sun. Everything else had been a dead end so far. Had it been anyone else but him, Myrna Glover would have laughed at his questions about Pumpelly Cave. "Of course it's a myth, Rob," she had explained. "Even I'm not sure how it started. But once when I was about ten or twelve my Dad told me he and two of his friends had invented it. I don't know if that's true, but I do know it doesn't exist."

The rest of the news from New Hampshire was as bad. When the ATQ team had moved in on the Sand Hill Farm complex in Peterborough, they had found nothing. All of the Falconer's people had long before left the scene. The equipment was gone. Even Gertmeyer's body had been taken from the site. When Pat Waters called in to report, there had been only one piece of solid data. Waters reported that the Farm appeared to have been warned. Someone, when taking a phone message, had written with enough pressure to leave the trace of a message on the surface of a table next to the phone. The message said "12:30 per Green." The scheduled raid had been for 12:30 that afternoon. When Joyce had relayed the report to Stephens she had closed her eyes briefly, and then touched him gently on the shoulder. "I'm sorry, Rob. I am really sorry."

Now the ATQ team was reduced to little more than waiting for the next lead. Police officers from almost all available state and local forces, augmented by FBI and ATQ personnel, were swarming over the harbor looking for any clue as to where the Falconer's boat had gone. Coast Guard and police Harbor Control boats were stopping every craft on the harbor. An E-3 sentry AWACS had been dispatched from Norfolk to help search for any air traffic that could not be accounted for by known flight plans. Every unknown plane in the sky was being contacted. More than a few private pilots who missed the radio call directed to them were shocked to see a fully armed F-16 out of Otis Air Force Base pull up on their wing to "get their attention."

For the hundredth time since he had returned to the deli, Stephens reviewed the facts. He could get small pleasure from the growing awareness that the old disciplines were starting to return. Very little was left of the person who, a week before, had been just a math teacher and soccer coach at Wendlandt. A part of him accepted that he was now operating on "auto pilot." Most of those things that made him an individual named Rob Stephens were pushed far into the background. There was no longer a place for a quiet evening reading Frost with Ned Mendoza in the loft over the library. Emerson's Chair on Mount Monadnock was a place that was ten thousand miles away now. It was as though every part of him that could be applied to the Falconer had been preempted. There simply was no room for anything else.

Stephens was staring intently at the ideas swirling around him, and missed the light knock at the door. He looked up and saw the outline of a BPD officer through the glass of the door. It was the head of the detail providing control of the area around the deli.

"One of you guys named Stephens?" the officer asked as he opened the door a few inches and stuck his head inside.

Everyone looked at Rob. "I am."

"Sir, normally we wouldn't bother you with this. I'm sorry if it's a crank, but we've had a lady just crazy enough to be real on the phone with our headquarters for the past fifteen minutes. We've been flooded with calls all day. This one was been bumped three, four times and finally managed to get through to the precinct HQs officer. Says she's got to talk to you. Someone there thinks it might be real."

"Any ID?"

"Said to tell you it's Myrna, and she has an answer. Made my captain promise to get you the message."

Stephens stood, walked over and fully opened the door. The officer stood, startled, half in and half out.

"Is she still on your phones? How do I talk to her?"

"No sir. You're supposed to call her. She said she'd keep calling us until we got you the message. You going to call her?"

Stephens didn't even answer the officer as he strode to the bank of phones. Joyce Patterson walked over to the door. "Thank you, officer. Tell your captain he showed outstanding judgment. You guys at BPD may have just helped us more than you can imagine. That's the first good news we've had today."

After all the frustration of the day, including the death of two of their own in the motorcade, it was the first good news of the day for the BPD as well.

"Myrna," said Stephens when the call got through to Dublin. "Rob Stephens."

Jacobi, Patterson, and Sanders surrounded Stephens as he spoke on the phone. Bradford listened intently from the corner. The call took only a few minutes. Stephens had to ask only a few questions. He grabbed for a pad shortly into the conversation and wrote down a list of names.

Stephens replaced the receiver and turned to Patterson. "Joyce. Get someone up to Dublin to meet Myrna Glover at the Yankee Magazine headquarters. We need two issues—June and October. She'll have copies of everything. Meanwhile, send someone to get the October issue, and anything else they can find locally. I don't want to wait for Dublin. There's got to be dozens of news stands at the airport that will have them. Check out the big bookstores downtown, too. This warrants helicopters and hand carrying. Have someone else get a hold of the USPS in Nashua. Find out anything they can about a PO Box 9954."

Patterson called for one of the runners stationed in the van outside. The sound of the first helicopter lifting off came less than a minute later.

"We have a key piece of the puzzle," explained Stephens. "Maybe just another dead end, but a key piece nonetheless. Sullivan had one of the people who picked up Green ask her about Pumpelly Cave. After he left Glover remembered an advertisement last June that stood out, plus another one from this month's issue. I think she's on to something. The June one was from some environmental group named "Environmental Clarity." It listed eight sites that were in danger and asked concerned people interested in volunteering to write letters to legislators to write to a PO Box. It emphasized 'No money, please.' The list included the Pumpelly Cave."

Bradford frowned. "Then is this place real or fake?"

"Oh it's fake," answered Stephens, "but most flatlanders don't know that. They think it's real."

"Flatlanders?" asked Sanders.

"People who come up only in the summer. Bostonians and New Yorkers. I think Falconer made a little mistake here. An easy one to make. Only someone like Myrna would catch it. He wanted something to make the advertisement relevant to Yankee Magazine, so he must have asked people about favorite local places. He didn't have a clue as to what the answers meant. The people he talked to probably didn't, either."

"You said there was a second ad?" asked Patterson.

"That's the breakthrough Glover made," explained Stephens. "She remembered someone placing an ad in the September or October issues that seemed strange at the time. For some reason it reminded her of the June add, even though it was from a different company. She's looking through the Yankee files to see if she can find it."

Sanders looked at the list. "So, what does it tell us? If there's no such cave, does it mean the item before or after it on the list is the right one? Is this just a coincidence? At least a couple of these places are real. I remember seeing a Deer Island near us when I looked over the maps of this place. Seabrook is a nuclear plant on the New Hampshire border. The Vineyard is probably Martha's Vineyard. I don't know what the heck the army annex is in Sudbury, but there is a town by that name west of here. The rest I don't know."

Stephens reached out and took the list. "The MacDowell Colony is in Peterborough. Cathedral of the Pines is just south of Jaffrey in Rindge. The Headwall must be either Tuckerman's or Huntington on Mount Washington. And Pumpelly Cave makes eight. Seven of eight real."

"You can't take a President to one of those," said Bradford "This is a bloody red herring. None makes any sense as a final destination. Climb Mount Washington with the President on your back? Give me a break."

"Maybe," said Stephens. "Maybe. But I'm not ready to concede this one yet. My instincts are rusty, but this one rings true to me." He turned to Bradford. "Can we put Sullivan on it? Fill her in on what we've got. See what she can figure."

"I agree, John," added Patterson. "This is the only thing we have that might be solid. And I agree with Rob's instincts. I'll call it in to Lowe and have him get her on it. Tell her to concentrate on comparing the June and October ads."

Chapter Twenty-Six

Stephens turned from where he was staring at the list of names when he heard the sound of a car pulling up in front of the deli. There were two people in the car. Even from a distance and through the dirt of the window he immediately recognized the silhouette of Harvey Green in the passenger seat. The smile that surfaced was natural and infectious. For the first time since he had left Wendlandt, he felt good just then. Jacobi and Sanders looked through the window and followed the progress of two people from the car to the door of the deli. Bradford and Patterson were out at the ATQ van. When they saw Green they started back towards the deli. Eaglestone was on the far side of the lot with the commander of one of the National Guard units now activated for the search. His SEALs had completed their gruesome search. Any remaining bodies were buried at the bottom of the tunnel where the explosion had caved in the middle third of the flat section.

When the door opened and Green looked in, it was with a smile that equaled the one on Stephens' face.

"Didn't think I'd leave you alone on this one, did you old buddy?" he asked as he limped through the opened door. "If you give me a hand now and then, I might just be able to bail you out one more time." Green nodded towards the driver. "Wesley wasn't too pleased about diverting me up here, but I managed to convince him of the error of his ways."

Stephens smiled in sympathy at the driver, a class three who had been assigned to pick up and escort Green from Myrna Glover's house the night before. He had been one of the three agents who had protected the room at Monadnock General Hospital all night, while the medical staff had begun to patch Green's body back together.

"Harvey's been known to be pretty persuasive, so I wouldn't worry about giving in to him," offered Stephens. "Everyone here will know you never had a chance!"

"Tell me about it," the agent said ruefully.

Jacobi had been near the door and walked over to Green. "I'm glad you made it, Harvey. At least you're still walking."

"Just, Pete. Just."

With Stephens' help Green slowly eased onto a chair. His face was tight as he tried to control the reaction to the pain coursing through his body. Jacobi and Sanders had stopped their work and were watching silently. The room was awkwardly quiet.

"You found him yet?" asked Green.

"Not yet."

"Leads?"

"None that are useful."

"I've been briefed on most of the tunnel action," said Green, staring intently now at Stephens. He leaned forward and dropped his voice. "With one notable exception. Not a thing about your friend. She okay?"

Stephens looked back at the dust and gravel of the parking lot and slowly closed his eyes. He could hear the approaching steps of Bradford and Patterson. The good feeling at seeing Green was pushed to one side and was replaced by loneliness. "Incredible," he thought out loud, "that I miss her right now."

"I'm not surprised, Rob."

He looked up at Green. "It show that much?"

Green didn't answer. He just raised his eyebrows and nodded his head twice. "I'm sure . . ."

"Green!" Bradford's voice was hard as he threw open the door. "What the hell are you doing here?"

"Well, I might not be healthy enough to take the point just now, John," Green answered, "but I'm in good enough shape to help out in some way."

"You're embargoed," said Bradford as he stepped directly in front of Green. "You can't help out in *any* way until we convene a council."

Joyce Patterson reached out one hand and placed it on Stephens' arm as he started forward. "Rob, don't," she said softly. "You know the procedures on this one. Harvey will have his chance. A good chance. I'll be there, too. But you've got to ride with it for now."

Sanders remained unusually silent again. Bradford stared first at Patterson, and then at Stephens before motioning towards Wesley.

"Wesley, what in hell are you doing?" Bradford ordered. "Harvey Green should be under close guard. Cuffs are called for. He's a six and you, I believe, are a three. So extreme caution and hostile engagement rules are in order."

"Mr. Bradford, I really don't think that . . ."

"Mr. Wesley! I'm not asking you to think just now. I'm telling you, as director of this agency, to put cuffs on this man and begin max-hold procedures until we know for certain just what we're facing. *Now*, Mr. Wesley."

When Stephens finally spoke everyone turned to face him. The voice was calm, laced with sadness. He was looking directly at Green, yet seemed to be looking well past him. All but Wesley and Jacobi recognized the look. It was the reflection of all the patterns coming together inside, and the answers finally becoming evident.

"I know who the mole is, Harvey. We *will* need to use the cuffs."

"You're ahead of me," said Green. "Try as I can I haven't figured it out yet. I'm starting to be suspicious of myself, old friend. All the hard data points right at me."

"It does indeed. And even that was a major clue. But your question, earlier, about my 'friend' is the heart of the answer." He paused for just a few seconds. "Sanders gave me the final pieces in the tunnel. Just a brief line or two that answered all the questions."

In stages, each member of the group pulled their eyes away from Stephens and faced Sanders. His eyes were wide open, at first, and then became angry and tight.

"Bullshit!" he said, looking from one to another before concentrating on Stephens. "I don't know what you think you heard, but you're higher than a kite if you're trying to nail me as a mole! What the hell are you trying to pull, Stephens? Same old anger? Foster again?"

When the rest glanced back at Stephens to see his reaction they saw that Stephens had pulled out his gun, and was pointing at the ground near Sanders' feet. Stephens nodded towards Wesley. The young class three was absolutely baffled by the conflict involving his ATQ leadership. "Wesley, please get your cuffs."

"Mr. Stephens, I'm not sure . . ."

"It's okay, Wesley," interrupted Bradford. "Get the cuffs." Bradford looked around the group. "We've got to respect Stephens on this one. If he says it's Sanders, and not Green, then we've got to ride with it."

"No!" Sanders' voice was an explosion of anger. "This is bullshit! There's no way in hell you can call this one this way!"

Sanders started to reach for his side where his own weapon was in a holster under his jacket.

"Carl, stop now, please." Stephens's voice was soft, but there was no question as to whether or not he was in command. Sanders stopped with his hand three inches from the edge of his coat.

"Joyce, please step over here behind me," Stephens asked. "Wesley, bring the cuffs over."

"Go with it Wesley," Bradford added. "This is Stephens' show. I back him all the way."

Stephens waited for Patterson to get behind him. "Wesley, please hand the cuffs to Mr. Bradford, and then step away," said Stephens. Jacobi, Wesley, Sanders and Bradford stood a few feet in front of Stephens. Green was off to one side.

"You want *me* to cuff him?" asked Bradford, taking the cuffs.

"Not exactly, John."

For the third time in the past five minutes, all eyes turned to lock on Stephens because of the tone and content of his voice. This time they saw that Stephens' weapon now had an active target. It was pointed directly at Bradford's chest.

"You mean John?" asked Jacobi incredulously. "Bradford's the mole?"

"Rob?" Patterson's question was almost whispered.

"John, put the cuffs on, please. You know the routine."

Bradford stood and stared at Stephens. Unlike the earlier confrontation with Sanders, Bradford showed no anger.

"Rob, I'm sorry," Bradford said with clear concern in his voice. "I should have expected this might happen with all the pressure after you've been out for so long. I guess I just didn't realize the strain and problems for you after so many years away. I should never have called you into this."

"The cuffs, John."

"Please. Don't kick away so much for this silly mistake. It isn't worth it Rob. My God, you know it can't be me! We've been at this too many years. You and I started ATQ. You're just tired. Burnt."

"John, I won't ask another time. Please put the cuffs on."

"Joyce, Carl, Pete, I'm sorry. Please restrain Rob. We'll have to go on without him. Wesley, you'll have to guard both Green and Stephens until this is over."

Only Wesley moved at first. He began to reach for his weapon when Harvey Green placed a hand on Wesley's arm. "Wesley, please don't do that." Wesley stopped in mid motion at the voice. "I doubt you'd have any way to know it, but when Rob takes a stand like this, you'd do better to wait just a moment. It will not have been lightly taken."

"Mr. Jacobi?" asked Wesley, confusion in his voice.

"Jacobi, he works for you," said Bradford. "Order him to take action."

When he finally answered Wesley's question, Jacobi continued to stare at Bradford. "Wait just a bit longer, Don. This has to clear up a bit before we choose sides."

"I'm over my head here, Mr. Jacobi."

"I know, Don. We all are."

The room went quiet as no one wanted to be the next to speak. Sanders looked back and forth at all standing there. He was still recovering from the dramatic events that had targeted Green, then himself, and then Bradford in quick succession. Like almost all in the room, Sanders was standing on the fence being pulled in all directions. Only Green had made his choice.

The room was silent. There were faint traffic sounds in the distance, and you could just hear the low drone of a plane leaving Logan Airport. With the tunnel closed and traffic diverted away from the area, it was strangely silent for downtown Boston. Stephens and Green waited patiently. Sanders glanced from face to face, as did Wesley. Patterson's gaze bored into the back of Stephens' head. Jacobi would look at one person in the group, then back to Stephens, then to another, and then back in a constant movement with Stephens at the center.

After nearly half a minute, it was Carl Sanders who first found himself staring at Joyce Patterson. A few moments later Jacobi also found himself looking over Stephens' shoulder to where her eyes were now locked on Stephens. Finally Wesley did the same.

"I'm sorry, Joyce," said Stephens when all the movement in the group had stopped and he saw that all eyes were focused on her. "You and I knew all along it would come down to you."

"I know."

"You have to make the call on this one."

"I suppose it's a coincidence that you have me standing behind you? You're pretty vulnerable this way."

"It's a way to make sure you know that it truly *is* your call. A 'gift freely given,' old friend."

"You certain about him?"

"Yes. No doubts."

"Why?"

"A lot of things, Joyce. Some of it was fact. Some was eliminating other possibilities. But the final proof I needed was something Carl said to me. What I've got is soft, and might not hold in any review. But I know it to be truth. Carl . . . what did you tell me about a woman with the Falconer."

"Just that we were trying to figure out who she was."

"How did you know that there was anyone with him?"

Stephens continued when no one answered. "Who was asking about her?"

"John," answered Joyce.

"Who made the report to him?"

"I don't know," she answered before looking directly at Bradford. "Who told you there was a woman?"

"Green, when he called in from Peterborough."

Green said nothing.

"That's crap, Bradford," said Stephens. "Why didn't he just tell the Falconer directly if he was the mole? You heard it from Falconer. That's the only way you could have known."

"Green called it in. Maybe he was just covering his tracks."

"And then, for show, let himself be nearly beaten to death?"

"Listen! Joyce, Carl. I don't know what these two are up to. Green must have known we were close to blowing him. Maybe Stephens is too blind to see it. But if Green knew we were closing in, he and the Falconer would have to make it look pretty good."

Green finally spoke. "That makes no sense."

"See! Green's still blocking our efforts! While we stand here talking, the Falconer gets farther and farther away. There's no choice here. You three have to take them into custody pending a formal review. That's policy. We have to get on with saving the President." Bradford's voice became hard. "Carl and Joyce, this has gone far enough. Wesley I can understand. But any more and you two cross the line to insubordination. No matter what comes of this you'll lose everything."

Carl and Joyce looked at each other for several seconds before Joyce finally broke the silence.

"You know what you're asking, Rob?" The question was rhetorical and an answer was not expected.

The silence that followed was brief. No one even looked up at the sound of Norm Eaglestone's approaching footsteps. Only Stephens looked over to see the assault rifle in the SEAL's hands. "There a problem here?"

"It's okay, Ned," answered Stephens. "You can put that away. This is under control."

Eaglestone looked back and forth at the members of the group before deciding what to do. Finally, he chose to keep the weapon ready, but slowly dropped the aim of the rifle to point at the ground. He then stood back a few feet away from the rest of the group and watched the scene intently.

Joyce Patterson finally broke the silence. "For what it's worth, Rob, my instincts have been the same for some time. I've been watching Bradford for more than a year now, but could never be certain. No matter how hard I studied it, I just didn't have any proof."

She moved to the left around Stephens, and all traces of hesitation or uncertainty were gone. Only Stephens realized the significance that she now stood with her back to him. "John, put on the cuffs. Now please."

Bradford didn't even try to answer. He knew the tone in her voice, and that there would be no change in that decision. Slowly Bradford locked one cuff on his right wrist, and then placed his hands behind his back. Green stepped over behind Bradford, locked the cuffs on the other wrist, and gave them a brief inspection before nodding. The cuffs were specially designed to provide maximum security. The wrist bands were wide, more like manacles, and shaped with a slight curve to match the shape of the wrist. There was a solid metal tube covering the chain between the wrists. The tube was eight inches long and ensured that the two wrists were held far enough apart that the hands could just barely touch finger tips, and could not reach the other wrist strap.

Green led Bradford over to the heavy door of the deli's walk-in freezer. He used a second set of handcuffs to link Bradford's cuffs to the freezer door handle. Next Green pulled a stool over next to the door for Bradford. Finally, he took a chair, turned it around so that its back faced Bradford.

"Looks as though I can be of some use after all," Green said as he sat down, straddling the chair with his arms resting on the back of the chair. "Let me sit here and watch this fellah. That frees up the rest of you for the dance with our old friend."

"Joyce, Carl, please give me a second," asked Stephens. "I'd like a moment with Bradford."

She looked at him briefly before her face relaxed into a wry smile. "Well, old friend, we're in deep shit on this one. Sure do hope we're right."

Stephens was not at all surprised by her use of 'we,' rather than 'you' in assessing risk and blame. Yet, he was powerfully impacted by her choice. He realized that it had not even crossed her mind to take anything less than full responsibility for the action with Bradford. He had never been one who was comfortable with the outward signs of his own strong emotions. But, despite the others watching, he was at ease this time with his reply.

"You know I don't take what you did lightly, Joyce." His voice was full of caring. "But I can't pretend to be surprised. You're stuck with who you are. You *have* to do what's right, even when it hurts. Harvey's the same." He looked up and into the distance for a moment before continuing softly. "If there's any good out of all this, maybe it's that I finally met two more like us."

Patterson stared back at him. She couldn't help wondering who was the second person. She had no doubt that Eaglestone was the one of the two. She scanned through all the names and faces in their past, and a slight puzzled look surfaced as she realized that she could not identify anyone close to that level of trust. "Whoever it is," she thought, "it's someone I'd very much like to meet." She gave a gentle grimace and a single shake of her head before walking away to join Sanders and Eaglestone, and the totally baffled Wesley, just outside the door.

Stephens walked over to the driver's window and stooped down to be at eye level with Bradford. "I owe Harvey an answer to an earlier question. What happened to the woman?"

There was no answer. Bradford briefly glanced at Stephens, and then turned back to stare blankly out the window. There was no expression on his face at all.

"Is she with him?"

Bradford leaned forward and used the edge of the freezer door to scratch an itch on the side of his nose. Then he leaned back and looked towards the right, away from Stephens, back out the window.

"Mr. Bradford, despite Rob's nature to play by the rules, I feel far less compunction in that area," said Green from his chair. "He's asked you a question."

Bradford turned his head slowly to face Green over his right shoulder. There was a trace of amusement in his eyes, followed by the hint of a slight, unpleasant smile. Then the face blanked again and he returned his gaze to the window. "You have nothing that will wash. All you've done is destroy yourselves, and taken Patterson and Sanders with you."

Stephens reached out his left hand and rested it gently on Bradford's shoulder. His voice was soft, almost as gentle as the touch. "I'm going after him, John. I don't feel as confident as I used to that I'll get him. But I have no doubt at all about getting you. You'll answer for this. You've caused the death of too many who should not have died. I can accept somehow, Falconer's role in all this. It was his job. Were all the deaths only because of him, then I could sleep tonight."

The grip on the shoulder tightened, and the voice lost any trace of gentleness. "But Kathy Whitworth didn't deserve to be a part of this. And Cynthia Lebart. You killed one of your own in Jim Peterson. And you killed more of your own in the tunnel. That I cannot accept. I will not accept it."

Stephens released the grip and stood up. He absentmindedly stretched his legs and lightly rubbed his side.

"If I come back after this, then you and I will have one last dance. And if you're right, if you've covered your tracks, then it will be up to me. It makes little difference to me whether you hang by the law or die by me. Except, if Cynthia Lebart does not come back with me, then I won't wait for the courts."

Bradford looked directly into Stephens' eyes. The slight smile returned, and then broke into the open. The smile was as unpleasant as had been hinted at before. There was no twinkle in the eyes this time, just hardness and hate. The voice was a low whisper, too soft for Green to hear just feet away, but plenty strong enough to carry the force of the message to Stephens.

"But first, Stephens, you have to come back. Don't you?"

—∞—

It was nearly ten that night when the call came in from Marilyn Sullivan in the ciphers group at ATQ. Bradford had been turned over to the ATQ Internals team upon the joint recommendation of Patterson, Sanders, Stephens, and Green. To the end, as he was loaded into the helicopter for transportation back to Virginia, he would say nothing. Wesley was taken to Logan for a separate trip back. The evening's impact had left him nearly useless as a guard or as an effective field agent on the case, and had him questioning whether or not he wanted a future in ATQ.

The Falconer's Boat had been found up in Chelsea tied to an old dock near the drawbridge not far from the base of the Tobin Bridge. It was a dead end. The Falconer and his people would have transferred to a van or waiting cars. They were well beyond the traffic jams and could be anywhere in a 150 mile radius by now.

"Rob, it's Sullivan," called out Sanders when he answered the phone. "She's got something. She's going to fax a copy of a page from the September Yankee."

Sanders dropped the October issue that he had read and reread a dozen times over the past hour. He grabbed the second Yankee Magazine sitting on the counter next to him. "Tell her no need. I have one. What page?"

"Forty-Seven."

"Ask her to wait just a second."

Stephens turned to the page and scanned the advertisement on the lower half of the page. He clenched his fist and shook it briefly by his side. "Yes! That's it." He walked over to Carl with his hand outstretched for the phone. "Sullivan! I owe you! That's brilliant! I read through that issue three, four times and didn't get it. I was working on October when you called!"

While he listened, he showed the page to Patterson and Sanders. "Next time in Virginia, dinner's on me. Thanks."

"I'd have missed it," said Joyce as Stephens hung up the phone. "No way I would have made the connection. She's good."

The advertisement was from a different company and had a totally different look and feel. The only similarity at all was the fact that there was a list of eight places in the ad. A company named "New England Selections" claimed to specialize in pictorial histories of interesting places. It would collect photographs for as far back as possible to trace the changes in a site over the decades. A quick scan of the list showed that all of these places were quite real and shared a unique characteristic. All were accessible and either abandoned or, at this time of the year, closed up. The seventh item in the list, corresponding to the placement of "Pumpelly Cave" in the first list, was Grace Air Force Base on the coast of Maine.

"We've got you," said Stephens so softly that he almost was not heard by the two agents standing right next to him. "I've finally got you."

Chapter Twenty-Seven

It was just before 2:00 a.m. when the first van arrived at the mobilization point in the Maine State Forest, twenty miles from the abandoned World War II air base. It pulled into a large field that was accessed by an old logging trail. Five helicopters, just barely visible in the darkness, were already waiting on the ground. Four were large CH-53 Sea Stallions that had brought the first loads of equipment and personnel. The fifth was a Super Cobra Gunship. There was a flurry of activity everywhere, faintly illuminated by hooded flashlights, as large tents were being raised and materials offloaded from the transport helicopters.

The field had been carefully chosen to be fully secluded, yet sufficiently large that nearly 300 people could operate out of it when the assault on the air base began. It was close enough to the old air base that transport of personnel and equipment would be fast and efficient, yet far enough that the pre-attack activities would not be seen if the Falconer had posted sentries around the air base perimeter.

The remaining vans, widely different colors and models sharing only the characteristic of having no windows in the back, would arrive over the next two hours. At the same time the rest of the dozen helicopters involved in the operation would be flown in at treetop level, each from a different direction over an hour's period. Spotters both on the ground and in a pair of specially equipped EF-111A Ravens flying at high altitude would warn approaching vans and helicopters in the rare case another car was near the entrance to the logging road. If there was any possibility of being seen, the vehicle would simply continue on past the site, and try again later. By 3:00 a.m. everything would be ready to insert the initial infiltration force. By 5:00 a.m. the entire force with all necessary equipment would be on the site and ready. In only five hours after they had first learned about Grace Airbase, despite no advance notice of the destination and with a long list of things that might have gone wrong but didn't, ATQ was ready to begin countermeasures. The ATQ Emergency Deployment system worked.

The cornerstone of the deployment was a set of plans that had been put in place years ago and constantly updated. It was not a system that required mobilizing the National Guard or desperately searching for equipment. Instead, ATQ kept a list of specific people around the country that had the special skills necessary for just such an event. A handful on the list were from ATQ. Many were FBI, Treasury, DEA, and ATF. Nearly seventeen hundred were active duty soldiers. The list was constantly updated as military assignments changed. It took less than fifteen minutes for Joyce Patterson to sit at a computer console and generate the initial list of people who could be transported to staging areas in the Northeast. Within half an hour the first seventy people had been confirmed and were on their way. Two hours later the complete contingent, including all necessary disciplines anticipated for the situation, were on the move.

If you were called, it was only necessary to follow instructions that would get you from your current location to one of the interim staging areas at airports in New Hampshire and Maine. All transportation was reserved and prepaid by the 'Premier Travel Agency' that operated out of the basement of ATQ headquarters. Vans would be waiting to provide transportation from your destination to the logging road site. Any required equipment, right down to clean underwear, would be waiting. A second list of equipment was prepared in parallel with the selection of people. Supply sergeants at Pease and Otis Air Bases, the nearest two facilities with the correct material and supplies, loaded CH-53 Sea Stallions with the equipment, weapons, and communications gear that was anticipated by the computer simulations. The three Sea Stallions, fully loaded with clothing, equipment, and individual weapons were in the air within ninety minutes of Patterson's first call. The fourth, carrying a team of two dozen ATQ personnel carefully trained in the process of meeting each arriving van and directing the occupants to the appropriate area, was airborne even faster. It took an average of just seventeen minutes to fully equip a new arrival the moment they stepped out of the van.

The system worked because of hard work and practice. Each of the 2700 people on the current list was involved in at least one practice deployment each year. Many participated in two. A call would be received and a location specified. The person would be given specific transportation instructions and would be expected to ". . . make the plane on-time, or else!" If a person could not be reached, the caller would move on to the next person on the list. If you were contacted, there were no excuses for missing the assignment. If you could not be contacted, the reason would be carefully investigated. The goal was to be able to have preliminary response to any location in the USA within three hours, and full response within six.

Stephens was asleep when the rest of the vans began to arrive on site. On the way up, as a passenger in the first of the four AH-1W Super Cobras assigned to the mission, he reviewed the maps and blueprints of Grace Air Force Base found in the Army Logistics Command archives. He had landed at the site just after 1:00 a.m., and had continued to study the blueprints until the rest of the ATQ contingent arrived on scene an hour later. He took five minutes to outline the basics of the plan he had developed to Patterson, before climbing into the ATQ van to catch an hour's sleep before the first assault would begin. Joyce would wake him when the rest of the team was at the site.

Grace AFB had been decommissioned just two years after the end of World War II. It had served as a key airlink in the flow of materials from the USA to England and Europe, and had been the northernmost base for the Catalina PBYs that had patrolled the western Atlantic searching for German U-boats.

The two airstrips were a half mile from the edge of a steep drop down to a wide beach and the Atlantic Ocean. There were five old buildings on the field. In the northwest corner, near the end of the end of one of the runways, was a large aircraft hangar. The remains of a two story building that held administrative and command offices was in the northeast corner 100 yards from the edge of the cliff. Between the large hangar and the office building was a smaller hangar, set back towards the middle of the field. The tower and barracks were south of the runways in the southwest corner of the field. Two pillboxes overlooked the beach at the northeast and southeast corners of the field. Under each pillbox was an ammunition storage room. There was a path carved into the cliff that slanted down to the beach and a small dock.

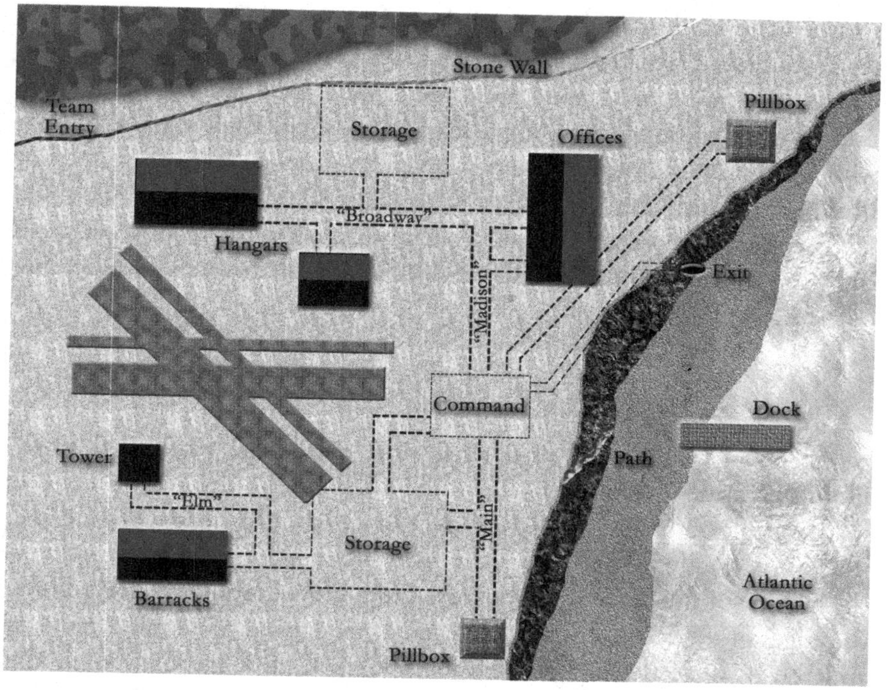

All of the buildings and the pillboxes were interconnected by a series of concrete tunnels that lay ten feet beneath the surface. These tunnels also connected to three large underground rooms—two for storage and one was a backup command post. One tunnel led directly down to the beach where it exited in a concrete and steel-reinforced enclosure designed to withstand the direct hit of anything short of a capital warship.

The three largest tunnels were all given code names by the assault team. The longest and widest east-west tunnel under the northern end of the complex was given the name "Broadway." It linked the two hangars and office building on the surface with a large underground storage area. The connecting tunnel running north-south between Broadway and the underground command center was named "Madison Avenue." The tunnel running south out of the command center was named "Main Street." Finally, the tunnel complex in the southwest corner linking the tower, barracks and southern underground storage area was called "Elm Street."

According to a two year old report by the Department of the Interior, the buildings were now little more than rusted shells. Grace AFB was far enough off the beaten path so that little vandalism had occurred, but weather and neglect had accomplished the same thing over time. The report indicated that the roofs of several buildings had long ago caved in. There were no reports about the underground facilities, except that the underground entrances remained sealed. The field itself was overgrown with weeds and the runways were cracked and broken from the effects of fifty years of unchecked winters.

Stephens was dreaming about the approaches to the field when Joyce slid open the door to the van. It was 3:00 a.m. and Stephens was the only one sleeping.

Stephens waited until the conversation in the large tent settled down. From the inside it would take a second look before you would believe this was a tent flown in and set up just an hour earlier. The floor was solid and the tent was fully lighted. Electricity was supplied by quiet generators on the far side of the field. Whiteboards, maps, and computer consoles lined the edges of the room. Inside there were three groups of people. Stephens and the ATQ leadership of Sanders, Patterson, and Jacobi were at the front of the tent. To the right was the small team of handpicked ATQ agents that would be part of the initial infiltration. To the left were the leaders of the forces that would make up the second wave.

Stephens looked at the twenty-four hour clock at the front of the tent. "Okay. Everyone grab a chair or find a place to stand. It's 3:15 and I want everyone fully briefed and all questions answered not later than 3:45. A few of us have to put on our make-up and be on the road by 4:00 for an early house call."

Sanders, like most of the people in the tent, was dressed fully in black. His pack and equipment lay on the floor under the whiteboard. After the briefing, he would only have to apply his camouflage paint to be ready for the raid.

"I'm going to cover the basics, and then let Joyce go over the layout of the airbase. Then we'll get into the detail on this dance. A few of us will miss the full briefing as we will precede the main assault."

Stephens walked over to the large map of the base on the front wall.

"Somewhere in this mess are the President, a civilian woman, and the most dangerous man any of you could possibly imagine. He is known only as 'the Falconer.' But while that might sound like a name from one of those old James Bond comedies, there's nothing funny about the Falconer. He is deadly. He's killed two dozen people in the past forty-eight hours. He's outsmarted me and the best of us at ATQ at every step of the way. There's not a man or woman in this room who can go one-on-one with him and live. Does everyone have that?"

Stephens looked around the room for any sign of false confidence. "Good. Because if you take this lightly, I'll pull you off this like a shot." He looked around the room once again before continuing. "Now we really don't have a clue how many we'll be facing. If you base it on what we think the Falconer took with him out of Boston, I'd say around a half dozen. But that guess would be a sucker's bet. He had three times the people in Boston that we anticipated. He's carefully planned and prepared every step of the way so far. I personally expect he had at least a couple dozen first class soldiers waiting for him up here, and wouldn't be that surprised if we ran into a force of fifty or more."

"Now we're going to have two small groups of six go in first. Team "A" will be me, Eaglestone, Stadfeld, Fischer, Wallace, and MeGee. Team "B" will be Sanders, Jacobi, Barlow, Soja, Kearnes, and Conte. We're going by van most of the way and walk the last mile or so. Team A will be inserted in the southwest corner to enter near the old barracks. Team B will come in the northeast near the offices. We're going to go it alone as long as we can. As soon as we're discovered, we'll call for all the help we can get."

Stephens walked over to a flip chart and turned over the first page to show six lists of names.

"The rest of you in this room will be leading the full assault teams shown here. These teams will wait here, fully ready in the helicopters. If we call, all six will come in straight and fast. You'll have to assume the landing zone is hot if we call for you. Each of the helicopters will have a designated landing site. All members of teams A and B will be authorized to order a diversion of a landing site in case a particular location is too hot. The code word will be "Frost." It will *only* be used to authenticate an order to abort or divert. Got that?"

All heads nodded. A few responses of "yes sir!" were heard around the room.

"Okay. What about objectives?" Stephens turned another page on the flipchart. "We aim to free the President of the United States, and to free him *alive*. That is the primary and *only* objective." Stephens took a deep breath before continuing. "There is also a civilian woman in there that is not part of the Falconer's team. Rescuing her is a low priority objective. Clearly we hope to free her as well, but if it comes to a trade-off between her and the President, the President is the issue. Clear?"

There were no questions.

"As to tactics, I'm going on the assumption that they're in the underground areas that Joyce will describe. I expect multiple hostiles on the surface as sentries. Teams A and B will have as our primary objective to remain undetected and to determine where the President is, or is not. Our secondary objective will be to identify and locate any hostiles on the surface to guide later forces. We won't attempt to eliminate hostiles as we go, because a mistake could announce our presence to the main force. We'll leave a person to mark anyone we do find, and if we are discovered the markers will take out all targets simultaneously."

"However, let's have a dose of reality here. The odds against us pulling that off are probably 80/20. We'll have to assume that one or two sentries will have to be taken out in order for the two teams to enter the base. Killing a sentry starts the meter running. Depending on how often they verify the status of their sentries, and when the last check was, I'd guess we'll have no more than ten or fifteen minutes before the next radio check lets them know someone is not answering."

"If we're lucky, the ultimate would be for the two teams to locate and remove the President without a major firefight. I think that's about as likely to happen as Madonna teaching a class on modesty. What might happen is that a couple of us can infiltrate the underground, and will have marked all hostiles on the surface, before we have to call in the reinforcements. If and when you are called in, remember you will be facing elite fighters. Because they are entrenched and capable, we will be in an unfavorable position as soon as we lose the element of surprise. I need everyone here to remember that we are the underdog no matter what numerical superiority or support we have."

Stephens let the assessment sink in.

"Good. Now we do have support. The four cobras parked outside aren't for show. Patterson will have the exact loadout, but these beasties typically carry Hellcat and TOW missiles that can stop anything we anticipate on the ground if we have to call them in. They also have a very nasty Gatling gun in their nose. We have F-15s out of Otis overhead just in case Falconer somehow planned to fly out of here. A Coast Guard Cutter is already a couple miles offshore, and a pair of Spruance class destroyers will be here by early afternoon. We'll have twelve people in the first two teams, another 180 in the six Sea Stallions of the main assault, and a reserve of fifty. Any Questions?"

Ned Eaglestone looked up from where he was quietly leaning against a tent pole. "I'd feel better if a few of my SEALs could close off that beach, sir."

"After seeing them in action in Boston, me too, Ned. But AWACS says there's nothing close that the Coast Guard cutter can't handle. Anything bigger than that, once spotted, would have to run a gauntlet of air cover that will not be passable." Stephens checked the time. "About ten minutes ago Pease had a new squadron arrive with Intruders and F/A-18s. That's overkill for anything within a thousand miles of here."

"Sir, why not surround them and wait them out?" asked a Special Forces captain.

"I'll handle that one, Captain," answered Joyce Patterson as she stepped forward. "We've danced with the Falconer for a few years now. Waiting him out will not work. He won't surrender. He won't release the hostages. He will not negotiate. What he will do is use any extra time we give him to his advantage. He's very good at that."

"If we found out he could stay down there, comfortable and warm for a year or two, it would not surprise me," added Sanders.

A hand was raised in the back of the room. "If they're underground, can we use gas?"

"Good question," answered Patterson. "One of the Sea Stallions brought in heavy loads of tear gas and something from Langley that's a form of sleeping gas. It's available as an option. However, based upon advice from the White House medical staff we don't think we can use either if the President's in the room. We have people checking on that."

"What's the condition of the underground passages?" asked a senior FBI agent.

"No one is quite certain," answered Patterson. "The best we have is an 'expert assessment' from someone in the Department of the Interior that they are 'probably' in pretty good shape. I'd rate that a SWAG at best—Scientific Wild-Ass Guess. Anything else before we get to the details?"

There were no further questions in the room.

"Good." Patterson picked up a pointer that was leaning against the back wall of the tent. "Let's study this map, and then the details of this operation."

—∾—

Stephens could not ignore the irony as he approached the overgrown stone wall that served as a fence at the edge of the airfield. Perhaps Frost would once again prove correct, and these fences would make good neighbors. But Stephens knew that they were more likely to make dead neighbors. Up to this point Team A had been almost invisible as it worked slowly and silently through the forest. Years of experience made them little more than shadows, deadly black wraiths like something out of Tolkien. Now the protection of the forest would end. For a few moments they would be fully exposed as they crossed the stone wall. Then there was a hundred foot open space between the forest and the barracks that loomed in the distance. The fence was a tangible dividing line between preparation and commitment.

Part of the silence was due to practice. Part was due to night goggles and following carefully in the footsteps of the person ahead of you. A large part was due to a simple device that had unwittingly been developed by a seven year old child. The boy was the father of a junior member of Lowe's cipher department. He and his sister loved to play hide-and-seek in the dark with their dad. One day, realizing that his father always heard him no matter how carefully he tiptoed around, the boy had taken some foam rubber that had been packing material for a new computer and wrapped it around his feet. It would be the first time ever that he was able to sneak up on his dad. The ATQ development team had at first laughed when told of the idea. Then they looked for ways to redesign it and make it tougher than ordinary foam rubber. The result was something the agents immediately named after the boy's description to his dad. They were "sneaky slippers." They slipped over standard shoes or boots, could be quickly removed, were deadly quiet, and gave the wearer just a bit more warning when stepping on something.

The night had decided not to cooperate. Instead it would alternate between teasing them and exposing them in the light of the quarter moon. It was partly cloudy with strong northeast winds at the altitude of the clouds. The clouds rushed across the sky, briefly darkening the area then letting the pale moonlight bathe everything. Even in full black and with every trick tens of years of experience could offer, the men would be highlighted against the rough grass of the open area. And Stephens knew that if the Falconer had equipped his sentries with night glasses, even the darkness could provide no help.

There would be only one way the two teams could enter the area unseen. Patterson had to make sure that the sentries were looking in another direction. It would have to be very convincing. That's where some special help from the Air Force would slightly adjust the odds.

As soon as Joyce had completed the description of the base, members of the two initial teams had left the meeting. The rest of the briefing would continue for another half hour. During that time the teams were transported by van to a point as close to the air base as possible without risk of detection. Because of their clothing and camouflage, the only thing that was not black was the whites of their eyes. Over the years the ATQ research people had never come up with an answer to that one. They had tried everything from contact lenses to black gauze overlays. But the bottom line was always that eyesight was the one sense that could not be at all compromised no matter what the gain. ATQ people could be trained to be nearly 100% effective even if they could not hear or smell or touch or speak. But diminish vision by just a small percentage and the odds of success plummeted.

Stephens motioned for the team to halt before the stone wall and carefully shielded his watch before briefly illuminating it to check the time. It was 4:25. If things had gone as planned, Sanders would have gotten to a similar position a few minutes before them. Stephens looked around at the rest of the team and saw that they were staying out of sight, not even trying to look over the wall. They had crawled the last fifty yards to this point. Anything else would have made them too easy to spot by anyone with night vision equipment watching the area.

Now there was little they could do except wait. The ATQ team could not even risk looking over the wall, because of the near certainty they would be spotted by sentries with night vision on the far side. Then they would have to cross a hundred feet of open area before they got to the barracks. It was a sucker's bet. Instead, Stadfeld carefully worked his way along the base of the wall until he could find a small opening that could be carefully enlarged by removing a single stone the size of his fist. Then he could search most of the area with a minimum risk of being discovered.

Stephens looked down towards the small mike on his collar and spoke one word. “Alpha.” A few moments later he heard a one word reply in his earphone. “Grass.” Sanders was in place, and according to the plan the teams now had a wait of about ten minutes before they would cross the wall.

A diversion that would attract the attention of professionals is nearly impossible. To work, it has to be believable and spectacular. Nearly anything would work if you just needed a couple seconds, and if you did not mind giving up all chance at surprise by announcing your presence to the enemy. Stephens and Patterson knew that the type of professionals they expected to meet at the airbase would recognize a phony diversion after about five seconds. It would only serve to warn the sentries that something was about to happen. If it looked real, but was not spectacular, then duty would overcome curiosity a couple of seconds later. Stephens and the two teams needed at least twenty seconds to enter their respective targets.

Eight minutes later another single word was heard in his earphone. “Tower.” At almost the same time the members of the team could hear the sound of a plane engine high in the night sky. The engine was clearly laboring. The plane engines slowed then sped back up, occasionally coughing, as the plane passed southeast over the base and out towards the sea. When the plane was about a half mile offshore and leaving the area the running and passenger lights of an airliner could be seen coming from the northeast. If anyone was watching, and Stephens knew that most of the sentries would have to keep glancing at the plane just to make sure it was not some kind of an attack on the base, they would see that the two planes were on a collision course.

At the last minute the engine of the small plane could be heard to race as the throttles were pulled to their maximum position. Then the small plane started to do a tight turn to avoid the collision. The airliner had not seen the plane and continued straight ahead. It looked as though the pilot of the small plane had made it. He pulled sharply up and to the left to pass safely over the airliner. But at the last minute the engine coughed again, and the small drop in airspeed was enough. The small plane caught the right wing of the airliner and exploded in a spectacular display of aviation fuel, lighting the sky like a dozen flares before the two planes spiraled to crash in the ocean a mile off shore. Stephens knew that the brightness was due to a large cargo of magnesium flare materials, carefully set off simultaneously with the crash of the two drone aircraft.

No members of the ATQ teams even saw the collision. They all had removed their night vision equipment and were staring down at the ground with their eyes covered. The sudden bright impact of the flares and crash would briefly destroy the night vision of almost anyone who was outside or looking outside. In buildings like the barracks that had no roof, anyone inside was likely to be temporarily effected. And if that person was wearing night vision equipment, even if looking away from the crash, the circuitry of the goggles would not be able to compensate fast enough before amplifying the brightness fifty-fold to send a searing stab of pain into the wearers eyes. Without the goggles, only night vision would be effective for five or ten seconds. With the goggles, the wearer might be nearly blind for ten times that length of time. In either case, Stephens knew he had to use those few seconds preciously.

As soon as the flash occurred, Stephens climbed over the stone wall and ran the hundred feet to the side of the old barracks. Eaglestone and the rest of the team remained below the wall. Entry was easy after the run across the exposed area. Stadfeld, watching through the hole in the wall with the help of night goggles, already knew that the doors to the barracks had long ago fallen off their hinges, and that no one was looking out through what was left of the windows.

Once inside the building Stephens quickly disappeared into the darkness. Almost by instinct, as soon as he stepped through the door he found cover where he would be able to hide while he used the night goggles to look for the sentry that he knew would be there. Little was left of the interior walls after fifty years of rain and snow. Old metal wardrobes and heating ducts were the only solid structures left. One wardrobe lay on its side a few feet from the wall centered on the door. He ducked past it to his right and sat on the floor in the shadow of another old wardrobe that stood against the remains of an interior wall.

Stephens spotted the sentry in his first sweep of the building. 'So that's why we didn't see you, my friend.' Stephens thought. 'Looks as though I was right not to underestimate you.'

The sentry was at the far end of the building against the same wall as Stephens. In the faint green picture in his night goggles Stephens could see him rubbing his eyes painfully. The sentry also had night vision equipment and had been looking outside when the two planes exploded.

The night goggles had amplified the light from the explosion many times over, leaving the sentry with painfully spotted vision. Right in front of the sentry Stephens could just make out a slightly shiny patch on the wall about two feet from the floor. What would appear to the team at the wall to be nothing more than a dark patch was actually the same one-way material used in limousine windows, but with the outside covered with a black web fabric to eliminate the reflection.

'We were lucky we were not seen,' Stephens thought as he quietly rose to his feet and padded noiselessly towards the far side of the barracks. '*It's about time we had some luck*.'

Stephens carefully worked his way along the far wall until he was directly behind the sentry about fifteen feet away. Then he froze and waited for the radio check that would have to come soon. While he waited, he wondered what impact the phony plane crash would have on the Falconer. "Will he buy it and think it will draw unwanted attention to his location? Will it force him to move up his schedule? Will he figure it out and know there's someone on the base? Would he have doubts?" One thing was certain to Stephens. Unless the Falconer got a conclusive report of infiltrators on the base, almost any impact would be good.

The radio check happened as quickly as expected. He saw the sentry touch his left ear and listen carefully.

"No. Nothing here," whispered the sentry.

Stephens could picture the double checking going on at each sentry position.

"I said nothing. Nothing at all. That crash was just shit luck." The voice never got above a soft whisper. "Does he think we'll have to move before this place is crawling with rescue people?"

Stephens could see the sentry's angry gesture in the air with his middle finger extended as he received a harsh response to the question. "Okay. Silence. Clear!"

The sentry lifted the solo finger to the air once again before pulling his night goggles back on and squatting down to look out the false panel. He carefully swept his eyes along the entire stone wall. Then he turned to his right where Stephens could now see another viewport that had been hidden by the sentry's body. The sentry carefully checked that direction as well.

When he was satisfied with both directions, the sentry stood part way up so that he would not be seen as he crossed below the windows to go to similar viewports at the opposite end of the building. Now Stephens understood the importance of the wardrobe that lay in front of the door to hide the sentry's movements from those outside. The sentry had taken careful precautions. Little mistakes were deadly in his business, and from what he had seen so far Stephens was pretty sure the sentry had made very few mistakes of any consequence over the past years.

In the end, the sentry really hadn't made much of a mistake this time. Sometimes there just is no answer to a problem. Perhaps if he had taken off the goggles, he would have had better peripheral vision and would have seen Stephens draw near. But without the goggles it would have been much harder to silently negotiate his way through the ruined building. He could not risk of making a noise that would have exposed him to anyone outside. And above all, his focus was outside the building, not inside.

The sentry never even realized that he was facing an unanswerable dilemma. When the pipe exploded across the back of his neck, and the lights and spots again flashed in his brain, a part of him drifted back into the scene a few moments before with the planes. 'How did I get up here,' he thought as he was now in the plane looking out at the explosion.

He never had the time to figure it out.

Eaglestone and the rest of Team A were inside the barracks thirty seconds later. Two members of the team silently took up positions at the front side of the building. Eaglestone and two others spread out in the eastern end of the building and began to search for the entrance to the underground complex. Stephens carefully inspected the inside of the building. He wasn't sure what he was looking for, but was reasonably certain he would find something. He needed to buy time, yet do it quickly before the dead sentry was discovered.

No one made a sound. There was no talking and almost no sound from their steps. Stephens assigned Fischer to lie on the floor next to the dead sentry, listening to the sentry's earpiece, to warn them if the Falconer's commanders tried to make another contact. Stephens was not even tempted to take the radio. There could be no doubt as to what had happened if someone, checking the body, found the radio missing.

The material over the viewports and the metal wardrobes gave him the idea. Stephens carefully repositioned the material over the largest viewport, and then cut away the excess. He removed one of the tacks from each of the two viewports. Then, motioning for MeGee to leave the search for the entry and join him, Stephens walked to the far western end of the building. He had MeGee help as he carefully and almost silently moved one of the big wardrobes up against the wall where a small hole could be seen. He then placed another wardrobe on its side against the first to form a giant set of steps. Next, he put several pieces of the old wallboard on the upper surface of both wardrobes, and then climbed up so that he could rest on the top one and look out the hole. The wallboard distributed his weight so that he made almost no noise as he climbed up. Stephens nodded once to himself before taking the extra material and tacking one end over the hole. Then, holding the tack so that it would not come out of the wall, he ripped the fabric back off the tack so that the tack remained in the wall and there was a two inch rip in the fabric.

When he climbed back down Stephens carefully crumpled the end of the fabric away from the tear. He looked at the position of the hole, and then the wardrobes, and dropped the second thumbtack on the ground three feet out from the wall. Then he went and with MeGee's help carried the dead body of the sentry over to where he had been working. Fischer continued to listen to the earphone as he awkwardly duckwalked along with them, trying to keep the earphone in his ear. Stephens sat the body on the floor, got behind it, and with a solid twist with both hands broke the neck of the dead sentry so that it was twisted at an ugly angle. Then he positioned the body where it had "fallen" onto the floor. The legs were sticking up against the wardrobe. Stephens made sure that the neck was twisted underneath the body. He placed the crinkled end of the fabric in the left hand of the body and closed the fist on it.

A light tap on his shoulder told him the entrance to the western end of the long tunnel called "Broadway" had been found. It was Eaglestone. Ned's voice was barely audible as he reported.

"Got it. But locked off. From the inside. No way to open it quietly."

"Used?"

"Definitely. It's active," he nodded to the body on the floor. "My guess is that's how your friend got here."

"Then we'll have to try the tower."

"Moving out."

"Ned, leave MeGee here. Someone will come as a replacement. Have him mark the new guy."

"Done."

The rest of the team had been gone less than ten minutes when MeGee heard the sound of metal against metal as the door to the tunnel was carefully opened. MeGee was almost directly behind the tunnel entrance, lying flat behind a pile of rotted lumber and wall panels in one corner. He could look out through a very small gap at the bottom of the pile, but would be invisible to anyone in the building unless they came right up to the pile.

The person exiting the tunnel entrance was equipped with night vision goggles. He carefully swept every inch of the building before turning back to look at the body crumpled on the floor.

"Trouble." The voice, less than fifteen feet away from MeGee, was soft but clear. "Henri looks dead. I don't see anyone else." There was a pause. "I can't tell. I'm going to check now. Richard's not here."

The soldier slowly left the tunnel and walked in a crouch over to the body. He inspected it briefly before walking down to the end of the building and looking out through the two viewports on that end. After a few minutes, he walked to the other end and carefully searched the area through those two viewports. Only when he was certain that the area was clear did he return to the body. He stared at it a few moments before pulling the ripped and crumpled one-way material from the body's clenched fist. Then looked up and searched the wall above the wardrobes. With the aid of the night goggles it was easy to discover the thumbtack still in the wall. For a few moments, the soldier stared at the opening above the wardrobe.

The soldier pulled Henri's body away from the wardrobe, laid it on its back, and carefully searched it. The he rolled it over and looked at every inch for a wound or sign of what had happened. He reached out and grabbed Henri's hair, and then twisted the head.

"Area's fully clear. I think the damn fool just fell. Broken neck. Radio and weapons still here. Looks like he was making a new spy port out of a hole about ten feet up. He fell off a couple cabinets he had piled here. But there's no sign of Richard. That doesn't figure."

The soldier stepped back towards the viewports at the end of the building nearest MeGee while he listened to the instructions. "Why the hell is that bastard down there? Who sent him? Tell Richard to get his ass back up here!" He crouched down and continued to sweep the area.

"Got it. I hope it was worth it to him. Who you sending instead?"

The sentry stood up to head towards the other end of the building. "Good. Get him right up here. Still clear everywhere else?"

MeGee was inwardly more relieved than he would have guessed at the answer the soldier must have received. When he heard the soldier reply "Good, Out" he knew that Team B had also gotten in clean. From what he had heard at the briefing, and from others while waiting, they were finally having some good luck since the mess began down in Boston. Now he would wait quietly until Henri's replacements would arrive to guard a wall that had already been breached.

Chapter Twenty-Eight

Team B had even been even luckier. Over the past fifty years the forest had begun to reclaim much of the north end of the airbase. Heavy woods came to within a few feet of some buildings. Tree branches touched the sides of both the large hangar and the old office. The small hangar was out of reach of the forest's inexorable invasion, but it too would be reclaimed in another fifty years. Sanders' group was able to get much closer to the buildings, and only had a few feet to sprint when the airplane crash occurred.

The office was a two story building running north-to-south along the cliff. The inside was in much better shape than most of the other buildings. The roofs of the office and the tower were made of corrugated aluminum, and had been replaced seven years back by the Department of the Interior when the base was under consideration for being reopened. So while the insides of the two hangars and the barracks had slowly been destroyed over the years, the office and tower had been far more protected.

There were six sentries in the office building, yet combined they were far less effective than a solo Henri in the old barracks. First of all, they were more visible and could be watched as they went about their routes. Second, they were far more interested in the sea approach, and the phony plane crash had only intensified their search of the ocean approaches. Finally, they had instinctively followed the wisdom of sentries since the start of time by seeking the high ground of the second floor. While they had a much better view of the approaches to the base, they were far more vulnerable should anyone get past their view. If someone entered the building unseen, then the advantage of the high ground would be a cruel illusion.

Sanders had split his group in half. He, Barlow and Soja has easily entered the office on the side away from the ocean. Jacobi, with Kearns and Conte, had crept along the back side of the office until they could slip into what turned out to be an unoccupied middle hangar. In half the time it had taken Stephens and Team A to clear the barracks, Sanders had stationed two marks on the sentries in the office, had cleared the middle hangar, and had found that the entry to the underground tunnels from the middle hangar was open. As a bonus, but of little practical value, they confirmed their theory about Falconer's escape from Boston when they discovered a van with in the corner of the middle hangar. Inside were eight sets of tanks, flippers, and wet suits.

Sanders spoke briefly into his microphone. "Gray one marked. Gray two clear and positive."

—∞—

Stephens reached over and tapped Eaglestone on the shoulder. The team was crouched in the entryway to the tower. Stairs led up from the entry to the tower's control room. A hallway beside the stairs led to the offices. There were three large rooms on the first floor. One room was on each side of the tower and the third was along the back wall facing the field. The team had split up to silently cover the first floor rooms.

Stephens and Eaglestone were in the room on the right side of the building. They could hear soft footsteps upstairs from at least four sentries. Like the office building, the tower was in somewhat better shape than the rest of the buildings on the airfield. The rooms were drier, and the walls were solid. Some of the broken windows had been repaired. Most of the holes in the walls had been patched. But in the years since those repairs, nature had started to win again. The cartons and old furniture littering the room had begun to rot and rust again. The walls were covered with dust and had large patches of moss on the outer walls. Within another three or four years nature would complete its victory and the tower would fall.

"Sanders is entering Broadway from the middle hangar," Stephens whispered. "He has people marking the office. No problems with the big hangar."

"Any sign we've been had yet?"

"None."

"Fischer found the tunnel entrance to Elm. Wide open. Do we enter, too?"

Before Stephens could answer, the sound of steps starting down the stairway triggered an instant response from all members of the team. Without a sound, Sanders and Eaglestone melted into the darkness on the far side of old bookshelves built into the wall that abutted the stairs. Both shifted the assault rifles slung across their backs so that they could get as close to the wall as possible. In the other rooms the rest of the team took the same kind of action. Every move was designed to be ready to engage the enemy, but have the priority be avoiding discovery if at all possible. Since Eaglestone ended up closest to the front where the soldier would enter if he came into the room, he raised his silencer-equipped handgun to the side of his face, resting it along the edge of the bookshelf. Then he waited.

When the steps got to the bottom of the stairs they stopped by the front door and paused. Another set of steps approached the top of the stairs, followed by a forced and angry whisper. "Not outside, idiot!"

A small grunt of anger could be heard, and then the steps went down the hall and entered the room where Stephens and Eaglestone hid. The enemy ducked beneath the window and walked to the far front corner of the room and stopped. A moment later Eaglestone and Stephens could hear the sound of a zipper, followed by the sound of water splashing against the wall of the corner. The smell of urine filled the room. When the sound stopped, the sentry waited almost a minute before zippering his pants. Then he carefully ducked under the window and headed back up the stairs.

Only when the soldier was back upstairs, and the sounds from the top floor had returned to the same patterns the team had categorized when they first entered the building, did anyone move. Eaglestone grimaced as he lowered his weapon and turned back to face Stephens.

"I hate this job," he said softly.

—w—

Sanders and the rest of his team deployed in the Broadway tunnel, entering via the door in the middle hangar, fifteen minutes before Stephens would follow suit in Elm Street. Sanders sent Kearnes and Conte along the tunnel to the west to where it entered the large hangar. There they would wait and would mark whatever sentries were stationed in the hanger. If Kearnes determined that there were no more than two or three hostiles in the large hangar, he would remain to hold that end of the tunnel and would send Conte back to rejoin Sanders and Jacobi.

Broadway was a quarter-mile long tunnel that connected to the office building at the east end, and to the large hangar on the west end. Midway along Broadway were two small branching tunnels entering Broadway about seventy-five feet apart. One branch ran north thirty feet to the underground storage area. The second branched south to the small hangar. At the far eastern end of Broadway, where it entered the office building, the tunnel branched south to interconnect with an underground command center.

Sanders positioned Jacobi just inside the southern branch to the small hangar. From there he could control the entire west end of the northern tunnel complex. The next step was to complete securing the northern system by clearing the underground storage area. As soon as that was secure, Sanders and Jacobi would be able to move down towards the office and prepare to approach the command center.

Sanders had taken only a few steps down Broadway when the team's good luck finally ran out. He was midway between the two entrances to the branch tunnels when two soldiers came around the corner at the east end of Broadway where it intersected with Madison Avenue. At first, he was able to simply stride purposely towards the shelter of the intersection just ahead. But when he saw both soldiers start to unsling their weapons he knew that more bluffing would not work. He sprinted the last ten feet, and threw himself into the opening just as two bursts of automatic shots streamed off the walls and down the length of the tunnel.

It was then, as he stood with his back against the east wall of the branch tunnel and exchanged his own silencer for the assault rifle on his back, that he first heard the excited voices to his right. Sanders twisted his head around and realized that the underground storage room was filled with soldiers. He could see tables directly in front of the opening and beds in the distance. He estimated fifteen soldiers were sitting at the tables or standing near them. At least half of them were already rising from their positions and scrambling for their weapons.

"Shit," he whispered to himself. Then he touched the switch that activated his microphone. "Jacobi. Send 'Blue Flag.' Then take out the two in the hall. I've got about five seconds before I need to be out of here."

Sanders spun around and squatted to face the opening to the storage area, and then let off a four second burst that immediately killed three soldiers and wounded more. More importantly, it quickly cleared the area. He waited until he heard a burst of fire behind him in the hall. "I hope that's you, Jacobi old friend. Else I'm dog meat."

Sanders let off another two second burst into the room, and then broke into the hall. The seventy-five feet to the other branch seemed to be a mile. He could not even dodge as he ran, instead having to keep close to one wall to give Jacobi a clear line of fire. It seemed like hours had passed for the short run before he jumped into the entryway with Jacobi. His back felt as though a crazed acupuncturist had filled it with pins and needles.

"Did you send 'Blue Flag?'" asked Sanders.

"Yes, but probably only Kearns and Conte got it. No line-of-site to outside. The radio can't carry here. You want to cover here while I go back to the entry to the small hangar, pop a wire and send it?"

"Do it." Sanders touched his own microphone switch and contacted Kearns and Conte. "K & C, mark now. Tunnel is hot. Repeat. The tunnel is red hot!"

Jacobi's 'Blue Flag' warning was unneeded. Long before he got to the tunnel entrance most other members of both teams knew someone had been discovered. Three separate groups would send 'Blue Flag.' By the time Jacobi sent his, all four Cobras were airborne and racing towards the site. The first of the six helicopters that would carry the main assault group was already off the ground and moving into a holding formation.

Barlow and Soja in the office building knew it when they heard the excited sounds upstairs and heard the instruction to ". . . get down and cover the tunnel. They'll come in through there." When the first soldier came down the stairs no one upstairs heard the sound as one silenced shot entered his head through the left temple. A second shot was unnecessary. Those left upstairs never heard any sound as the two agents crept up the stairway. Less than twenty seconds later the room was cleared, and the Falconer had no 'eyes' covering the northeast sector of the airfield.

For Conte and Kearns at the large western hangar, it was much easier. Five minutes earlier they had found the opportunity to sneak into the large hangar to wait silently. When the message came, five quick close-range shots silenced the northwest corner of the field. At the same time, MeGee took out Henri's two replacements in the southwest corner.

Wallace and Fischer in the tower had almost the same experience as Barlow and Soja—except the sanction was far more difficult. No one made it easy by coming downstairs. A brief peek around the corner and up the stairs made it clear that the agents would not be able to sneak up and take out the sentries. The soldiers had placed a thick metal table on its side so that it covered the opening at the top of the stairs. Through a one inch gap on one side a sentry could lie on the floor and cover the whole approach. The solution to the standoff was not even clever. It was just another of the scenarios ATQ had practiced many times. Wallace went around to the back room of the building until he was directly below the soldier at the top of the stairs. Then he unloaded a full clip of armor-piercing slugs up through the ceiling. When Fischer saw the rifle at the top of the stairs jump, and then sag, he ran up the stairs and now had the table on his side. From that point it was easy. The whole middle of the airfield had now lost its eyes.

And for Stephens, Eaglestone and Stadfeld it was clear that all surprise was lost when they heard many feet running towards where they crouched just inside the west end of the southern underground storage area. They had just entered the room from the Elm Street tunnel that led west another 200 yards to meet with the barracks, and beyond that to the tower. The room was full of supplies, and was packed to the ceiling with a maze of boxes and containers so that they could not see the exits on the north and east sides of the room. They had just ducked behind boxes near the Elm Street entrance when they heard fast moving steps midway across the room muffled by all the boxes in between. A second later the first soldier ran into sight, running towards the Elm Street tunnel to the barracks and tower. Even though the Falconer's soldiers knew about the breach in the northern tunnel system, Stephens hoped to buy a bit more time in the southern complex by using his silencer to take out the soldier. But it turned out to be a wasted precaution. Just after his single shot dropped the man, three more soldiers came into sight near the middle of the room and the sound of many more could be heard at beyond the boxes at the far side of the storage area. Any chance for surprise was lost as Eaglestone had to open up with automatic fire to stop them.

Without wasting even a second to regret the loss of surprise, Stephens began to calculate options and possibilities for a room that was a maze of huge boxes and crates. He guessed that there were already at least twenty enemy soldiers lurking and moving inside, against the three of them. Stephens saw nothing that he could use to balance the odds.

"You cover the door, I'll try to reposition," he said to Eaglestone. "This doesn't look good."

Eaglestone checked his magazine before answering. "You ever have any easy ones, Rob?"

—∞—

The Cobras remained in a racetrack pattern as they waited for any signs of counterattack on the surface. The big Sea Stallions had reached the area unopposed, four landing at each corner of the field, and two deploying on the main east-west runway in the middle of the airbase. Immediately, one quarter of the force made its way to the tunnel entrances in the tower and the two hangars to help in the firefight underground. The rest began the process of securing all above-ground portions of the base.

Within fifteen minutes all surface buildings had been verified and cleared. The task was accomplished with only one injury—a broken leg when one of the ATQ assault team fell through a weakened section of floor in the office building. The initial ATQ teams had already silenced all sentries in the buildings.

As soon as the buildings were clear, the surface force split into three interrelated actions. Two groups of fifteen were sent to positions around the pillboxes at the northeast and southeast corners of the field overlooking the beach. The rest of the force, 130 strong, spread out over the airbase and began a step-by-step sweep of the rest of the area outside the buildings. With the Cobras patrolling overhead, additional ground troops swept through the forest to the north, west, and south to make sure that there was no counterattack possible from those directions. Nothing would be taken for granted. A "surprise" counterattack from the forest when the ATQ team was concentrating on the tunnels would be deadly.

When the forest out to a half mile from the base was secured, the bulk of the force pulled back, leaving three concentric rings of their own sentries to watch the area. The returning force split up once again, with half staying in strategic "ready" locations on the surface, and the rest strengthening the positions that had been taken overlooking the beaches and the pillboxes.

The beach would be difficult to secure as long as the pillboxes dominated the area. Small groups of twenty each were sent north and south along the cliff edge to make sure that those approaches were clear. When they were a half mile past the pillboxes, at too sharp an angle to be seen, each group rappelled down to the beach and waited for a signal to proceed. It was a miniature version of Omaha beach fifty years earlier. Until the pillboxes were silenced, any force inserted on the beach would be slaughtered. But this time there could be no bombardment to clear the way, even though pinpoint laser bomb drops or even precision bombardment from the sea could have easily destroyed both in seconds. Until the location of the President was determined, most of the force operated with hands tied. All the heavy weaponry that had been brought to the site—the explosives, gas, Hellfire and Tow missiles—along with a wealth of options available if the Air force or Navy was called in, was totally off limits.

The primary rule of engagement was what the ATQ staffers called "whites-of-eyes." It meant hand-weapons only to known and identified targets. "If you can't see it and identify it, don't shoot it." Mass-kill weapons could be used only if an area had been determined to be 100 percent unfriendlies. Even the Cobras patrolling overhead were little more than bluff and bluster. They were not even allowed to return fire, unless specifically directed to do so by one of three designated members of the command team.

Stephens knew that unless the reinforcements arrived soon at the entrance to the southern underground storage area, they would be of little help. Whoever controlled the rooms would control the long, open expanses of tunnels leading up to it. Right now Stephens estimated the odds were at least twenty to three. It would be only a matter of time before those odds proved conclusive.

The underground room was 200 feet square with exits out the west side to the barracks, the north to the command post, and the east to the southern pillbox. In between was a jumble of boxes piled to the ceiling in irregular rows. There was little if any pattern to the layout, and no long clear lines of sight. The process of clearing the room would require box-by-box, row-by-row action. Grenades, either fragmentation or stun, were nearly useless in the combined space. Because the boxes reached all the way to the ceiling, there was no clear space to throw a grenade. And with all the turns and jags in the irregular rows, you had at most six to ten feet of clear aisle to roll a grenade. Using a grenade would be equally as dangerous to the attacker as to the defender.

The ATQ forces were at a serious disadvantage since the defenders had already moved their people into two-thirds of the room. Stephens, Eaglestone, and Stadfeld were forced to take purely defensive positions to hold onto their small section of the room next to the entrance to Elm Street. Eaglestone was positioned just outside the room in the tunnel with Stephens to the right of the door and Stadfeld to the left. If they were pushed back out of the room, or eliminated entirely, then the reinforcements would face the prospect of coming down a long exposed hall while the defenders would be fully protected. Under those circumstances a single Falconer defender would be all that was needed to control Elm Street and prevent any of the ATQ forces from entering the area.

The standoff was complete. All three of the ATQ team had repositioned boxes to give themselves strong defensive positions. They could cover all angles while remaining out of the line of fire. With night vision equipment being used by both sides there were few surprises that could occur. One surprise that would not happen would be the same trick with the flares that had briefly disabled so many sentries when the two planes crashed. Eaglestone, from his commanding position in the entryway, was the only ATQ member wearing the goggles. Stephens had little doubt that the Falconer's men had learned their lesson as well. Most of their team would be operating without the lenses. Ironically, it was in the interests of both sides to leave intact the bulbs that dimly illuminated all the underground rooms and tunnels.

For most of the time waiting, there was only sporadic action. The Falconer's commanders would send one or two soldiers at a time to try to work their way close enough to attack the ATQ agents. It was a gruesome game of hide and seek where the losers often died and the winners just got to wait it out a bit longer. Three of the Falconer's soldiers had died in the attempts. But with each attempt the Falconer's troops gained a few more inches of ground, and consolidated their hold on the room.

Ten minutes before the reinforcements arrived, the Falconer's soldiers had tried one major attempt to clear the ATQ agents from the room. With a strategy more like something more out of medieval times than the twentieth century, they had used heavy boxes on dollies to make battering rams. Stephens heard the movement of boxes at the far side of the room as the Falconer's troops slowly opened up the space in their side of the room, and eventually created a barrier wall running diagonally from southeast to northwest. The middle four feet of the wall were on the dollies. Their plan was simple. Like a siege of a castle, they would use brute force to make an opening, and then overrun the area in a war of attrition that would be won by the side with the most people. Then they would hold the room, and control the vital tunnel leading to it.

Stephens was looking at Eaglestone, listening to the sounds of movement and shrugging his shoulder to show "I haven't got a clue," when soldiers began to push the dollies. The crash of boxes falling and being pushed aside echoed in the confined space. All soldiers in front of the barrier lay down covering fire at the ATQ's critical point—Eaglestone in the tunnel entrance. With Eaglestone pinned, the wedge could be pushed forward, claiming even more precious space and forcing Stephens and Stadfeld farther and farther back towards the corners. Behind the pushers, soldiers worked like scurrying ants to remove boxes on the sides of the path that was being cleared, and carried them back to line the Main Street tunnel leading out the north and east side of the room. When they ran out of ability to push more boxes, the soldiers would draw back a few feet and get a running start with the makeshift battering ram. And the boxes would fall and be pushed back a few more inches.

Stephens and Stadfeld had little option but to burrow into whatever cover they could find. For the next three minutes they would crawl from box to box, constantly change position, and wait for the opportunity to fire at any soldier that might briefly be exposed by falling boxes. Very few made that mistake, and when they did it was so brief and under such confusion that there was little time to even aim before firing. Half of the battle was just to make sure the "other guy" had as little time to aim if he saw you. Of the hundreds of shots fired in those three minutes, only seven hit their targets. But even though those seven hits resulted in five less attackers, Stephens knew they were losing the fight.

Stadfeld would be the first ATQ death of the day. Like Henri in the barracks, it was not because he made a mistake. It was just there was too much to process, too many variables. There were too many directions to look and too many attackers. Time and again his instincts had saved him. But this time, when his peripheral vision once again saved him from one of the four soldiers that were starting to encircle his position, there was no safe answer. He saw the two shapes rise to his left, and immediately dove to his right. But this time there was someone waiting and watching on the right. Stadfeld was looking directly into the eyes of his killer when the bullet entered his brain. And like so many before, in places like Vietnam or Borneo or Waterloo or Thermopile, death was just a quiet statement of fact with no laurels and no glory, no triumphal fanfares. There was just the almost indiscernible sound of a last soft breath slipping into the air.

Stephens immediately knew Stadfeld was dead by the shift in the patterns in the room. Suddenly the left side of the room was quieter and he could see boxes being moved into position where Stadfeld had once been. In a few more seconds he would be trapped in a full crossfire.

Stephens touched his microphone and spoke softly. "Stadfeld is down."

"I figured," came Eaglestone's equally soft reply.

Stephens looked at the shifting boxes and knew that there was no easy answer. A part of him started to consider the possibility that he had simply lost. No cavalry would come in time. They never had a chance. But the rest of him did what it always did. It kept studying the facts, trying and discarding option after option. It was like his one recurring dream of trying to save his family from a car that had gone off a bridge into a river. First he would roll down the windows and they would all swim out. But then the dream would suddenly change, making the problem ever more difficult. The windows would become electric and would not go down, so he'd crack open a door. Then the dream would then change and the door would be buried in the mud. Sometimes there would be ice on the river, or he would have two small children who could not swim, or his wife would be unconscious. One time he even had a dog trapped in the car and the "rules" of the dream meant he had to save the dog, too. The permutations were endless.

In a strange way the dream was important. He wondered about it now and then. It was almost as though the dream was a gift from some guardian angel who was helping to train him for times such as this. Sometimes, while sipping Bordeaux late at night, he would be fascinated by the implications of the dream, and would mentally debate whether it was significant, a gift or a curse, or just the result of a "bad piece of pepperoni." But this time, there in the room, it was a gift that would save his life yet another time.

He had almost made a deadly blunder by not revisiting an old decision. He had discounted the use of grenades, because he had determined when he first entered the room that they were ineffective in an enclosed space like this. But now the layout of the room was far different than just those few minutes before. It was now possible to see across the room to the far side. Many of the boxes had been dragged out of the room to line the sides of Main Street, or had been pushed out of the way. They no longer reached to the ceiling in most places. Conditions had changed, and the fifth iteration through the options brought him back to the grenades that were so useless just minutes before. "Damn," he thought to himself. "Someone on the other side of the room is going to figure this out any second, and I'll be the one eating grenade fragments."

Stephens glanced over to where Eaglestone stood by the entrance and spoke softly into his microphone. "You have room for me in there?"

"Yup. Won't be easy for you to make it back here though."

"Clear a bit of the side. I'm coming."

"Won't be much better from here, my friend." There was resignation in Eaglestone's voice. "I figure a few minutes and they'll have clear sight of me."

"Get out a handful of frags. When I signal, start three or four fusing. I'll wait and join you. When I break through, fan them. I'll leave a few on the right side, and a few presents as I move that way."

There was a slight pause. "The boxes are down! Got it. Might just work. At least for a while till they try again."

"Maybe we'll have help by then."

Stephens pulled five fragmentation grenades from his backpack, placed one on the floor in front of him, and looped his finger through the four remaining loops before speaking into the mike.

"Now!"

Stephens pulled all the loops at once and lobbed the first one to the far side of the room. It had not landed before the second was in the air. The result was just as expected. In three different languages he heard the scream that warned of a grenade, and then the room became a blur of action. At the left side of the room where Stadfeld had been he saw three shapes rise up and begin to crash their way towards the back of the room. The battering ram stopped its movement. From a dozen feet away two soldiers who had worked their way close to Stephens without being seen opened up with long bursts at his position. There were the sounds of running and crashing throughout the room.

Two seconds later he lobbed the last of the grenades to land next to the two soldiers still firing at him. The firing stopped and he could hear more crashing from their position as they ran towards the south wall. Stephens reached down and pulled the pin on the final grenade, placed it on the floor by his feet, and then crawled as quickly as he could towards Eaglestone. In his mind he could hear the counting that was now at "seven" and would stop at "ten." He heard the sound of more grenades falling as Eaglestone added to the effort. The count in his head was at "eight" when he reached the door and pulled himself behind the boxes. A burst of fire from his old position winging past his legs let him know, as expected, the final destination of some of the people running for a safe place in the room. He and Eaglestone threw themselves on the ground ten feet from the opening to the room just as the fragmentation grenades exploded.

The barricade of boxes Eaglestone had erected was thrown back into the tunnel entrance, slamming against them as they lay there. But the same boxes that would add so many to the bruises already on Stephens' body also absorbed the fragments of steel that were careening around the room. Five seconds later even the echoes of the blasts were gone. Neither Stephens nor Eaglestone waited before running back to begin re-erecting a new barricade part way into the room. In the confined space the grenades had cleared almost the western third of the room. Those Falconer troops who had been behind the diagonal barrier, or had made it there in time, were alive. But now it would be much harder to dislodge Stephens and Eaglestone. There was a thirty foot wide clear field of fire for the two defenders, and the soldiers would be slowed by the rubble and fully exposed.

When the reinforcements did arrive a few minutes later, led by Wallace and Fisher, the smell of explosives, and a wispy gray cloud of smoke up near the ceiling, lingered in the area. Eaglestone and Stephens did not even turn around. They kept studying the room beyond around the edges of the boxes. Both knew that there was no use in looking. If the Falconer had circled around them, there was nothing more they could do about it.

"Sure hope that's the second shift, Rob."

They were only mildly relieved when they recognized the voice of Wallace. "You boy's appear to have been busy. And just a bit destructive."

"We had a difference of opinion with a couple people in that room."

"What do you want from us?"

Stephens didn't stop looking at the area. "Replace us and keep sweeping the area. Shoot anything that moves. I think there's a dozen or so on the far side of the room."

Wallace handed Stephens one of the radios taken from the soldiers in the tower. "You might want this. They went from plain text to code words a few minutes ago so it's a lot less helpful. But you can still get the gist of things. One thing seems pretty clear," he said, motioning to the debris in the tunnel. "They sound pretty confident that they can hold out. No sign of any change."

"Falconer try to contact us? Any demands?"

"Nothing at all. Silence."

It would not be until much later that Wallace and Fischer realized that Stephens and Eaglestone had left a few details out of their report. They accurately described the situation in the room and the loss of Stadfeld. They laid out the basic tactic of a pincers through the southern pillbox that would be the key to taking the room. They said that there had been a firefight before the reinforcements arrived.

But they had never indicated how close it had been, nor said anything that would indicate seventeen enemy bodies would be found in the room, clustered around the positions the three ATQ agents had held for twenty minutes.

The situation in the northern system of tunnels was also a standoff, although the ATQ control of the surface would prove to be the key to ending the impasse. The ATQ forces held the west end of Broadway, and the Falconer's troops held the east end. The middle was still up for grabs. The long exposed expanse of tunnel was a great equalizer. It didn't matter how strong a force might be available for either side. No more than a couple people could be at each end, peering around the safety of the corner, waiting for anyone to try to advance down the open area. The rest of the forces could do little more than wait out of sight until something changed.

The middle of Broadway was equally balanced. A sole member of the ATQ assault force in the south branch tunnel to the small hangar could keep an eye on one end. His counterpart was in the north branch to the underground storage room. Both had dozens of people waiting to back them up, standing uselessly a few feet behind the doorways.

However, the ATQ control of the surface gave them two advantages in the battle for the northern tunnel system. First of all, they controlled all of the exits to the surface, including the entrance in the office building that accessed the east end of Broadway. The entrance on the beach was in full view of snipers on cliff overlooking it. Second they had mobility. While the Falconer's troops were trapped in the underground command post and in the underground storage areas, the ATQ forces could move freely on the surface and deploy to any location that was needed. They could bring in whatever manpower, equipment, or weaponry was called for. The Falconer's soldiers had to use whatever they had, wherever they had it.

Those two factors were more than sufficient for Carl Sanders to design a plan to take the northern tunnel system. It was no more than a simple chess exercise, where one side had developed his pieces to dominate the board and the other was in a tight defensive position with little room to move. When that occurs in chess, the solution is always to identify and break down the defensive kingpin, and then watch the rest slowly collapse.

Broadway and Madison Avenue fell less than twenty minutes from the start of Sanders' plan.

The entrance tunnel from the office building allowed ATQ forces to attack the soldiers controlling the east end of Broadway from behind, and place them in a crossfire that started the first domino in the series to fall. The connecting tunnel from the office was twenty feet long, and joined Madison Avenue twenty feet south of the intersection with Broadway. Two Special Forces sergeants were able to control the short branch tunnel, and in so doing prevent any additional Falconer soldiers from passing north to reinforce those guarding the eastern end of Broadway.

The process was right out of the book. As soon as the ATQ sergeants were in place, two stun grenades were more than sufficient to eliminate the three Falconer troops guarding the inside of the branch tunnel without damaging the structure. ATQ troops used those few seconds to enter the connecting tunnel, and move to where they were now ready to enter Madison Avenue behind the Falconer forces at the east end of Broadway. The next step was to bring down into the connecting tunnel two thick panels of Kevlar that had been airlifted onto the field. The panels, the size of a four-by-eight piece of plywood, but able to stop anything short of mortar or missile fire, had small slots along both sides. The ATQ forces simultaneously slid both panels out into Madison Avenue, creating a safe area between them and cutting off the fire from the south at the command post. The Falconer troops at the intersection were eliminated long before they could recover from the initial stun grenades.

ATQ forces now controlled both ends of Broadway, and had split the Falconer soldiers.

From that point it was a simple matter of logistics to complete the capture of the rest of the northern tunnel system. Kevlar shields were inserted into Broadway from the small hangar branch so that two ATQ snipers could now comfortably watch and control the entrance to the underground storage area that had been used for a barracks. The enemy inside could no longer even monitor the hallway. They had to drop back within the storage area and set up a line of defense. Barlow and Soja were uncontested as they hugged the northern wall and approached the entrance to the storage area. They were still uncontested when they pulled the pins on two fragmentation grenades, waited six seconds, and lobbed them around the corner and down the tunnel.

When the smoke from the grenade had cleared, the soldiers in the storage room saw that there was now a Kevlar barrier across the entrance to their tunnel as well. The fall of the rest of the dominoes was now inevitable. The senior officer of the soldiers knew that there was no effective course of action left to him, and there was nothing left to gain by fighting. He had only eleven men left in the room, including four who were wounded. He had no place to escape, nothing to protect, and no way to defend against more grenades. He had lost. The only option was to surrender.

The next domino that had to fall was control of the two pillboxes. They were vital to the Falconer's remaining control of the area for two reasons. First of all they dominated the beach and prevented any action from the sea. Second, and more importantly, if they fell the tunnels linking them with the command center would provide yet another way to attack the remaining Falconer forces. The tunnel from the south pillbox, Main Street, also had a branch leading to the southern underground storage area. That branch tunnel was the key to Stephens' plan to end the stalemate there.

It was 7:40 a.m. when the assault on the pillboxes began. Morning had finally come. Now the sun was as much an ally to the ATQ forces as the darkness had been earlier. The long morning rays of the sun came directly out of the east and into the eyes of those looking out from the pillboxes. The rays wouldn't hurt the pillbox view of the ocean, but they did ensure that no shadows of the attacking forces up on the cliff would show on the beach and give away the movements of those preparing the attack. Thus, the classic weakness of the pillbox would be exploited. It was no different from what the French had discovered seventy-five years earlier with the "impregnable" Maginot line. A pillbox could only face one direction. Those inside could do nothing about what lay in the other.

Scouting the pillboxes did cost the lives of three more men. Once again Patterson and Stephens had underestimated the Falconer's preparations. One of the Super Cobras was diverted back to the staging area to add a full visual reconnaissance pod in place of half of its missiles. The pod allowed both visual and infrared imaging with live telemetry to a van back in the staging area. In the van, the images would be captured, stored, and analyzed on site. Equipment and specialists back at the staging area could do sophisticated image enhancement that would get an identifiable image out of even very poor quality photos. For backup, the feed would be retransmitted to ATQ, and from there to NSA specialists who could accomplish even more enhancement and analysis.

The pillboxes were a mile apart. Because the pod was mounted on the right side of the helicopter, it started at the northern end of the beach. It would stay a mile off shore and traverse parallel to the beach at its top speed of 195 mph. The cameras used a self-correcting laser guidance system that was a derivative of the guidance system used in M1 tanks. The pilot had no need to keep a steady course. He could bob and weave as necessary, and as long as the electronics specialist kept sighting a laser beam on the target, the cameras would aim and focus at the correct area. The cameras would have to focus on each pillbox for only a few seconds to accomplish the mission. Then the helicopter could safely leave the area.

The electronics specialist had just changed his sight from the northern pillbox to the southern when the trail of smoke exited the northern pillbox. The pilot instinctively began to dive the helicopter to surface-skimming level, and then turned the nose of the helicopter to point towards the missile. This gave him two increased chances to live. Most surface-to-air missile guidance systems get confused by terrain if they have to operate down at low altitudes. Turning towards the missile slightly lessens the heat signature for those missiles that use infrared homing. With the shoulder fired SAM accelerating to 1100 miles per hour there was no time for anything else.

The pilot guessed right on one, and wrong on the other, and neither guess impacted the final outcome. He was correct that the missile would lose target lock near the ocean's surface. He was wrong about the infrared. The missile used semi-active radar homing to lock onto the target. But neither mattered. The missile was passing harmlessly overhead on its way to crash in the sea beyond when a proximity sensor detonated it thirty feet above the helicopter. The combination of the blast, the angle of the rapidly descending helicopter, and two small pieces of shrapnel did the rest. The helicopter was driven into the ocean at full speed. The reconnaissance specialist kept his laser beams and cameras on target until the helicopter hit the water. He died while still sending excellent images of the inside of the pillbox.

Three minutes after the impact, the assault on the pillboxes began. The pictures from the helicopter were excellent. The morning sun flooding the interiors made it easy to determine that the President was not inside either one. Each held four well-armed Falconer soldiers. The photos were so clear that the analyst was able to identify both the type of shoulder-fired SAM missiles and their source by the markings on the side. They could also see the antitank weapons stacked in the corner of the northern pillbox. Shortly after the assault began the full identities of all but two of the soldiers inside were fully established.

Those in the pillboxes sat protected by almost three feet of reinforced concrete. They had sophisticated weapons that would defend them from planes, tanks, and even smaller ships. From their vantage point high over the beach they could easily destroy any force of men sent foolishly against them. Eight men, in two pillboxes, could totally dominate and control anything that occurred in front of them to the east.

But they could do nothing against men who walked up casually along the bluff from the west. As soon as it was determined that the President was not inside, their position became hopeless. Like any pillbox, they relied on others to protect their back and sides. But those forces had long ago been eliminated. The ATQ forces did not even have to call in outside help. Instead, a pair of demolition experts strolled out to the top edge of the pillbox, and casually prepared their charges. With the sun in front of them there was no shadow to give them away. The thick concrete, designed to withstand five inch navel shells, meant that no one inside heard anything that would indicate someone was there. Yet, it was the nature of pillboxes that the knowledge would have made no difference. Had those on top announced their presence to those inside, there was nothing those inside could do.

When the demolition men were ready, the small Special Forces contingent moved towards the edge of the pillbox and waited patiently to rappel down the cliff. The demolitions men did not have to come up with a complex solution. Instead, they used stun grenades tied to the end of lengths of cord. They made up a half dozen of the grenades. They would pull the pin, wait until there were four seconds left on the fuse, and then use the cord to swing the grenade down over the top of the pillbox and into the slot.

It didn't matter if the first few failed. If they missed, the demolitions men would just let the grenade drop to explode harmlessly to the beach below. If those inside blocked them or caught them and threw them out, they'd just try again. If they ran out of grenades, they'd just pause and uncrate some more. But eventually one would get through. Then another. And then the Special Forces sergeants could rappel down the face and crawl inside unopposed.

The south pillbox fell quickly. The first grenade got through and knocked out all inside. Ten seconds later ATQ forces were inside and the second set of reinforcements were repelling down the face of the pillbox. Soon, before they began to attack the southern underground storage area from the backside, the flow of equipment needed for the assault had started to be lowered down the face of the pillbox.

The northern pillbox took longer to fall. By chance the first grenade missed and bounced harmlessly off the face of the pillbox. Those inside, once warned, then managed to block the next five. The spread out across the slot, first using hands, and then the sides of ammunition cases, in a crazed video arcade game with very high stakes. During the lull when the demolitions experts began to make additional grenades, one of the Falconer soldiers in desperation tried to extend out of the slot to lob grenades of their own onto the top of the pillbox. He was killed instantly, just as he pulled his arm back to throw the grenade, by an ATQ sniper a half mile down the beach. The grenade fell out of his hand and fell to the beach, below, with him a tumbling few feet behind. The lifeless body had just hit the beach when the grenade exploded beneath him.

With only three men left to defend the slot, and with multiple grenades being swung into the opening, there was no chance to hold out further. Because those inside did not surrender like their compatriots in the northern underground storage area, the rest of the assault had to be brutal. There was none of the glory or elegance found in stories of warfare. It was just deadly and effective. Men refused to surrender, so men died from overwhelming force.

The northern pillbox soon fell. The ATQ forces now controlled the entire surface and most of the northern and southern tunnel systems. The Falconer's soldiers held only the command post and part of the southern underground storage area. Both areas were now the target of attacks from multiple directions. There was only one final domino to fall before the Falconer would finally run out of options.

CHAPTER TWENTY-NINE

Joyce Patterson's expression was calm and matter-of-fact. Only those who knew her best would have understood the intensity in her eyes, and the tightness around her eyebrows, as she held out one of the small captured transceivers towards Stephens. "Rob, he's using his own net. Asked for you. He even asked us to '. . . please wake him up' so you could talk."

For a few moments Stephens continued to sit with his back against the base of the old tower, eyes closed, with the morning sun bathing his face. He tried without success to let the beauty of the Maine coast wash over him, just as he had let the winds flowing up the west face of Monadnock comfort him so many times in the past. It was warm for October in Maine. Had Stephens been able to hear it over the rancorous clatter of the pneumatic drill a thousand feet to his east, the ocean waves upon the beach as the tide came in kept up a steady soothing rumble. Had he been able to look at the woods with anything other than the clinical eye of a soldier, he would have seen that those leaves left in the trees were the deep rusty brown that marked their very last days. He didn't notice as they caught the morning sun and shimmered with the light breeze, many falling gently to the ground below. Nor did he see the innumerable pines that were gloriously green in contrast. Try as he might Stephens could not recapture the healing feeling of Mount Monadnock.

Stephens opened his eyes and gave a small smile to Patterson standing over him. "He always was confident. And he sure predicts his enemy's moves better than I do."

"Yup. Didn't even waste time identifying himself."

"Sir," interjected the colonel who headed up the surface force, "with all due respect there might be something we've overlooked. He must have an observation post we've missed, and just saw you sitting there. Sounds like a cheap psych job."

"With someone else, perhaps," answered Stephens, "but not with this one."

"Colonel," added Joyce, "it might turn out that you're right. But it's ten-to-one the Falconer just worked it out in his head by knowing his adversaries. He's that good. That's why this is only the second time in thirty years that he's ever been cornered. Any that's why I'm not counting any chickens just yet."

Stephens stretched and rolled his head on his neck to loosen the muscles that had tightened from too much activity and too little rest. Then he slowly rose and reached out to take the transceiver. When he spoke there was no triumph in his voice, just tiredness.

"It appears this is almost over, Falconer. It's finally coming to an end after all these years."

"Perhaps so, Stephens. Perhaps so. Unless this is another London."

"Up to now, maybe. But the ending has to be different. This time there's no floor safe for you to crawl into. And there are more than just Green and me here to seal off the area."

"It's funny. I had always thought that, in the end, we would face each other without the others."

Stephens faced the ocean. He stared at the waves stretching to the horizon. He could see the Coast Guard cutter three miles off shore. "So did I," he answered quietly. "But it's better this way. At least it'll finally be over."

"Yes. At least there will be that, Stephens."

There was a flurry of activity a few feet away at the command post. Patterson listened intently to a report coming over her headset and pulled a large map of the area out onto the field table. She turned towards Stephens, and then motioned with one finger across her neck for him to cut off the conversation.

"Rob, AWACS has a small boat about thirty miles northeast, coming fast. They say it can't be any larger than thirty or forty feet for it to get that close without being spotted earlier."

"His? Identification?"

"None yet."

"Where are the Spruances?"

"Still too far out. Rounding Cape Cod about now."

The colonel spoke out. "Divert the Coast Guard. That's got to be his ride out of here. We don't want the boat close enough to give him something to bargain with."

Patterson looked at the officer and nodded before turning back to Stephens. "Good idea. Rob, I'll have them intercept."

Stephens was staring out across the ocean far to the northeast and didn't answer. Pieces were starting to come together in his mind and he knew that he was close to understanding another part of the Falconer's plan. Like so many times in the past, a "know-so" was forming. It was one of those times when, even if he did not know the full answer, he had started to understand enough of the framework to at least rule out many of the options. He could never quite define how it worked, but at time like this, even if he did not yet know why, some things were just "wrong" or were "right." They would fit, or not fit, a pattern that was just starting to take form.

Stephens nodded once to himself, and then focused back on Patterson. "No. Not yet. Keep the cutter here and send out choppers."

Patterson could see the intensity of his look. "Rob?"

"Stephens," came the voice over the radio, "you still there? Plotting and planning?"

Stephens looked at Patterson and raised one finger in the universal sign for her to wait before he spoke into the transceiver. "Yes. Both."

There was a slight laugh over the radio. "Aha! The truth! I guess there is really little need for secrets between us, old friend."

Stephens spoke to Patterson. "No! For once, let me get it right. He's out-guessed me and pulled my strings at every turn so far. That boat *is* his. I'm sure of it. But it's a red herring. Joyce, have one of the Cobras equipped with a recon pod again."

"How could you possibly . . ." said the colonel before Patterson held up a hand to cut him off.

"Rob, what else is there?"

"I don't know yet," answered Stephens. He thought for a few seconds before lifting the radio back to his mouth. He continued with the same quiet tone. "Lehar, there are no options left. Release the President."

"Some of my people think that would be a good idea. They figure that your drill will get through this bunker in another half hour or so. I take it you've finally decided to use gas."

Stephens looked over near to where he could see the top of a large yellow pneumatic drill that was working at the bottom of a ten foot hole. You could just see the top two feet of the piston as it kept up its stead banging. The big scoop loader that had created the hole sat quietly to one side. Both pieces of equipment had been airlifted to the field from a highway construction site just outside of Bangor. 'Patterson anticipated that one well,' he thought. The previous day the machine had been drilling into granite outcrops. Tanks of a compressed sleeping gas, finally cleared early that morning by the Bethesda medical staff as safe for the President, were in a Harrier VTOL Jump Jet less than twenty minutes out.

The southern storage area had fallen quickly once the ATQ forces could attack from a second direction. A handful of the Falconer's soldiers had been able to retreat into the underground command center to join those already there. The bunker was the last area not yet secured. However, the command center had been designed to be defensible. Ten feet of ground lay above three feet of reinforced concrete to protect it from above. The old rusted doors to the center lay against the wall in the corridor. They had been replaced by strong new ones that allowed the defenders to stand in a fully protected position behind gun ports that made it easy to ensure no ATQ forces could get near the doors. With the President inside the relatively small room, the use of explosives would only accomplish the Falconer's job for him.

"We have all the tunnels leading to you covered. Men are in the pillboxes. We cover the beach. The exit by the dock is now under our control. Continuing is senseless."

"Sounds like I can't get out. But neither can you get in. A standoff."

"Is the President in there with you?"

"You know, Stephens, he's an old man. Gas might not sit too well with him."

"Is the President in there with you?"

"Then, of course, we could just wait it out with air tanks of our own."

Stephens' voice remained quiet. "Lehar, if we use gas, you and I both know we've had more than enough time to specially select one that won't harm an 'old man.' And if you have tanks, even if you have *lots* of tanks, that only delays things until the air runs out. It wouldn't change anything."

There was a short delay before the Falconer answered. "Yes. He's here with me."

"And the woman?"

There was silence for several seconds before he answered. "Yes, Stephens, she is in here as well. I envy you on that, you know? Do you have any idea what you have there?"

For a moment, Stephens felt the unreal sensation that he was somewhere else. For the briefest of moments he was not thinking of the Falconer, the President, or anything else except the phrase 'what you have there.'

"She is incredible. Worthy of you, old friend. And very much in love with you. I regret that you might never know the things she was able to do for you, and others things she tried to do. I wonder how my life might have chosen different paths had I ever tasted love from one such as her."

Stephens looked down at the ground and closed his eyes. He held them tightly closed while he concentrated on returning to the events along the Maine Coast. When he finally opened them and looked up, in his mind he could see the Falconer huddled in the command bunker.

"If we use gas, Lehar, you're an easy target in there."

"I think not so easy, Stephens. This command post will be difficult for your people to take. Unlike the rest of these tunnels, this one has thick doors that protect my men as they control the halls. And I have a President standing right next to the doors, making some of your earlier tricks, shall we say, 'inappropriate.' Even the gas will not be a surprise to us."

Stephens stared through the ground towards the Falconer. He allowed himself one brief moment to relegate the President to second priority.

"Does she have to die as part of this?"

"No Stephens. That will be my gift to you. Regardless of outcome, she will live. She will walk out of here this day."

The moment was over.

"And the President?"

"That has yet to be seen."

"Lehar, it accomplishes nothing, any more. You know that. He's not leverage for you."

"I cannot trade him for my demands?" The voice had traces of humor in it.

"What were your demands going to be, anyway?"

"A lot of money, TV coverage, evacuate the Middle East, release anyone I could think of."

The start of understanding finally began in Stephens. "You mean 'impossible demands.' Ones that could not possibly be met. If you thought they might be met, then you'd increase them."

"Excellent, Stephens. The key to the whole thing was that they could not be met."

"So the President would have to die, after all. Probably video on TV in gruesome color?"

There was genuine respect in the reply. "My old friend, you almost *do* understand. It would take something quite like that to finally bring terrorism home to the Americans. For the first time they would feel what happens each day, each hour, *each minute*, in my home. Never again would the next two generations of your people be able to sleep without knowing the meaning of fear. They would never feel safe again. Anything we might do in the future would have a new measure of significance. Everything would change in the fabric of America. The shield of isolation would be broken."

The voice on the radio gained intensity. "I wish every man, woman, and child in America to know fear. I want them to be afraid. Gut-level fear. I want them to know the shame of being afraid. Then things will start to change. You would no longer be a nation wrapped in a false shield of invincibility. You would know vulnerability."

"You know that we won't let that happen. There will be no video."

"Perhaps. But there still can be a death."

Stephens looked into the distance again, and then back through the ground to where the Falconer was. Finally, he nodded once again as another piece of the puzzle fell into place.

"Yes. But you could not have your public spectacle if the President was already dead. You would no longer have a threat."

The humor returned to the Falconer's voice. "Aha. He is not in my bunker then? He drowned, perhaps, in the tunnel? You would make it so?"

"The divers could find his body there. Even the first lady would confirm it."

"Then there is no choice. I must get out of here to make that video."

"Yes, Lehar. We both know that. Your task is to escape with the President and make your film. Mine is to prevent it. The dance is easily understood by all."

There was no reply for more than a minute. A squadron of high clouds was moving in from the northeast. They were the spectacular high stratus clouds that can become brilliant interlocking shafts of white blazing in the sun.

"Stephens, do you realize the irony that you and I so want to delay the inevitable to sit here and talk? I think I have the answer. I know why."

Stephens did not reply.

"It's because we both know the other believes fully in what he is doing. We do these things not for gain, but for principles. And even though we are opposites, that makes us the same."

Stephens reply was to Patterson, with the radio off. His voice was almost a whisper. "Devil and angel. Each hoping he is the angel, and both terrified that he might be the other."

"And that, Stephens, is why I know that this won't end quite the way you think. It must still come down to just you and me. It's fate. Like your cruel God, letting Satan toy with Job and destroy all his family and possessions, '. . . just because.' It is simply fate. No way around it."

"Then set the President free. Let this be between you and me."

"No! He has killed so many of my people!"

"How?"

"His fleet is there. He sends cannons against a mosquito."

"He's protecting innocent shipping from your attacks."

"The ships are attacked because they support our enemies, and fight against us for you Americans."

"We must protect our allies. What would you have us do?"

"You follow the chain back how far, Stephens? When does it end? The Shah? Before that?"

"I don't know. It goes back forever. Maybe until the dawn of time itself? There has been good versus evil since before man began."

"But which of us is the good, Stephens? When does the chain become satisfied? What act of man can *break* that chain, forever?"

Stephens stared across the distance again before answering. "I don't know. None. Maybe never. There are forces that exist only to perpetuate the chain. The President dies as the latest link in the chain, so we retaliate with something. An air raid? Bomb something? And then what do you do?"

"I don't know. I think that if I were to understand the answer to that question, then many things would become clear."

Stephens stood up and looked up at where the clouds now streaked across most of the eastern sky. In a few more minutes the airfield would be in shade. He looked south towards Boston, where Dublin Lake and

Wendlandt Academy lay nestled far to the southwest. He could picture the soccer field at Wendlandt and half expected to see his soccer team playing walk across the old airfield towards him. He absently glanced at his watch. It was 9:00 a.m. and he was close to the end with Falconer. Stephens realized that soccer practice, if it were held today, was four hours off.

Chapter Thirty

The choppers found the boat twenty minutes later. A two-second burst of the Gatling gun by one of the Cobras was enough to cause the skipper of the boat to kill his engines. The tracers roared past less than fifty feet in front of his course, whipping up large plumes of water as they ripped into the waves. The message was unmistakable even without the warning from the loudspeaker mounted in the Sea Stallion. While the gunships carefully covered the forty-foot cabin cruiser from the four and eight o'clock positions, the Sea Stallion dropped a half dozen troops on the deck. There was no resistance. The search was over in less than five minutes.

"Rob, the choppers found the boat. They report nothing obvious, but the Special Forces captain leading the raid says, quote, '. . . it doesn't smell right.'"

Stephens reached for the microphone. "What's his name?"

"Urban."

"Captain Urban," he spoke into the mike, "this is Stephens. What have you got there?"

"Sir, this boat is clean. On the surface there's no tie to your dance back there."

"On the surface?"

"Sir, I'd be willing to bet my left one they're dirty as hell."

"Why so, Captain?"

"It's a lot of little things. I'm a boater, sir. This craft is out in the ocean fifty miles from nothing, yet it has no extra supplies. Hell, there isn't even any beer on board, sir. And not one of these people has any ID on them. No wallets. No credit cards. No checkbooks. Just some cash, about three, four thousand."

"Who do they claim to be?"

"Won't answer. Playing the part of the 'indignant citizen.' The party line is they won't answer anything until they have a lawyer and know what they're charged with."

"Smugglers? Drugs?"

"That would fit, but then I'd expect either more cash or some contraband. We came in low from three directions. Maybe we missed it, but I think we surprised them and I'm convinced they never dumped anything overboard."

"What *do* they claim?"

"That's another thing, sir. The answer is smooth and believable. They just rented the boat for a day trip out of Eastport. But they all, separately, used almost the same words." There was a small pause. "Too smooth, if you know what I mean."

"Captain, get them all on deck and have them smile nice for the recon Cobra. We're going to take some pictures before we decide what to do."

Stephens turned to Patterson. "Joyce, how fast can we ID them against ATQ files?"

"If they're in our files, maybe fifteen minutes, max."

"Do it."

Stephens stared out to sea again. He tilted his head to one side, looked down, and then closed his eyes as he concentrated. He clenched his fist and brought it up to gently prod his lower lip. Then he stopped, with his fist against his lip, and opened his eyes. He looked back towards the beach, dropped his hand, and smiled ever so slightly.

"Get Eaglestone up here. Quick!"

They all stood around the field table next to the old tower as Stephens tacked a map of the surrounding area next to a sketch of the airfield that already was on the wall. Sanders and Jacobi had rejoined Patterson and the colonel. Stephens stepped back from the map and watched Eaglestone stride across the field to take up a position standing casually to the side of the ATQ leaders.

"Listen, we're ten minutes from being able to insert gas into that bunker and the Falconer is about as concerned as a baby at a bottle. Yet, we have him completely surrounded. He's not even tried to work a deal."

"What other option is there," suggested Sanders. "He knows we won't deal."

"Unless he's not in there?" suggested Jacobi.

"Good, Pete. Good," answered Stephens. "That really is a possibility. All we have is a voice on the radio. Using landlines and repeaters, that could be coming from anywhere. He could be in Boston and still let us talk to him here."

"Then we've lost him again?" asked Sanders.

"No Bill. I don't think so. I believe he *is* down there. In the command bunker."

"Gut?" asked Patterson.

"Gut."

Patterson answered. "Then the only other option is for him to escape with the President."

"How?" asked the colonel. "There's absolutely no way to get out of there. My men have everything sealed tight."

Stephen's voice was matter-of-fact. "I don't believe that any longer, colonel."

"Sir, with all due respect once again, we're dealing with the President here. It's not a time to go on hunches!"

Stephens walked back to the maps on the tower wall.

"The colonel is right. But I think this is a bit more than a hunch. I've just been too dim to put it all together until now." He pointed to the map of the field. "A few minutes ago I finally asked myself the right bloody question. 'Why this airbase?' How did he plan to get out of here? It isn't by plane. Nothing but VTOL could land here. An unknown VTOL jet heading this way would scramble half the fighters out of Northeast Air Defense. A helicopter could land anywhere, and doesn't need a runway. So he didn't choose it because it was an airfield."

Stephens turned back towards the small group. "He didn't choose it because it was well hidden, either. Any of us could come up with a hundred places he could have used that were even more obscure. There's only two answers, and they only make sense if you think the way the Falconer thinks. It's because of the sea and all the possible red herrings."

Patterson was the first to get it. "You mean, it's easy here for him to get us looking in so many different directions that we'll miss the right one."

"Yes, Joyce. This is a virtual candy store of possibilities. Tunnels, airstrips, roads, forests, airfields. And, of course, the ocean."

Patterson finished the thought she had started. "Then you're saying that the only thing unique, or needed here, is the ocean."

"That's right. Joyce, there's nothing else."

"Then it's the boat, after all," said Jacobi.

"No, Pete, I think that's just another of the red herrings. It's too simple. For days, he's totally outplayed us at every turn. There's not a single step along the way where he didn't have a fallback option. At every step he faked us right, and then went left. Or left, then went right. But the bottom line is simple. He never once assumed the obvious plan would work, and never once went the direction that seemed obvious. Why should this be any different?"

"But Rob, the sea is closed off to him," said Sanders with some confusion in his voice. "He can't even get down to the beach."

"Sir, my men have it totally surrounded," said the colonel. "Even if he somehow got out I've got dozens of men between him and the dock, and up on the cliffs overlooking the beach. My snipers would have a field day. Sir, he couldn't even use the President as a shield with that many snipers."

"He could wire the President with some form of dead man's device so that we couldn't use snipers," suggested Sanders.

The colonel would not let go of his certainty. "But he'd still have nowhere to go."

"And no boat is going to get anywhere near here without our knowing," added Sanders. "Look at the boat those choppers . . ." Sanders stopped in midsentence as he noticed the way Stephens was staring at Eaglestone, and that Eaglestone was staring back at Stephens.

Finally Eaglestone nodded slightly. "Well, old friend, I think I'm finally with you. Been in the slow group up to now."

"Ned, you were right all along. We should have brought your whole team."

"No time to cry now. Where do we get equipment?"

"Have Pease fly it in?"

"Would take an hour. Think we have that much time?"

Patterson broke into the conversation. "Think you two might share a bit of this private conversation with the rest of us?"

"Sorry Joyce. We need to get some divers offshore, now! Full underwater weaponry. And we need some Orions here ASAP."

"Orions?" asked Jacobi. "The sub hunters?"

"Yes," answered Stephens, staring out at the ocean again. "He's going out by sea. I'd be willing to bet that there's a sub out there waiting right now."

"Rob, he can't cross the beach to get to the sea," stated Sanders.

"Then he plans to cross under it."

There was silence in the group until Patterson got up and walked over to the maps. She stared intently at the sketches of the airfield before deciding.

"Colonel, call Pease and get them cracking. Orions and a full complement of Eaglestone's SEALs. Tell them they need to be airborne *yesterday*. Pete, you contact the cutter and have them do whatever they can to check the area for a sub. Does the Coast Guard even have sonar?"

"I don't think so," answered the colonel.

Eaglestone answered the question for her. "Ma'am, they won't have sonar, but they will have some underwater gear. Wouldn't take more than a few moments for one of your helicopters to ferry it ashore."

"Mr. Eaglestone," she said, nodding respectfully, "you just earned your pay for the day. Again."

Eaglestone didn't answer. We simply walked over to the side of the tower and studied the maps.

Eaglestone and Stephens were already on the beach to meet the helicopter from the coast guard cutter when the drill poked the roof of the bunker. The carbide drill had been designed to cut into the granite outcroppings of New Hampshire and Maine to carve roadways through the mountains. The fifty year old concrete of the bunker had been far easier. The drill was self-propelled on a pair of treads. It was half way up the ramp that the scoop loader had made into the hole when the explosion occurred. On the surface, it was almost unnoticeable except for a plume of dust that shot through the drilled hole like a small geyser. Down in the tunnels it was much louder.

"Patterson," came Wallace's voice from his position with the troops in the south approach to the command bunker. "We have a small explosion down here in the command post."

"Damage?"

"Can't tell. It was inside the bunker."

"Repeat, please. Did you say inside?"

"Inside. It makes no sense. No effect out here."

The next voice on the network was not from the ATQ team. "Yes, Patterson. Inside. Just a small demonstration. Your President was barely hurt by this one. I'd put him on to talk to you himself, but he's having some difficulty hearing just now. Seems we forgot to give him earplugs. He was the only person in the room we forgot."

Patterson raised one eyebrow before turning aside to speak quietly to Sanders before getting back on the radio. "Notify all commanders. Switch to comm two, now. Use scrambler tango. But make sure we keep enough traffic on this net to keep him interested."

"Done."

"What's the point Falconer?" She did not ask how he had tapped into their command network.

"Stephens, you there?" asked the Falconer.

Stephens, down on the beach, cut into the conversation. "Yes. But Patterson's running the show."

"Not quite correct, Stephens. I'm running the show. So, let me tell you what will happen next. My men have put a temporary plug in the hole you so carefully made. It won't do much to stop you if you really want to use it, but it'll give us a couple second's warning if you do. That's all I need. The next time your President will be holding a small explosive taped into his right hand. If you continue, or if there is a next time, then I guess we'll just have to go forward without the video after all."

"Even if we stop it buys you nothing, Falconer," answered Patterson.

"Ah yes, but it does. I only need a little more time. Then you will let all of us out of here. On my terms."

Patterson waited a few moments while she considered which approach to take. Finally, she turned to Sanders again. "It's time for us to push a few buttons and see what we can learn."

"Falconer, let's make things clear. Do you play chess?"

"Why yes, Patterson." There was amusement in his voice. "I did. Once a long time ago."

"Then you understand the concept of a forced mate."

"Ah yes. You announce your moves, because there's no way out."

"Yes. Exactly. I have men on the beach. I have snipers on the cliff. And we intercepted your boat twenty minutes ago. Help is *not* just over the horizon."

There was almost a minute of silence before the Falconer replied. "Interesting, if there was really a boat."

"Oh there is, or was, Falconer. Five men. Forty footer out of Eastport. Three of them have already been identified, including your old friend Heinrech. Two we don't know . . . yet. There is no rescue coming."

Again there was a long delay. "Well, that does change things a little. Interesting. Do you ever read the prophets Patterson?" He did not expect a reply. "Well, it is said there is no sense in damming a mighty river. For there are a thousand paths it can find down the mountain."

"That is all very interesting, Falconer. But all I have to do is be patient, now. You see, *my* prophets say that all things come to those who wait."

There was genuine laughter over the radio from the bunker below. It continued on for several seconds. "Patterson, that is good. I'll now get off and think through all this. But I'd like to leave you with just one more quotation, if I may. From your own Abraham Lincoln. He once said almost the same thing, that 'all things come to those who wait.' But he added something. He said that usually they only find what is left behind by those who hustle."

The radio went dead.

Jacobi shook his head from side to side. "How the hell could he know a quote from Lincoln?"

"Joyce, I've got Stephens on comm two."

Patterson switched the channel selection on her radio. "Rob, what did you make of all that."

"You did well to bait him. I think you caught him a bit off guard for a change."

"But I don't think we learned anything from it."

"Maybe. Except for that little bantering at the end."

"Yeah. One-upped by a quote from Lincoln."

"Yes. But the key was the laughter. That was just a bit too genuine for my taste. Not at all forced."

"Meaning?"

"Joyce, he's not worried. I'm going into the water."

"What was the explosion? Any ideas that make sense to you?"

"Not a clue, Joyce. Not even one. It's your call, but I think you should go ahead with the gas. I'm going swimming."

"What do you have?"

"The Coast Guard had three sets of tanks and equipment. No spearguns, just knives. Ned and I, plus a seaman named Gardner who's the size of a small house, are going in. Any report about a sub?"

"Nothing. But it would be the longest of long shots for the cutter to find it. A couple Orions are a half hour out."

"Then we better get him first."

"If there is a sub, Rob. Sanders spoke with Navy. They claim it's simply not possible. They have sensors all over the sea bottom in this area as part of SOSUS. There's nothing in any of the sensor logs going back months that could be a sub slipping in here. At least one, and usually two of the new Improved Los Angeles class subs patrol this area continually. According to some admiral in Norfolk, there is no way a sub can cross the Atlantic and get here without getting known. Even the Russian Typhoons and Deltas leave some trace."

"I know."

"And how does he get to it? If he rushes across the beach, he won't have a chance. You said so yourself."

"He has an alternative, then."

"Rob," she said gently, "this doesn't compute."

"There is a sub, Joyce. I can feel it. And he's already on his way to it. Use the gas as you planned. But when you get in there, you'll find you're holding an empty bag."

Stephens, Eaglestone and Gardner entered the water next to the decrepit dock just as the hose from the first gas canister was inserted into the hole to the bunker. The plug the Falconer had inserted in the hole offered little resistance. The gas would fill the room in a matter of minutes. Anyone without breathing equipment would be asleep within seconds of breathing it.

"Wallace," spoke Patterson into the radio, "any reaction down there?"

"Nothing."

"What about an explosion?"

"Nothing here."

"Barlow, anything up at the north end?"

"Nothing here either."

Patterson put down the microphone and turned to Sanders and Jacobi. "This smells. Nothing on comm one, either. I'd expect at least a threat."

"Then we wait?" asked Jacobi.

"No. We can't afford to. If we wait, the advantage slips back to them."

"Joyce," answered Sanders, "we have to know the status in that room."

Patterson picked up the radio again. "Wallace, any sign of life at your end?"

"None. Can't tell if they're watching through the slots in the door."

"Barlow?"

"Same here."

"Okay, both you. If they're awake, I need them to be concentrating on you for a minute or so while we drop fiber optics through the hole. Can you move towards the doors."

Barlow answered first. "If they have air tanks and masks in there, the tunnels will still be covered."

"I know. What about the Kevlar bit again. It was useless for attacking the doors, but might let you get a man up closer to them."

"Wait one," answered Wallace.

Patterson turned to Sanders. "Get the FiberCam ready. Leave the gas pipe in there and slip it down next to it."

When all three locations were ready, men in urban assault protective gear with Kevlar shields started down the north and south tunnels towards the command bunker. At the same time, Sanders carefully slid a quarter inch diameter fiber optic cable with a miniature camera on the end down the hole drilled through the concrete roof of the bunker. Next to him was a video display that let him see the progress of the fiber optic snake down the hole. At first, all he saw was dim shapes from the side of the thin shaft as the camera was aimed horizontally out from the snake. It was set up so that when it cleared the hole, he would only have to twist the cable to rotate the camera to see all parts of the room.

The two ATQ soldiers were half way down the tunnel when Sanders saw the camera gingerly poke into the bunker. He carefully kept it just barely into the room. The whole point of risking the lives of the two men approaching in the tunnels was to buy a few seconds to see what was in the room before someone saw the camera and destroyed or disabled it. The men had only one goal—to distract the Falconer's soldiers. While they were as protected as possible, they had no better than an even chance of surviving if the soldiers opened up at close range with armor piercing shells, or simply rolled a grenade out of the slot at the bottom of the doors. Both men, as well as Patterson when she ordered it, knew the odds and the likely result.

Sometimes there is quiet heroism in events that is never known because nothing ever happened. A child, afraid of the dark, might pass through a field of "monsters." A friend might dive into the waters to save a friend, and find the waters to be shallow. A soldier might walk through his fears towards an enemy strong point, and find it undefended. The heroism existed. The honor and nobility of one ready to make a sacrifice was real. But it is unknown to anyone else. Even to the person involved it is quickly forgotten, ironically replaced by shame at the fear that was felt. Within a few seconds of the camera's entry into the room it became clear that the two men carefully working their way down the tunnels were never at risk.

"Shit! Joyce, I have three bodies, nothing else! Give me a second."

"Barlow and Wallace, keep down and wait," commanded Patterson. "Hold your position wherever you are."

"Joyce, that's confirmed," continued Sanders. "Unless there are traps, the room is clean. I have no one standing. Three bodies on the floor, all near the doors. I can see two of them clearly enough to see there's no breathing equipment, so I have to assume they're out cold. I can't see the top half of the third."

"Any ID?"

"The two I see are unknown, but certainly Falconer's people. Not him. Not the President or Lebart."

"No sign? They're not in there?"

"Nothing Joyce. We've been had again. The rest of the room is empty."

"Barlow and Wallace, move in on the doors, stat! You are not, repeat, *not* covered by anyone in the room. Three inside, all apparently unconscious. Assume all three are faking, and that everything, repeat, everything in the room is trapped. I need to know what the hell is happening in there *now*!"

Patterson turned to the colonel and Jacobi. "Colonel, I want your people to re-sweep the surface of this airbase, millimeter by millimeter. Check and double check everything. Jacobi, you drive a sweep of the underground. We've missed something and I want to have it found!"

She picked up the radio. "Is Stephens in the water?"

"Yes Ma'am," came a voice from one of the soldiers on the beach. "He's out of reach."

"Damn."

When the doors were forced open to the command bunker it turned out that Sanders' assessment was very accurate. There were only three of the Falconer's soldiers left in the room, and all three were asleep from the effects of the gas.

"Patterson, Wallace here. The room is clean. We're going to search for traps, but there's just the three bodies. All three are unknowns. However, we might know where they all went. There's a set of stairs leading down from the east side of the room to the start of a tunnel heading to the beach. The tunnel at this end is all caved in. We have a landline buried in the dirt coming out of the collapsed tunnel to a radio in the bunker. My bet is that they're on the other side of the cave-in, and were talking to us through that landline setup."

Patterson stepped over to the maps on the side of the tower. "That the tunnel to the beach?"

"Yes Ma'am."

"Beach, report in."

"This is Major Jackson, Ma'am. The beach is clear. The entrance to the tunnel is still sealed, and looks as though it is so rusted it would need explosives to open. My men are all over this area."

Patterson turned to Jacobi. "Get down there and personally take charge of the bunker end." She picked up the radio. "Sanders, get down on the beach. I'm going to the edge of the cliff where I can see what the hell is happening."

"You think the explosion was the tunnel collapsing?" asked Sanders on the radio.

"That I do Bill. It happened just as we drilled through. That's one sure way to block off the gas from his position."

"Then we've got him trapped, finally. There's no place else to run."

"Bill, it looks that way, but I'm starting to have a glimmer of what Stephens has been saying."

"Joyce, Rob could be wrong. It's been a long time. Everything points to that section of tunnel. There's no other alternative."

"That's what's bugging me. If he's there, he really bought nothing except a little more time. We can just drill again. Through the top of the beach entrance, or through the dirt in the tunnel."

"Then we have him."

Patterson's voice was tired when she replied. "I've thought that a half dozen times over the past two days. Let's dig, but I have a bad feeling we'll have Rob's empty bag, after all."

Chapter Thirty-One

The three divers had been crisscrossing the area for fifteen minutes, when Stephens saw the black shapes rise out of a jumble of rocks a hundred feet off to his side. He had passed within twenty feet of that same location minutes before, and had not seen the small tunnel entrance that had recently been carved into the dirt and rocks. It had been well camouflaged by large boulders and smaller rocks that had been carefully muscled into position. The rocks lay two hundred feet offshore in twenty feet of water. The Falconer had needed almost three weeks to dig an additional tunnel that showed on no maps of the old complex. It started midway along the tunnel that led down to the beach from the command bunker. Once in underwater equipment, The Falconer had only to walk down a mild slope to the new tunnel, and swim out.

As Stephens hovered close to the sea bottom, he saw that there were eight shapes in all. It was not hard to identify the President and Cynthia. The President was supported by two divers, and slumped limply between them. Even from a distance it was clear to Stephens that the President was partly drugged. There were two divers also holding onto Cynthia, but it was obvious that it was not for support. He could see her struggling against them, and twice saw the divers shake her violently. In front of the two groups of three were two separate swimmers. One was a large man who swam easily and gracefully despite his bulk.

The other glided through the water like a predator. Stephens could not help but think of a shark slipping silently beneath the waves. "You were right, Falconer," he thought as he watched them start away from the rocks and head east out towards the open ocean. "*It will be just the two of us after all.*"

Stephens was southeast of the Falconer with Gardner fifty feet to his left towards the beach and Eaglestone to his right fifty feet farther out.

The remains of the old dock was just beyond Gardner. Stephens glanced right and saw Eaglestone also hiding on the bottom, partly shielded by a small ridge in the ocean floor, watching the Falconer. Stephens signaled to wait and Eaglestone quickly acknowledged. Stephens had just turned to his left when the large diver at the front of the pack saw Gardner. He grabbed the Falconer's leg, twisted around and pointed. The Falconer then pointed to the divers holding the President and Lebart and gestured for them to attack.

Immediately Stephens signaled Eaglestone and Gardner to close in. The divers holding the two hostages at first stayed with their charges. Then the Falconer swam over to the two holding the President, grabbed him, and pushed them off. They swam at full speed towards the ATQ team. The Falconer gestured for the large man to take Cynthia Lebart, so that the two holding her could join the attack. For just a moment, they both hesitated before one let go and started off to attack Stephens and his team. The large diver was still ten feet away when Cynthia reached out, pulled the mask and air hose off the distracted diver's face, and scratched as hard as she could against his face. A small cloud of blood spread to surround his head. While he tried to reach behind himself and catch the air hose, she pulled away and accelerated towards the shore.

The large diver began to follow her, but pulled up as he reached the struggling diver. He knew that the woman was a low priority compared to the President and the three shapes closing in on them. He grabbed the whipping air hose, pushed it into the diver's hand, and then swam to the bottom to retrieve the lost mask. The large diver glanced briefly to where Cynthia could be seen receding into the distance. Then he swam over and took the other side of the President. He and the Falconer began to swim towards the east again, out to sea. The fourth diver shook his head once and cleared his mask, and swam to join the fight.

Underwater, had all four of the Falconer's soldiers been experienced divers, their one-man advantage would have proven conclusive. It would simply be too big an edge. There would always be at least one extra man who could circle behind an opponent who was occupied with a threat in front of him. While the target defended against an attack from the front, the extra diver could slip in from the back. If the target turned to defend his rear, the first would now have a clear path towards his back. Either way the result would be the same, and then there would be two extra men.

But there were three factors that more than countered that advantage in this fight. First, the Falconer's men were soldiers, and not divers. On the surface it might have been different. But under twenty feet of water none of their exceptional skills could be applied. Second, Cynthia's actions had served to delay one of the divers, and the remaining three had not even considered defying the Falconer by waiting for the fourth to catch up.

And finally, had all the rest been equal, Ned Eaglestone was one of the three they faced. He was as comfortable underwater as the soldiers would have been on land. More importantly, of the seven divers facing each other he was the only one with experience in underwater combat.

Even though he was the farthest away, Eaglestone was the first to close on the three lead divers. With powerful strokes he pulled directly in front of them, and then hovered just above the sea bed. The three divers stopped fifteen feet from him, and then fanned out as Stephens and Gardner caught up and took positions on both sides. The diver in the middle looked back over his shoulder and saw the fourth diver still fifty feet away. He finally realized that he should signal the others to wait until they had the numerical advantage.

Eaglestone did not give them that chance. He switched his knife to his right hand and charged through the water at the middle diver. Stephens and Gardner were both caught by surprise at the swiftness of the move, but began to move in on the two outside divers, though much more slowly. When Eaglestone was five feet from the middle diver, he threw both arms out, and with a powerful backward movement brought himself to a dead stop in the water. He let himself sink to the bottom. The middle diver, confused by Eaglestone's sudden start and now the equally sudden stop, had been moving slightly forward to parry the attack. Now he looked quickly back over his shoulder to see if the fourth diver was yet in a position to help him against the SEAL. The middle diver hovered six feet off the ocean floor waiting to see what would happen next. His years as a soldier made him realize that he was in trouble against a very dangerous adversary. His years in combat told him that the only chance he had was to keep the high ground and make Eaglestone come up to him.

The diver was wrong on the first point, and dead wrong on the second. Had he had more experience in underwater fighting, he would know that up and down are useless concepts. Had he been more observant, he would have seen that Eaglestone had sunk even lower, until he was crouching on the bottom. Had he thought more about the what he had already seen his adversary do, he would have realized that he faced a powerful swimmer.

Eaglestone waited a few more moments until he saw the middle diver make the "normal" move of adjusting his position to be straight up and down in the water rather than "unnaturally" leaning forward. That was all Eaglestone needed. With one powerful lunge he sprang off the bottom with his right hand stretched out ahead of him. He crossed the space between the two men in less than a second. The middle diver had time only to raise his knees before the knife entered his chest just below the ribs. The diver's own knife, even at full extension, fell almost a foot short of the top of Eaglestone's head. By the time he had the chance to twist his body to be able to attack Eaglestone, he had already begun to die. Eaglestone reached up and pulled the knife out of the weak grip and let it sink to the bottom. He didn't bother waiting for the diver to die before letting go and looking to see where to attack next. The middle diver slowly sank to the bottom, watching Eaglestone all the way down. His last thought was a question. 'How could this be? He had to come to me?'

For the next few moments, there was little movement. In the ten seconds it had taken Eaglestone to attack and kill his adversary, Stephens and Gardner had been carefully jockeying around the other two divers. Now both of Falconer's divers propelled themselves rapidly backward through the water until the final diver caught up with them and the odds were even again. The opposing figures hung silently in the water in two lines that were twenty feet apart.

Stephens looked over at Eaglestone with increased respect for the SEAL's skills. He realized that Eaglestone was the right person to make the decisions as to how to attack the remaining three divers. He raised his hands, palm up, to his side and shrugged his shoulders to signal that he was waiting for instructions. Eaglestone looked at Stephens briefly, and then nodded once in agreement. Eaglestone turned and scanned the position of the three divers for several seconds before turning back to Stephens. He pointed to Stephens, and then in the direction where the Falconer had headed less than two minutes earlier. Then he pointed at Gardner and himself before pointing to the three divers.

Stephens hesitated for only a few seconds before he started to swim to the northeast to follow the Falconer. He knew that his departure would make the odds three-to-two against Gardner and Eaglestone. A part of him could not help but think of an old television show, *The Wild Wild*

West, where the hero was always far outnumbered. "The bad guys don't have a chance," he thought.

—m—

Stephens' side and shoulders started to ache again as he swam as rapidly as he could to catch up with the Falconer. He tried to pick a speed that would conserve whatever strength he had for when he did find them. He had no false hopes that Eaglestone and Gardner would be able to join him in time to make a difference. The three divers they faced would be far more careful this time. They would backpedal and defend one another. They would delay and defend. If they managed to hold out for even a few minutes against Gardner and Eaglestone, that would be more than enough.

It gave Stephens no satisfaction to realize that he had finally figured out the Falconer's plan. He was too tired, and his body ached too much. The direction of the Falconer's underwater course provided the last piece of proof. He had been heading almost directly out to sea. Stephens knew from the survey maps of the area that the sea bed had a very gentle slope. It reached a depth of only thirty feet even a half mile off shore. At that point there would be another rapid drop over the next hundred yards to a depth of ninety feet and another small underwater plateau. A mile off shore the bottom dropped rapidly heading into the depths of the Atlantic ocean. Stephens realized that there was only one possible reason to head directly out to sea instead of up or down the coast to escape. There were only two questions that remained for Stephens. Could he catch up with the Falconer before he got to the sub? And what could he do if he did?

Two hundred yards later he spotted the shapes in the distance, still heading almost due east. The Falconer and the large diver with him spotted Stephens at the same time. They had been constantly checking back over their shoulders as they pulled the limp form of the President through the water. Stephens saw them begin to swim faster, but he continued to close the distance. The two divers could only swim with one hand each as they held onto the President. That, plus the near dead weight of the President made their progress painfully slow. Finally, when Stephens had pulled to within a hundred feet of them, the pair stopped and the large diver let go of the President. He turned, and headed directly for Stephens. The Falconers continued on alone with the President. Stephens could see the vague darkness another five hundred feet beyond where the ocean began to drop down to the second plateau. He knew the sub must be waiting there.

The diver coming at Stephens looked huge in the water, nearly the size of Gertmeyer back at the farm. Like Stephens, he had only a knife as a weapon. "Unlike me," Stephens thought, "he probably doesn't have any broken ribs, and slept well last night."

When the two divers were ten feet apart, they both slowed and cautiously worked closer. Stephens let himself drift towards the bottom as he had seen Eaglestone do earlier. But the large diver matched him and drifted down at the same pace. When he reached the bottom Stephens pushed off his right leg to move rapidly to the left. The diver matched him, carefully keeping between Stephens and the rapidly dimming shape of the Falconer and the President receding into the distance.

Stephens considered the possibilities as they did a graceful pairs ballet thirty feet beneath the waves. In the shape he was in, and given the size of the diver in front of him, he would have no chance if it came down to a hand-to-hand struggle. Stephens had no doubt that should the diver be able to grab his arm, there would be little Stephens could do to prevent the diver from taking his knife. And while, in the movies, it always looked good to have the good guy and bad guy each holding the other's knife hand in a test of strength and determination, that would be a sucker's bet here. Stephens had no illusions about who would win a foolish 'mano-a-mano' duel. The only approach that might have a chance would be to carefully and slowly probe for a mistake or an advantage, but he was running out of time.

The shapes disappearing to the east took away that option. There was no time for caution. If the Falconer reached the sub and got the President onboard, then even the Orions that were on their way would be of limited value. He had no choice except to attack the diver, even though he knew he had the worst possible odds of succeeding.

As Stephens moved closer, he could see the divers eyes clearly. They were calm and confident as he waited. Stephens was within five feet of him when the basic idea of a plan came to him. The part of him that was always a 'third-party observer,' standing at a distance watching himself, chuckled wryly. "It's a damn small chance," he heard himself say. "I think I should bet on the snowball."

Stephens transferred his knife to his left hand and reached behind himself with his right. He rotated his body so that he was leading with his left hand and continued to move slowly towards the diver. He had no hope of fooling or bluffing the soldier now three feet in front of him. He only hoped to draw his attention away from analyzing why Stephens had switched the knife to the left hand. All he needed was a little surprise. Just a second or two of misdirection.

When he was within striking range he brought his right hand back out in front again. He had his fist clenched and bent backward as though holding something. He swung his right hand out towards the diver's face, pulling his left hand with the knife farther away as he rotated his body. As he hoped, the diver hesitated just slightly as he watched both knife and empty hand. Then with all the strength Stephens had left, he violently twisted his body, opened his right hand, and lunged to clamp his grip on the diver's right hand holding his knife. He yanked the wrist forward. At the same time, using the pull on the arm as a counterbalance, Stephens kicked out with both feet into the diver's chest to hold him away. Before the diver could react and begin to fight to free his knife hand, Stephens attacked his real target. Instead of aiming for the body, Stephens used his own knife, safely out of reach in his left hand, to drive into and through the forearm of the diver. Then he pulled it out and struck again, this time into the upper arm.

Two seconds later the diver's knife was dropping to the ocean floor and the diver had only one effective arm to use in defense. Both knew that the fight was over at that point. The diver's arm hung lifelessly by his side, surrounded in a thickening cloud of blood. The salt water in the wound seared the exposed muscles and tissues. Stephens moved back a few feet and pantomimed pulling off his own mask, and then dropping it to the sea bed, then pointing up. The diver considered the demand only briefly before removing his own mask, letting it drop, and painfully swimming to the surface.

Stephens waited until he saw the diver reach the top and start swimming towards the shore. He picked up the mask and carried it with him for the first hundred yards as he resumed his chase of the Falconer. For the first two hundred yards he kept checking back, both to make sure that the large diver was not following, and in the faint hope he would see Eaglestone and Gardner coming to join him. When it was clear that neither was true, he dropped the mask. He headed towards where the sea floor began to slope down and a submarine would have enough room to sit and wait, unobserved, on the bottom.

He had lost another three minutes. He hoped that wasn't fatal. In looking back towards the large diver would be on the surface, and to the southwest where Eaglestone and Gardner should appear if they were coming, Stephens never looked to his north. Thus, he never saw the faint shape of a diver swimming parallel to him, hugging the bottom, at the extreme range of his vision.

—∾—

When he reached the top of the slope Stephens saw the sub resting silently on the bottom. It was a small diesel sub, just over 200 feet long. As he started down the slope, he could see the Falconer struggling to tow the President through the water. He was thirty feet from the sub and there was no other activity visible. Stephens quickened his pace. He was gulping large amounts of air, now, and saw that he only had a few minutes of air left on his tank. The Falconer had not been involved in the underwater combat, and even with the exertion of towing the President would have much more air reserve.

When the Falconer saw Stephens come over the crest of the ridge, he dropped the President and swam rapidly towards the side of the submarine. The President drifted slowly towards the bottom, arms moving weakly as he tried to orient himself. When he reached the sub, the Falconer used his knife to bang hard on the side several times before turning around and swimming rapidly back to the side of the President. Then he waited for Stephens to draw near, and for help to arrive from within the sub.

Stephens heard the clang of metal on metal from three hundred feet away and knew that he had little time left. As he slid through the water, he concentrated on getting his breathing under control. We wondered if the sub would have divers waiting and ready to come out, or would need a few minutes. Either way, Stephens had to close in. But a part of him knew that it didn't matter—that he had lost. Even if he defeated the Falconer, and was able to do it quickly, it would still not be enough. Divers from the sub could intercept him and recapture the President long before he could get out of the area. The President was too drugged to do much more than breathe and float. He would not have the ability to swim away, on his own, during the action.

When Stephens drew up within ten feet of the Falconer, he once again experienced the feeling of facing an underwater predator. The Falconer hovered a few feet above where the President slouched on the bottom. Falconer's eyes were calm and confident. He could picture what Stephens had been through in the past fifteen minutes, let alone the prior two days. He could easily assess the status of Stephens mind and body. The Falconer knew that even without help from the sub, he would have a substantial physical advantage. He saw Stephens' chest heaving, and the explosions of air being exhausted into the sea.

The two moved carefully towards each other. When they closed to within three feet, each began a series of thrusts and feints. They circled slowly, like fighters in a ring rather than underwater. They probed and pushed, looking for any pattern or weakness they could exploit. Again Stephens tried to use the approach he had seen Eaglestone use of dropping to the bottom and lunging forward at an angle, but the Falconer did not make the same mistake. He kept even with Stephens, always wary and prepared.

Finally, Stephens knew that he could wait no longer. He knew there was no use in bitterness at having the action forced for him yet again. It would accomplish nothing and change even less. Once again all the odds would be stacked against him. But he had no choice.

Stephens moved in closer and began to force the action. The knives got closer now. Instead of feints that missed by a foot, they would often get within an inch or two, and twice Stephens felt the painful prick of a knife point that was just short of puncturing his skin. Yet, he moved in ever closer. He switched his knife to his left hand, and saw the Falconer mirror his action. He reached one hand behind his back, and saw the slight smile cross the Falconer's face. Stephens immediately discounted the option, and brought the hand back out on front of him. They both switched the knives back to their right hands. Then the Falconer circled a little closer.

The Falconer's attack almost worked. Stephens made only the slightest mistake. When the Falconer quickly switched his knife back to his left hand and lunged towards Stephens' right side, Stephens' left knee came up, instinctively, just a few inches. The Falconer's right hand shot out and caught the knee, and pulled hard. Stephens was twisted around to his right, his knife arm now uselessly on the opposite side of his body from the Falconer, almost with his back to the Falconer. Only by twisting violently was he able to turn enough so that the Falconer's knife entered his lower left side, rather than his middle back. The four inch blade sunk in up to the hilt, with the point sticking through the far side by a half inch.

Stephens dropped his own knife and whipped his right hand around to catch the Falconer's hand. Inside he screamed silently as the knife was ripped back out. He pulled himself around to face the Falconer, and concentrated every ounce of his effort gripping the Falconer's arm. He forced himself to shut out the fire and flame coursing through his lower back. Slowly he became aware of the ever loudening cry that he heard in his head. "No! No! No!" continued in an endless loop. He was shouting to himself and to all the unfair fates that had gotten him this far, yet now had condemned him to failure.

And in that instant, Stephens finally crossed over the line and became the Falconer's equal.

His mind had totally closed out the pain in his body. The shouts of "No!" covered all other sounds. He reached his left hand down to help the right, ignoring the Falconer's free hand ripping at his mask and face. He wrenched the Falconer's knife hand until The Falconer had to choose between maintaining his grip on the knife or preventing his wrist from being broken.

When the knife fell on the sand beside them as they grappled inches off the sand and rocks, Stephens pushed off with his feet and drove them several feet away from the knife. They were now just twenty feet from the submarine, with the President half drifting, half walking along the bottom away from them. They tumbled against a jumble of rocks strewn against an outcrop of granite. Both were fighting to get a hand free as they twisted and turned, smashing first one, then the other, against the rocks.

When the Falconer finally pulled one hand free, both reached for the other's face. Simultaneously they each ripped the other's air hose out of the other's mouth. The sea over their heads was filled with a fountain of bubbles as the two hoses floated just above, and behind each head. The Falconer began to reach back over his head with one hand while trying to push off with the other. In the background, Stephens could hear the sound of metal on metal as a hatch cover was being turned. Time had run out. Divers from the sub were on the way.

It was then, facing the prospect of yet another standoff, that Stephens knew it was time for a lifetime of waiting to end. He almost did not care which way it ended—just that it was finally over. He knew that it could not be allowed to continue. Most of all, he knew that he did not have the strength left in him to battle the Falconer once again in the years to come. One way or another the end had to come.

Stephens stopped reaching back towards his own wildly dancing air hose, and instead shot out his hand to catch the Falconer's forearm and prevent the Falconer from recapturing his own hose. Then Stephens wedged his left foot between two of the rocks beneath him, and turned to look into the Falconer's eyes.

At that point, there was nothing short of death that would release Stephens' grip. Both were locked there, tied to the bottom, without air. Once again he saw a slight smile from the Falconer, and knew that he understood as well. The Falconer stopped fighting to break free to capture the air hose, and shifted his right hand that had been reaching for the hose to now equally grasp Stephens' wrist. Anyone watching would have found it comical to see two men without air, holding each other in the two handed fireman's grip, while their air hoses flapped uselessly just above their heads.

Neither would let go of the other.

Given all of the exertion, it took only fifteen seconds before Stephens began to feel as though his chest would explode. He didn't take his eyes off the Falconer. His head began to throb, and his ears were filled with the roaring sound of jet engines planted in his brain. He stared at the Falconer, drawing strength from the face before him, and the animal determination that he could not let go, no matter what. Stephens felt his legs start to get numb at the same time he saw the first signs of struggling on the face of the Falconer. It was just a slight twitching around the mouth, and creases from a clenched jaw. The area started to get darker, and Stephens mind began to wander slightly as he wondered why it was harder and harder to concentrate on the Falconer.

Finally, he felt the Falconer's grip loosen a small degree. The instincts that were now driving him made him clamp onto the Falconer's wrists even more tightly in case it was a trick. Then he saw a sad smile cross the Falconer's face, followed by a small nod. Stephens realized that the nod was a salute, a show of honor, and realized that it was now over. A moment later there was a burst of bubbles from the Falconer's mouth as the lungs could no longer hold. He saw the water being sucked in as the lungs automatically tried to carve air out of the water around them. Then the Falconer pulled left then right, before going limp.

Stephens did not release his own grip. His mind and lungs were screaming at him, but he screamed back as he forced himself to count to five. Inside he was swearing, screaming, and insulting himself. "One, asshole, just keep going." He could barely keep his eyes open. "Two. Wimp, that's two." He felt his own grip slipping, but did not dare to let go before he was certain that the Falconer could not be faking. "Three. Just two more, wuss!"

He let go of one hand and reached up for the air hose. It was still tumbling and he could not seem to get a hold of it. He would reach, and miss. The hose would be in his hand, but he could not catch it. His hands seemed crazily programmed by some mad computer to do the opposite of what he wanted. His right hand could not release his grip on the Falconer in order to help capture the air hose. And his left hand could not close in a grip even when he could see the hose resting in his palm.

When he saw the shape of the diver materialize behind him, he knew he had lost even with the death of the Falconer. Stephens knew the President was only a few feet away, and could easily be recaptured. He knew he had run out of time. Oddly, he wanted to cry. He had failed, and so many would now pay the price for his failure. And he would never know what might have been with Cynthia Lebart. Then he could see her face in front of him. 'My God, you're beautiful' he thought. He saw her reach above him for something, and then felt something forced into his mouth. 'If I'm to die, I am grateful I dreamt that you'd be here to save me,' he thought as he slumped towards the bottom where he ended up next to the body of the Falconer.

Then, long before he would reach the count of five, he mimicked the final actions of the one whose life had been so intertwined with his for the past decade. His lungs ejected the stale air and gulped in the sea.

Except it wasn't sea water. It was air.

Stephens looked as though he was praying as he supported himself against the rocks and let the air recharge his body. Slowly he felt some strength returning. The body of the Falconer was drifting slowly out to sea off to his side. As his body recovered a little, and his mind began to focus on the events around him, he heard the clang of a hatch being opened from the submarine. Then he remembered a diver from the sub had given him back his air hose, and wondered how many they had sent out to get the President. He turned towards the President and saw the diver holding the President's arm. It was only then that he realized that the diver was not from the sub, and for the second time it was not a dream that he had been rescued.

He was staring at Cynthia from ten feet away when she pointed over his shoulder towards the sub behind him. Stephens turned and saw one diver coming out of the sub. Stephens gestured for Cynthia to bring the President to the surface, and then began to swim towards the sub. He was halfway to it when the diver coming towards him realized something was wrong. He had only been sent out to help bring the President on board and was unarmed. When he saw the body of the Falconer floating down near the bottom, two divers working their way towards the surface, and another slicing through the water towards him, he decided to retreat. By the time Stephens reached the deck of the sub, the hatch had slammed shut and the diver was on his way back to the relative safety of the interior.

Stephens waited for two minutes before starting to slowly rise to the surface. He wanted to make sure that no one else exited, this time better prepared, until Cynthia and the President were on the surface. He didn't know what he would be able to do against a well armed force, but really didn't care anymore. He was past the point of caring. His actions had been switched to autopilot and instinct.

As he started up, he began to hear the sound of the Coast Guard cutter engines echoing through the water from a distance. He knew that Cynthia and the President had been spotted. He could see them seventy feet above him, and could just discern the froth on the water that had to be caused by a chopper hovering just above the surface. Next he saw two bodies crash into the ocean near them, and then swim over next to the President. A moment later he saw the President disappear as he was lifted from the water.

Stephens was thirty feet off the bottom when he heard the sub engines start up, and saw the sub lift slightly from the bottom. He was amazed at how quietly it moved as it began to turn beneath him. He could almost not hear the engines as the sound of the Coast Guard cutter got closer. Then he saw a small burst of bubbles from the front of the sub. As the sub turned to face the oncoming cutter, one of the torpedo tubes along the port side of the sub had been opened. Stephens looked back up to the surface and realized that Cynthia was still in the water with the two divers.

The hopelessness closed in once again, as he realized that the sub planned to attack the cutter. The helicopter would drop the President at the closest point, the cutter, in order to get back quickly for another load. He could now just make out the hull of the cutter as it closed in on their position. And below him, he could see the sub turning to line up a torpedo shot. The cutter would not have a chance.

Stephens was already diving towards the sub as fast as he could swim before he had any idea what he would do. The sub was creeping along at five knots. It would not even need a periscope bearing to fire a torpedo. Passive sonar would easily track the oncoming cutter. He landed on the front deck of the sub and pulled himself along the deck to the bow. Then Stephens lunged over the bow and caught the open door on the torpedo tube. It was only then that he stopped to ask himself what to do.

It was an irrational act born of desperation. He felt tiny and insignificant pinned against the bow of the sub. A fly on the side of an elephant. Even as he was shouting "Why?" to himself, he began to remove his air tank. Keeping the mouthpiece in, he shoved the tank part way into the tube where two feet away he could see the deadly snout of the torpedo. He used the strong straps of the tank to tie it to the torpedo tube door. Then he took three deep breaths of the air and began to stroke to the surface.

He was halfway up when he heard the whine as the torpedo engines started, followed by a slight 'thwunk.' He stopped swimming for a moment and instinctively curled up his body to withstand the explosion. Had the explosion occurred, the position would have been a useless effort. He would have been far too close, and the concussion would have crushed his body. But there was no explosion. And when Stephens heard the insistent tapping of the torpedo trying to get past its restraint, he began to swim upward with renewed effort.

When he reached the surface there was no one left in the water. He could see the helicopter hovering over the deck of the cutter that had slowed to a stop in the distance. He lifted himself out of the water again and again to motion the ship to move away. He could see sailors on the deck waving back, unaware of the message he was trying to give. He screamed, but his voice did not carry far enough. He could see Cynthia Lebart turn and move towards the railing, and then she began to wave, jumping up and down like a schoolgirl.

The helicopter had lifted off and was halfway to him when the explosion occurred. The submarine had continued towards the cutter as the torpedo raced its motor in the closed confines of the torpedo tube. Inside, sailors were rushing to close off all watertight hatches and get to life support equipment. The torpedo would not arm itself until it went 1000 feet from the sub. It would know that when the motor had taken a preset number of turns. Inside a simple counter was slowly working its way to the point where another switch would turn the torpedo from just a fast fish into a weapon. It was a foolproof system that made sure a torpedo could not explode too close to a sub. However, it was a system that assumed the torpedo was not running in place.

The sub had moved another fifty feet from Stephens when the torpedo armed. Then, another tap against the air tank was enough to explode the device. The bow section of the sub would have been destroyed by the single torpedo. But when it set off two more that had just been loaded to be ready if the first had failed, the result was a massive explosion that instantly killed the entire crew, except for six sailors in the rear engine compartment. The explosion, so close below Stephens, threw him with a giant bubble of gas and water fifteen feet above the surface of the ocean. The shock from the explosion struck him like dozens of full sandbags being thrown at him from all sides.

But he knew that the President and Cynthia were safe. And that the time of the Falconer was now past. And for the first time in as long as he could remember, he was at peace. His final thought before there was only blackness was "Thank you. It's finally over."

Epilogue

Cynthia Lebart pressed her face against the window as the helicopter made its way through the night to the landing pad in the southwest corner of the Camp David compound. Had she not known they were landing she would have missed it. When the Marine lieutenant sitting next to her pointed, she could only see a few lights from the camp. There was nothing that would make it stand out. Even the landing zone was marked with just four simple lights at the corners. The pilots were trained to land with no lights at all, or at best with the light of a single flashlight on the worst of nights. They would be guided in by an electronic beacon until they were close enough to land visually. The small beacons for night landings were more for the benefit of queasy passengers than for the pilots.

The grass rippled and flowed from the down draft of the rotors, swaying first one way then another. Just before the wheels touched down the grass blades were whipped around in a crazed dance. Finally, as the helicopter came to rest and the rotors were allowed to slow down and stop, the cabin became very quiet again. She could hear soft voices up in the cockpit speaking on the radio. Outside, in the distance, she saw a door open and two figures leave the building to approach the landing zone. When she was helped out of the helicopter she felt very alone and out of place. "I so wish you were here, Rob," she thought as figures drew near.

The lieutenant had flown with her from Boston on the shuttle, and then from Dulles to Camp David. He politely extended a hand to guide her down from the helicopter, and then escorted her towards the two approaching figures. She drew within ten feet before she could recognize Ned Eaglestone in the darkness. She had to smile, and ran the next few steps with her arms out.

"Ned, I'm so glad you're here!" She wrapped her arms around the big SEAL, and was lost in his huge hug. "I was hoping I'd see you. After the airlift, I didn't know if we'd ever be able to track you down again." She leaned back and smiled as she gently touched his face. "After all, now that you're stationed at the White House, I figured you could afford a better class of friends than deadbeats like me."

Eaglestone continued to hold her waist with his right hand while reaching up and to lightly squeeze her hand. His voice was soft and very caring. "There is no chance of that, lady." Then he drew back and straightened up into the position of attention. His voice became formal as he stepped to the side so that she could now see the second person who had been standing quietly behind them. "May I present the First Lady."

Cynthia stopped awkwardly when she saw the First Lady step out of the shadows. "Ma'am, I'm sorry. I didn't recognize you. I didn't mean to . . ."

Before the Boston tunnel, the First Lady had been known only as a strong, capable person. In the four weeks since the President had been rescued, she had replaced him at many public functions while he was recovering, and had become one of those rare people who would be remembered and cherished by a generation. In a way that only those old enough to remember Dallas in 1964 could understand, she had become a figure that could not quite be defined, yet was treasured by all. Like Shane, she would never be able to go back to what she had been. No one could ever look at her the same way again. As she approached and put her arms around Cynthia, it was a mark of what she had become that none of that showed. At that moment she was far more a mother than a First Lady.

"Dear, first things first. I, too, would want to hug Sergeant Eaglestone after all you two went through together."

"Thank you Ma'am."

"I'm so sorry that Rob could not be here today," said the First Lady, drawing back from the warmth of the hug a little while still keeping her hands on Cynthia's shoulders. "I'll always owe him a debt of gratitude that I couldn't hope to repay."

"Ma'am, Rob could never see it that way. He couldn't turn away from them any more than you could, I think. He'd call it a no-brainer—something that is so obvious that it takes no thought. Perhaps," she said with sudden insight, "it's like some of the things you must do as a President, or as a First Lady."

The First Lady thought a few moments before slowly nodding. "Perhaps. Just a little. But neither my husband nor I would compare anything we've done to that. And I'd still like to thank him, not as First Lady, but as a wife whose husband is alive because of him."

"Yes, Ma'am. That part would mean something special to him."

The First Lady pulled close for another brief hug, and then put one arm around Cynthia and turned her towards the door. "Well! Come dear. Let's have a bit of tea with the President. Mr. Eaglestone, would you please join us?"

"That would be a pleasure, Ma'am."

The First Lady laughed wryly, and even in the darkness you could see the sparkle flashing in her eyes. "At least my husband could order Mr. Eaglestone to be here. Perhaps I'll ask him to reinstate the draft so that Rob will have less choice next time."

"Ma'am, I doubt even that would work," answered Eaglestone. "He'd find a way out. Only Rob would turn down an invitation to Camp David."

The three walked quietly towards the light of the doorway. When they reached it, the First Lady stopped and stared past the helicopter in the distance, towards the small school she could picture nestled in the hills of New Hampshire.

"No," she said softly. "Let him be. He has kept all of the promises we asked him to keep." There was a measure of sadness in the words. "For that one, it would be a sin, somehow, to ask of him another. Let him go back to his books."

Dublin Lake was mirror-quiet that early in the morning. The sun had not yet cleared the trees so the smooth water was colored with long shadows from the east. Small ripples from a light breeze came with the dawn, causing the shadows to wave back and forth like thin silk in a light breeze. There was almost no noise, except for the wind and the early birdcalls. There was no traffic on route 101, just a few hundred feet from the deserted Dublin Lake Club beach. Thanksgiving was just two days away, and the flatlanders had long ago left for places to the south. The club was boarded up, the two rafts pulled out of the water and stored well above the ice line in preparation for winter.

To the southeast Mount Monadnock stood sentinel over the lake. Stephens stepped backward along the beach until he could see the profile of the mountain through a gap in the trees surrounding the beach. Only in the past couple of days had he started to feel at home again in his beloved woods and mountainside.

The fall wind picked up for a moment, and Stephens awkwardly tried to button his shirt against the cold. The sling on his right arm kept getting in the way. He pressed his lips together as he concentrated ever harder each time his fingers were unable to close on the collar buttons. He tried several times before finally dropping his hands to his sides and shaking his head with frustration.

The doctors who had hovered over him for the past four weeks now felt that he would almost completely recover. It had not appeared that way when his unconscious body had first been airlifted into Mass General Hospital. Most of the right side of his body carried evidence of how close he had been to the sub explosion. The broken right arm and near drowning could be treated effectively on the scene. The explosion had broken three more ribs, and re-fractured the rib Gertmeyer had crushed up in Peterborough. Two of the ribs had punctured the lungs. He had bleeding from his left ear. The force of the explosion had left him unconscious for three days.

The previous night, the lead physician flown in from Bethesda Naval Hospital had announced that the only permanent injury would be significant hearing loss in the left ear. The cast on his arm was due to come off the next day. Stephens was beginning to think about teaching and coaching again.

Stephens turned away from the view of the mountain and walked to the large boulder on the left end of the beach. He carefully lowered himself to sit leaning against the rock, where he could look out over the lake spread before him. He reached over and touched the book resting on the top of the boulder, and then pulled his hand back, leaving it where it lay. He once again wondered at the insight and understanding in the gift from the President and First Lady. "It only seems right that you hold on to this," read their inscription.

Somehow the book of Frost poetry was the only way to have ended the events of the past weeks. The Falconer's body had never been found after the explosion had destroyed the sub. To Stephens, that seemed right, somehow. "There shouldn't be a body," he thought. "No reminders, no links to the past. Let it be over and forgotten."

The sub was a Kilo export. Joyce Patterson had told him, the day he left the hospital, that it had taken all of the three weeks he was there for the Navy to figure out how the sub got past the SOSUS net. In the end the answer came from information John Bradford offered as a bargaining chip to counter the charges against him. The sub, barely able to make twenty knots, had crossed the Atlantic directly under the hull of a Libyan super tanker that also provided cover when the sub had to surface. The cover, plus the Kilo's anechoic coating and extremely quiet engines, let the sub be undetected until it was in position off the Maine coast. SOSUS and patrolling US subs would only hear the sounds of the tanker. The same tanker had returned to the Maine coast the day after the sub explosion, and finding nothing, had continued across the Atlantic. It was now safely docked in Tripoli.

The sun was just showing above the trees and the lake was coming alive. A car passed by on route 101. At the far side of the lake Stephens thought he saw brief movement, and for a moment wondered if the loons would dance that morning. "It's a cold November morning, Stephens," he chuckled to himself. "There will be no loons here today!"

He rose carefully and picked up the book. He turned a few pages until he came to the poem he was looking for. He didn't need the words on the page to remember Frost, but it was reassuring, nonetheless.

"*Promises to keep*," he thought. "*Promises to keep*."

He looked back to the west towards the school as he closed the book and put it under the sling of his right arm. He thought of where Cynthia would be sleeping in the warmth of their bed. And as he pictured her he was once again stunned by how beautiful she was when she was sleeping. He remembered how often in the past days he had found himself reaching out to touch her face or hair. Or how often at night he would lie there, hoping he would not wake her up as he stared at her in wonderment.

Stephens reached up and this time his left hand easily buttoned his collar against the wind. He looked at his hand in surprise as he opened and closed it easily several times. "It's starting to be over," he thought. Stephens reached under the sling with his left hand for the book of poetry. He opened it carefully and read the inscription once again. He looked out over the lake, and then towards the school. He smiled softly, and gently rested the book on the top of the boulder. The early morning breeze slowly turned the pages.

Stephens left the book on the rock as he turned towards the school and started walking back to the dormitory room where Cynthia waited.